Praise for
The Murder of Harriet Monckton

'I loved *The Murder of Harriet Monckton*; what a *tour de force*! I'm blown away. Elizabeth Haynes completely transported me to that time and place. I also found the novel incredibly moving and I'm so glad to know Harriet's story. The novel is an absolute triumph.'   — Elly Griffiths

'Elizabeth Haynes evokes the language and world of the 1840s, and lifts Harriet from obscurity with a damn fine tale. In these #MeToo days, her rich and magnificent imagining of a long-forgotten murder connects the past to the present as if it were yesterday.'   — Lesley Thomson

'Elizabeth Haynes is one of the top storytellers in a genre bursting with the best tale-spinners in the world. *The Murder of Harriet Monckton* is a page-turning mystery, charged with compassion, wisdom and a modern understanding of human nature and psychology. It is both a humane defence of women of all eras who choose not to conform and a celebration of their trailblazing. This is an important book, one which I just could not put down. If spirits exist, Harriet's will take some comfort knowing that Elizabeth Haynes has set her trained, empathetic, forensic eye to vindicate her.'   — Julia Crouch

'A historical whodunnit with heart; a story that was begging to be told. I can't get poor Harriet out of my mind. Wonderful.'
                                                        — SJI Holliday

'Elizabeth Haynes's real-life story of a young Victorian woman who was systematically wronged by those around her resonates powerfully in the current climate. Moving and brilliantly written, this is a must-read from one of the most talented crime writers out there.'   — Cass Green

'The writing is exceptional: I spent much of the book in a state of visceral terror for Harriet... Haynes captures the age perfectly and she's particularly good on the precarious life of the unmarried woman, virtuous or not... The plot has a sense of completeness about it and the ending blew me away: it just seemed so right. In real life the murder might remain unsolved, but Haynes' solution is neat, realistic and entirely plausible. Perhaps the highest praise that I can give this book is to say that it won't be too long before I reread to see how it was all done.'   —*The Bookbag*

'Absolutely brilliant! Elizabeth Haynes has brought to life a wonderful array of characters, recreated a truly authentic Bromley and given a voice to an intriguing mystery surrounding the death of a young woman. Highly recommended.'
                        —Tracy Fenton, *Compulsive Readers*

'This page-turning whodunnit based in compelling historical reality reads like a modern psychological thriller, with all the resonance of the #MeToo movement. Haynes is a can't-miss author for me.'   —Alexandra Sokoloff

'Intricate and evocative, with such resonance for the age we are living through. Harriet will haunt you in the best possible way.'
                        —Sarah Hilary

'A poignant and gripping reimagining of a real-life case from 1843 which skilfully evokes Victorian England in all its petty conventions and dark hypocrisy. *Brava*, Elizabeth Haynes.'
                        —Rachel Rhys

'What a fascinating and deftly created novel. Drawing on real reports and statements from the time, Elizabeth Haynes recreates the final hours of a young woman murdered in Bromley in 1843. Authentic and intriguing.'   —Anna Mazzola

'Dark, troubling and richly evocative. Elizabeth Haynes has reimagined the case of Harriet Monckton to startling effect.'
                        —Colette McBeth

THE
MURDER

of

HARRIET
MONCKTON

Elizabeth Haynes

First published in 2018 by
Myriad Editions
www.myriadeditions.com

Myriad Editions
An imprint of New Internationalist Publications
The Old Music Hall, 106–108 Cowley Rd,
Oxford OX4 1JE

First printing
1 3 5 7 9 10 8 6 4 2

A CIP catalogue record for this book
is available from the British Library

ISBN (hardback): 978-1-912408-03-0
ISBN (trade paperback): 978-1-912408-04-7
ISBN (ebook): 978-1-912408-05-4

Designed and typeset in Perpetua
by WatchWord Editorial Services, London
Map of Bromley 1843 by Jo Hinton Malivoire

Printed and bound in Great Britain
by Clays Ltd, Elcograf S.p.A.

for Harriet, and her son
not forgotten

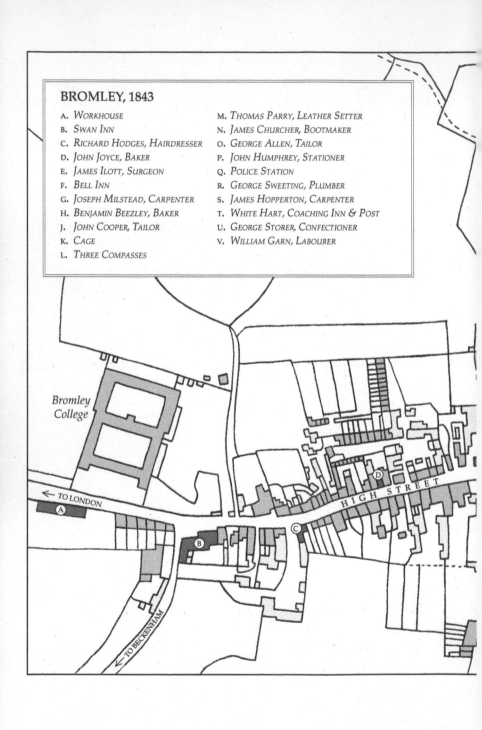

BROMLEY, 1843

A. *Workhouse*
B. *Swan Inn*
C. *Richard Hodges, Hairdresser*
D. *John Joyce, Baker*
E. *James Ilott, Surgeon*
F. *Bell Inn*
G. *Joseph Milstead, Carpenter*
H. *Benjamin Beezley, Baker*
J. *John Cooper, Tailor*
K. *Cage*
L. *Three Compasses*

M. *Thomas Parry, Leather Setter*
N. *James Churcher, Bootmaker*
O. *George Allen, Tailor*
P. *John Humphrey, Stationer*
Q. *Police Station*
R. *George Sweeting, Plumber*
S. *James Hopperton, Carpenter*
T. *White Hart, Coaching Inn & Post*
U. *George Storer, Confectioner*
V. *William Garn, Labourer*

Bromley College

← TO LONDON

← TO BECKENHAM

HIGH STREET

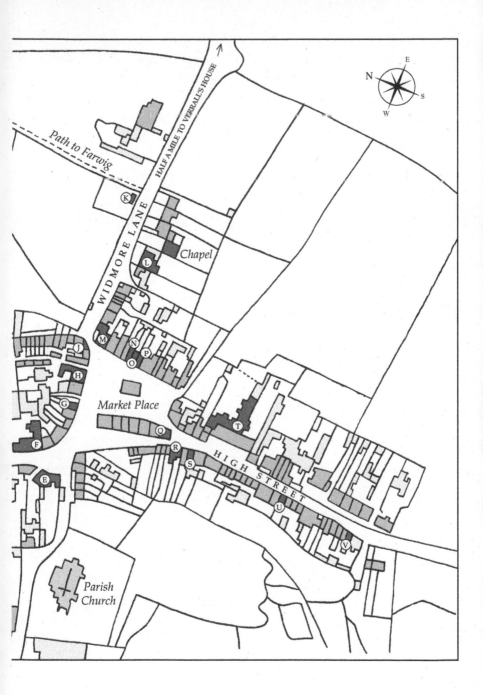

Path to Farwig

HALF A MILE TO VERRALL'S HOUSE

WIDMORE LANE

Chapel

Market Place

HIGH STREET

Parish
Church

Contents

Prologue 1

I: 1843 7

II: The Confession of the Reverend
George Verrall, a Gentleman 205

III: 1846 237

IV: The Diary 341

V: 1843 467

Epilogue 481

Afterword 487

Prologue

Monday, 6th November, 1843

When Death comes to visit, he arrives clothed in the most unexpected of disguises.

Harriet Monckton did not have time to think this, or remark upon something as profound as Death and Life. She did not even, in the end, have time to say her prayers or ask for help or confess her sins.

But at least she was not alone. Such a privilege is not afforded to all; perhaps this act visited upon her was one of mercy.

She did not deserve it – mercy, that is. Standing straight-backed, proud, a small frown as if she had been interrupted in the act of prayer, instead of what had actually just taken place, something far more earthly. The very air around her was filthy, contaminated. She reeked of sin.

There had been conversation, a little of it: hushed, although this late and in this place there was nobody to hear. Perhaps someone might be walking home from a visit, along the lane, some thirty yards away, but, here, they were entirely alone.

There is something else I could do to help you.

She said, 'I thought we agreed—'

You're not the first girl to find herself in trouble, you know. It's obvious to anyone with an eye and half a brain. Look at you.

She even looked down at herself. Dresses hide a great deal, but there comes a point when the swelling of a girl's belly lifts the bottom of her stays and the whole shape of her looks odd. Looks wrong.

'If I just had enough money,' she said, 'then I should go away and not trouble anyone any further ...'

*This is a better way. Solves the problem altogether. Do you
want it or not?*

'What is it?'

*A draught. It will help you get back to the way you were;
the effect is very quick.*

She considered it. She even looked at the bottle, although
she did not read the label. If she had, she would have seen
this:

THE CORDIAL BALM OF SYRIACUM

For treatment of those who have fallen
into a state of chronic disability.

Nervous disorders of every kind, sinkings,
anxieties, and tremors which so dreadfully
affect the weak and the sedentary will, in a
short time, be succeeded by cheerfulness
and every presage of health.

Provided by R. and L. Perry, and Co.
PERRY'S PURIFYING SPECIFIC PILLS
19, Berners Street, London

The Cordial Balm of Syriacum, of course, was not what the
bottle contained.

'Surely it would be a terrible sin,' she said, but already she
was wavering.

The look on her face. Dismissal, followed by doubt.
Whatever plans she had made herself, they were not
foolproof. Things could always go wrong. And how much
easier it would be to wipe clean the slate, to start again. She
would do things differently, of course. And her life could slip
back to the way it was. She would be respectable, whole.
She could go to Arundel, as she had planned to, before her
problem manifested itself. She could still – although she was
getting on in age – make a fair match.

All of these thoughts visible on her face.

'Will it hurt?' she asked, and Death rubbed his hands with glee, knowing she was almost his.

A little, perhaps. Not much worse than you suffer every month. It will be quick.

It wasn't a lie, not really. At least this particular suffering would be over with swiftly, and she would, actually, get back to the way she had been, albeit the state of existence before she was born. The state of oblivion.

There was a moment's hesitation, but then she uncorked the bottle and drank the contents down. Her last act on earth was a brave one. Perhaps that would make a difference.

The look upon her face at the end, after the initial spasms and the shock of the pain that seared down her gullet as the poison took effect – thirty-five grains of it, they would estimate, when three-quarters of a grain was supposed enough to kill a man – was almost one of peace. Surprise, perhaps, that it should end thus. And here, of all places, illuminated only by a guttering candle. The supplier of the poison could slip away unnoticed. The agony was swift and profound. The spasms caused her to bite down on her tongue and arch backwards as she fell. There were no screams. Nothing but a squeak, and some rasping sound like someone trying to clear their throat. By the time she hit the floor, she was already dead. Dark blood bubbled from between her lips, the colour of varnish. Her eyes were half open, glassy.

For some moments, there was silence.

She would have to be moved, of course; she could not stay here. The second part of the plan was set in motion. Half lifted, half dragged ... but then the small bottle that had been clutched in her spasmed fingers slipped free and clinked on to the stone floor, along with some coins.

She was heavier than she looked. Perhaps she could be left, after all.

The world would forget about Harriet Monckton. Within a few years, even her family would cease to talk about her.

Just another girl who had fallen into sin, like so many others. It was better this way. After the initial shock, her family would thrive without her; her friends would be able to resume their lives in peace. The town would go back to the way it was, eventually: honest, righteous, sure in the knowledge that order had been restored.

There had been no other choice. For the greater good, it had to be done.

From outside the chapel came the sound of footsteps on the flagstones.

Someone was coming.

I: 1843

Tuesday, 7th November, 1843

Frances Williams

At first light I sent a boy to Harriet's mother, to ask after her. Half an hour later, he returned with a note. Harriet was not there. She had not been seen by them since yesterday morning, when she went there to change her dress.

The reply washed over me like cold water, and I knew then that something ill had befallen my dear friend.

The conversations you have with yourself, at times such as this: you try to remain rational, to think through the events in a logical order. Last night, she had gone out to post a letter. She said to me she would be back soon, and she would make me some gruel. I was feverish, thick with it, not concentrating. She told me to get back into bed, to try to rest. She said she would not be long.

I must have fallen asleep, then, for I woke and the room was cold, the candle burned low. And she was not there. I was dazed. I was shivering with the fever. I got out of bed and searched, in case she had returned and left me a note, telling me she had gone out again.

But there was no note.

I tried to sleep some more. I was not worried, not then; so many things might have happened whilst I slept. She might have been called away. She would not have woken me to tell me that, and perhaps she had not had time to leave a note. She might have expected to be back again before I woke. She might just have stepped outside for a moment, to speak to someone.

But by then it was four o'clock. Too late to be out, too early to be out. It was dark night outside, still.

In the end, I went back to bed and lay there, listening for her tread on the step outside, listening for conversation out there in the night, but all was quiet.

And then, eventually, the message to Farwig, to Harriet's mother, and the reply, and she was missing. Who would take my place at the school? Harriet had promised to do it. She said she would take the girls' lessons until I felt better, until I could manage to speak without coughing.

I sent the boy to the schoolhouse, to warn Mr Campling that my deputy was missed; I told him the pupil teachers would have to manage for today.

Oh, I went through all possible emotions, that morning. I was curious, I was vexed; I was fearful for her. Exhausted from another wakeful night, I knew my thoughts were not rational. *Think, think*, I told myself. *You must know where she has gone. She must have said something, last night, something you missed. That she was going to visit someone else*; but there was nothing like that. She went to post a letter. She said she would come back, to make some gruel. She said she would not be long.

And then my thoughts turned to him, to Tom Churcher; outside, on the step, asking for her. I told him: *Harriet has gone to post a letter.* He wanted to wait. I told him he could not. I told him he should talk to her in the morning, and, in the end, he left.

Perhaps he had seen her? Perhaps they had met, in the street? Perhaps an accident had taken place, somewhere; she had fallen, in the dark, injured herself and lain in a ditch, insensible, unable to cry for help?

You think so many things. You try to find the right solution, to a mystery, and you can never quite confront what must be the truth. You veer away from it, because facing it is too terrible.

Reverend George Verrall

I was in my study working on the series of lectures I have been delivering on the subject of the Lord's Last Supper, when through the blanket of my fierce concentration I heard the knock upon the door.

Now when the even was come, he sat down with the twelve. And as they did eat, he said, Verily I say unto you, that one of you shall betray me. And they were exceeding sorrowful, and began every one of them to say unto him, Lord, is it I? And he answered and said, He that dippeth his hand with me in the dish, the same shall betray me. The Son of man goeth as it is written of him: but woe unto that man by whom the Son of man is betrayed! it had been good for that man if he had not been born. Then Judas, which betrayed him, answered and said, Master, is it I? He said unto him, Thou hast said.

Thou hast said.
It is you. It is you.
And then, my wife at the door.
'What is it? I asked not to be disturbed.'
'Mary Ann Monckton. She insists upon seeing you.'
I turned from my desk. 'Well, show her in.'
Sarah paused, then returned to the hallway. I heard Mary Ann's voice insisting that she would not stay, and then she was shown into my study. I bade her sit beside the fire.
'Sorry for disturbing you, sir,' she said, refusing the seat. 'I am looking for my sister.'
'Harriet?'
Afterwards I thought it a mistake to utter that name. Mary Ann had three sisters; that I knew Harriet more intimately than any of them was not something that should be brought to attention under any circumstances, least of all these.

Sarah Dorset, born Monckton, and Elizabeth who is now Elizabeth Carpenter, and Mary Ann
and then Harriet last of all
best of all

'Yes, Harriet. She was to have stayed with Miss Williams last night, and yet she did not. Miss Williams thought she must have come home, but she did not.' The young woman appeared in some distress, struggling to offer even these few words.

'Perhaps she has gone to some other friend?'

'We cannot think of anywhere else she could have gone. We have enquired of everyone; no one has seen her.'

I offered her a smile. 'As you can see, she is not here.'

My mind was still upon the word of the Lord. *One of you shall betray me... Master, is it I?*

Mary Ann stiffened at my humour. 'That's what Mrs Verrall just said. If you don't mind me saying so, sir, it isn't very kind. I fear something terrible has befallen my sister, and, sir, if you're not able to offer me any assistance in locating her, I should be grateful if you could remember Harriet in your prayers.' She headed for the door.

'Wait, please.'

And she did not turn. She could not bring herself to look at me. It brought back a sudden memory of Harriet doing the same thing; late summer, the heat of it, stifling. Looking at the back of her neck, the whiteness of the skin, and the sheen of perspiration upon it.

'I'll see what I can do. To help with the search.'

one of you shall betray me

Thomas Churcher

I was working in my father's shop. I saw Mary Ann Monckton come through the door, her face pale, shawl clutched tight about her.

'Have you seen Harriet?' she asked.

'No,' I said.

It was not yet nine o'clock, and I was the only one present. Father was gone to the tanner's.

'Is she not at the school?' I asked, because that was where she was most likely to be. 'She is helping Miss Williams.'

'I'm aware of that, Tom Churcher,' she said, in that cold way she has. She thinks herself so fine, Harriet's sister. She thinks ill of men like me. 'She is not at the school.'

'Well, she is not here.'

'But you do not know where she is?'

'No.'

'And Clara?'

'She is not here either.'

And she tilted her head to one side and spoke to me as if to an imbecile.

'I can see that for myself. Perhaps Clara has seen Harriet. Where is she?'

'At home.'

'Very well,' she said, and made to leave the shop.

I stared after her, thinking of Miss Williams, and that thing she said. They all believe me to be a fool. I am not clever like some of them. I am good at music and I am good at making and mending boots, and I am good at listening.

Neither Harriet nor Clara paid it any mind, but I took it into my heart and I have thought about it much since then. *You shan't go to Arundel, Harriet. I won't let you leave me.* She said it lightly, with a smile, but her hand on Harriet's arm was gripping.

Mary Ann should have asked me for help, I thought. Had she asked me to come and search for Harriet I should gladly have done so. After all, I know Harriet. I know the places she likes to go, her secret places. I know her secrets. But her sister thinks me a fool, and for that reason I stayed where I was and waited for my father.

13

Reverend George Verrall

There being no sign of the girl, at half-past one o'clock I went to the police station and spoke to the officer behind the counter, a young man with sparse pale whiskers on his long chin.

'Help you, sir?'

'I understand a search is being made for a member of my congregation,' I said, 'a Miss Monckton.'

'Yes, sir.'

A thought crossed my mind that this youth could, should he be so inclined, clap me in irons and throw me into a cell. He was scarcely older than my eldest boy. I licked my lips. 'And there has been no news?'

'Not so far, sir.'

'I am very concerned about it,' I continued. 'Her state of mind, in particular. I fear something terrible must have befallen her. Poor child.'

'What makes you say that, sir?'

It was said with nothing more than an idle curiosity, vague interest, but my senses were brought alert. 'Just that – a young woman, alone … and she has been somewhat … how to say it … a little troubled, perhaps.'

stop fumbling over it, man

say what you mean … Harriet is lost, entirely lost

Satan has found her and taken her for his own, and she must be found

none of that

it won't do

it won't do at all

'Troubled, sir?'

'It would be as well to consider that the Bishop's Pond should be dragged. I wonder if that has been thought of? Perhaps I could speak with the inspector?'

'He's very busy, sir.'

14

'Or the sergeant?'

'Out on enquiries, sir.'

'Quite, quite.'

'I'm happy to note down your concerns, sir, or perhaps you should like to leave a note for the sergeant when he comes in?'

don't overdo it, George

just a hint

just a suggestion

you don't want them thinking this is all a bit suspicious

I waited.

After perhaps ten minutes, the sergeant emerged from the room at the back. Out on enquiries? Or just avoiding me, most likely. Samuel King, once a member of the chapel, but no longer. Full of his own self-importance and much in want of judgement.

'Mr Verrall,' he said, booming. 'How can I help you?'

I told him something of what I knew, and left as soon as I could. Outside, the day was still grey and cloudy. This time last year it was snowing; the beginning of November, and this curious warmth in the air, the smells of the town hanging in it like threadbare laundry, no breeze to disperse it.

Tom Churcher was watching me from the doorway of his father's shop. When I met his glance he gave me a nod. I felt a spike of fury, crossing the road with a purpose, striding fast and only just missing the butcher's cart.

'What are you doing?' I hissed at him.

'Nothing!' he said, alarm written all over his face. 'Nothing. Have they found her?'

'What do you think?'

'I've heard nothing,' he said.

I softened, then. Poor Tom, poor sad boy, had he forgotten already?

'I suggested they should drag the Bishop's Pond.'

'What for?' he asked.

'For Harriet, of course.'

He looked at me, cow-eyed, blinking. A slick of perspiration on his pale brow.

'Leave it until it gets dark,' I said to him. 'If there is no news by then, take someone with you, to look for her. Someone sensible.'

I thought he was going to protest, but he stopped himself.

'I will pray for you, Tom. I will pray for all of us.'

That seemed to alleviate some of his distress. I went back to the house for dinner. The house was echoingly quiet, and I sat alone in the cold dining room wondering if everyone had left. At length I heard footsteps coming up the corridor and the door opened. Even though her presence was expected, she startled me with it. Sarah came in, and without speaking a word placed a plate upon the table in front of me. A mutton chop, and potatoes. She made to leave the room.

'Where is Mrs Burton?'

'Her sister is ill. Again. She has gone to Sydenham; she said she would be back in the morning.'

'That's probably for the best. And Ruth?'

'Visiting Miss Gent. She has another chill.'

'You're not eating?' I asked her.

She paused in the doorway, her back to me. 'Lost my appetite,' she said, and left, closing the door behind her. Footsteps retreated back towards the kitchen.

I offered my thanks to the Lord, and, almost as an after-thought, asked Him to bestow His Grace upon Tom. After a moment's reflection, I prayed for Harriet's soul. Then I ate the mutton, which had the unusual quality of being both tough and greasy at the same time. The potatoes chased each other around the plate. My breath caught in my chest.

Lord grant me thy peace
why will no one look me in the face any more?

I ate half of the potatoes and the cutlery clattered on to the plate. I wiped the grease from my lips with my handkerchief, folded it and replaced it in my pocket. I took out my watch and observed that it was two o'clock exactly. The watch ticked, hard and fast.

Frances Williams

At two o'clock Thomas Steers came with a note from Mr Campling:

> *There has been no word from Miss Monckton. Mrs Campling has been kind enough to take the girls this morning, but please ensure that you attend the school tomorrow at the usual hour. I should like to discuss the matter with you before lessons begin. No further absence will be tolerated.*

I sent the boy back again with a message to say I had understood. What else should I say? Perhaps the fever would take hold once more; perhaps I would be dead by tomorrow. Perhaps at any moment Harriet would stroll in, smiling, telling me she had gone to this friend, or that friend, and she had told me as much last night, and how very silly I was, for worrying so. I still wanted so very much to believe that all was well.

But the hours continued to pass without her, and the evening grew dark again, and I lit the lamps and told myself that she must, surely, be safe and warm somewhere. There comes a moment when you stop lying to yourself, and you start to think about the secrets you've buried, the truths you've discovered, the ones you keep close to your heart.

The truth that there was not one Harriet, but two: the Harriet you knew and loved; and the other Harriet, the girl with the secrets, the girl you did not really know at all.

Reverend George Verrall

By half-past five, it was dark. I had been out intermittently, visiting church members, asking after Harriet. The opinions were varied: that she had left the town, for some nefarious reason; that she had gone to Arundel early. Several were of the belief that some ill must have befallen her.

'We can none of us know the will of the Lord,' said Samuel Taylor darkly.

indeed

'I will pray for her, that she is found swiftly,' said Elspeth Taylor, crossing herself like a Papist. She has never quite got the hang of nonconformism. I let her get away with it, because she is generous with her tithing. Not all of them are.

pray for her, I will pray for her

Echoes throughout the town. No real sense of the urgency, not yet. Missing was just that: missing. She might have changed her plans at the last minute. She might have gone for a walk, lost track of the time... maybe she has turned her ankle, taken shelter in a barn. Fallen asleep.

But, by then, everyone had retreated inside. Fires were lit, although the weather was still mild. Candles flickered in windows as night descended.

I walked the short distance to the Churchers' workshop. James Churcher was at the counter, noting the day's business neatly in his ledger. Through the doorway at the back I saw Tom sitting on a bench, his hands hanging between his knees, a cat twisting its skinny body around his ankles.

'What can I do for you, Reverend?' said old man Churcher.

not so very old

less than ten years on me, although he looks older

looks worn

'No word yet on the Monckton girl,' I said. 'It's very perplexing.'

'She'll be found in a ditch somewhere,' he said, adding, 'God rest her soul,' as if that made it less blunt.

Tom Churcher stared. 'Good evening, Tom,' I said.

He nodded, in response. 'Perhaps I can help with the search,' he said. 'Seeing as I'm done here.'

James Churcher frowned. 'If you must. Although what you're going to see in the dark I couldn't say. Better off waiting for first light, if you ask me.'

Tom took up his hat.

'Take someone with you,' I said to him. 'Take Sweeting. He will be at home, if you go there now.'

As he passed me, he took a deep breath in.

now he is over the worst of it

he is stronger than he looks

he can bear the weight of the world upon his shoulders, that boy

Thomas Churcher

George Sweeting did not want to come with me. His wife was cooking a stew, he said, and his youngest was unwell. He had better things to do.

'Reverend bade me come,' I said. 'He told me you would go with me.' He pulled a face at me and collected his cap.

I had thought about where to go, in advance. Up Widmore Lane, across the fields towards Farwig and her mother's house. Then back down past the workhouse and the college, back to the Market Place. It should not appear planned. It should be thorough.

'Funny business,' was the first thing he said to me.

I had not trusted myself to speak up to then. What did you talk about, anyway, when you were looking for a girl that had gone missing?

'Yes it is,' I said.

'I reckon she's gone to London,' he said, out of breath. We were in the field at this point, Sweeting's lantern swinging shadows across the bare earth, although the moon was full once more and we could see lamplight in the windows of the houses up ahead. He was looking for a body, a collapsed pile of clothing, somewhere in the field. If she had been there, someone would have seen her in daylight. 'Or that mad Williams woman has done something foolish. If you ask me, she don't belong in Bromley. All of this happened since she turned up.'

'All what?'

He ignored my question, and asked me one in its place. 'And she said nothing to you?'

'No,' I said. Then I added, 'Why should she?'

I could hear the smirk in his voice. 'You and her were close. By all accounts.'

I stopped walking then. It took him a moment or two to react, before he stopped too and looked back at me, holding up the lantern.

'I'll not hear you say that,' I said. 'It's untrue, for a start. Such things hurt those I care about.'

'Like who?' he laughed. Then, 'Ah. Yes. Emma. Well, she'll be glad Harriet's gone, if gone she is. They'll not be fighting over you any longer.'

'Nobody's been fighting.'

I heard him chuckle at it. We carried on. There was no point talking to him. He thought himself better than I. Why had the reverend prompted me to bring him, of all people? We had never been friends. Even the reverend knew that...

I stopped walking again. *That* was why he had told me to bring Sweeting. Had I taken a friend, I should perhaps have found myself with someone to confide in. There was no way on God's green earth I would share what I knew with this man.

'Hurry up, man,' Sweeting said. 'What you dawdling for?'

At last we came back down the High Street and into the Market Place. Still busy, people everywhere. And the White Hart with the late coach outside it, the light above the door showing the steaming horses and the people stepping down, the smell of warm bodies and beer, laughter because there were still people who were happy, even if I was not.

'Well, that's that,' Sweeting said, looking at the pub. 'We've done our bit. No sign of her. Now you can go 'ome, and so can I.'

'We should look in the chapel,' someone said. Perhaps it was me. It sounded like my voice. 'The Lord Himself knows she spent enough time there.'

'The gate'll be locked,' Sweeting said. 'She can't have got in.'

Despite his objection we walked down through the Market Place and turned left into Widmore Lane, back to where we had started. In front of us stood the brick building that housed the parish fire engine, and beyond it the Cage, now defunct. It would have been a good place to hide a body: two cells, opposite each other, dank and cold and open to the elements. It had not been used since the police station had opened in the Market Place, a couple of years ago.

Sweeting shone his lantern inside: it was empty, of course.

The chapel came into view, pale in the moonlight, ghostly, hiding behind the beech tree and the horse-chestnut in the churchyard, both of them almost bare of leaves.

The gate was not locked. I pushed at it, and it swung open.

'Who was last in there and didn't lock it?' Sweeting said. 'We should make enquiries. Beezley will know.'

'Mr Beezley isn't the only one with a key,' I said.

'You mean the reverend? He is most meticulous about locking up, and I should know; you remember last summer when I was clearing up the books, and he locked me in? Four hours I was in there, till Eliza went to enquire of me at the Manse.'

Sweeting handed me the lantern and tried the main door of the chapel, but that was locked. I thought he would give it up at that point, turn back to the road, but then, without my even having to prompt him, he led the way up the path to the side of the chapel.

Back here, in the shadow of the chapel, it was properly dark. I kept behind him and tried to use the light from the lantern to pick my steps carefully between the potholes and uneven slabs.

He was at the back door, then, twisting at the handle. He banged it with the flat of his hand. 'See? Proper locked, both doors. Nobody in there.'

'Perhaps I should go and get the key,' I said. 'She might have gone in to pray, got locked in as you did. Perhaps she fell asleep.'

Sweeting guffawed at this. To make a point, he knocked again. 'Harriet!' he called. 'Harriet Monckton, are you there?'

No reply, of course, although from the road outside the Three Compasses I heard a woman laugh and a man pass some comment.

'Check round the back,' someone said, with my voice. 'Now we are here.'

And so I let him take the lead once more, towards the privy, knowing what lay there, waiting for us. For a moment I believed my own lies. I thought perhaps we should open the privy door and find nothing. That perhaps she was not dead at all, but in a faint; that she had recovered and wandered off somewhere, or got on the coach to London; nothing to worry about, nothing of any consequence. Harriet was alive and well, just somewhere else. Somewhere far from Bromley. Maybe she had never existed at all.

But then Sweeting pushed open the door, and I heard him shout, 'Hi, what's this?' or something like that, and then he screamed like a girl and I knew it was true and she was really dead and nothing would ever be the same again.

Reverend George Verrall

Churcher came to the Manse, out of breath.

'Harriet's been found,' he said. Wild-eyed. 'In the privy, at the chapel.'

'Lord have mercy,' I said.

'Sweeting has gone for the surgeon.'

'Have you told the police?'

'No,' he said.

fool, you should have gone there first

'I will go with you,' I said. 'Sarah! My coat, my hat.'

She was there anyway, listening in the hallway, standing motionless, frowning.

I went to the police station and raised the alarm. Together we walked quickly back to the chapel with the benefit of the sergeant's bull's-eye lantern to light our way. The surgeon was already there and the narrow path running beside the chapel was crammed full of people. Sweeting was there, and George Butler too for some reason, and another figure, and Jasper Tarbutt the drayman, Jenner, Alfred Garn, and then all of us besides. I could not see her, just glimpses through the dark mass of bodies. Her boot, beside the door, a tiny snail clinging to the edge of it. The corner of her dress.

the blood all black in her mouth

dear God

And all the while my heart hammering as if it should burst from my chest, muttering prayers and not even aware of what I was saying.

dear God have mercy

'Someone get me a light, for God's sake!'

The sergeant pushed forward and illuminated the scene for the benefit of the surgeon, who was crouched over. I saw her bonnet, pushed down over her face. Perhaps it was a good thing, for her face was obscured. It might be a pile of rags, a boot, propped up as a facsimile of a human being.

'What's that, in her hand?'

'How did she fall, thus? Did she strike her head?'

'In the privy, of all places ... '

And one of them was sobbing. Girlish gasps, shudders. I could not see which of them it was but at least it was not Tom Churcher, who was beside me, tall and still, the side of his face lit by the moon, carved from marble.

get a grip, man

whoever you are

The surgeon stood up. 'I shall need a strong man – Jasper, you'll do. And the sergeant. The rest of you should go home.'

Nobody moved for a moment, but then Tom turned and walked back down the path, and Sweeting followed and then Butler and the others and then it was just the few of us remaining.

'Reverend,' the surgeon said, noticing me at last. 'A terrible thing to happen here.'

'A terrible thing to happen anywhere at all,' I said. 'I should like to go to her mother.'

'Of course, of course. We need to move the body to allow a proper examination. You are willing to inform her family, then?'

'I am willing. A sorry business, but I am the man for it.'

They agreed to follow at a slower pace, once a blanket had been obtained to cover the body. I set off across the fields for Farwig, thinking of the words I should use to break the sad tidings. I had done this before, of course, many times. Informing people of a death in the family is a sorrowful duty to have as a pastor but I relish it, for it is a privilege, seeing people at their most raw. Fathers who have lost sons; children killed, illnesses, accidents. Mothers, howling at their loss.

I did not know Harriet's mother well. She did not attend chapel, and rarely came to the town. What would be her reaction? Harriet was fond of her as a dutiful daughter should be, but she was a little afraid of her. Her father had died two years ago, and since then her mother had hardened.

And this, the worst of all news to bring to a family home. It was right and just that I should be the one to bring it.

'Mrs Monckton,' I said, as soon as I had been granted entry 'I am most sorry to inform you that your daughter is found, but the Spirit has fled.'

They both stared at me; the mother and the daughter, dark-eyed like Harriet. Not as pretty.

'What?' said the girl, rudely. 'What are you talking about?'

I addressed the older lady, sitting still beside the fire. Had she even heard me? 'My sincerest condolences, madam. They are bearing her home to you as I speak.'

'She's dead?' the girl asked.

'She will be here presently,' I said.

'But she's dead?'

'Yes, I am afraid so.'

'How? How did she die?'

'The surgeon should be able to inform us, once he has had a chance to examine her more closely.'

'Was it an accident?'

is this girl stupid?

'I'm afraid it's impossible to say.'

'Where was she found?'

I coughed. 'Outside the chapel,' I said.

'Outside? But how was she not seen? We've all been looking, all day. Someone looked at the chapel. Someone would have seen her.'

dear God grant me patience

'She was – forgive me – somewhat concealed from view.'

That shut her up. Something about the word 'concealed', it implied a third party. Dangerous. Her mouth shut tightly; she would say nothing else. Nothing at all. She did not trust me.

And then, the knock at the door, the sound of shuffling and breathing from outside, and from the girl a wail like an injured beast; and Harriet came home.

Thomas Churcher

My mind was empty. I poured it out like milk, all those thoughts, the picture in my mind of Harriet lying there. I poured it all out into the gutter and walked home with a mind clear and dry like a washed pot.

They all looked at me as I came through the door and something broke; perhaps I had not poured it all out as well as I thought I had because it was all there again, and I could smell her dress and her hair, how it felt damp in my hand and how her eyes had looked at me in the chapel those times when she was supposed to be praying but her eyes were open all the same.

'Thomas,' my father said.

And I could hear her calling me that, *Thomas, Thomas*, and laughing with her small white teeth and the dimples in her cheeks that you only saw when she smiled.

'Thomas,' he said again. 'Take off your coat, lad.'

I could still move; I could still hear them. But in my head it all swam together like mud in a puddle, swirling and mixing. Harriet at Miss Williams's room, looking at me while she was drinking tea and listening to me – not like they do, properly *listening* to what I told her like I was teaching her something, and not the other way around; and Harriet with her smile at the tail end of the summer in the fields, the smell of the harvest and the turned earth, and then we went by the river and into the shade, and the pine needles underneath us warm and springy and smelling like a perfume.

'She's dead,' I said.

And then Harriet lying on the flagstones in a bad way with her eyes open but not seeing, her bonnet tied under her neck but hanging off, her fingers curled, and how heavy she was to lift, and I've lifted her before but she felt heavier, she felt *dead* like an animal, not like Harriet at all. A snail worked its way along the edge of her boot, and I wanted to brush it gently away, as she would have done herself if she had still been breathing.

'Something's wrong with him,' my brother James said.

'Tom, sit down.'

And Clara, coming into the parlour from the kitchen. 'What's happened? What's wrong with Tom?'

'They found the Monckton girl,' my father said. 'Dead.'

'Harriet?' Her hand, over her mouth. 'Dead? Oh, no, no. Please, dear God no.'

I went through to the parlour and hung my hat and coat up and went to sit down on the chair but instead I sat down on the floor and curled tight because then I might disappear. I did not know what to do, how to be. I curled up and I didn't cry because I am a man and men don't cry, even when bad, bad things happen. But then not crying made my stomach turn and I uncurled and went on to my hands and knees and was sick on to the floor.

They were all watching me.

Reverend George Verrall

Sarah had locked the door, which meant she had gone to bed. She had left a candle lighted on the hall stand, and I carried it upstairs. From the boys' room, all was quiet.

other men come home drunk and insensible

for my abstinence you should consider yourself fortunate, wife

But she was not asleep. I took off my clothes and laid them carefully upon the chair. She stirred as I pulled the nightshirt over my head, and as I turned to the bed she sat up and looked at me.

'I went to the Moncktons,' I said, although she had not asked. 'Poor, poor woman, her mother. She has barely recovered from the death of her husband.'

'I wasn't aware you knew the family so well,' she said.

'I don't, to be truthful with you.'

'Just Harriet,' said Sarah. There was an edge to it.

'And no longer Harriet,' I said. 'The poor girl is gone to be with the Lord.'

'You think that's where she's gone?'

'Sarah, please. Be kind.'

'And she was in the privy?'

'Yes.'

I made myself comfortable and blew out the candle. After a moment my eyes became accustomed to the dark, and the light from the moon visible at the edges of the curtains painted the room in a pale grey light.

'How did it appear that she died?' Sarah asked.

'They are not certain.'

We lay side by side in the darkness. In my head the thoughts of Harriet, living and dead, twisting around each other.

the last time I saw her she was weeping
and then silent, nodding her assent

'It's still so interminably warm,' I said. 'Surely we shall have winter soon.'

her mouth, dark with blood

'I'll not wish for it,' she murmured.

Her tone had softened, and I thought perhaps she might be willing. Something about the day, the horror of it and yet the constant, constant reminders of Harriet, who she had been, and that I should never see her alive again. If I were a man given to sentimentalities, I should be in need of a wife to give me comfort at such a time of loss. I thought about saying this to her, but instead I turned in bed and put my arm about her waist. She did not move, but I felt her tense.

'Sarah,' I said.

She had but rarely refused me. That, I would say, was to her credit. Men often came to me for advice, when their wives had grown cold towards them. Telling me that they had to be forceful, to push themselves through thighs gripped together, holding their women by the wrists. A symptom of getting older, I would tell them. Of childbirth, of tragedy. And I counselled the men to persist but to be gentler, and I counselled the wives to remember their oaths. But I took it as a sign of a successful marriage and a pure heart, that my own wife did not deny me my conjugal rights.

And yet even before the boys, the three living and the two who have gone to the Lord, all she did was lie there, inert, waiting for me to finish. She could not even bring herself to lift her arms about my neck, lying there with her fists clenched into balls. In the dark I wanted to think that she could be someone else, but the thinness of her, the bones of her hips that dug in, the flat, slack skin of her belly, was too familiar.

small wonder I sought release elsewhere
how is a man supposed to function
without the relief of it?

Not a word was spoken. I lay in silence, my breathing slowing, thinking of Harriet.

Frances Williams

It was Beezley who told me the news. In my heart I knew, already, of course. She was nowhere to be found, for a whole night and a whole day, during which I looked out of the window and wished that she had gone to London early, without telling anyone; or perhaps had gone to Hackney to see Maria Field, or that she had gone already to Arundel. But there was only one possibility.

And outside all day the grey skies and the unseasonably warm temperatures, and the breeze blowing bad news up the lane.

At ten o'clock Tom Churcher had been outside, talking to Mrs Beezley. I saw him look towards my window, and then she turned too. Shortly afterwards he came to my door.

'Mr Beezley says Harriet did not come back last night?'

He did not ask how I was feeling. Perhaps he could tell by the sight of me; he looked pale and ill himself. He said he would make enquiries of her, in the town, and that he would pray. Fine help that would be. By eleven I guessed that half the town would be at prayer, or making a show of doing so at least. Hypocrites. How I despised them! Or, specifically, the adults. Not my girls.

But by noon even I was making an attempt at a prayer, for there was nothing else to be done. *Please let Harriet come home. Please, God, if you can hear me, let her be safe, after all.* But to me it was like speaking underwater: nonsense, breathless, soulless; empty words.

Then, at last: after dark – almost a full twenty-four hours since I had last seen my friend alive – Beezley rapped at my door.

'You heard the news? They found Harriet.'

As if standing where Beezley stood I pictured my own face, like stone. White, still, cold marble. 'Where is she?'

'In the privy at the chapel. Tom Churcher found her. With Sweeting.'

'In the privy!'

'Dead as dead. Poor child.'

My face, like stone. My lips, like marble. Would not move.

He was expecting something else. I tried to sculpt a different expression. Shock. Horror at it. 'Dead?'

'The surgeon has had her taken to her mother's.'

30

'Poor, poor Mrs Monckton. Poor Harriet. My dear friend. What can have happened to her? She was well enough just yesterday.'

'I reckon you must've been the last person to see her alive, Miss Williams. She was here last evening, was she not?'

Beezley's face, florid in the light of his lantern and leering, inches from my door. His door; he owned it, after all. He missed nothing, between him and his vixen of a wife – good or ill, the business of Bromley town was conducted under their judgemental scrutiny.

'Yes, indeed she was, Mr Beezley. She left to post a letter. When she did not come back, I thought perhaps she had gone back to her mother's.'

'She's a good girl, to tend to a sick friend. Sorry. She *was* a good girl, right enough. God rest her soul.'

'Mr Beezley, if you will excuse me.'

I had been trying to close the door as he spoke, but the excitement of bringing the news had rendered him ruder than usual.

'Of course. Our condolences to you, Miss Williams. I know you and she were very close.'

I closed the door without thanking him. For a moment my visage held its stony composition.

Then it shattered, and I stuffed my fist into my mouth to stop the noise.

Wednesday, 8th November, 1843

Frances Williams

The next morning I dressed before dawn. I had lain awake most of the night wondering what to do, how to act. Many things required my attention, but there was one task that was more pressing than all others.

I wanted to see her and yet I could scarcely bring myself to contemplate it; I wanted to remember Harriet as she had been, not as she was now. Not dead. But propriety dictated that I should pay my respects to her family and so that was a good place to start.

After that, I would have to go to the school.

I made tea and left it to go cold, standing at the window, looking out over the street as it came to life. Dark shapes, moving in the gloom. All these people, going about their business as if nothing had happened.

At six it was light enough to see my way and I left the house to walk the mile or so across the fields to Farwig. It was not cold, unusual still for November. Soon the weather would break and the winter chill would set in – short gloomy days and long, dark nights. And Harriet was dead.

The door to the rooms where Sarah Monckton lived with her daughters – no, her daughter, Mary Ann – had black crêpe draped over the lintel. Just a scrap of it, like a veil, to signify the tragedy that had befallen the household. I knocked at the door and in a moment Mary Ann opened it. She was dressed, but not yet in mourning. A black shawl was all she had managed to find.

'Miss Williams,' she said, both as a greeting and as announcement to her mother, who was sitting in a hard-backed chair beside the fire, which had burned low. Despite that, the room was stifling. The body was laid out on the bed in a corner of the room, a sheet covering it. Neither Mary Ann nor her mother could have slept at all, unless they had dozed in the chair or on the floor.

'I am so very sorry,' I said, my voice as soft as I could make it.

I have been accused by some of hardness of temperament, of being brusque and opinionated and cold. This has never mattered to me: in the schoolroom my manner is useful for keeping unruly girls focused upon their lessons; in the market, the barrow boys don't try to short-change me. It pays to be seen as formidable.

But here, with my dear Harriet dead and cold, under a sheet, and her mother and sister apparently so bereft, a gentler tone was called for.

Mary Ann went to speak, but her mother interrupted. 'Thank you,' she said.

'There is to be an inquest,' Mary Ann said.

'Indeed?'

A look passed between them, a warning perhaps.

'It is to be begun this morning, at the workhouse.'

I swallowed hard, experimented with my new, soft voice. 'Forgive me, but Harriet had some books from the schoolroom. I must take them back there today. Is it possible they are here?'

Another glance from Mary Ann to her mother. Then she said, 'Come with me.'

The back room was smaller, another two beds within it, pushed against the wall with a narrow space between them. Perhaps the two women had slept after all. Perhaps they had left Harriet to sleep alone. The thought of it choked me. Mary Ann lit a candle, for there was scarcely any light here.

The glow made things look even more shabby, although it was, at least, clean. Mary Ann indicated the second bed, a trunk underneath it. I pulled the trunk clear of the bed, and opened it. Mary Ann stood over me, with the light. I reached up to take it from her.

'I'll hold it,' she said. 'You need both your hands.'

The school books were on the top of a pile of clothes. She could see them as well as I. I removed them and touched the dresses that lay underneath, pressing down to feel for anything solid that might lie below. All was softness. I ran my hands along the edges, where perhaps I should have tucked a book, had I wished to conceal it.

'What are you doing?' Mary Ann said. 'You have your books.'

I looked at her directly. People do not challenge you when you look them in the eye.

'There is another missing. An arithmetic primer.'

'Well, you won't find it hidden, I'm sure. If it's not there with the others, then you must have misplaced it somewhere else.'

There was a catch in her throat; close to tears, perhaps, or anger. The candle flickered.

'Very well,' I said, getting to my feet, the books clutched close to my chest. 'Thank you.'

I placed the books on the bed and closed the trunk, sliding it back under the bed. Mary Ann was already heading for the door, the room slipping into darkness. My desperate eyes, chasing around the room in case I should see it lying on a shelf. As I took up the books I ran my hand over the bed, under the feather pillow. Nothing.

There was nothing more to be said. I joined her, and her mother, and Harriet, in the other room. They both stared at me.

'I apologise for the intrusion, Miss Monckton, Mrs Monckton. Perhaps if the arithmetic book should be found you might have it sent to me?'

A curt nod from Mary Ann.

'Once again, my sincerest condolences. Good day.'

The sky was grey, light spreading from the east. People were on the path but I met the eyes of none of them. Hurrying, hurrying to get to the school where for a few blessed moments I could be alone with my thoughts. There was scarcely a half-hour before Mr Campling would arrive; in that time I should light the stoves in both the school rooms, prepare for the lessons, wash my hands and face and make tea. Routine would save me. Once I was there, in familiar surroundings, taking the lessons as I had done every day for the past eighteen months, I might feel safe.

But on the path, in the school room, even an hour later when the girls were beginning their day by reciting the poetry Harriet had helped them learn just two days before, the thoughts were crowding upon me, tumbling over and over in my brain like pebbles churned by the waves.

Where is it? Where has she hidden it?

Thomas Churcher

Emma called at the house twice.

'She called at the shop,' Clara said. 'When you weren't there, she came here.'

I said nothing.

'She's worried for you, Tom. She wants to see you.'

'Not today,' I said.

Emma did not want to see me. She was only calling to gloat at my condition.

I stayed in my bed, shivering. I heard the door slam as Clara went out. I felt as though I had caught a chill, one that made my stomach bad. My head ached and I could not think; my hands shook. I could not work.

An hour later, my father came.

35

'Get up now,' he said, his voice low. 'Mrs Verrall is here to see you.'

I got up without arguing, and found a clean shirt, pulled it over my head, and tucked it into my trousers. I washed my face in the bowl and dried it.

In the parlour Mrs Verrall was seated in Father's chair, her skirts spread about her. Her face was pale, and pretty, and she had a gentle smile. She made to stand when she saw me, and held out her hand.

'Tom,' she said. 'I heard you were suffering.'

My father was standing in the doorway. She gave him a look, and said that Ruth was waiting outside, and perhaps he could go and see that she was all right? He left us alone.

'You must be brave, Tom. For you are such a good man, and such a friend to Jesus. The town is looking to you, for you were her friend.'

'I know, miss, and that's what makes it so hard.'

'You know you are not alone. So many people here love you. And the Lord takes care of his own. Psalm Sixteen, Tom: the Lord wilt not leave thy soul in hell. Only pray, and trust, and look to the Lord, and all will be well.'

'How can it be? How can anything be well again?'

She had hold of my hand, and her grip was so gentle and so firm, I felt the tears starting. 'I will pray for you, and the Lord will send you comfort. In the meantime, be strong. We know that all things work together for good to those that love God, to those who are the called according to his purpose. So it shall be with Tom Churcher.'

I bent my head, so she should not see my fears. Behind me I heard the door open and my father's voice saying to someone – Ruth Verrall, I guessed – that she should warm herself, and I wiped my eyes and let go of Mrs Verrall's hand.

'Here he is, Ruth,' Mrs Verrall said. 'And what a fine young man you have raised, Mr Churcher, that does such good and such kindness in our community. A credit to you.'

'He is that,' said my father, although he sounded surprised.

She got to her feet, and Father was asking if she was sure she didn't want tea, and he was only sorry that Clara wasn't here to help, and Mrs Verrall was insisting that it was quite all right, and they had many calls to make, and she was only sorry to have interrupted our morning.

At the doorway Mrs Verrall took my hand again, and smiled, and said, 'You really should see Emma, Tom. She should be like a rock to you, at such a difficult time.'

My head was a writhing mass of thoughts, like a bucket of worms.

Harriet's face, dark blood between her teeth; Harriet smiling up at me, turning her face up so I could kiss her. How she tasted. How her hand felt, small and delicate, inside mine. The sensation of her heart, beating. My finger on the skin at her throat, the pulse beneath it. She was so full of life! Harriet pleading with me, tears in her eyes. The Cage Field at night, the smell of the turned earth, still warm, underneath us. I said to her, *I'll not do that, I cannot*, and she said, *You should, Thomas, you must.*

She called me Thomas. They all called me Tom, well, most of them; apart from my father, when he was angry with me about something, or wanted my full attention. She called me Thomas and sometimes Mr Churcher, which felt like she was poking fun at me, only she was not. She made me feel more than I was.

She made me feel like a man.

Reverend George Verrall

I returned to the Monckton house on Wednesday morning, at nine o'clock sharp. I brought with me my Bible and a basket containing some fresh bread, baked in my kitchen, and cheese, both of them wrapped in muslin cloth by my wife.

Mary Ann Monckton opened the door to me. Someone had made an attempt to dress the house in mourning, but it felt half-hearted.

'I have come to offer my sincerest condolences,' I said, 'and to bring you some prayer, and some sustenance.'

'You came yesterday,' she said, but after some sound from the room behind her she opened the door and granted me access.

The room was full. Mrs Monckton sat in the same chair she had occupied last night, when I came to deliver the sad tidings. Standing at the mantel were two young men, one of whom looked sufficiently like Harriet's deceased father to be her brother; the other I did not recognise.

On a low bench beside the fire, Mary Ann's elder sister, Sarah, sat knitting. Her eyes were red as she looked up at me.

'Do forgive the intrusion,' I said. I offered the basket of food to Mary Ann, who took it.

I shook hands with the two men; as I suspected, one was the eldest son, Stephen. The other was George Dorset, Sarah's husband. They had only been married a year, and were living a short distance away, in Plaistow.

Harriet's body was still lying on the bed where it had been placed last night. A sheet covered it. I wondered if she had been undressed, and washed. If her teeth were still clenched over her tongue. If her eyes were closed.

if she has been washed clean
if she has my scent upon her skin

'I wondered if arrangements had yet been made for the funeral,' I asked Mrs Monckton.

'None,' said Stephen. 'We can spare no money for it.'

Sarah glared at him. It felt as though I had intruded into a conversation.

'It may be, sir,' I offered, 'with your sister having been a regular attendant of my chapel, that some of our funds could be made available to you to facilitate, perhaps, a simple coffin. I can make enquiries, if you should wish me to.'

'We are not members of your church,' Sarah said haughtily.

'Yes,' Stephen replied, at the same moment. 'Paying for the coffin would be appreciated most warmly, sir '

a thank-you from your mother would not go amiss either

I was about to offer to lead them in a prayer when there came a knock at the door.

Mary Ann went to open it. 'Never had so many callers,' she muttered.

Two men came in, removing their hats as they did so. One of them was older, grey-haired, with a jowly, sagged face like a wax cast that had been placed too close to a stove, the other taller, sallow, clean-shaven. He introduced the elder man as the coroner for Kent, Mr Charles Carttar. All in the room stood, even the ladies. Carttar bade them sit.

'My dear lady,' he said, addressing Harriet's mother. 'My deepest condolences upon the sad loss of your daughter.'

'Thank you,' she responded. I believe it was the first time I had heard her speak. Her voice was high, and querulous.

'I do require a formal identification to be made. Perhaps now, if you would be so kind.'

The woman looked alarmed at the thought of it. I wondered if the sheet had even been removed from Harriet's face. If she had looked upon her dead daughter.

'I'll do it,' Stephen said.

The coroner nodded. The two men crossed to the bed. I accompanied them, for the sake of comfort, and so I saw what they saw.

it does not look like her
it is not her

The eyes had been closed but not fully; beneath the lashes a sliver of the eye still visible, dull and waxy.

they need to place pennies on those eyes to close them

39

The skin of the face was white and mottled with blue, cheeks slack, but the mouth still closed. A half-inch of the tongue still between the teeth. Black with blood, a line of it trickling down one side to the chin and down the neck. On the side of the throat, the ghost of a bruise. A fly landed on the face, walked across to the corner of her eye. Stephen Monckton waved it away.

her eyes her cheeks her face her neck
don't do that again, she said
it leaves a mark
someone will notice
but I ignored her and did it again

'This is my sister, Harriet Monckton,' Stephen said.

'And when did you last see her alive, sir?'

'Saturday last.'

'And she was well?'

'Well, and in good spirits.'

The coroner looked around to his assistant, who was taking notes, and caught sight of me.

'You knew the deceased, Reverend?'

'Yes, sir,' I said. 'She was a member of my congregation. A most virtuous girl.'

Carttar nodded, looking down once more at the body. 'I shall arrange for her to be removed, so that the surgeon can perform a post-mortem. Perhaps later today.'

'A post-mortem?' Stephen asked.

'She shall be returned to you in due course, for the burial.'

'Is a post-mortem entirely necessary?' I asked.

'Yes, indeed,' the coroner said. 'The cause of death must be determined.'

The room was silent. All of them were looking at me, looking to me to support them, in their hour of most desperate need. I was the one who must speak up. It fell to me to represent them, to speak up for Harriet.

40

'But the family,' I said. 'I speak for the family. Their poor dear daughter lies here in peace, awaiting her transformation into glory. Surely there is no need to disturb her rest?'

'I'm afraid there is no other course of action to be taken, sir.' He glanced behind me. 'My dear lady,' the coroner continued, addressing Mrs Monckton, 'I'm afraid we shall have to trouble you further today. Once the jury has been sworn in, they are required to view the body. That may well be as soon as this afternoon. If you would prefer it, we can remove her remains to the workhouse and the viewing can take place there.'

'She should remain here,' Stephen said. 'Let them come.'

'As you wish, sir.'

The coroner nodded to his assistant, and they took up their hats once more. I offered my hand to Stephen Monckton, acknowledged the ladies and wished them well, and followed them out.

'Sirs,' I said, to attract their attention. A closed carriage was waiting for them outside. 'A moment, if you please.'

'Reverend?'

'Verrall is the name, sir. I am pastor of the chapel, in Widmore Lane. Miss Monckton was a regular attender.'

'Yes, as you said.'

'Forgive me, sir; I had wished to mention this to you, but not in the presence of her poor family, who have suffered so, by her sad loss.'

'What is it, man?' The coroner had one foot on the step, ready to leave. He took it down. The assistant took out his pencil.

'That I saw the girl on Sunday last, sir. That she was in a state of some excitement, and vexation. That she was – in fact – troubled, sir. When I heard she was missing, I went immediately to the police station – immediately, I say – and suggested that they should look for her in the Bishop's Pond. I thought she must have taken her own life.'

'Indeed?'

'Yes, sir. And so, you see, there is really no need for the delay of a post-mortem, after all.'

The man raised one eyebrow, and did not speak.

'I feel quite certain that no other has had a hand in her unfortunate demise, sir. Quite certain. And on that you have my oath, as a Christian and a gentleman.'

Moments passed, and he continued to regard me, as if contemplating my words with the greatest care.

'Mr Verrall,' he said at last, 'I am grateful for your candour. And yet I am afraid the matter is quite resolved. A post-mortem must and shall take place. And your thoughts will be put to the inquest, and your opinions and knowledge of the deceased and her state of mind will be given due consideration.'

He turned and climbed the step, pulling the door closed behind him. 'Good day, sir.' A knock upon the roof of the carriage, and the coachman nudged the horse with his whip, and they were gone.

why does nobody listen to me?

Frances Williams

Sixty-four girls in attendance this morning. Eliza Sanger was sent home to fetch her school pence, which were a full week in arrears. She did not return. Mrs Campling stayed in the girls' room for an hour, to supervise the older girls' needlework, which is to be sold next week. Ann Voakes and Priscilla Draper were sent to the corner for gossiping. Mr Campling beat two boys for poor work. Alice Jessops is absent with scarlatina. Mr Campling wishes all the Jessops children to cease attending until the sickness is passed from their household, so I was obliged to send the three girls home with their brothers.

In the morning, Mr Campling spoke to me about my illness and my failure to attend the class yesterday. My voice was hoarse and I was still feverish, but he appeared to overlook this.

'Mrs Campling,' he said, 'has been greatly inconvenienced by your lack of commitment to the school.'

'I did suggest that the pupil teachers would manage well enough,' I said.

He does not like it when I stand up to him. He had begun his lecture from his usual position, a few feet away, and was so incensed by my response that he took a stride forward, the better to fix me with his stare, apparently forgetting in his fury that I am some six inches taller than he, and he was thus forced into a disadvantageous position.

'If you should fail to attend in future, Miss Williams, you should look for a position elsewhere.'

I thought of answering, but what was the point? He needed to assert his authority, and it was quicker and easier to just let him do it, so I could get on with the business of the day.

'And you should not expect a favourable character.'

With that, he turned his back on me, which I took as a dismissal. He was full of bluster and ill will; he ruled the boys' room with violence because it was the only way he could maintain discipline. He was shorter than most of the older ones, and, if they were to see through him as I do, they would turn the cane on him and get their revenge.

Fortunately the girls were so pleased to see that I was to take them, and not Mrs Campling, that they behaved beautifully. It was just as well: I had not eaten, scarcely slept. The cough that had troubled me for weeks and had caused me to take to my bed, and have Harriet as my nurse, had worsened. Every breath was painful. My heart, broken into pieces inside my chest, and the pain spreading within me, seeping into my bones.

And Harriet's diary was nowhere to be found.

Reverend George Verrall

The inquest is opened at the Bromley workhouse. I will say this: the man wasted no time. Scarcely twenty-four hours have passed since Harriet's remains were discovered by Churcher and Sweeting, and yet already the coroner has found and sworn a jury, no doubt brought them to the Monckton house to view the body, and set up the first meeting.

I was in attendance, of course; my duty was to ensure Harriet's welfare, even after her unfortunate demise.

This morning, over breakfast, Sarah had asked if she should also attend.

'Under no circumstances,' I told her.

'But I shall be expected,' she said. 'If you are there, I should be by your side, to support you, and those others who are suffering because of this dreadful business.'

'On the contrary. You must stay here. Minister to the town if you insist, but stay away from the inquest.'

She bit her tongue and said nothing else. She meant well, but I feared she might say something, unintentionally, which could be misconstrued.

Eventually the coroner entered. He appeared a serious, steady type. His assistant was most business-like about the whole affair, bustling into the meeting room at the workhouse and ordering everyone about. A long table had been set up at the front of the room, a single chair in front of it, two rows of chairs to the left, under the window, for the jury.

At the back of the room was another line of seats, to be occupied by the elderly ladies and gentlemen of the town, those not so noble as to find the whole matter distasteful, and yet sufficiently respectable as to qualify for a seat. I noticed a cohort of ladies from the Bromley College, their maids standing behind; I recognised Miss Holgate – *that old toad* – Mr Patello, Robert Latter, the attorney; Abraham Nettlefold, Mrs Carter of Bromley Lodge, Mr Lawes. Another whose name I always forget – the lady who walks with a glass-topped cane.

Behind them a rope strung across the room held back the crowd who had come to gawp. The working day was all but over, lending an additional throng of the curious, those who had nothing better to do with their evening than indulge their righteous indignation at such a horror, taking place as it did right under their inquisitive noses. The air fragrant with the press of unwashed bodies rubbing up against one another; I looked up longingly at the windows, but they were beyond my reach and should have required a pole to draw up the sash.

The coroner watched in silence as the jury took their seats. I felt sorry for the man, to have to breathe in this reeking air. Perhaps he was accustomed to it.

Fifteen men, good citizens of the town of Bromley. I knew them all to a man; five of them are members of my congregation. Among them three deacons: Thomas Parry, a leather-seller; James Sherver, watchmaker, and Robert Cooper, who leads the men's prayer group. Also Daniel Biggs and Thomas Costin, both simple men, labourers, but trustworthy. I trusted them all.

To my mind, it was a favourable jury, for our purposes.

First came Harriet's brother, Stephen, who had little to say beyond the identification of his sister, and that he had last seen her on Saturday, and that she had been in good spirits. After he was dismissed, Susannah Garn was called—

of all the people

—who testified to the deceased calling at her house at around twenty minutes past seven on Monday night. That Harriet had told her she was planning to go to London on the following day, and had come to bid her farewell. And that she was quite well and in good spirits.

Next to be summoned to appear was George Sweeting. He approached the seat in the manner of a man who was eager to appear humble, whilst simultaneously being bloated spherical with his own self-importance.

'Your name, sir, and occupation?' asked the coroner.

'George Sweeting, of Bromley. I am a plumber and a glazier, property-owner and deacon of the chapel.'

pompous oaf he is

'You heard the deceased was missing, and went in search of her, did you not?'

'Indeed, sir, I heard that the deceased was missing and on Tuesday morning enquiries were made after her. During the day I did all I could to enquire after her.'

you did all you could

did you, man?

did you?

'I understood the police had been made acquainted with her absence and in the afternoon about five o'clock I saw one of the policemen, who told me that he had searched, but could not find her, and had heard nothing of her. I then accompanied Tom Churcher in search of her. We came by the chapel gates and I said, "Are the gates open?", and I tried them and went in and we went down the passage at the side of the chapel to the back part of it. The privy is at the extreme end in the corner of the yard at the rear of the chapel and out of sight as you pass down the passage. The back door of the chapel is close to the privy. I had to pass the back door to get to the privy door. I found the privy door open and I saw the body of a woman lying or sitting up partly on the floor.'

At this he paused, and glanced about the room. All present were listening to him intently, and for a dreadful moment I thought he was going to break into a smile at being the focus of such rapt attention.

'What did you do then?' asked the coroner.

'It was too dark to recognise her, and I was alarmed and drew back. I did not touch her or go into the privy. I ran out with Churcher into the street and called the police and we returned together. Mr Ilott the surgeon came directly afterwards.'

'Thank you, Mr Sweeting.'

He stood there proudly, until the coroner was obliged to add, 'That will be all at the present time.'

All eyes were upon him as Sweeting left his seat and came to stand next to me. The noise in the room swelled with conversation. His face was pink with the excitement of it all, and he looked up at me as if he wished me to say 'well done' or some other word of encouragement. To that end, after a moment, he nudged me in the ribs, and nodded to me.

'A man's pride shall bring him low, George,' I said. 'But honour shall uphold the humble in spirit. Think on that.'

And at that he flushed even darker.

Thomas Churcher

I shall have to answer to God for my sins. The reverend told me that. He preached a sermon about the last day, I cannot remember when, months ago, perhaps. I listened as I always listened and I remembered what he said: that on the last day we shall all be called to account.

I remember thinking, strangely, of my friend Joe Milstead and the time he stole a penny from John Cooper's jacket. He had no reason to. It was just there, and he could. I told Joe that theft was a sin and that he should repent, and give the money back, but he laughed, and then I laughed because I could not stop myself.

But stealing a penny is one thing; eating too much at the chapel field day, pulling my sister's hair, telling a lie about the tear in my breeches, all of them sin by degree. Keeping my eyes open during prayer.

That last one was not even a sin, but it feels as though it should be. It made me think of Harriet.

The first time I noticed her was in the chapel, a long time ago. Years; she cannot have been but sixteen. She had been attending a while, alone – her family being worshippers at the parish church instead – and I knew her name, for Bromley is not large and she went to my sister's school – but I had paid her no mind. I was not interested. And then I looked across the congregation while Daniel Biggs led the prayers, and she had her eyes open, unfocused, but when she saw that mine were open too she looked straight back at me.

I pray best with my eyes open. I always have. I am not distracted by the world around me; I draw inspiration from it. If anyone asks me, that is what I will tell them. And yet, this girl, in the congregation, had her head up and her eyes focused upon me. She did not smile. I did not smile. But for what felt like a full minute, though it may only have been a few seconds, while Daniel Biggs asked for Christ's blessed Mercy to rain upon the people of Bromley, Harriet Monckton and I were staring at each other.

I thought no more of it until the Thursday night prayer meeting. I sat with the others on hard chairs in the Sunday schoolroom at the back, in a rough semi-circle, as by turns we brought our troubles to the Lord and prayed for each other, for the chapel, for our pastor, for the poor, for the missionaries bringing the Word of the Lord to the dark places of the world, for Her Majesty the Queen, for the people of our town and for our families. And Harriet was there. I kept my head down until I could bear it no longer, and I looked up, and her gaze was fixed upon me. I frowned. James Hopperton was praying, one of those that went on and on and repeated itself at least three times before it reached its conclusion. All other heads were bowed, eyes closed. Just myself and Harriet, staring at each other. At any moment someone could look up, and interpret our wordless communication as a sin, or as, at least, something indelicate.

I bowed my head once again and broke the spell.

That so much could come from such a moment – even now it takes me by surprise. That look between us, a connection, born silently, in the sight of God and in the presence of the Holy Spirit – surely such a thing is Holy itself?

After that, I spent all my time thinking of interesting things I could say to her, but on the few occasions I found myself in her presence the words would not come. One fierce February afternoon when there looked to be a storm brewing I offered to accompany her home. I helped her over the stile and she took my hand and my heart buzzed like a bee in a bud with it, the feel of her. If she noticed, she never said, for she was kind-hearted. I asked to walk her home whenever the opportunity presented itself, just so that I could have those joyous moments in her presence; sometimes she accepted, sometimes she had other things to do, or said she was happy to walk by herself. I liked to think that we had an understanding, wordless, perhaps, but an understanding nevertheless.

I must have been mistaken, though, about that; for one day I heard that she was gone to London, and she never even told me she was going. A few times she came back for visits, and went away again, and when she left my heart was sore without her. For all that Emma Milstead stepped in to keep me occupied, I never stopped thinking of Harriet Monckton, all of the long months she was gone. When she came back to stay, there was a moment when I thought that this time would be the death of me. Or her. How I felt about her, it was too much. Too fierce. And then she smiled at me again and the sun came out and the worry of it was all forgotten, until the end.

But it did not matter, now. I had been right, with that morbid feeling I had. Harriet was dead. All of the good things were past, and done with. None of it was important. Not any more.

Harriet wrote in her journal most evenings, when she stayed with me.

It was a small book, bound in green leather, with creamy-white paper within it. She said it had been a present from a dear friend, so that she could record her thoughts, and she carried it everywhere with her, lest her sister should find it, and read it, for she said that she sometimes wrote unkind thoughts in it to get them out of her head.

I asked her if she ever wrote unkind thoughts about me. Half-joking, of course, for by then we were firm friends.

She laughed and said she never wrote a bad word about me, and, on the contrary, that she had written at length about our friendship and how much she cherished it.

'Let me see,' I said.

And she clutched the journal to her chest and shook her head, still laughing, and said that I should think her very free with her words, and she was embarrassed by them.

She relented, though, eventually, when we had grown closer still. Those nights when we lay still, listening to the rain outside, my arm about her waist. How warm and soft she felt, the shape of her, beautiful, under my hands. I became very good at pretending to be asleep. I learned to deepen my breathing, to sigh, to mumble as if in a dream, and as Harriet lay there, still awake, my arm would move, seemingly involuntarily. Sometimes she would move my arm gently away, and then I would turn in bed and leave her in peace. But not always. Sometimes she moved my arm closer, or stroked it; once, she kissed my hand, which was near her face.

There was one night when I woke up to find the lamp burning low at the table, Harriet sitting up in her chemise, with her journal.

'What time is it?'

'Past three,' she said. 'I could not sleep.'

I got out of bed and found my shawl, and placed it about her shoulders, so that she should not catch a chill.

'What are you writing about?' I asked.

'Just the events of the day.'

I watched her writing: tiny little letters she had, filling each page. It had not been an especially eventful day, as I recall; but she continued, bending closely over her words, writing page after page.

'Oh, Frances,' she said, at last. 'Do you want to hear some of my thoughts? I think you shall like them.'

I told her I did.

She turned back through the book, looking for the right place, and then she found it, and read aloud. '*Frances is the most excellent teacher I think I should ever know. She loves her girls, by which I mean she does not indulge them, but she disciplines them so well and praises them so fulsomely when they work hard, or try their best, that they want to improve and so work even harder for her. She knows them all as individuals, and loves them dearly, although she cannot tell them so except by giving them what they most need: the gift of an education. She defends them against Mr Campling's more vigorous complaints, and if any one should speak ill of any of them she becomes a veritable warrior in their defence. I declare that is exactly what she is: Frances Williams, Warrior for her Girls.*'

I smiled at this, and perhaps I blushed a little.

'See how very highly I regard you? And this part, too: *If I should ever be a teacher half as fine as Miss Williams is, I should think it some achievement. I shall never be as good!*'

'You flatter me, Harriet,' I told her. 'Of course you are an accomplished teacher already.'

Later, when I knew more of her past and of her secrets, she shared with me other pages too: although always letting me read a particular passage and then taking back the book, lest I read on to something that was too personal for me to see. I liked that she trusted me with her words, but I worried about the journal falling into the wrong hands. I thought, perhaps, that the pages she would not let me read contained secrets about me. She knew how I felt about her, that my love for her was not the same as her love for me. What if she had written about it? What if someone else read those words? My reputation would be destroyed, my position as a teacher would be impossible, and with that my life would be at an end.

I told her that I was afraid her journal would be mislaid, or stolen, or fall into unkind hands. She said she always kept it with her, and she would never lose it.

And now Harriet is dead, and the journal is lost. And every day I wait for the consequences of that to unfold.

Reverend George Verrall

On my return home, Sarah was in the drawing room with Ruth, who was at her sewing. She got to her feet and said she would fetch me some supper, for which I thanked her.

'Well,' I said to my wife, taking the seat next to the fire, 'the inquest is begun. And the coroner – fool that he is – insists on calling for a post-mortem.'

'A post-mortem! What does he expect to find?'

'The manner of her death, one assumes.'

'You told him she had destroyed herself, I presume? What further investigation is needed?'

'I suppose he has to be thorough.'

Ruth came back into the room with a tray: a pot of tea, cold meat, bread and cheese on a plate with a round, red apple. She took up her sewing once more. I expected her to ask about Harriet, but she did not. My sister, the only person in Bromley able to mind her own business.

'I visited the Churchers today,' Sarah said.

I looked up from the plate. 'Did you now?'

'The poor boy is in a bad way. He is refusing to see Emma Milstead. I told him he should make his peace with her.'

'Why must you meddle so? Leave the boy be.'

'You know he needs guidance, George. He cannot be left to blunder through life like that. He is, as you rightly say, a sensitive boy.'

The fire crackled in the grate. I swallowed down my anger, a hard lump of indignation, doing my best to ignore Sarah's increasing habit of challenging me in front of my own sister. She knows I will not rise to it, not unless we are alone. It has become like a sport to her. The bread was stale, the cheese hard at the edges. No amount of chewing would soften it further than a sticky lump. I washed it down with tea but I could still feel it, a ball of putty in my chest.

her eyelashes wet with tears

her begging on her knees before me

'I shall write to the coroner,' I said.

'To what end?' Sarah asked, but I was already on my feet.

'To insist that a post-mortem is entirely unnecessary,' I said. 'The man's a fool if he can't see it. The jury will do as he says, all he has to do is suggest it.'

'You're too late for the post,' Ruth said. But I went to my study nonetheless, as much to escape the pair of them.

you could save me and you choose not to, she said

I shall pray for your soul

Thursday, 9th November, 1843

Reverend George Verrall

'Where are you going?'
   'Go back to sleep.'
   'What hour is it?'
   'Past four. I need to pray. Go back to sleep.'
I lit a candle on the landing to light me to the kitchen; Mrs
Burton was not yet awake. I sat beside the range, which was
quite cold, the candle upon the worn oak table that had been
in this same kitchen for years, years before we moved in and
would remain in it no doubt for years to come.
   if I am spared
My bare knees objected to the cold flagstones but I paid
no heed; I prayed for forgiveness, called out to the Lord for
mercy. I repented for my treatment of her, for turning her
away when she asked for my help. I asked the Lord whether
the path I had chosen was indeed a righteous one, or if I had
slipped from it through pride, or thoughtlessness. I prayed
for calm, for a steady head, that I should minister to my flock
with all of my heart and soul, that I should not let anyone else
fall away from the path of righteousness.
   By that point my knees had grown numb and getting to
my feet again was intensely painful; no less than I deserved.
   Harriet on her knees before me in the chapel
   her eyes raised to mine
   I could not deny it. I had lusted after her; whatever I
called it – Holy Fire, a Gift of Grace from the Lord – it was
still lust.

filthy with it
filthy with sin

I took my candle to the study. The fire had been swept and freshly laid, so it was a matter of a moment to light it using a taper from the mantelpiece. The warmth spread from it quickly as the fire rose and crackled, and I drew comfort from it. I felt, perhaps, a little forgiven. I felt blessed.

I could not put it off any longer: I had to write to Richard Field.

At my desk I lit the lamp and drew forth notepaper and a pen.

Bromley, 9th November 1843
My dear Sir,—

and how should I write to this man
this man who apparently loved her once?

We are suddenly plunged into the depths of trouble.
Our dear young friend, Harriet Monckton, who was
expecting to visit you yesterday, to arrange about going
to Arundel, was found on Tuesday afternoon, about
half past 5, within the privy of Bromley chapel, quite
dead—

quite dead
how odd that sounds
you are either dead or not dead, how can you be quite dead?

—and had apparently been so some hours. The jury sat
last night, and have adjourned until tomorrow (Friday)
evening, at seven o'clock, to allow a post-mortem
examination to be made, to ascertain whether any thing
has been taken to hasten death. We are of opinion that
she has died in a fit—

a fit you call it now, George?
a fit of excitement
what else can I say?

—produced by excitement at the sudden change from depression of spirits at being so long out of a situation, and the contrary, in expectation of so soon getting into one. The examination today will throw some light upon the business. The enemies of the Cross are alert in this place of abounding infidelity and High Churchism. Pray for us, that, in the event of her having taken any thing improper, the blow may not fall on our dear Zion's cause. My poor people, not to say the poor afflicted mother and sister, are greatly excited. Harriet was a favourite with everybody for her exemplary conduct—

I stopped writing for some time and stared at the page, at my letters so neatly formed, the ink drying as I watched. How best to phrase the last part? This letter might well be made public. Everything I said and did had to be thoughtfully considered now, lest someone should be called under oath to report upon it. Even – or perhaps especially – Richard Field. For now, the man was in blissful ignorance as to the fate of his dear Harriet. His dear young friend. There he was in London, no doubt sleeping deeply in his warm bed, next to the virtuous Maria. He had no knowledge of what was to come. And here was I, writing a letter which would throw him into a state of considerable distress.

—I have strong evidence to present myself of great mental excitement under which she has been labouring for some time—

yes, George, that's good, that's right

56

*—and which was calculated to produce a fit of some
kind, or temporary insanity, but which, of course, will
not be presented to the jury unless it is necessary—*

*necessary being the moment when you stand up and tell them
about me, Richard*

*—I do not know whether you could add any thing to
that evidence or not.*

*and if you do so, let it be favourable
for your sake and for mine*

*—I will send you word what verdict the jury may
decide upon.*
    I am, yours truly,
    George Verrall
    P.S.— You will, of course, inform the Arundel folks.

I sat back in my chair. The fire, untended, had burned itself
low. I should have fuelled it further but my mind had been
consumed with the task in hand, which, now completed, had
quite exhausted me. I took up the letter and read it closely,
considering whether he would fully understand my meaning.
How difficult it was, to express so much earnest desire and
hope, whilst writing about a subject so terrible and so tragic!
    But he was an intelligent man. He would understand.
    It was a letter of warning. A letter of instruction.
    I heard the creaking of the stairs followed by the sounds
of someone – Jessie, or Mrs Burton – in the kitchen. Here
I sat, attired only in my nightshirt. I addressed the envelope
and sealed the letter inside it before I could doubt myself still
further, and took the candle back upstairs to the bedroom.
    Sarah was still and quiet. She was not asleep.

Frances Williams

The weather remains warm and dry, but overcast. Fifty-nine girls in attendance. Four girls absent with scarlatina, not including the Jessops children, who remain at home. I fear there may be another outbreak, like the one we suffered in February. Selina Lucas fell in the yard and tore her dress, and was sent home to mend it. The Reverend Mr Newell visited the girls' room to hear them sing. They performed passably. In the afternoon I tested the older girls on their letters; further work is needed. At the end of school I heard some of the older children playing 'murder' in the yard. I went to speak to them but, by the time I got out, they had gone.

By now, Harriet should have gone on from London to Arundel. Someone would have written to them, of course; if not Mrs Monckton or Mary Ann then Mr Verrall would have seen to it. They would have to find another schoolteacher.

For a moment a thought crossed my mind: that I should write to the board at Arundel and offer them my services in Harriet's place. I could not stay here. It wasn't the school; I had taught in far worse establishments. But here, in Bromley – with memories everywhere, and with the rest of them, the hypocrites and the gossips, the women with their false manners and the men with their filthy minds – I should die here, die of misery and heartbreak, were I to stay.

That evening I ate a chop with some Beezley bread ('beastly bread', Harriet called it, with a laugh) that tasted of chalk and mould. At seven, when I was preparing for bed, there was a knock at the door.

'It's Clara,' came the response when I asked who it was.

Clara was possibly the only visitor I could have tolerated that evening; the one remaining decent woman in the town. I opened the door to her and she came in, wide-eyed, carrying a bottle. 'Well, my dear,' she said, taking off her bonnet. 'What a dreadful, dreadful thing to happen. How are you?'

I was so tired, I could not manage to arrange my face appropriately, and she could see for herself how I was. She gathered me into her arms and held me close against her. I tried to relax but was unable to, and after a moment of standing there stiffly she released me.

'Did you hear the coroner has been called?' Clara said.

I put the kettle on to the stove. 'Yes. Mary Ann Monckton told me.'

'The inquest began yesterday. After an hour the coroner adjourned it.'

'Why?'

'It was late, I think. They have much to discuss, or whatever it is they do in such circumstances.'

'So they believe it was ... murder?'

'The surgeon thinks she was murdered, perhaps with poison. There is to be a post-mortem. Can you imagine?'

I knew this, too. Of course there would be a post-mortem. Harriet would be stripped and examined, her skin cut, the secrets of her lovely body given over to the gaze of men. The thought of it made me feel sick.

'Perhaps it was yet accidental,' I said, for want of something else to say. 'How can they tell it was at someone else's hand?'

From the look she gave me, I regretted my choice of words immediately.

'Accidental?' she echoed. 'How could that be?'

Too tired, not thinking straight. I should keep quiet. Instead, I added, 'Perhaps she thought she was taking something else: a draught, maybe, or a tonic. And in the darkness ... ?'

'But in the privy, at the chapel? Why on earth?'

'Better surely than to think that we have a murderer amongst us.'

I busied myself spooning tea into the pot, and setting out cups and saucers. They would all know, soon enough. If a surgeon was examining her, then he would soon discover more than just the cause of her death. To pre-empt these revelations in idle conversation was more than just foolish, it was dangerous.

'You know Tom is in a bad way,' said Clara.

'Tom?'

'He found her, with Sweeting.'

I bit down on my lip, tasted blood. That he had been the one to find her, of all people! Or had one of them known where to look?

'Father says he has never seen Tom in such distress.'

'He should be careful, showing his feelings; Emma shan't like it.'

'He broke it off, didn't you know? A few weeks ago.'

I did know, of course. Harriet told me. But perhaps I had denied the reality of it. Emma Milstead had always had her heart set on Tom Churcher, everyone knew it, and he'd liked her well enough. If he hadn't had his head turned by my Harriet, perhaps none of this would have happened.

The kettle rolled into a slow boil. My father's clock, on the wall above the mantle, ticked a steady beat. I took the kettle off the stove and poured water into the pot. Clara gazed at the lamp.

'We are all of us quite done in by it,' I said briskly. 'You too. You look quite ashen.'

She stood and retrieved the stoneware bottle that she had left by the door. 'I almost forgot,' she said. 'I brought us some gin.'

We added a tot of gin to the tea and it revived me somewhat. Just three nights ago, Clara had taken tea with Harriet and me here, in this very room. My cough had been very bad, and Harriet was to stay the night with me to tend to me. On leaving, Clara had said she would return with some gin to try and help me sleep. But she had not returned; instead she had sent her brother.

'Tom told me you were unwell on Monday, when he brought the gin,' I said now, to Clara. 'Are you better?'

'It was just a chill, my dear. Thank you, I am quite well.'

She sipped her tea, thoughtful, as if preparing to say something difficult.

'Will you attend the inquest?' she asked.

I pulled a face. 'I shall not. Unless I am pressed.'

'But aren't you curious about what happened?' she asked, leaning forward in her chair. She put the teacup down on the table and reached for my hand. It took me by surprise; I was not quick enough to move away.

'Not curious, no. Horrified, shocked. But hearing poor Harriet's life and death dissected by a collection of men – I cannot imagine a worse spectacle.'

Clara looked at me, surprised. I had gone too far. Perhaps it was better to be inquisitive? Perhaps it was more acceptable to be a gossip, to pore over the business of the good people of the town for your own amusement?

'Besides,' I said, in a milder tone, 'I must attend to the school. Mr Campling will dismiss me if I fail him again.'

'You are such a good person, Fanny,' Clara said, releasing my hand at last. 'I said as much to Father last night. Harriet was fortunate to have you as a friend. Oh! What shall become of the school, at Arundel? And Mr and Mrs Field? Do you suppose they know?'

Richard Field. That man. I tried to suppress a shudder. 'I am quite sure someone will have written to them. Mr Verrall, I expect. He always seems to take these things upon himself.'

'God bless him. He is a man of such strength and virtue. I daresay he will have words of comfort for us on the Sabbath. Although he must be terribly upset himself. He and Harriet were such close friends.'

Clara had no concept of the truth of the matter. She had no idea of Harriet's state of mind, of her condition, of any of it. If she had the slightest notion of what these *good men* were really like, she would not bring them into the conversation. I thought of the inquest tomorrow, of the men of the town being sworn in to pass judgement upon the case, and I felt quite ill. Should I be there, to see it? To observe them all, salivating over the gossip concerning my poor, dear, dead friend?

Not I. Let them do that without me. I would find another situation, somewhere far away from Bromley. As soon as I possibly could.

Reverend George Verrall

Thursday evening, lecture night at the chapel. Beezley had already unlocked the gate. He has taken it upon himself to guard the keys with his life. He accompanies all who wish to use them, and returns to lock up again afterwards.

'Can't take a chance any more,' he said darkly, when I asked why he was here already.

rather too late for all that now
but he means well

It had been my intention to deliver a sermon on the subject of our dear sister Harriet, of the example she gave to us in life and of the opportunities for growth afforded to us by the occasion of her death, but, as the inquest had thus far failed to deliver a verdict, I supposed now that it might not be prudent.

In previous weeks the lectures had been well attended, in fact by most of the congregation. Tonight, however, the attendance was limited to the deacons. If their wives had intended to accompany them, perhaps they had been told to stay at home.

'Gentlemen,' I said. 'Had you mistaken the evening? The deacons' meeting is not due this week.'

Beezley spoke first. 'It seems we have much to discuss, Reverend. But by all means deliver your lecture, if you feel it might help us.'

I drew my lips tightly together, and paused.

breathe, man

slow and deep

'You are right, of course,' I said. 'The lecture can keep for another evening. Benjamin, perhaps you would lead us in prayer.'

I tried to focus my attention on Beezley's words, asking for the Lord to bless our meeting, but all the while my thoughts strayed to the men gathered here and what their opinions were. My heart raced, which meant my conscience was troubled by some fear. That they were here in judgement of me. That they thought me no longer suitable to lead the congregation.

'Amen,' I said, as the prayer drew to a close.

'Well,' said Sherver. 'This is a proper to-do, is it not, Reverend?'

'We should pray for our sister,' I said. 'Before we go any further. We have lost a dear member of our congregation, and a good friend.' Before any of them could interrupt, I began. 'Lord God our Father, who came to love us poor sinners, we commend to you the soul of our sister Harriet. May her short life here with us serve as a testimony to the women of our church, and that she be remembered by us all with love. May she rest in peace until the day when you return to us in Glory, in the name of your son Jesus Christ, amen.'

'Amen,' they muttered.

Sweeting was red in the face.

'The coroner called upon me to testify,' he said. 'I did not wish to do it. I had no choice.'

All eyes turned to him.

'The coroner is conducting everything quickly,' I said. 'We should take that as a good sign. The verdict will be reached soon enough, and then we can continue with our lives, and bringing the Gospel of the Lord to the people of the town.'

There was a pause. I believed then that they had been talking about the situation, before I arrived. Perhaps they had even arranged to meet early, for a discussion, without consulting me.

'What should we do, Reverend?' asked Sherver.

'Do?'

He cleared his throat, then. I stared at him. This felt like a challenge.

'The girl was found in the chapel grounds. Having, to all appearances, drunk poison. It does not reflect well upon us.'

'Indeed,' I said.

'Look here,' said Sweeting, 'I've been to her mother, this morning. I suggested we might raise a subscription, to help with the costs of the funeral. The poor woman, she is quite overcome with grief.'

'What did she say?'

'Very little. I gave her three shillings.'

'Good of you,' said Cooper.

Sweeting shot him a look.

'Gentlemen,' I said. 'We are members of a fine, blessed chapel. We make all welcome, regardless of their circumstances. We are Christians not only in word, but in deed. We share what we have; we minister to the poor and to those in need. Charity should not only be offered to those whose hearts are joyful. We weep with them that weep, do we not?'

Murmurs of agreement from some. James Churcher looked up at last, his expression fierce; his eyes were shining, and for a moment I fancied he might have been overcome with emotion. Then he looked down again.

'But it's a sin,' said Sherver. 'Suicide is a mortal sin. Self-murder.'

Sweeting scoffed at this. 'What are we, Papists? There's no such thing as mortal sin. For all have sinned, Joseph, and fall short of the Glory of God.'

Cooper's face, like stone. 'The town is full of it. Of her. Why did she choose to undertake the deed in the chapel? Of all the places. Why could she not go into a field, if she wanted to kill herself? Throw herself in the river, maybe, or do it at home?'

They all looked at him.

'There is no point speculating as to her thoughts,' I said. 'All we can do is pray for her soul, and rejoice in the knowledge that she has found peace.'

'You're certain, then?' said Cooper.

'Of what?' I asked.

'That she took her own life.'

Around the table was silence. They all looked at me, anticipating my response.

'What else?'

'All those I have spoken to say she was quite happy,' said Cooper. 'You'd think, if she was planning something of that nature, she would have appeared low.'

say it, man

say it

I dare you

None of them spoke.

There were moments when they needed a clear direction. They might all be adults, men of the community, but they were still sheep, and they required a shepherd to guide them. They needed a stern voice, the authority of one who knew the Lord, their pastor as well as their friend and servant.

'You all know Harriet had been visiting me privately. Indeed, some of you may have noted that I spent some time with her on Sunday, here in the vestry.'

They were silent for a moment, then Cooper said, 'It did not pass unnoticed.'

I glared at him. 'Then you should also know that Harriet was severely troubled. To outward view she presented herself to all as a woman filled with the Lord's grace, joyful and happy to serve the Lord in every possible way. And this she was. Yet it was also true that she was deeply unhappy, and she came to me for advice and comfort. And I kept her confidence, and will continue to keep the details of it so. You should all respect that, as I have ministered to each and every one of you in times of trouble. Should you like it now, were I to bring all of those private discussions to the meeting for our consideration?'

They remained silent. I felt as though I had won a small but important victory.

'Well, then,' I said. 'To business. Mr Sweeting, we shall arrange for a subscription, and you shall take charge of collecting it. I will mention it to the congregation on Sunday, and I shall press the coroner to reach a verdict of suicide as swiftly as possible. The work of the Lord in Bromley shall on no account be disrupted. Harriet would wish for that least of all.'

The rest of the meeting, thankfully, proceeded without incident. Sweeting closed the meeting with a prayer and we emerged back into the night later than usual, subdued to a man. I waited with Beezley until they had all passed through the gate.

'Bad business,' he said, as we turned into the lane.

here he goes again

'Before you arrived, Reverend, James Churcher was telling us young Tom is in a bad way. He don't know what to do with him.'

'The shock of it, no doubt. Of finding her, like that.'

'Sweeting's all right.'

'Sweeting is a man of mature years, Benjamin. Tom Churcher is little more than a boy, in his head at least, if not in stature. Such things affect us in unexpected ways.'

'Even so ...' he said, and paused.

spit it out, man

'Folks like to talk. You know how it is.'

We were outside the bakehouse. I saw the light of the candle beyond the flimsy curtain, a shadow behind it undoubtedly that of Lottie Beazley, listening to every word. Above, at the front, the room occupied by Frances Williams and, occasionally, by Harriet. I had been in there, once.

someone will see you, she said

then we must be careful

my hand

over her mouth

to muffle the cries

'*Let no corrupt communication proceed out of your mouth,*' I said to him, '*but that which is good to the use of edifying, that it may minister grace unto the hearers.* Ephesians, Chapter Four, Verse 29, Benjamin. Perhaps you and Lottie could use that text to inspire your evening prayers?'

He mumbled something in response, which might or might not have been 'goodnight'.

I left him and walked to the manse, my heart heavy. Tom had been seen, walking with her after dark. I knew this. Other people had told me, more than once.

he is a good man, she said

am I not also a good man?

'I shall visit tomorrow,' I said aloud, although there was nobody to hear. 'I shall visit them, and pray with them.'

Friday, 10th November, 1843

Richard Field

The baby cried all night and all morning until I was ready to smother it; instead I went out.

I should employ a wet-nurse. I had thought this more than once; today I resolved to do something about it, for Maria's sake as well as mine; she could not escape as I could. How did women stand it? They were a fathomless mystery to me.

I sat in the lounge of my club and ordered coffee and brandy, the former to bring me to a state of full consciousness, the latter to make me less willing to care. It had been a hectic week; I always slept badly when away from home, and then to come back to a household full of noise and general malaise had made me peevish and overtired.

The trouble was that we could ill afford it. Earlier this month the cook had left, leaving us with Annie, the maid, who was practically useless at anything other than putting together a milk pudding and burning the potatoes. By not replacing the cook we had spared enough to pay the butcher's bill for the first time in more than a year; it had been something of a relief. I could happily live on tick – in fact, I have done so most of my life – but debt made Maria anxious. And when she was anxious the pitch of her voice rose, and, in consequence of that, the baby screamed.

I ate a kipper for breakfast at the club and then returned home. All was quiet. Maria came to meet me from the back parlour, her finger pressed to her lips to shush me before I had so much as uttered a sound.

'He's asleep?' I whispered.

'At last,' she said. Then, 'A letter arrived for you. From Bromley.'

'Another?'

She had already turned away. 'It's not from her, this time.'

I took the letter into the drawing room and closed the door. The handwriting was unfamiliar to me, the script a loose scrawl.

My dear sir, I read, and then turned to the second page to read the signature. *Geo. Verrall.*

It was to do with Harriet. I knew that straight away; and then soon enough I came to those fateful words:

quite dead

Should I have been more surprised? Should I have been, perhaps, distraught? I had rather the sense of sudden understanding, that a puzzle had finally been completed, and the entire picture revealed.

Harriet should have been here in London by now, but Harriet had sometimes been delayed before, or she had muddled her days, so we expected her whenever she arrived. That she was late this time had been something of a blessing, with the child so fractious and Maria exhausted with it.

This had been Harriet's home for many months. She had lived here and worked a half-mile away at the school in Hackney; we two – we three, once she suggested her friend Maria might join us – had shared dinners and breakfasts and suppers, we had had lively conversation and laughed together, and played cards, when the mood took us to do so. She was a handsome young woman and she was intelligent, quite the brightest girl who has ever been in my company. We could discuss anything from the nature of faith to the current political situation; I taught her music and painting, when she was so inclined, and in her turn she taught me about love.

I found that I was weeping. Not for the Harriet who had been found dead in Bromley, but for the Harriet who had been here, with us. And, I am a little ashamed to admit, for myself.

Maria came in a few moments later and found me thus, collapsed by the hearth.

'She's dead, then?' she asked. She sounded cold.

Thomas Churcher

'The reverend is here to see you, Tom,' Clara said. She closed the door behind her.

The room was dark with the curtains drawn but she pulled them aside. I blinked at the light. Just for a short while, I had slept, and she had disturbed me. I wanted to cry like a child at it.

'Get up,' she said, her voice low. 'Wash your face. I'll make the reverend some tea, and so help me, do not leave me to speak to him on my own. You be quick.'

My sister does not use that voice often but when she does, even with my head a writhing mess of thoughts and aches, I listen. I washed and dressed and ran my hands through my tangled hair, and came through to the parlour.

Mr Verrall stood when he saw me. 'Ah, Tom,' he said.

'Reverend.'

I shook his hand, and we both sat. Clara disappeared into the back room. He waited until the door closed behind her. I felt dizzy, perhaps through lack of sustenance, perhaps from fear.

'Let us pray,' he said, with no warning.

I bowed my head. Kept my eyes open, looking at his shoes, wondering who made them. Some London bootmaker, no doubt; they were well-tooled, polished.

'Our heavenly Father,' he said, 'who loves us even when we are mired in sin, look upon us both as sinners and grant us your grace, and your mercy, and your forgiveness. Bless us with your Holy Spirit, so that we may learn from the terrible events of the past few days, and that we may use them as an opportunity to witness to the good people of our town, to bring them closer to Christ. Grant us strength to fight against the Enemies of the Cross. And we ask that you receive the soul of our dear sister, Harriet; we ask that you forgive her for her sins, and take her to your right side. Bless and comfort her family, Father; may they grow closer to you through the power of your Holy Spirit. In the name of Jesus Christ, your son … Amen.'

I moved my lips but could not quite form the word. If he noticed, he did not say.

The house was silent. The reverend stared at me, his eyes keen. 'How are you, Tom?'

'I'm afraid I do very ill, Mr Verrall.'

'And why is that, boy?'

I wanted to tell him I was a man, but I was afraid to. That he should call me *boy*, at the age of three and twenty … I had no words, not even angry ones.

He sighed. 'The deacons are all worried about you, Tom.'

He leaned forward, placed his hand upon my knee. The feel of it burned. He gripped me tightly, so that I should listen, so that I should pay close attention. I felt his breath upon my face. I could not look at his face, so I looked at his hands, at the white knuckles, at the brown hairs that were on the backs of his fingers. Thought of where those fingers had been. What they had done.

'You must be quiet, but not silent. You must be as you always are, Tom. Just a little sadder, perhaps. A very little bit sadder. That is the only way we shall all get through this terrible, terrible time. Do you understand?'

I stayed silent. I breathed.

His hand gripped still tighter. 'Do you understand?'

'Yes,' I said, at last.

'Good,' he said, and relaxed his grip. 'Good boy.'

And he smiled, and patted my knee, as if in comfort where he had just injured me.

Frances Williams

Forty-nine girls in attendance today. The Jessop girls are still absent, although I saw three of the girls playing in Beezley's yard this morning. They ran off when they saw me, before I could speak to them. The Harrises were all absent without explanation, so I sent one of the Judd boys with a note for their mother. Lizzie Finch took the girls for needlework whilst I took the younger ones for arithmetic. They have all fallen behind and seem to be distracted; the whole class had an uneasy feeling about it today. Many of the girls were disruptive; I had to speak to several of them about whispering.

The jury has been sworn in. Beezley told me, this afternoon. I have no particular desire to have the details of the inquest relayed to me by a man of questionable morals and dirty fingernails, yet he feels it is his duty to keep me informed.

How quickly one becomes accustomed to circumstances! Less than a week ago, Harriet was here with me, sitting in the chair beside the fire, reading through my schoolbooks. I had brought them home with me, so that she could look them over and decide which particular ones she might require for her work with the infants at Arundel.

'You will need a simpler copybook,' I remarked. 'They won't be able to read, or write, when you first take them.'

'I understand some of the older girls are quite advanced, Mr Jackson informed me.' Then she turned to me with the brightest of smiles. 'I hope they are not more intelligent than I am, Frances, can you imagine?'

'I am quite sure that will not be the case.'

She was so excited, so thrilled to be going. My heart was heavy with it, with the loss of her, my dear Harriet. How much my life had been brightened by having her in it! I went out to the market to get potatoes and some vegetables to make a soup. When I returned, Harriet was seated at the table, writing in her diary. She was so distracted with it, she did not acknowledge my greeting.

She wrote everything down. Sometimes she would show me a page wherein she had written down a lively conversation she had had, or an intriguing event at the chapel. 'Do read, my dear. I've expressed it so much better on the page than I can hope to relay in speech.'

She had a skill with words. I saw it from the start, how she could be persuasive, charming; how she was able to hold an intelligent conversation with all who chose to address her. And she had a talent for poetry, too. She showed me some verse she had written about the school, about my girls.

The first time I saw her I adored her.

There, I have admitted it. Perhaps that might help me to understand how this has happened, to admit to my feelings. To admit that when I saw her my heart beat faster. That, when we became friends, my whole life became brighter and more worthwhile.

I should have met Harriet soon after I arrived in Bromley, but circumstances had worked against us. I was to begin work at the National School on the Monday morning, taking the girls' room alongside Mr Campling in the main room. Clara, who had been teaching the girls of the town at Sunday School for some time, had been instrumental in encouraging the subscribers of the school to advertise for a schoolmistress, and she had written to me in advance of my arrival, to tell me how much she was looking forward to meeting me. Mrs Campling had been taking the girls for lessons, but then only intermittently, as she was often unwell.

Harriet had been at the Churchers' the very same day that I had been invited for tea with Clara, just a few hours before. I was told of her in passing, that she was a friend who was also a teacher, and that she had secured a position at a school in Hackney. That she was leaving for Town that very afternoon, and that she should be very sorry indeed to have not had the opportunity to make my acquaintance. That was all I heard of her. I stored the information vaguely in some part of my brain, this person called Harriet who existed and had lived in the town, but now she had left and therefore was of no importance to me.

If only I had known! How very different things might have been, had she tarried a little and taken tea with Clara in the afternoon rather than in the morning. Or, if I had been a little earlier in my arrival, perhaps I should have met her.

And what then? No. Things happen for a reason, albeit not one dictated by some mythical deity. I may not publicly call myself a Christian, but I do see patterns in my existence and the world at large that suggest purpose. Fate, perhaps. Let us call it that. Thus I did not meet Harriet for eighteen months; but it was time in which I learned the town, the people in it; I grew in confidence as a teacher, loved and cherished my girls, even during the times I disciplined them with a hard hand and a harsh voice; and, perhaps most important of all, it was a period in which I learned about myself. Who I was. What I needed.

I arrived with no expectation, but Bromley was larger and busier than anywhere I had lived or worked before. I had come directly from a village school in Leicestershire, a classroom of twelve boys and girls of all ages from five to fourteen; most of the children attended irregularly, depending on the season, or on the requirements of the home, or on the availability of money to spare for their pence.

Whilst Bromley was still some miles from London, it was busy with coaches back and forth to town; there was a thriving market, attended by tradespeople from the surrounding area. There were six public houses in the town itself, three of them coaching inns offering accommodation. The main thoroughfare which took travellers to London to the north, and Tunbridge Wells to the south, snaked through the Market Place, where there were businesses bordering all sides of the square. I had never lived in a place with so many opportunities to spend money.

Besides the shops, there were some good houses further out, along the Widmore Lane, and to the north, in parks of their own. The Bishop of Rochester had his palace there, with fine gardens surrounding it. The church held a strong grip on the town with its various denominations, but the focus for the residents of Widmore Lane and the Market Place was the Dissenting Chapel, a new white building in a Gothic Tudor style, with turrets at the corners. It looked beautiful, and oppressive.

Of course, it's easy to find it thus in hindsight. At the time, I thought it was almost magical, bright, beside so many squat redbrick buildings. Like a palace, perhaps.

In advance of taking up my position I had arranged a room at a boarding house in Mason's Hill, a hamlet close to the school, which itself was in a location south of the town commonly known as the Gravel Pits. The school board had made the necessary introductions; the house was owned and occupied by two spinsters, the Misses Mercier, who were related in some capacity to one of the subscribers.

The house went by the confusing name of Hill House Farm. The land which must once have belonged to it had long since been sold off, leaving behind a rough acre of lawn bordered by a tall yew hedge. At the time of my arrival the grass was yellowed and tussocky; the yews, the darkest of green, were overgrown, and patchy with some type of blight. The house was built of grey stone and in need of some attention. The guttering was broken in two or three places, which meant rainwater ran down the exterior walls and had stained them a darker grey. It looked as though the house was crying.

Inside it was even more dismal. The house was draughty, dark and cold, smelling of damp, with several rooms unoccupied and shut off; besides the spinsters, there was a maid of all work, Amelia Carpenter, and another lodger who at the time of my arrival was away visiting a sick aunt.

I did not much like the house, nor the obsession the ladies had for prayer and contemplation. It was bad enough that I was expected to educate my girls first and foremost with the catechism and the Bible, but to be forced to continue with the charade outside of school was harder to bear. Before we were served meals in the evening we were expected to pray. Afterwards, the ladies would retire to the drawing room for an hour before bed, where Miss Lucy Mercier would read aloud from the Gospels whilst Miss Mary Mercier would sew shirts to send to missionaries in Africa. It was made clear to me that I was expected to lead a contemplative Christian life whilst living under their roof: absolutely no callers, gentlemen or otherwise. Worse still, I was to attend the parish church with them, twice on Sundays.

I then learned that the schoolmaster and his wife, Mr and Mrs Campling, not to mention their brood of eight daughters and one son, lived in a house adjacent to the school, and directly opposite Hill House Farm. I could see their front door from my bedroom window.

Before I had even passed a single night in the house, I had resolved to seek alternative accommodation, even if this would take me an inconvenient distance from the school. My tea party with Clara Churcher was the ideal opportunity to set this plan in motion; I had resolved to recruit her to assist me in escaping from the virtuous Misses Mercier.

Clara was a fine, tall woman with a pale complexion and an earnest demeanour. She made efforts to put me at ease and smiled when I told her that Hill House Farm was perhaps a little farther from the town than I had anticipated. 'I take a long walk every day, and it does me the power of good. Being so close to the school, and to Mr and Mrs Campling … I feel I should like to be a little further away. I should be very happy to walk from the town, and back again. You understand my meaning, Miss Churcher?'

'Indeed I do. Please call me Clara.'

Clara had two elder brothers and one sister already left home, and two younger brothers, Thomas and James, who still lived at the house. Their mother had died some four years past, and Clara's chief occupation was to keep house for their father. Running the Sunday School at the chapel was her solace; a responsibility that kept her sane. I liked her immediately. Her opinions, on all matters other than religion, accorded so much with my own that I felt I had made a firm friend. She promised to look for a room to let in the town, and assured me that we should be able to pay each other visits and enjoy lively conversations much more easily than if I remained at Hill House Farm.

I recall that, as I left the house to walk back to Mason's Hill, Clara said to me, almost in passing, 'To be honest with you, Frances, I have no idea how Miss Frisnell can bear it.'

'Miss Frisnell?'

'Your fellow boarder. She is away at the moment, I believe. No matter. You'll meet her soon enough.'

Matilda Frisnell. It was a week before she returned; and of course, once she was there, I had no desire to move closer to Bromley after all.

It pains me still to think of Matilda. It was a difficult time in my life, one I have preferred to try and put aside, and yet, if there had been no Matilda, it seems likely that there would also have been no Harriet.

On the following Sunday, I had reluctantly attended the parish church with the Misses Mercier, and sat through a silent meal of beef stew. My attempt at conversation was met with silence and glares; apparently talking on the Sabbath was discouraged. After luncheon we sat together in the drawing room reading whilst the grey light was still sufficient to see the text. At length I excused myself, claiming to have a headache. Miss Lucy told me to be downstairs at five o'clock sharp; the evening service began at half-past.

Thus was I upstairs when the front door received a hammering. After a minute of peace the hammering started again, and, assuming Amelia to be indisposed, I made my way downstairs to answer the door myself. I was halfway down the stairs when Amelia rushed across the hallway to open the door and Miss Matilda Frisnell entered.

'Where on earth is everybody, Milly? Need I ask. Are they both praying again?'

She caught sight of me at the same moment I saw her. Her gown was muddy at the bottom. I noticed this because it was bright, peacock-blue, her shawl orange with a gold fringe. Her hair, underneath a fancy straw bonnet with a feather, was golden and shiny. And her smile – radiant.

'Well, hello there. Who are you?'

I reached the bottom of the stairs, offered my hand. 'How do you do? Frances Williams.'

'Matilda Frisnell. How do you do, Miss Williams? Delighted to meet you. Are you the new girl?'

I must have blushed. 'I suppose I am.'

Matilda turned to Amelia, who had a strange little smile on her lips. 'Can we have some tea? What do you think, Milly? Shall we take it in the kitchen, where we can talk?'

I cast a glance towards the drawing room. Surely the Misses Mercier could hear this exchange between us?

'Oh, don't mind them. They can carry on with their holy business; let's go and have a proper chat!'

Matilda was also a schoolteacher, and three years older than myself. She had been a governess, and had subsequently taught at a finishing school in France. She spoke French like a native, and Latin and Greek; she also had some German and a little Russian. She had been to most countries in Europe, having toured with friends. For the past year she had been employed as a schoolmistress at a private school for the wealthy families of Beckenham; she had charge of eighteen girls, and had additional responsibility for foreign language tuition. She was glorious, and clever; witty, and colourful. I found her by turns alluring and frustrating; she made my heart sing for joy, and cry out in despair. Our friendship almost immediately became something intense; that first night we sat awake in the warmth of the kitchen, long after Amelia had retired for the evening, discussing art, literature, the role of women in society; the pressures of finding a husband when there were no men attractive or intelligent enough to satisfy us.

Eventually I went to my room but hardly slept. When it was barely light I was dressed and making my way to the school. That evening, the Monday, I retired to bed after supper and not long afterwards Matilda knocked softly upon my door. I recall how my heart thudded in my chest as I let her in. How I looked at her, expecting her to enquire after my health, or demand that I return to the kitchen so we could converse some more; how I thought she would laugh or ask me about my day, or tell me about hers. How she did none of these things but instead took my hand in hers and lifted it to her face, her eyes never leaving mine, and placed her lips tenderly upon the inside of my wrist. And then how she smiled, questioning, as if asking for my permission for something I scarcely understood. And how I nodded, because I felt that nothing would progress without my doing just that, and knowing without understanding that whatever it was she proposed was something I wanted desperately.

If Amelia noticed that Matilda's bed was no longer slept in, she never remarked upon it.

My room was smaller, and warmer because it was above the kitchen; hers, at the front of the house, was next to that occupied by the Misses Mercier. I often thought it odd that they shared a room, and a bed. Hill House Farm had any number of bedrooms, most of them no doubt perfectly pleasant. Perhaps, as sisters, they always had and therefore found it difficult to sleep alone; perhaps it was in the interests of economy. But, with my new experiences of the delights of sleeping with another, a new curiosity at their odd sleeping arrangements emerged. Perhaps they were not sisters at all; who was to say? And their religious devotion – was it real, or a pretence? They certainly seemed completely unconcerned by Miss Frisnell and her liberated opinions. Perhaps the rule concerning gentlemen callers had discouraged a certain type of lodger?

Never mind my suppositions; it did not matter. None of it mattered, except for Matilda. The greyness of Hill House Farm became somehow warm and golden and bright when she was there. All thoughts of leaving were banished; the walk to school every morning was a desolate trudge, the walk home again was almost a dance.

Matilda Frisnell, my love, my first love.

I suppose Matilda was to me as I was to Harriet. Our closeness, however, which was everything to me, was commonplace to her, and when her appointment came to an end three months later she applied for several positions and casually accepted the most enticing, even though it was in Yorkshire, which might have been in another continent as far as I was concerned. I hid my dismay, pride and self-control standing me in good stead as they always do, and I wished her well, and on the day we parted she was moved to tearful expressions of undying affection but it did not prevent her leaving and so, I think, cannot have gone very deep.

Despite everything that transpired between us, I remember her fondly; after Harriet came into my life, Matilda Frisnell began to seem in many ways like a dream. When I think of her now, it is in the manner of some exotic bird. Sometimes she is caged; sometimes she is free.

Or perhaps that is I.

Reverend George Verrall

The inquest resumed this morning, the room much as it had been on Wednesday last. If it was possible, I fancied that even more of the townspeople were present, presumably having forgone their labours on that day to pack themselves into the meeting room. More than half of the room was taken up with spectators, and still more seats had been provided for the gentlemen and ladies of the town, which now included John Joyce, the high constable, and Long Bob Sutton, the bailiff.

To begin the day's proceedings the coroner summoned Mr James Ilott, the surgeon. The room buzzed with gossip such that the coroner had to strike the flat of his hand upon the desk to get them all to be quiet.

The surgeon was duly brought forth, and bidden to sit in the single chair. He was a young man, fair-haired and vigorous, with cheeks that flushed crimson when he beheld the size of his audience.

'Your attendance is most appreciated, sir,' the coroner remarked, once the man had identified himself. 'You have examined the deceased?'

'I have.'

'And perhaps you can begin by explaining the circumstances under which you were called out.'

'Of course. I was sent for on the evening of Tuesday last, to attend at Mr Verrall's chapel yard in Widmore Lane. I went directly. I found the deceased lying in the privy. To my knowledge she had not been touched prior to my arrival.'

One of the ladies at the front, fanning herself vigorously, made a noise of distaste at the word 'privy'.

'And your immediate thoughts as to the condition of the deceased?'

Ilott unfolded some sheets of paper that he had brought with him, and referred to his notes. 'She had apparently died from some convulsive action, or effort. The pupils of the eyes were dilated, the tongue clenched firmly between the teeth. There was a dark viscid fluid escaping from the mouth. The hands were clenched; her right hand was behind her. Her left hand was in front of her body and a clean white handkerchief was either in her left hand, or between it and her body.'

that one occasion she turned away from me
wiped her mouth with her handkerchief
she thought I didn't see

'She was in a semi-recumbent position, sitting on the floor of the privy in the right-hand corner with her left side against the seat. Her face was towards the door, which was open. The right leg was against the door and prevented it being closed; the left leg was bent.'

I glanced around the room. Not so much as a whisper disturbed the proceedings now; everyone present was open-mouthed and intent on hearing the details of the corpse.

Harriet's corpse

'Her head was bent rather forward, her chin being on her chest. Her bonnet was on, and the front of it was bent down over her face.'

Ilott cleared his throat. Someone in the room, taking advantage of the pause rather as one does between acts at the playhouse, coughed. The coroner's assistant was taking notes, and Ilott seemed to be aware of this, for he paused regularly to allow the scribe time to catch up, although the man did not appear to be writing in a hurried manner.

'Her clothes were not disarranged. She had boots on, and she did not appear to have walked very far, as the mud was principally confined to the sole of the boots. I should say, there is one seat in the privy with two holes in it; both were open.'

Miss Holgate gave out another 'tsk', slightly louder than before. It did seem to me rather as though Ilott was obsessing over the nature of the building, and thus avoiding the business at hand.

'Do go on, Mr Ilott,' the coroner said, glancing at his scribe. 'You must not worry about Mr Gregg here, he can quite easily manage to keep up, can't you, George?'

The scribe looked up, briefly.

a face that could curdle milk

Ilott coughed again. 'The body was quite cold and stiff. She had been dead some hours, I should say at least fifteen to twenty hours. I gave directions for the removal from the privy to her own home, and I was very particular in observing that nothing fell from her when removed. I examined the floor directly round about, also the surface of the night soil, which was encrusted and hard. I found no vessel of any kind, a bottle or any broken pieces of china or glass.'

A murmur had started up amongst the throng at the back of the room. I caught whispers, a single word, repeated: 'murder' … 'murder' …

that she had not taken her own life
for that we must be grateful

'No vessel?'

'None at all.'

'Pray continue.'

'I proceeded with the body to her mother's home and made a careful examination externally. I found no marks of violence. I had her clothes removed. She had been in the habit of tight lacing.'

my hand upon the flat of her back
solid like a board my fingers tracing the lines up to her neck and at last the softness
the warmth

83

The Holgate goat tsked again. All this talk of privies and lacing; whatever should come next?

'I searched her pockets and found a penknife, her thimbles, a purse containing five fourpenny pieces and a small silver coin of Bogotá-de-real; one penny piece, a ticket of a Sunday School and a letter signed "Richard Field", which I delivered to Sergeant King of the police force.'

and no half-sovereigns

Mr Gregg duly noted the list.

Richard Field, Richard Field

Oh, that I could tell all that I know about that man

fornicator

liar

moral bankrupt

'When the body was stripped there were no marks of violence on it. I noticed a smell from the mouth, apparently that of prussic acid.'

Here Ilott paused again, and cast a glance towards the crowds of us gathered at the back. He seemed to notice me for the first time; his eyes widened and, I thought, he gave a tiny nod in my direction. The flush on his cheeks darkened further.

what now?

what next, man?

'Do continue, Mr Ilott.'

'It — it so struck me, at the time, that the mammary glands were enlarged, and that there was a dark areola around the nipples. I was able to squeeze a few drops of serous fluid from them. The abdomen was enlarged, but from the rigidity of the muscles I could not make out the uterus. I was told her health had been very good.'

The murmuring began again, like a low hum rising from a chorus. One or two of them gasped. I heard Jane Walker mutter, 'What's he saying?' And Miss Holgate said, 'Well, I never did' and made to stand. The coroner gave her a look that brought her immediately to her seat once more.

a dark areola around the nipples
I was able to squeeze them
squeeze them

'I yesterday, pursuant to the orders of this court, made a post-mortem examination of the body, between fifty and sixty hours after death.'

The coroner held up his hand to interrupt. 'Ladies and gentlemen, but ladies in particular, I should mention at this point that the testimony of this witness is liable to include some medical details of a somewhat delicate nature. It is important to the duty of the court that these details be aired openly and without hesitation. Therefore, if anyone in the public gallery would wish to absent themselves at this point, I should be grateful if you could do it now, rather than to interrupt the proceedings at an inopportune moment.'

Nobody moved, or breathed. I glanced at them all, staring at the coroner. Even the Holgate woman was silent. At the back, old Sarah Churcher – grandmother to Tom – growled, 'What did he say?' but, other than that, not a sound from any of them.

vultures

'Very well, Mr Ilott. Pray continue.'

'As I said, sir. I examined the body. My father, a surgeon, and Mr Sparkes, also a surgeon, were both present with me. But little change had taken place in the body. I opened the head. The membranes of the brain were healthy with no effusion below, although the vessels on the surface of the brain were rather congested. The brain was, however, perfectly healthy with no effusion into the lateral ventricles, or at its base.'

No sound, save the scratch-scratch of Mr Gregg's nib against the surface of the paper, and the occasional chink as he dipped his pen.

'I opened the chest, and abdomen. On opening the cavity of the abdomen the impregnated uterus was seen occupying the lower part, the intestine being pushed up by it. I fancied there was the smell of prussic acid.'

prussic acid
prussic acid
her mouth full of blood

'There was a small quantity of one and a half ounces of serous fluid in the pleura. The lungs were congested with scarcely any adhesion, otherwise quite healthy. The heart, about its ordinary size and healthy. The large veins of the chest were filled with blood. I removed the stomach and oesophagus with their contents for further examination, previously securing each end carefully by a ligature. The liver, the spleen and the kidneys were all in a perfectly normal state. The pancreas was rather congested, and the lining membrane of the larynx reddened. The tongue was dry on the surface and firmly clenched between the teeth, partly protruding from the mouth and wounded by the teeth.'

she bit her own tongue
what pain must there have been, before she fell
before she fell

'... the papillae distinct, and the stomach contained about four ounces of thickish fluid with scarcely any solid matter. The contents smelled strongly of prussic acid. I put the contents carefully in a clean bottle and corked it tightly. The lining membrane of the oesophagus was intensely reddened, plexus of vessels distinct. The stomach at various points, but more especially near to the oesophagus, was inflamed and congested. In some portions of the small intestine, similar patches were visible ...'

I glanced across at the faces. At Miss Holgate, her expression aghast but fascinated, like all of them. They wanted all the detail and yet were disgusted by it. *You all have the same insides*, I wanted to shout. *God's creatures, all of you, tainted by drink, and vitriol, and sin.*

86

'I examined the uterus and its appendages. From the general appearance of the foetus, a well-formed male, I am of the opinion that she was between five and six months advanced in pregnancy ... '

a well-formed male

a well-formed male

' ... the ovaries were small ... '

for unto us a son is given

between five and six months advanced

five and six

And someone muttered, 'God bless the child,' and someone else besides said, 'Pity the poor girl.' And amongst them too, someone clucked and yet another said, 'For shame.'

'The bladder was empty and the vessels at its neck congested. On making a section with the knife into the vagina, a small quantity of whitish mucus escaped and flowed out. I had not time to collect this for further examination and analysis before it mixed with some blood that had previously flowed, but this mucus could indicate, and, perhaps, lead me to suppose, that the deceased had had sexual intercourse just prior to her death.'

A grimace had fixed itself upon the face of Miss Holgate; too much for her, perhaps. Or maybe not enough.

'I have examined and analysed the contents of the stomach so far as time will allow me at present to do, and I am satisfied of the presence of prussic acid, and to that a very considerable quantity. The dose must have been an extraordinary one, producing, I should say, instant death. The strength of the acid must have been powerful, and the quantity large, for the smell to be so easily perceptible. All of which is very unusual, since by that time it was a full sixty hours after death.'

'And what, Mr Ilott, would have been the action of this quantity of prussic acid upon the deceased?'

'I am most decidedly of the opinion that the deceased could never have had the power after taking the poison to get rid of, or cast away, the vessel out of which it must have been drunk. Almost before the poison could have flowed down her throat her power must have been prostrate, and when down on the floor she would die as she fell, without the ability to alter her position.'

Murmuring, again.

'I also cannot account for the front of her bonnet's being bent down on to the face. If she had fallen, it would have been more natural that the back part of it should have been crushed, but that was perfect.'

'Thank you, Mr Ilott. One further matter, if you would spare us a few moments longer. I understand that Sergeant King of the police has provided you with an item of evidence?'

'Indeed, sir. I have received from the sergeant a one-and-a-half-ounce phial, apparently containing common smelling salts. From present examination I cannot speak of what it may have contained, but there is no odour at all of prussic acid. I shall be able to state with certainty after analysing the contents, but from present appearances this phial seems to have been embedded in the night soil for some considerable time. I will carefully examine and analyse the contents by the time the inquest next meets.'

'Very well, Mr Ilott. We are most grateful to you for your diligence.'

The surgeon got to his feet and the murmur of the gathered crowd rose into an excited babble of voices. I heard snatches of conversation, words here and there, grasped by my desperate ears as a hungry man might grasp at a morsel of bread.

'…in the family way!'

'…and her, of all people…'

'…always so very pious…'

'…pity the poor child!'

and its mother
and pray for the soul of the father too
whoever the hell that might be

And then there he was, standing before the table with his hat tucked under one arm, straight as a poker, moustaches stiffened to a point, hair parted neatly and combed flat against his skull. Sergeant Samuel King.

Frances Williams

It took a matter of an hour for the word to spread from the workhouse to Widmore Lane – that Harriet had been pregnant. The surgeon estimated five to six months advanced. As if that wasn't intrigue enough, the further revelation that she had had relations with a man shortly before her death made it all the more salacious.

I heard it from Beezley, and then from Alice Isard the butcher's wife, and from Lizzie Finch, whom I had recently appointed a pupil teacher, since she was a good reader and had a firm hand with the younger children.

I stretched my face into an arch of surprise, because that is what was expected of me.

'I heard she was six months gone,' Alice Isard said. She was not addressing me but Ann Metcalf who was standing beside me, mother of Mary Ann, one of my more disruptive pupils.

'That's what happens when young women go to London without proper supervision,' said the Metcalf woman. 'You cannot trust them. And her, such a pious girl! It reflects badly on the chapel, and on the school.'

'Of all the people,' Alice Isard muttered. She was looking at me as she said it.

'And that she had been helping out at the school! I shall speak to Mr Campling about it.'

If I had been in any doubt that Mrs Metcalf knew I was standing next to her, that doubt vanished as she turned to me, expecting me to issue some challenge, or defend my friend in some way. What could I say? Afterwards, of course, I thought of any number of responses – that if they considered themselves Christian women they should guard against casting judgement; that Harriet was a better woman than either of them and their daughters had been privileged to meet her at all; that they should speak to me if they had an issue with the standards of education there and not trouble Mr Campling.

Instead I did none of those things. I walked out of the shop and shut the door fast behind me. As I did so, I heard one of them laugh.

Later, Beezley said something about 'the sainted Harriet' and how the town's opinion of her would change from this point on. 'Proper virtuous, she seemed to be,' he said. 'Always at chapel, always looking at us like we were something beneath her. Turns out she's a filthy sinner like the rest of us.'

He was red in the face, as if Harriet had somehow affronted him personally. Yet, as far as I was aware, Harriet had scarcely passed the time of day with him.

The sergeant came to the schoolroom at a few minutes after noon. I had not yet rung the bell, and lessons were in progress. Lizzie was examining the younger girls on their sewing, and the older ones were learning a poem with me. The room was peaceful, and when the door opened and the sergeant entered – with merely a cursory knock – all was disruption.

'Girls, girls. Back to your work,' I said. It is a rare day that I need to raise my voice to them now, once they have settled to their tasks, but the sight of the uniform seemed to inspire a kind of madness in them. My own heart was beating hard and fast, thinking perhaps he had come to arrest me. I forced myself to breathe slowly; blinked once. Took my time to respond.

'Rebecca, perhaps you will take over the supervision. Miss Finch, keep your girls in order, please. I shall be listening out for you.'

I took the sergeant outside and closed the door. Before he could speak, I held up my hand to silence him, and listened for uproar within. Nothing. All was quiet. They were either terrified, or listening at the door.

'How can I help you, sergeant?'

'It's the inquest, miss. Coroner requests your attendance at one o'clock.'

'But that's in an hour! I cannot possibly dismiss the school so early.'

The sergeant stared back, resolute.

'I have no replacement,' I hissed, 'since my own deputy was murdered.'

I saw him blink. Perhaps he was noting my dissent; he would report it back to the coroner. Some penalty might be imposed.

'I am able to attend at three, and not before,' I said, by way of compromise. 'Perhaps you could inform the coroner.'

I left him standing there and went back inside. The girls' heads were all bent studiously to their tasks. If I had regained my composure, I should have addressed them directly: *Listen and learn, girls. When you are afraid, you simply pretend that you are not, and it is very difficult to tell the difference.* And the other lesson: *You do not always have to do what men tell you to do.*

Thomas Churcher

Harriet was dead.

I saw her body myself, with my own eyes, and yet in my dreams she was still walking and talking as if she was not. Every night I dreamed of her, and awoke bereft again, remembering. Losing her afresh every day. I walked the fields late into the night, trying to exhaust myself so that thoughts of her would not haunt me, and yet each time she was there, just before the dawn.

I caught her in snatches, fragments of memory or half-remembered things.

Her hands, how they were so delicate, slender fingers and pale skin. Holding her hand and feeling the bones in it, like a bird's, the softness of her palm turned up to my lips so that I could kiss it. Hands accustomed to holding books rather than tools; hands that guided others.

From the doorway of the shop once, years ago, when she was still a girl, I saw her in the market talking to a woman with two children, an older girl and a baby, just barely on its feet, its hand fisted around the girl's index finger. And the girl was laughing with Harriet and her mother, and Harriet's hand on the baby's head. I had watched her hand and thought how gentle she was, how tender, and yet how strong.

'You are a brave man, Thomas,' she said, more recently. She was laughing when she said it but she meant it nonetheless. We were sitting on the bank of the river with our faces to the dregs of the late autumn sun. I should have been working but Clara was in the shop and Father was away, so I told my sister I was going to call on our grandmother. And after that I called on Harriet.

'Brave,' I said, 'I don't think so.'

I had told Emma; broken off our association. In the end, it had been easy. I had Harriet's words in my mind, the promise of her. If I had Harriet, I had no fear of anything, not even the fury of Emma Milstead. *I cannot be with you any more. You should find yourself someone who is worthy of you.* I had said it kindly, and at first Emma was tearful, and then a very short time after that she was angry. I knew she would be. She had been angry with me before. *Why?* she asked me. I could have told her any number of things. That I did not want to have children with a woman who had such a violent temper; that I did not like her mother; that I thought she was too beautiful to be with a man like me. I could have told her any number of truths, but instead I said, *I don't love you, Emma*. The tears dried and her face reddened with rage, and she shouted and called me fickle and cruel, and said nobody in the town would have anything to do with me, once the truth was told. Then she had stamped her foot, and turned and run away, back to the town. I'd watched her go and I should have felt more — sadness, perhaps, or a horror at what I had done — but instead all that remained was relief.

'I didn't think you would do it,' Harriet said.

'You asked me to,' I said. 'I would do anything you asked. Anything.'

She kissed me, then, or perhaps she did not; perhaps this is one of those misremembered dreams. It does not matter now. I can imagine that she kissed me for a long time, her hand soft against my cheek, and how good that felt, to be that free. 'You are a good man, Thomas Churcher,' she said to me. 'You are a good man, a kind man, and you deserve to be loved.'

I dreamt that she was drowning in the river, that I jumped into the water to save her and it took me too. The last thing I saw was her face beneath the water, her arms outstretched, delicate fingers clutching for my hand, black blood between her teeth. I woke in a panic, my heart pounding with it, the same thought that I had every time I woke: Harriet is dead. I cannot save her. I am too late.

Reverend George Verrall

'I swear by Almighty God...' Sergeant King began.

He said he was at the Station House between one and two o'clock. He said that the Reverend Mr Verrall of Bromley Chapel, accompanied by the superintendent of the chapel — that's Churcher, Thomas, although he was not the superintendent, he had no such title but what was the man to know about such things? He saw me, and Churcher, and assumed that he was my deputy.

'Mr Verrall said they had been searching for her since ten o'clock in the forenoon and that she was...'

And the man looked down at his notebook and consulted it for the exact words I am supposed to have used, although through the mouth of the police sergeant they do not sound like my words at all.

'He said she was "a pious and a modest girl" and he feared she had "destroyed herself".'

yes, yes I feared that
I told you I feared that
lie upon lie George
may God Himself strike me down

Thomas Churcher

She was afraid of him, of the reverend.

'Why?' I asked her. 'He is a godly man.'

She looked at me, a wry grin twisting the corner of her mouth. 'I think that he is not. He is a man who tries to be godly, and falls a little short.'

'We all try, and we all fall short, except for the Son of Man himself.'

Her gaze dropped to her hands, open and loose in her lap. I took hold of one of them and held it tightly for a moment. I did not understand, of course. I understood nothing then, except for how this made me feel; how my heart soared like a bird when I was with her.

'Has he hurt you?' I asked her.

'It's not that,' she said. 'You mustn't think badly of him. He is your pastor. He will still be here long after I am gone.'

'What am I to think, then, that you are afraid of him?'

She was quiet for a while, her hand still inside mine. I wanted her to turn to me and kiss me but she was deep in thought; wisps of hair curling over the back of her neck, under her bonnet.

'I told him something once, in confidence.'

'Yes?' I said, encouraging her.

'I rather think that it was a mistake.'

'A mistake?'

'He forgets nothing, even those things you would prefer him to forget.'

'You are afraid that he will not keep your confidence? Surely he must; it is the obligation of his profession.'

And she turned her face to me, and smiled. 'Let's talk of nicer things,' she said.

I thanked God for the warm evenings, although the days were now short and we were meeting more often in the dark. We took advantage of the days when I finished work early, meeting in our secret places: the furthest reaches of the river, the woodlands behind the Archbishop's Palace, the chapel. The space behind the chapel, when there were too many people around. We sat on the ground with our backs to its southern wall, talking in whispers because on the other side of the wall was the back yard of the Three Compasses. Once we sat and listened to an entire conversation between a drayman and one of the barmaids, neither of them any the wiser. We watched each other's eyes, holding our hands over our mouths to stop any sound from escaping. Once, meeting earlier in the day, we listened to some men in the field behind, singing and telling stories. Once, she fell asleep there with her head upon my shoulder, whilst I sat motionless and holding my breath lest I disturbed her.

She told me of Miss Williams, how sweet and kind she was. I replied that the rest of the town thought her rather fierce, myself included. Several times she had scolded me like a child for getting in her way, or standing too long in one spot, or – once – for 'looking oafish'. That made Harriet laugh.

'She is the loveliest woman alive,' she said. 'I wish I were more like her.'

'You are lovelier,' I said.

She blushed and pulled a face, and pretended to push me away. 'But of course she'll never marry. Not Miss Williams.'

'Indeed, she is too old,' I said in reply. 'If she hasn't found a husband by now, I can't see as anyone will take her. He'd need to be a brave man to do it.'

'Why?'

I hesitated, choosing my words. 'She likes to keep control of those around her. The same way she takes her lessons. She does it with you, too, Harriet.'

'What do you mean?'

'She keeps you on a very tight rein,' I said.

She looked thoughtful, and did not reply. It was growing dark, and I offered her my hand to help her up the bank, lest she lose her footing and fall into the river.

'I should like to marry,' she said, climbing to my level. She placed her hand on my arm for support. I did not move away.

'Would you?'

'I should like to promise to love one man above all others. And to be loved in return.'

I felt my heart beating in my chest at the closeness of her. Her dress felt smooth, silken. The evening was salty, dusty, the air full of the scent of bare earth and dry leaves.

She was twenty-three, the same age as me. I should have asked her, then and there, for my heart had been beating warm and strong for her for seven long years. But I did not ask. It was only seven days since I had broken off with Emma. I thought I should wait a little while, speak to my father, speak to the reverend.

And I waited, and because of that I lost her.

'Mr Verrall? Are you quite well?'

I found myself outside, in the yard. There was little breeze to stir the air, and I was seated upon the steps of the workhouse, my head bent low. Albert Richardson was next to me, his hand upon my shoulder.

'Reverend?'

'Quite well, thank you,' I said, but even to my own ears my voice sounded feeble. 'Rather warm in there, I felt.'

'Yes indeed.'

Without asking my leave, he took it upon himself to perch on the step next to me. 'You must be feeling this worse than any of us,' he remarked.

I flexed my jaw for a moment before responding. 'What do you mean?'

He fixed me with his insipid blue eyes, widened for effect. 'Just that you and she were friends, were you not?'

so it begins

'She was a member of my congregation, Mr Richardson.'

'Of course, of course. Nobody's saying nothing else, Mr Verrall.'

liar

liar

I waited, in case he went away, but he did not.

'What did he say?' I asked, at length. 'The sergeant. What else did he say?'

'Just all the places they looked. And then how Mr Sweeting and Mr Churcher came running up to him to say she had been discovered in the chapel.'

'In the privy,' I said. 'Not in the chapel itself.'

'And how he sent for the surgeon and how he guarded the body in the meantime so that none should touch it. And then how he went rooting about in the night soil and came across a bottle that had been tossed in there. He gave the bottle to the surgeon, to check what was in it. Surgeon said it smelled of salts. I reckon it smelled of night soil myself.'

like he got close enough

'Quite.'

Behind us, the doors opened and the crowd began to issue forth. Albert and I jumped to our feet to avoid being trampled. The great throng of Bromley gossips went forth to spread the word. At the back, Maud Richardson with her daughter.

'There you are! Where'd you go running off to?' she demanded of her husband.

'I was just seeing that the reverend was well,' he said. 'Thought he looked a bit peaky, rushing out like that.'

Maud noticed me then. 'Good heavens, yes. You do look most peculiar, Reverend.'

'I assure you both, I am fine.'

'What's gone on?' Albert asked his wife, tilting his head to the door.

'They are stopping for dinner. This afternoon they are going to call Miss Williams, I told Mary we'd come back. Three o'clock sharp.'

now there will be a tale to hear

Frances Williams

I dismissed the girls at half-past two; an hour early. Mr Campling sighed and grumbled at it, but even he is not belligerent enough to argue with a court of law.

I could sense the atmosphere in the Market Place as I crossed it, and outside the workhouse where they were gathered in groups. I caught snippets of conversation as I passed, angry at myself for failing to meet their eyes and show them my defiance. Too late, I wished I had attended the inquest earlier, to understand the proceedings, to get a sense of it all. I was coming into this blind, and I was – to my own bitter disappointment – afraid.

My usual response to feelings of fear and discomfort is to react with yet more determination and stoicism, and today was no exception. I should perhaps have apologised to the court for my failure to attend when requested, but one glimpse of the old man who sat in judgement of us – of Harriet, and of me – made the tatters of my heart harden. *Your dusty grey wig does not make you my better, Mr Carttar*, I thought.

'Miss Williams, thank you for taking the trouble to attend.'

He was expecting me to apologise, and this was my opportunity. I raised my chin instead.

'If you would be so kind, pray tell us how you knew the deceased.'

I cleared my throat to begin. 'I was well acquainted with Miss Monckton. She was assisting me in the management of my school. We met eighteen months after my arrival in Bromley, as she had been employed for some time at a school in Hackney. We were introduced upon her return.'

'And you became friends?'

'Yes. Good friends.'

From somewhere behind me I heard a snigger, and a shush. Despite my resolve, I felt the heat rise in my cheeks.

A deep breath, then another.

The coroner said, 'And now, Miss Williams, if you could tell us everything you recall about the night of the 6th of November.'

Another breath. Do not gasp. Do not hesitate, or stumble over your words. You are fluent. You are eloquent. You are recalling a memory of another person, nothing else. This is not difficult. All you need to do is state the facts.

'Harriet had stayed overnight with me on the Sunday night, and she was to have done so on the Monday night too.

She had taken my place at the school on Monday, as I was unwell.'

'Unwell, Miss Williams?'

'I had a bad chest,' I said, and once again I heard a murmur, a snort coming from behind me. Surely my girls are better behaved than these, their loutish parents!

'And the deceased?'

'During Sunday and Monday she was in perfectly good health and spirits. Better than normal if anything, which I attributed to her having procured a situation as teacher at a school at Arundel in Sussex.'

At the right hand of the coroner sat another man, a sour-faced clerk with thin black hair plastered wetly over his skull. Until that moment I had not paid him any attention, but now I realised he was writing down what I was saying. At my continued silence the man looked up and glared.

'She took tea with me and Clara Churcher at about six o'clock on Monday evening,' I said. 'And then, at about seven o'clock, she said she would go out to catch the post and return shortly. She had been writing a letter.'

And in her diary. I could picture it; Harriet bent with her head low, writing in the journal she carried everywhere with her. The letter lay unfinished before her, and I had wondered what sudden observation had caused her to break off the writing of it and transfer her attention to noting some private recollection.

I had been dozing in the chair by the fire, having hardly slept the night before. I did not see her finish the letter. I did not see where she put her journal.

'I fully expected her back long before nine o'clock, but I did not see her again. She never returned.'

I felt the emotion of it rising up in my chest, threatening to spill out. I swallowed it back down again. Not here, not now. Later I could cry. Later I could wail and scream and beat my fists against my forehead; not now. Retell the facts, I thought. Just that: the facts. 'She never returned, which very much surprised me. I supposed she had gone home to her mother's.'

I wished desperately for a glass of water, something to swallow down the tide of anxiety, the fear of saying the wrong thing. Of giving away some detail that should attract their attention.

'Thank you. Now you are no doubt aware that the surgeon has conducted a post-mortem on the deceased?'

'Yes.'

'And you may have heard that the surgeon concluded that the deceased was found to be five or six months advanced in pregnancy, is that the case?'

'I have been told as much,' I said.

'Were you aware of her pregnancy before that?'

Liar, liar, Frances Williams! Do you dare?

'I had thought her rather stout of late, but I did not know, nor did it occur to me, that she was in the family way.'

'And her emotional state at the time did not betray her condition to you?'

'On Sunday evening she was in high spirits.'

'Why do you suppose that was?'

Harriet, in my room, singing and dancing. Often on a Sunday she was subdued; something about attending the chapel three times made her melancholy. Or perhaps not that; perhaps I should say reflective. But on that last Sunday she was different. She was almost joyous. *What are you about?* I had asked her. *What's this, girl, so much joy?*

And she said, *In a few days I shall be free of all this. In a few days I will escape.*

Escape me? I asked, dreading her answer.

Of course, not you. I shall miss you, Frances. I shall miss you so very much.

And she had taken my face in her hands and kissed my mouth quickly. Oh, that she had lingered! Sometimes she did, in a tease. Her lips on mine, held there as if she had forgotten what she was doing and was distracted by the sensation. And then I would move, and the spell would break and she would leave me. I should do anything – *anything* – to prevent that.

Is Bromley really so very dreadful, I asked her, *that you should long for escape?*

And then her smile dropped a little. *I need to be free*, she said.

Of me? I asked.

Of him, she said.

Who?

And she shook her head and pulled out her journal, and read something and smiled again.

I could guess at it, though. I could guess at the man who troubled her this severely, that she should long for a strange place in preference to her home.

'And did she have other close friends, Miss Williams?'

I cleared my throat. 'She was a regular attendant at Mr Verrall's chapel,' I said.

'She was to leave for her situation shortly, as you understand it?'

Behind me, the crowd stirred. I wondered if Verrall was present. I had not noticed him as I came in, and that was unusual. In any given room, the reverend stood out. Not for appearance, for he was as a man, in my opinion, quite nondescript, with his brown whiskers, bare at the chin, tallish but not too tall; average in every possible way. But he had an energy about him, a fervour, perhaps you could call it that. He drew people to him, and his congregation swelled.

I felt it, and I resisted. I always resist compulsion.

But that is not true at all. I was compelled to love Harriet, and I let myself do it. Perhaps that is why she died.

'I understood from her that she was going to Arundel in a few days,' I said.

'Apologies for the delicate nature of my questions, Miss Williams, but do you know of any man who had expressed a particular fondness for the deceased? Anyone to whom she had grown attached?'

I paused, took a breath in. 'I heard nothing of any person being in love with her.'

It's always best to avoid an outright lie, if you can. But presenting a half-truth can prove difficult if you are called upon to elaborate or explain. I had not answered his question, preferring instead to answer another. I heard nothing, for scarcely anybody spoke to me, especially not to gossip. Doubtless if the coroner asked the same question of Susannah Garn, or Lottie Beezley, there might be said to be any number of people in love with her. Perhaps they might even include me, although I doubt they should name me thus in a courtroom.

I heard nothing of any person being in love with her. I saw it, of course, all the time, if indeed that was what it was. Infatuation, perhaps; lust. I saw that all the time. I saw it and knew it. But love? Perhaps that was just me.

The coroner dismissed me after that, and called Alfred Garn, Susannah's half-witted brother. I was almost tempted to join the throng at the back of the room, for curiosity's sake, but I felt them staring as I walked past and I had no wish to stay.

Reverend George Verrall

The mind is a curious device; one that enjoys torturing its host. I can never quite comprehend it, the efforts the mind goes to, to undermine one's own sense of wellbeing. If it is not questioning decisions, judging one's physical appearance or creating pains and chills that have no apparent cause, it is imagining phantoms and creating nightmares with which to disrupt the only time one should expect peace and quiet.

I woke from a dream, sitting upright in bed, my nightshirt soaked with sweat, breathing hard. It took a moment for me to come to my senses, to realise where I was, and not where I thought I had been.

Sarah turned in bed. I had forgotten she was there. 'What's the matter?' she asked.

'Nothing. A dream. Go back to sleep.'

I tried to settle but found I could not; after a few minutes of lying motionless, my heart still pounding, I rose and took a blanket from the chair. With that about my shoulders I went downstairs, found a candle on the hall table and lit it. The fire in the study was barely glowing, but with the door closed and the silence all around me I fancied it was almost comforting. At times like this I regret my vow of temperance; a tot of something, brandy perhaps, would be just the thing to send me back to sleep.

But alcohol was the fuel of the Devil, and the Lord Himself knew that I needed no further assistance from that quarter.

The room looked very different, now, from how it had looked in my dream. In my dream it was bright daylight, five or six or seven policemen in here, searching through all of my things. The sunlight allowing nothing to be hidden: dust and papers and books thrown into the air whilst I pleaded for them to take better care. My cries went unheard, as if I were not there at all, or I had turned invisible. The couch was overturned, the upholstery rent with a pocket-knife, and I protested and protested, unheeded. I did not ask what they were looking for, or suggest I could help them in their search. I just wanted them to stop.

And at the height of it, when the table lamp was thrown to the floor and smashed into a thousand glittering shards, scattering across the floorboards, I saw the object of their search: on the mantelpiece was a glass bottle with a large label proclaiming 'POISON'.

Still they searched; I tried to turn them from their task, tried to push them from the door, but they ignored me – and the bottle. But surely it could only be a matter of moments before one of them turned to the fireplace and saw it, and a further moment before they charged me with the ownership of it, I who had denied it all …

At that moment I had started myself into wakefulness and the dream dispersed.

I felt little short of exhausted here in the study, but I did not want to return to bed and to sleep. Instead I sat on the couch – which was, almost to my surprise, fully intact – and looked to the mantelpiece as if expecting to find the glass bottle there, or for it to appear before my eyes like a parlour trick.

I was a foolish old man, to be thus affected. And by a dream! None of it was real. In a few days or maybe a week the inquest would reach a verdict, and all of this would be at an end. I would rest easy again, and Bromley would return to the way it had been before Harriet even arrived. It had to be so, because the alternative proposition was too hideous to contemplate.

To pass the time until daylight, or until I could sleep again, I tidied the papers on my desk, reading through the notes for future sermons that I had made in the weeks past. All seemed pathetic, uninspiring, vapid. I had written so much better! What had happened to me? I thought back to the time before Harriet, to Phoebe; in those days I had produced the best sermons of all. The Lord had spoken to me then in a way that He had not done since. Perhaps I should have tried harder with Phoebe; then Harriet might have been just a brief interlude, someone to keep me in mind of the nature of the Lord whilst I waited for my Fire and Glory to return.

Perhaps Mrs Burton knew where Phoebe was. I resolved to ask, in the morning. Perhaps we could find her, bring her back to Bromley, and then everything would be as it was before all of this sorry business had begun. The sooner it was ended, the better.

I stared once again at the mantelpiece with dry, tired eyes, and in that moment inspiration struck me.

dear God!

thank you, thank you

For the unravellings of my fevered mind had given me an idea after all, one that came from the Lord Himself. Inspiration. The bottle. The search for the bottle.

I took up my pen and found some notepaper in the drawer, addressed the note and dated it, and asked of Mr Carttar the coroner to consider whether it were possible that the deceased had taken the prussic acid in some other manner than as a liquid; whether the poison was obtainable as a powder, or as a pill, or as a dragee; and, that being the case, whether the search for a bottle had been entirely unnecessary, and its absence not therefore a conclusive defence against self-harm. After all, the most likely answer to the dilemma was yet that Harriet had taken her own life. She was unmarried, and with child; she had secured a position that she could, in her condition, never have taken up. What further reason did she need to wish to depart this life?

The letter written and sealed, I felt a sense of deep relief. That was it, then: what the Lord had been trying to tell me, through the medium of my fevered dreams.

I should be better at listening for His Voice.

Saturday, 11th November, 1843

Thomas Churcher

Father and James left me in bed this morning. I was pretending to be asleep, although they made enough noise getting up and dressed. I had been dreaming about Harriet, and I wanted to stay with her for as long as I could.

That day we went to the woods instead of the back of the chapel or by the river, and walked through the trees, talking. I was telling her about boots and shoes and how they are made, and why our boots are better than Ayling's or Burgess's, because of the quality of the leather. She said she should never buy shoes elsewhere as long as she lived, and I smiled and said in that case she might be my best customer.

We walked away from the paths and deep into the woods where the ground was uneven, thick with pine needles that were soft underfoot like a mattress, soft and fragrant and smelling of the rich earth and the cool wind. I found some cyclamen and gathered up some flowers for her, and she smiled and thanked me, and by and by we got to the edge of the wood and walked along the hedgerow back towards the town, picking blackberries and vying to find the biggest and the best, until my fingers were stained with the juice and her mouth was dark with it, and I kissed her, tasting the warm sweetness of the berries in my mouth and hers. I felt the heat rising up inside me and I wanted her. She was in my arms and I moved my hand to her waist and I felt something, like a stiffness, perhaps, or a hesitation. It was enough. I held her again and kissed her but I did not force her. I thought she would come to me when she was ready, and, if that happened, I would be waiting.

When we parted I looked at her and in the dappled light of the sun her pale skin and dark eyes and the red of her mouth were so beautiful, so lovely.

And the darkness of her lips made me think of the blood and then all I could see was dead Harriet instead and I had to get up and get dressed and go for a walk to get the picture of it out of my mind.

Dark blood between her lips, like varnish, her eyes glazed, her skin still warm.

Reverend George Verrall

I woke late and lay for a while listening to the sounds of Sarah and Mrs Burton discussing the purchase of new linens. Jessie would be with them, standing there wide-eyed and dumb, waiting for something that sounded like an instruction. Phoebe would have involved herself in the discussion from beginning to end; perhaps she was in a new house now, as a housekeeper, with Mrs Burton's no doubt effusive letter of introduction to assuage any doubts as to her character.

I heard Sarah's voice grow louder as she came out into the hall: ' ... that girl needs a job to do.'

That girl needs help, George.

She had said that to me the night before Harriet died, sitting in the parlour after supper.

'That girl needs help.'

'I do not see,' I said petulantly, 'why I should be the one to do it.'

She put down her work and stared at me. 'Because the Lord calls you to help those in need, George. Do I really need to explain it to you?'

'I'll thank you not to take that tone, Sarah. You are the first to say that charity should be for those who are in need through no fault of their own.'

'And is this situation her sin alone?' She set her mouth in a line. 'You should think, perhaps, of the consequences of your actions, and of your inaction.'

And she bent her head to the embroidery once more. A dozen remonstrations filled my thoughts but I could give none of them voice. What did she mean? That the chapel would be tainted by the association, once it came out? That I might be suspected of putting a child in her belly?

you should have helped her when you had the chance to

It was too late to do anything to fix it now.

That evening we had sat in silence for a long while, until the tangle of my thoughts unravelled to the sudden horrifying idea that if I did not offer some sort of practical solution, then Sarah might well seek out Harriet herself and offer some sort of assistance, as part of her pastoral duties. If I did not take care of it, then the matter would escalate out of my control.

'I shall see her in the chapel,' I told Sarah. 'Tomorrow evening. I will pray with her, and offer assistance. Will that satisfy you?'

And she had nodded, and offered a curious sort of smile, and said no more about it.

too little
too late

Richard Field

Maria joined me for supper, which pleased me greatly. I tried my best to lighten the mood with conversation, but she kept her head down and spooned her soup.

I had spent the morning at my club, scouring all the newspapers for any mention of the dreadful events in

Bromley. That I found nothing at all was a good sign; perhaps the journalists would steer clear of it. And yet it made me feel sad, too, that Harriet's untimely death was something so unremarkable as to go unreported.

'What I can't get over,' I said, chewing, 'is what she was doing with that Williams woman.'

'For heaven's sake,' Maria said, but quietly.

We had discussed it already at some length. We knew of Miss Williams, of course, from Harriet's letters to us. At first we had been pleased that she had found a friend, for at first her letters back from Bromley had been full of melancholy. She had complained of her mother and her sister, of feeling lonely; of the townsfolk being cold and ignoring her. She said that she thought it was because she had returned wearing London clothes and having clearly expanded her own means, which had made Maria snort. I recall one letter in particular where she had said quite clearly, 'I am not well liked.' She had mentioned the Churchers, a family she had known for years, and other members of the chapel; but none who seemed to be close friends.

But then she had made the acquaintance of Miss Williams, a spinster more than ten years her senior, and everything had seemed to change. All her letters were about Miss Williams: how she talked, what she ate and wore, what lessons she was teaching to the girls in her care.

'You cannot complain of her making new friends,' Maria had said to me, at the time. 'After all, if she had not been the kind of girl to nurture intimate friendships with her own sex, you and I would never have been introduced.'

'That is true, dearest, and I'm not complaining,' I had replied. 'I just think it a little odd, for a woman like that to attach herself to a younger female.'

'Attach herself! What on earth is that supposed to mean?'

I did not answer. I could not say why I felt so uneasy about it.

'Anyway, you haven't even met the lady in question. She must be perfectly decent, if Harriet likes her so much.'

Nevertheless, in my letters of reply I asked Harriet more questions about Miss Williams, to satisfy myself that she was not being led astray. All enquiries were answered joyfully; it seemed there was no limit to the brilliance and resourcefulness of her new friend. And then within a short matter of time Harriet was spending the night with her, ostensibly to avoid the walk back across the fields to her mother's house, and yet that in itself seemed very odd, to me.

Her final letter to us, which arrived just this very week, showed the extent of the woman's manipulative skills – Harriet had delayed her travel to us in order to deputise for Miss Williams at the school because she was supposedly unwell. Who knew but that Harriet's life might have been saved, had she only made the journey as she had originally intended?

I said as much, again, to Maria as Annie cleared our plates.

'I do wish you'd stop,' Maria said, as the door closed.

'But I can't help but see the significance of it,' I insisted. 'That she was sleeping with her! Do you not see it?'

'All I know is that my friend is dead, Richard, and we must accept some responsibility for it.'

Her words had a cold finality about them, and she stood up – a little awkwardly – and left me to sit at the table and enjoy a pipe and a glass of port on my own.

She was right, of course. Harriet was dead. And, the more you looked at it, the more it became my fault.

Sunday, 12th November, 1843

Reverend George Verrall

The attendance at the morning service was poor, very poor. There was not even bad weather to account for it, for the Sabbath day was grey and cloudy, not at all cold. The air hung outside much as it did within the glorious walls of the Lord's house, gloomy and turgid. That morning, in my dressing-room, I had taken myself in hand and indulged myself in the hope that my sermon might be enlivened somewhat by it; my original talk had had to be put aside following the terrible events of the week, and I feared that my own grief at the loss of Harriet would prevent me from delivering the Lord's Word to my flock in a manner which they would find enlightening.

'Perhaps you should send to Camberwell,' Sarah had said to me, over dinner the previous evening, when I told her of my fears. She meant that I should ask the Reverend Boyce to come to preach on my behalf; he was soon to take up a ministry at York, but for the time being he was travelling between parishes to preach. 'Or ask one of the deacons to do it in your stead.'

'I don't think they should like that very much,' I said glumly. 'No: I shall have to do it. The Lord will guide me in the right words to say.'

She looked at the pear she had sliced into quarters on her plate and said, to it, rather than to me, 'Let us hope so, for all our sakes.'

I feared I was never very far away from Sarah's disapproval; this had occurred to me some years ago and once the thought had been formed I could never quite get rid of it. Over the years of our marriage it had solidified into pure fact, and now it had become a daily pastime to discover what it was I would get so terribly wrong before the sun set once again.

Alas, even the casual indulgence in the dressing room did not inspire me to produce a sermon worthy of Harriet. The congregation stared at me as I spoke from the pulpit, as if daring me to tell the truth.

'Our dear sister was a woman of rare kindness,' I said, beginning with truth, and then veering slightly away from it. 'She was generous in nature, spiritual and holy, and a fine example to set to us all. And yet, even the best amongst us are called unto the Lord at a time of his choosing. We cannot know the day or hour, nor the reason why our loved ones are taken from us. We must, as the Lord himself tells us to do, trust and obey, and know that our sister has been translated into Glory, and that one day we ourselves will follow her, and see her once again.'

Where there had been silence, I heard a noise – perhaps a cough, or a snort. I looked over the faces, expecting to see a reflection of the same emotion I felt myself, and yet they were all set to stone.

'And now, my brothers and sisters, our next hymn: "I Know That My Redeemer Liveth".'

There was a pause as I stepped down from the pulpit. At the organ Tom Churcher lifted his hands to begin, and the music filled the chapel. I felt relief that the sermon was over, allowing my voice to rise to the familiar words of the hymn. The congregation were not in such fine voice; if I had been at all uncertain before, the weak and faltering sounds of them singing confirmed it.

At the closing of the hymn I felt anger rising in my breast, and as I stepped forward once again to offer them a blessing I had to choke it down. There was a pause for a moment of silent prayer, and eventually Tom began to play a gentle melody that usually sounded peaceful and yet joyous; today it sounded mournful.

I rose from my seat and made my way to the chapel door, ready to shake hands and wish them well as they departed. But, to my dismay, many of them chose to exit via the rear door – the one nearest to the privy – which had been opened for them by Beezley. From my position I could see them, scurrying for the back of the chapel.

Joseph Milstead took pity on me and came to converse with me while the rest of them trooped from the passage at the side of the chapel and made their way to the gate.

'It's a worrying time for everyone,' he said.

'Indeed,' I replied. 'How very disappointing it is. At a time when we are so sorely tested ... '

'People work things out in their own way,' he said mysteriously.

'But the Lord provides us with guidance, and support, through the Word ... '

'If there is one who speaks the Word, Reverend.'

what are you getting at, man?

spit it out

if you have something to say then say it

At length Sweeting came to stand beside me. I noticed within the gloom that a few of the men had stayed behind: Churchers, father and son; Beezley; Brigley; John Joyce.

'What's this?' I asked.

'We would speak with you. Perhaps in the vestry?'

I followed them back inside, wordless, feeling my blood pounding through my veins. Perhaps this was how the Lord himself felt, I thought, being led to Calgary. Or perhaps how he felt in Gethsemane, knowing that he was about to be betrayed. I had recently preached a sermon on it. Had they been listening?

They gathered in the vestry and chairs were brought in from the hall. Tom sat at the back with his head down. I felt that whatever had been discussed between them had passed over his head; he was here by default rather than by his own will.

I took a deal of trouble choosing my seat and moved it to the head of the room, in front of the desk I used for chapel business, wishing by this action to indicate that this was still my place. I smoothed my trousers and my gown before I sat, and lifted my chin.

'Well, brothers? What's this about?'

'You know well enough,' said Sweeting. His colour was high; I fancied with little provocation he might actually explode.

'I'm afraid I do not.'

John Joyce spoke then. 'You saw for yourself, Reverend. Attendance today was perhaps half what it usually is for a Sabbath. The town is in uproar over it. The gossips—'

'Do we listen to gossip?' I demanded. 'Have we ever listened to gossip?'

'No,' James Churcher said, quietly, 'but we do address the cause of it. *If thine eye offends thee, cut it out and throw it away.*'

he is talking about me

they wish to cut me out and discard me

I smiled, inside praying for the Lord's peace and for wisdom to deal with this in the most effective way. 'The cause of the gossip does not lie within these walls,' I said.

'Does it not?' Sweeting said.

I got to my feet as the Holy Fire of the Spirit rose in my chest, a rush of pure, righteous anger. 'Have you forgotten who you are? You are God's children! You are responsible for bringing Light and Life to this community, and yet you are fractured and broken because of one woman's suicide! Pull yourselves together!'

They were all staring at me in shock, except for Tom. He had not moved.

115

'Are we to let Harriet's death destroy everything we have built here? Are we to let Satan use her for such ill? Gentlemen, we are being tested, can you not see it? And that testing is showing that we are wanting, brothers, we are very much wanting.'

Sweeting breathed in sharply through his nose.

'We have a choice,' I said, more calmly. 'We can watch and pray, thank God for Harriet Monckton's life, mourn her passing and carry on as we have before, ministering to the godless and the destitute, following our Lord's example and bringing hope to the hopeless; or we can give up, fall apart and turn our faces away from Him who loves us. What is it to be?'

There was a pause.

'He's right,' said James Churcher.

Beezley had been watching me closely. 'This meeting,' he said, 'was called by us because we are deacons of this church and we can all see the danger in what has transpired.'

'You think I am blind to that danger? The Enemies of the Cross are all around us, brother. They are all waiting for us to make a mistake, to fracture, to show ourselves as half-hearted. We cannot let them win. We should stand together, trust in the Lord with all our hearts, and come together instead of drifting apart.'

There was silence for a moment. I sat down again.

'If any of you wish to ask me anything,' I said, quite calmly, 'then this is the time to do it. I will answer you.'

They shifted in their seats, none of them speaking for a moment.

go on
I dare you
ask it

'If it were not for the circumstances,' Beezley said, 'it would not be so very bad. I mean, her death is one thing, but the manner of it, and more importantly her condition – that's the problem.'

'I'm fully aware of that,' I said.

'The question is, Reverend,' Beezley went on, 'were you aware of it before she passed into Glory?'

I hesitated before answering. 'I was aware.'

Churcher and Beezley exchanged a glance between them.

Joyce said, 'And were you the cause of it? The surgeon was not certain of the exact timing of the...initiating event, after all.'

The anger rose within me once again but I swallowed it back down.

how dare you how dare you think that of me?

'I was not the cause of it, no.'

There was a collective exhaling of breath in the room. They were relieved! But to my very great surprise they believed me, to a man. I felt the anger subside and in its place was a sensation of warmth towards them all. They wanted to trust me; I was their shepherd, and I was steering them through the very darkest of valleys. All they wanted was to know that I was still guiding them in the right direction.

Sweeting then ruined it for us all. 'If it's not him,' he said, 'then it must be Tom.'

Everyone in the room turned to look at Tom Churcher, at the back. He looked up for the first time, his expression one of horror at being thus exposed.

James Churcher said, 'Sweeting. This isn't—'

'Well, Tom?' Joyce asked. 'The reverend has answered; now you must, too.'

'Answer what?' he asked, desperate.

he hasn't been listening

leave the boy alone

'You walked out with Harriet often,' he said. 'You were sweet on her even before she went away, were you not? Perhaps you picked up where you left off, as soon as the girl came home from London. For all we know, you may even have been the reason she returned to Bromley.'

'No,' Tom answered. His initial shock at being the centre of attention in the room had given way to anger at being cornered. 'I liked her, is all.'

'Answer truthfully, boy,' Sweeting said. 'Did you lie with her?'

'Sweeting,' James said, his voice low. 'Please.'

'He knows what I mean, James, he's not a child.'

'I did not!' Tom said. Anger had driven him to his feet, made fists of his hands. He took a pace towards Sweeting, who shrank in his seat. 'I would not!'

'Tom,' I said, 'that's enough. Sit down.'

At that very moment there was a knock at the vestry door. I turned towards it, wondering who else could possibly wish to join in with this ghastly spectacle. Beezley got to his feet and opened the door, and behind it, hat held in his hands, was Sergeant Samuel King of the Bromley police.

I got up and faced him. 'Samuel,' I said. 'What brings you to our door?'

'I asked him,' Beezley said. 'Take a seat, Mr King. I'll fetch another.'

Everyone shuffled round to make room, except for Tom, who had sunk once again with his head clutched in his hands, his ears covered.

Sweeting could no longer contain himself. 'I never thought it. Never thought such a thing.'

he hates to think he has been fooled by a girl

'And I gave her mother three shillings,' he said. He was in such a fearsome rage that he could barely get the words through his bared teeth.

'Calm down, man,' I said. 'You also promised to raise a subscription to pay for the funeral. I notice you made no mention of that in the service today.'

Sweeting's eyes bulged. 'Under the circumstances—' he began.

'The circumstances are that a girl is dead,' I said.

They were all staring at me. I should perhaps have bitten my tongue, but I was so far down that road that I could no longer turn back. 'A girl has lost her life here in this place, in the Lord's house, at her own hand or by the hand of another. A young woman whom we all knew, and called a member of our congregation. Yes, she was a sinner, but so are we all, every one of us. If any of you think that you are more worthy than she, then I should ask you kindly to depart this place and never return. Do I make myself clear?'

Nobody spoke.

that was a mistake, George

were you not thinking?

were they not listening?

I addressed the sergeant. 'We have nothing to hide. This terrible event has befallen us, and we have no choice but to deal with it as best we can. But you should know, sir, that what has happened here has come as a terrible shock to us all.'

'I understand,' King said.

how I loathe that man

slow-witted

insensitive

the basest of base men he is

'Then you must forgive us, sir,' I said, 'if you find we take exception to the intrusive nature of the inquest. It feels quite as if we are all put on trial for our lives.'

'No need to be quite so dramatic, Reverend. We just want to find out the truth, is all.'

'None of us here has any responsibility in her death, and that's the truth of it. If you and the coroner wish to look for another's hand at work in this tragedy, then you will need to look elsewhere.'

King stared at me. 'I look for evidence, sir. Nothing besides that.'

We all sat in silence for a moment.

'Our work here in Bromley is important,' I said. 'It is the Lord's work. We preach the Word of God to the ungodly; we lift up the downtrodden, we tend to the sick, and we share what we have with the poor. Unlike other churches, we turn nobody away who is in need.'

Joyce shot me a look that might have been warning. Samuel King had left our congregation just a few months after my own arrival, in order to renew his membership of the parish church. Fool that he was. I could do nothing about his stupidity, but to pander to his own High Church allegiances was beyond me.

King got to his feet. 'I appreciate your taking the time to reassure me, Reverend,' he said. 'Nevertheless, sir, I have a job to do, and I will on instruction of Her Majesty's coroner continue to do it.'

The rest of them stirred and got to their feet, as if taking his cue. The meeting, such as it had been, was apparently at an end. Despite his apparent hurry to leave and get back to his work, King dawdled in the vestry talking to Beezley. Beezley stayed to lock the doors and the sergeant walked out with me. I had nothing further to say to him, but instead he addressed me.

'The boy seems very distressed,' he said.

'Tom Churcher? Yes, indeed he is. He has taken it very badly.'

'Because he was the one what found her?'

I paused, and looked around me. James Churcher and his son had gone through the gate and were some fifty yards ahead of us, walking quickly back towards the Market Place. The rest of them had already dispersed to their homes. Behind us, Beezley had gone down the passage to the side of the chapel to check that the back door was securely locked. We were quite alone.

'Yes, partly. But Sweeting was there at the same time, and his manner, as you have seen, remains very much as it once was. Tom Churcher, on the other hand, has quite fallen apart. Tell me, sergeant, what does that suggest to you?'

His eyes narrowed. 'I don't know what it is you're getting at,' he said, and he was lying.

'His feelings towards Harriet ran very much deeper than anyone quite realised,' I said. 'I do believe he thought himself in love with her.'

'My understanding of the matter was that he is promised to another young lady in the town,' King said, generously.

'Emma Milstead, yes. He was promised to her. But he broke it off, and he spent a lot of time with Harriet over the last few weeks. They were regularly to be seen walking across the fields together, as I'm sure you know, if you have asked around the town.'

'Are you suggesting—?'

'I'm merely stating a fact, Sergeant. You deal in evidence, you say. Then you should look to those who spent the most time with her, and who are the most affected by her death.'

Richard Field

Maria was unwell after our meal, and did not come down at all today. The child, at least – perhaps out of pity for me – was less fractious and even at times smiled as I dandled him on my knee during the endless hours of Annie's half-day.

I found he was inclined to wail as soon as I left him alone, and so he accompanied me about the house, lying on the rug in front of the fireplace in the drawing room while I read the paper aloud to him, or balanced upon my hip whilst I made tea in the kitchen, all the time cursing the poor state of affairs that has led us to have only one servant, and no sign of another.

Such time alone allowed me to think of Harriet. I had told Maria, through my shameful display of emotion, of Verrall's letter: she had read it herself. If, indeed, there had been some element of warning cloaked in those sentences, she gave no indication that she had noticed it. Her initial reaction seemed to be shock, rather than grief, for she was detached and quiet. She held me dutifully as I sobbed, and wiped my face with her handkerchief, then helped me to the chair. 'We will get through this,' she said. 'We will survive it, as we shall survive any crisis.'

Her words were those of a loving wife, but her tone was distant.

After the tears, I felt somewhat better, as though the knowledge of it had bedded in. It was a terrible thing, but it had happened, and now here we were, Maria, myself, and our son: and we would continue. Later that evening, though, I heard Maria sobbing in our bedroom. I went to her, but the door was locked. 'Maria?' I called.

The sobbing stopped. I heard her sigh, and breathe, and a quavering voice came back. 'I'm quite all right, Richard. I just need to be alone for a while.'

I left her, and the sounds began again, breaking my heart. We had both loved Harriet, each in our own way. We would both miss her.

The child slept on the rug and for a little while I was able to lie on the settee and indulge in my own thoughts in the quiet of the afternoon. Harriet and I had made love where the babe now lay, on that very rug. Not once, but several times. And here, too, upon this seat: my trousers dropped to the floor, her across my lap, her legs either side of mine, riding me like a horse. She was a vigorous and an attentive lover, in the end. When she first came to me she was a virgin and yet I did not press my advantage: she came to me, rather; curiously, wishing to know.

Those rather desperate days — I remember them well. I was feeling my age somewhat, having hosted a dinner party for some of the gentlemen students at the Hackney College;

Harriet had only recently begun to lodge at my house, having taken up her position at the school. She was a shy girl, and yet once she felt comfortable with you she was able to engage in lively and intelligent conversation, such that you forgot quite quickly that she was still very young. Then, I think, she was just twenty-one years old.

I remember asking her by what manner of means her parents had sought to educate her, for they were not wealthy, although they were respectable. She said she had been fortunate enough to learn much at the village school she had attended – that she had had an inspirational lady teacher, who had encouraged her a great deal. From a young age her own earnest desire had been to pass on that spirit of encouragement to others, such that girls – in particular girls – should feel able to push themselves to learn, if they were capable of it, no matter how poor and humble had been their beginnings.

At that dinner, with young men of character and, in some cases, wealth, seated around our dining table, she chose to converse with me. Afterwards, as the men retired to the drawing room, she hesitated in the doorway, and wished us goodnight.

I had only been in the drawing room for a matter of minutes when I excused myself and went to find her. She was in the dining room, reading a book.

'I thought you had gone to bed,' I said.

'No,' she said. 'I find I am too excited to sleep just yet.'

I laughed at her. 'Too excited? By all that male company?'

She had the grace to flush, just a little. 'Perhaps. I find conversations very enlightening.'

'As do I.' I sat next to her at the table. 'What are you reading?'

She showed me the book – a translation of the Greek tragedies. 'I borrowed it from your library. I hope you don't mind.'

'Of course not,' I said.

You have to remember, then, that she was twenty-one years old and I was a full thirty years older. I had been married, once, and had no intention of marrying again. I had indulged my desires with whores when the need pressed itself upon me, and I had on several occasions had love affairs with women, some of them younger, some of them older. But not for some time.

Harriet put down her book. 'I fear you must think me very naïve,' she said, quietly.

'Naïve?'

'In matters of the heart,' she said.

And that was how it had begun.

I woke from my reverie to find the baby fidgeting and grumbling, so I lifted him and shushed him against my chest in the hope that he would not rouse himself to a full scream. All was quiet in the house. I took the child upstairs to the bedroom. The curtains were drawn and the room was dark, just the sound of Maria's deep breathing. I was reluctant to disturb her, but the child's mewling started her instantly into consciousness and she raised herself to a sitting position.

'Richard.'

'I'm sorry to wake you,' I said, passing the baby to her.

'Needs must,' she answered. As she loosened her bedgown to accommodate the hungry child, I went to the curtains and drew them a little. The greyness of the day outside did nothing to brighten the room.

'You've kept him very quiet,' she said. 'I thought you must have gone out somewhere with the perambulator.'

I laughed at the thought of it. 'To the park? Like a nurse-maid? That would make a fine spectacle. I should be laughed out of the neighbourhood.'

'Annie will be back this evening,' she said. 'But thank you, for letting me sleep.'

Her mild tone made me feel able to broach the subject that had been troubling me since the letter had arrived on Friday.

'I feel I should go to Bromley,' I said.

She did not reply immediately. I turned back to the bed. Her head was bent over the child's, watching him as he suckled. 'When?' she asked, her voice low.

'Sooner the better, I fancy. I should pay our respects to Harriet's mother; attend the funeral perhaps.'

'If there's to be an inquest, the funeral may be delayed. Or perhaps it has already taken place.'

'If you don't want me to go, I'll…'

I did not finish my sentence. She had not interrupted me. I realised I did not want her to come up with a reason for me to stay, although there were plenty: the child was very young, my wife was unwell, we had limited help in the house; we had very little money to spare on a hotel and coach fares back and forth. Harriet was our friend but we lived far enough away for nobody to expect us to attend; in fact, for me to attend at all – a married man, who had counted an unmarried young female among his close friends, might be looked upon with some suspicion.

'When?' she asked, again.

'Perhaps tomorrow, then,' I replied. 'I'll ensure Annie is here and able to attend to you.'

There was another little pause. The air in the room felt heavy, scented with something foul that I could not name.

'I should like a drink of water, Richard,' she said quietly. 'Perhaps you might fetch it for me.'

I left the room and closed the door quietly behind me. I fancied I heard her make some sound: I thought she was talking to the baby in the strange, high voice she uses when she lifts him and plays with him, but then I realised it was something else. A cry, perhaps.

Monday, 13th November, 1843

Frances Williams

Thirty-two girls in attendance today. The room felt so empty I was obliged to move some of the girls from the back of the room to the front, to fill in the space. Lizzie Finch now has just twelve younger ones in her group. If the numbers dwindle further, I shall have to send some of the older ones to her to even things out. There are so many absences it is hard to keep track of them all; I have sent notes home for many of them, but have had few replies.

Mr Campling spoke to me after school. He said he has had four letters today and another four last week, six of that number unsigned, suggesting that the parents are unhappy with me teaching their girls. I felt my heart sink at that news. This – my position being endangered – was a consequence of Harriet's death that I had not foreseen. I felt foolish for not having considered it earlier. Perhaps, if I had known, I might have handled things differently.

After school I had intended to eat a supper of bread and cheese, but I had no stomach even for that. The room was not cold enough to light the fire, and inside my room it felt stuffy and too quiet. I could hear the Beezleys arguing. Shouts from the street. Laughter. In the end I took my shawl and the bottle Tom Churcher had brought the night Harriet disappeared, now empty, and walked across the Market Place with my head down in case someone should approach me. I could feel eyes upon me, sense the way people fell silent as I passed. I felt contaminated by it, by shame.

Clara opened the door, just a crack, and then wider when she saw it was me.

'Forgive me for calling unannounced,' I said. 'I couldn't stay at home.'

'You know you are welcome at any time,' she said, taking a cloth to move the kettle on to the stove. 'How are you?'

'Well, under the circumstances. And how are you – and Tom?'

'Tom keeps to his bed, when he is not dragged to the shop. I don't know what to do with him.' She looked to the door that led to the back parlour.

'He'll come round,' I said, not entirely sure if that was likely. Other women might call it a shame, for such a fine young man to not have the sharp wits to go with it, as though the face should reveal the character. I have never known that to be a universal truth. People can be beautiful, and deceitful; and ugly people can be the kindest of all. I am not prone to note the attractive features of the male, and yet even I can acknowledge that Tom is handsome. A man who wears his honesty on his face, who is no more capable of subterfuge than a child.

I say that, of course, but I have known children capable of attempting the most elaborate of deceptions. What I mean is that I can always see through them.

The kettle boiled and Clara poured the water on to the tea leaves in the pot, setting out their china cups and saucers for us both. 'Will you have some cake? Mrs Verrall brought it.'

'Is that a good thing, or a bad thing?'

Clara laughed. 'I am sure it must be very good. Although I doubt she made it herself, with those porcelain hands of hers.' She cut a thick slice from the cake and halved it, offering a piece to me on a small china plate.

'She has visited you, then?' I asked.

'Twice. She brought us this – and some bread. She gets her flour delivered direct from the mill, I believe.'

'Very good of her, I'm sure.'

'Oh, Frances, don't take that tone. She is really very kind. She doesn't make a song and dance of it, just comes and offers help, and prays for us. And she doesn't need to; she could stay in her lovely house and because she is a lady nobody would think anything of it. Caroline Cooper told me Mrs Verrall brought her a bundle of herbs from her own garden to make a poultice for her grandmother's leg, and said nothing about it to anyone in the town, or the chapel.'

I wanted to ask why Mrs Verrall was bringing cake and bread to the Churcher household, since they had not been bereaved, or fallen ill. Why had she not bothered to visit me? I knew the answer to that question, of course. I was a newcomer to the town. A stranger, still.

'Emma Milstead has called for Tom,' she said, 'several times.'

'Oh?'

'He won't talk to her.'

'Why not?'

'I don't know.'

'Perhaps he thinks she will judge him harshly,' I offered. 'For his friendship with Harriet, I mean.'

'It's not just that. I think they all suspect him, everyone,' she said, and to my surprise she let out a sudden sob, and clutched her hand to her mouth.

'My dear,' I said. 'Nobody can seriously believe him capable of such a thing. Not Tom!'

'Not you, perhaps,' she wailed. 'But the gossips! And, worst of all, the police, the coroner. They don't know him. They just hear the rumours, that he was walking out with Harriet, and that's why he and Emma broke off their engagement.'

'It wasn't a proper engagement; he hadn't even spoken to her father,' I said. Ever the pedant.

'Nevertheless, Emma took it as such, and she took Harriet to be the interloper between them.'

128

'In that case, perhaps Emma should be suspected, and not Tom. Why would he harm Harriet, if she was dear to him?'

Clara bit her lip, tears trembling on her lower lashes. 'You know why. Because she was in the family way.'

'But surely ... '

'I know, it's hardly even possible, but that's still what they will say. Perhaps one of the gossips has told the coroner that Tom was associating with Harriet from the moment she returned. Everyone knew he was always sweet on her, he couldn't hide it. They will believe the worst of it. Our supposed friends. Our customers. The newspapers, even. People who don't know Tom as we do. They will make out that he didn't want the scandal; that she was demanding assistance from him.'

'What does he say about it?'

'Nothing. He won't speak to any of us. If we go in there, he pretends to be asleep.'

'Do *you* think the baby was his?'

My words were out before I had properly considered them, and now at last the tears spilled over and ran over her cheeks. She wiped them away with her handkerchief.

'No,' she said, firmly. 'I do not.'

I held my breath for a moment, then let it out in a sigh. 'No,' I said. 'Nor I.'

Clara smiled, then, and reached for my hand. 'You are a good friend to me, Frances.'

I was no such thing, to be fair. I did not believe Harriet's pregnancy was caused by Tom because I did not think her capable of consorting with a man who was less than her intellectual equal. But I could not admit as much to Clara.

And of course I had known Harriet was with child, perhaps long before anyone else did, possibly even before she knew it herself. I shared a bed with her, after all. I saw her in her chemise and sometimes not even that. I noticed because I noticed every little thing about her. I saw the way

129

her hips rounded; I saw the shape of her belly, a gentle curve at first that I loved, that grew into a bump which in the end even her stays could not properly disguise. I saw how her breasts swelled, like ripening fruit; how her nipples darkened in colour. After a while there was nothing else that could explain the changes.

Besides, I knew that she was not a virgin. She had told me that, at least.

'Who, then?' Clara said.

I had been lost in thought, remembering Harriet. Irritated, almost, to be brought back here to the Churchers' parlour and Mrs Verrall's fruit cake and the cup of tea that was already growing cold, I snapped, 'I have no idea.'

'But surely … I mean, you knew her best of all. She must have had a secret lover. If we knew who that was, we should know the murderer.'

Let her think that, I thought. If she believed it, then perhaps everyone else would, too. That Harriet's pregnancy was the motive for her murder, and the man responsible for the former logically must be responsible for the latter – well, it seemed highly probable. And, whilst they suspect that, they cannot suspect me.

Thomas Churcher

A knock, upon the door. I had been sleeping, and it startled me awake.

'Tom?' Clara's voice, outside. 'Tom, can you come out?'

I struggled to find some words. 'What is it?' My mouth felt dry, my tongue swollen.

'Emma is here.'

I closed my eyes again.

Another knock, and then the door opened and closed again.

'You can't stay in here forever. Look at you!'

'Leave me in peace.'

She sat on the edge of the bed. 'You're still dressed. Are you ill, or no?'

I breathed in and sat up, with difficulty because she was in the way. I rubbed my hand over my face, through my hair. And then finally I looked at my sister.

She put her hand on my arm. 'I'll tell Emma you will meet her at the pump. Yes?'

This time I did as I was bid; I could not avoid Emma forever. I would see her and something would happen; she would say everything was now concluded between us, that she no longer wished to have any association with me. She would look at me, and see, not the man she thought she loved, once, but rather someone broken.

She was waiting for me at the pump, as Clara said, and the smile when she saw me approach died on her face as I came closer. I felt exhausted, despite spending so much time in bed.

'What happened to you?' she asked. Fair hair, blue eyes. She looked as pretty as she always had. I had wanted her to love me, once, and I was the one who had pushed her away.

I shrugged, and that seemed to be enough.

We walked towards the chapel, then took the footpath into Cage Field. The land opened up to the north, the earth bare, spread wide. I had walked this way with Harriet. I had walked this way with Sweeting, just a few days before, looking for Harriet. Everywhere I looked, memories of her spun sticky webs in my head.

Now the path was wide enough for us to walk side by side. The trees and hedges edging the field were bare of leaves and the path was dry. I could not look at her, although I wanted to.

'Are you well?' I asked her.

'Yes,' she said.

'And your father and mother?'

'Also well.'

She laughed, and tried to take my hand. At first I jumped as if she had burned me, but then I smiled at her and took it, and squeezed it. We had held hands before. Despite the season, I felt sweat upon my brow. I was not feverish in the body, but perhaps in the brain. Perhaps I really was ill. Perhaps I would die, and then all of these thoughts would die with me, and I could be with Harriet again.

'What is it, Tom?' she said. 'Why won't you talk to me?'

I said, 'Does things to you, finding a body. Of a murdered person.'

'Was it ... dreadful? Was she injured?'

The question took me back there. 'I don't like to talk about it,' I said.

She looked sulky, then. 'Don't you like me any more, Tom?'

I stopped and turned to look at her. 'Like you?'

She looked almost afraid.

'Of course I like you. I'll always like you, Emma, how can you ask me such a thing?'

She set her mouth. 'You don't like me as much as you liked her. You liked her even before she went away to London, before you even noticed I existed. Don't deny it.'

'It was different.'

She took a deep breath in. 'Tom, I have to ask, I can't bear it ... did you?'

I looked at her for the first time. There were tears in her eyes. I tried to feel something, and my heart was like a lump of coal in my chest, dried and hard and still.

'Did I what?'

'Did you ... do it?'

My breath caught and I turned away from her. I heard her steps on the bare earth, hurrying behind me.

'If you can't tell the truth, I can't trust you,' she said.

'Don't, then,' I said, without looking back.

We parted in the Market Place without another word spoken between us. All the way back I had tried to think of something to say, to try and mend what was broken, but all I could think of was Harriet, and my heart cold and dry and hard, and my head full of her.

Emma said something as I left her, but I did not pay her any heed. A shout, from behind me – 'Tom!' – and a wail, like a shriek, like a bad-tempered child stamping its foot in the street. There were people standing at the stalls and in doorways and on the corners and I could feel their eyes on me, like a freak in one of the tents at the fair. Staring and whispering, loud enough for me to hear. I walked back home and all I could think was that I would go to the bedroom and shut the door and cover my head and hide from them all.

But that did not happen. I opened the door and he was standing in the parlour.

Clara got to her feet.

'Tom,' she said, 'the sergeant has come to ask you a few questions.'

Reverend George Verrall

I should like to say I remembered Harriet from the first time she came to the chapel, but I am afraid that I cannot. She was there as an older girl, sitting with Clara Churcher. Her parents worshipped elsewhere, I presumed at the parish church, so she had begun to attend of her own volition, perhaps as a form of rebellion, or experimentation. She was a serious, quiet girl, who rarely spoke out and only spoke to say goodbye and thank you to me after the services.

At some point she was no longer there, and I believe that must have been when she went to London to teach. She would occasionally come back to Bromley to visit her family at the weekend and would appear at the chapel for the Sunday morning service. She grew into a fine, attractive young woman. I believe teaching was good for her, because her confidence grew and on the occasions that she visited she would sometimes speak to myself or the deacons after the service about some matter of interpretation, or to ask for us to pray for her, or her father, who was ailing.

Eventually she returned from Hackney, and after that her attendance at the chapel was very regular indeed. I dare say she did not miss any service or meeting at the church at all.

All of these things I shall say to them, if they ask. And the other things I shall keep to myself.

Clara Churcher was pleased with Harriet's return from London, for she had been badgering me for help running the Sunday School for weeks, and Harriet, as a teacher, was the perfect person. After a morning service Clara came to me again, this time to ask permission to approach her friend about the Sunday School, and I told her to bring her to speak to me after service.

That very evening, Clara brought the girl to the vestry after the service. I recall I was in something of a hurry to get home.

'Reverend, I believe you know Harriet Monckton. She is willing to help me with the school, while she waits for her next position.'

I looked up from my desk. Was I peevish? I don't recall, but I must have felt something. Annoyance at the interruption, perhaps. Cross that Clara had clearly told the girl that she would be given the position as Sunday School teacher, when I had told her I wanted to speak with her first. That it had all been rushed through, and taken out of my hands.

Perhaps I tutted. Clara had set her mouth tight and thin, expecting something, an argument. Disagreement. And, behind her, a dark-haired, dark-eyed vixen, smirking.

'Very well,' I said, or something similar.

Disturbing, that was what it was. I had mixed feelings about her, from that moment on. I couldn't say why. She was perfectly pleasant, and kind to the children, and good at keeping them in order. She joined in with the prayers, and sang well, and looked up at the pulpit, listening to every word. Yes, that was it: she listened. Sometimes I would look out over the congregation and despair of them. George Sweeting, waiting intently for the messages that he could take and twist for his own ends. Mr Joyce, asleep. Mary Ford, head down, either asleep or daydreaming but in any case certainly not concentrating on the Word. Not listening. I can bring fire and damnation into it, I can shout about the hellfire that awaits them, sinners all, I can call them pilgrims and penitents and lambs and disciples, but half the time they are thinking about their dinner, or the conversation they had with their children last night, or the price of fruit at the market. They are *not listening*, not really there.

is that my failing or theirs?
forgive me Father for I have sinned

There she was, just behind Clara Churcher, standing in the open door.

'Well, Miss Churcher, you can leave us in peace.'

She turned and left, and closed the door behind her.

'Am I disturbing you?'

'No, not at all. Come in, Miss Monckton. Take a seat.'

'I wished to compliment you on a most enlightening sermon.'

fixing me with that dark-eyed fathomless stare
like a fox looking at a rabbit

'Thank you. Praise be to the Lord for his blessed Word.'

'I give thanks for it.'

'And you wish to help with the Sunday School?'

'I have been teaching at a school in Hackney, and I should like to help Clara until I find a new position.'

'Why did you leave your situation there?' I asked, thinking that if it were a matter of discipline or dubious morality, I should know about it.

Her face flushed and she could not look at me, but instead addressed her hands, clutched in front of her, and said that she had grown homesick and that since the death of her father her mother needed her at home. I did not believe a word of it. I supposed there to have been some failed romance, or some dispute with another teacher. But she seemed intelligent enough, and so I told her she should begin to assist Miss Churcher, and resolved to keep a close eye on her.

She came every Sunday. Sometimes she helped with the Sunday School but if there were not many in attendance she would sit for the whole service. George Sweeting, the superintendent of the Sunday School, said she was perfectly adequate, although occasionally a little free with her manner. I asked him what he meant by it. He said that she was always eager to do singing, and the reading of stories from the Gospel, and less keen on leading the children in silent prayer.

She was always at the chapel. She became part of the building, almost. I recall a men's Bible study and for a moment I was about to say, 'Where is Harriet?' for the sole reason that her presence was almost ubiquitous.

Of course, her presence disturbed our status quo. Especially for Tom Churcher. When Harriet Monckton went to London he seemed to mature: he took over the chapel music, grew in confidence, spoke up at chapel meetings and started to court Emma Milstead. I thought he had forgotten Harriet entirely, but of course I was wrong. If I believed in such superstitious notions, I should have said that she bewitched him.

For the rest, she was to all appearances a pious girl. Serious-natured. Thoughtful. If you had asked the congregation what they thought of her, that is most likely what they would say.

She was good at fooling people, even from the very start.

'My father will be back soon,' I said to the sergeant. 'Or we can go to the shop. Ask me questions there.'

'No need for that, lad,' he said, slowly, like he was talking to a simpleton. 'I'm here now. Just sit down and I'll ask you a few questions and you can answer them and then I'll be on my way.'

I looked at Clara. She nodded.

'I've told you what happened,' I said.

Clara was staring. I looked at her, desperate. 'Sit down, Tom,' she said.

I sat. My knee jumped a merry dance. He looked at it. I put my hand on it but it would not stop.

'You said you spent the afternoon looking for Harriet,' he said.

I thought hard. What to say, what to say? Say nothing was the best thing to do, but here he was and here I was and there was nothing for it.

'Yes,' I said.

'Who asked you to do that?' he asked.

It was a trick, I thought, he wanted me to say Mr Verrall, so I did not. 'Nobody asked me. I wanted to help.'

He looked like a kind man but he was big, red in the face, like a farmer or a smith, not a police officer with his uniform and his tall hat.

'When did you hear that Miss Monckton was missing?'

This was easier, I had answered this one before. 'Mr Beezley told me. He said she was expected back the night before – Monday night – and she did not come.'

'And what did you think had happened to her?'

I frowned. What had I thought? I had thought nothing. Nothing at all.

He went, eventually. The questions went on and on until I couldn't think straight any more and I think he saw that.

He said he would come back. I told him I needed to speak to my father. And he looked at me oddly. Perhaps I had said something wrong.

After he had gone I sat for a while with Clara drinking tea but she would not stop talking about Harriet and I could not listen. It was as though Harriet was hers. It felt as if they all thought Harriet belonged to them. Mr Verrall, Mary Ann, Mrs Monckton, Clara. Miss Williams. They each had a Harriet but it was not the same as the real Harriet, who belonged to me, and only me.

Richard Field

In the public bar at the White Hart I had to wait to attract the attention of the landlord, who was deep in conversation with two other men, one wearing the leather jacket common to hedge-cutters in the countryside, the other dressed more for town, and inebriated, judging by the slump of his frame against the counter.

'...there should be none of it. He lords it over the town, like he owns the place, and owns us,' said the man in tweeds.

'Right enough,' said the hedge-cutter.

'For all that posturing...'

'If he di'n't do it, then someone put her there for him to find, I reckon.'

The landlord noticed me then and straightened, and left the two of them to their opinions, and came to serve me. His name was Pawley, and he was kind enough to pretend to recognise me from my previous visits, as well as being in receipt of my letter asking him to keep a room for me.

'My apologies, sir,' he said, as we climbed the stairs, 'if you found the conversation in the bar somewhat ... indiscreet. You can imagine how people like to talk when something like this happens.'

'Indeed,' I replied. 'What has the reaction been, in the town?'

'Everyone is quite undone by it,' he said.

Pawley was a man I considered quite stoical in nature, one of those for whom the need to throw a drunkard out of a door comes as easily as serving him a jug of ale not a half-hour before.

'I am most terribly sorry for it,' I said.

Pawley looked me in the face. 'You and she were good friends,' he said. There was no judgement in his words. Like many others, he looked at my greying hair and my stoop and considered that my relationship with Harriet could be nothing other than paternal.

'Indeed we were. She lodged at my house in London for more than a year,' I added, although this was perhaps more information than he required.

'You'll be staying for the funeral,' he said.

'Has it been announced?'

He shook his head. 'The inquest resumes on Wednesday, I'm told. Perhaps we shall know more then.'

'Have you been attending the inquest, Mr Pawley?'

He gave a short laugh. 'Not I. Where do you suppose I get time off to sit in the workhouse and listen to all of that? Will you be wanting a meal?'

By the time I had taken refreshment it was quite dark, and late to be making private calls, but now I was here I could not rest. I walked from the White Hart down through the Market Place, empty now that the traders had packed away their barrows, and entered the narrow gap into Widmore Lane. I had planned to walk across the fields to Farwig to pay my respects to Harriet's mother, but it was only then that I appreciated how difficult it would be to keep to the path without a lantern, much less how I should tell the correct dwelling without disturbing perhaps several households. The street was lit by a lamp hanging over the door of the Three

Compasses, and I had just resolved to sit in the public house for a while, and perhaps drink an ale, when I noticed that a second lamp over the gateway which led to the chapel was also lit.

My feet carried me almost unbidden in that direction. Through this very gate Harriet must have passed on foot for the last time. I placed my hand on the gate and to my surprise it swung open. I walked into the chapel yard, thinking perhaps that there might be some prayer meeting going on. From the chapel came nothing but silence.

The door, when I tried it, yielded easily to my touch. Inside, the building was quite in darkness save for a light coming from a door at the back.

'Who's there?' came a voice from that very room.

'Mr Verrall?' I called.

The door opened wider and the man stood framed in the doorway, his face in shadow, and yet it was undoubtedly he. I stepped forward.

'You must be Richard Field,' he said. 'I wondered if you'd show your face.'

Reverend George Verrall

He offered me his hand but I did not take it.

Instead I stepped aside and he entered the vestry, looking about him as if he had come to buy the place, hat in his hand, proprietorial.

'I wished to thank you for taking the time to write to me,' he said.

I ignored his thanks. 'I assume you informed the school.'

'Of course.'

'And you are well?'

'Yes, indeed. Although very much distressed by your letter.'

'And your wife?'

He flinched at this, but recovered his composure swiftly. 'She is better than she has been of late, thank you.'

'For that I am glad.'

why has he come here?

what does he mean by it?

As if he had heard my thoughts, Field said, 'I called to ask, sir, if there is any news regarding the laying to rest.'

'Not yet,' I answered him. 'Unfortunately that matter remains with the coroner.'

'I understand. Are they near reaching a verdict?'

'That is something you will need to ask him.'

We stood in silence for a moment, facing each other. There were many questions I had for Field, of course, and I have no doubt that he had many questions for me, too, but at that point we could not express them.

'And Harriet's mother,' he asked, 'how does the good lady?'

I narrowed my eyes before replying. 'How do you expect? She has lost her youngest daughter, in quite the most horrific fashion.'

He left, shortly after that, and who could blame him? I felt rather sorry for the man. Of all of us, perhaps, he had loved Harriet the best, and yet of all of us he had let her down in the worst way. If one could trace the course of events back in time to try to find the source of the tragedy, then Richard Field's behaviour towards Harriet must have been the very beginning of it. Had he not behaved as he did, then Harriet would undoubtedly still be among us, living and breathing.

I watched until he closed the door of the chapel behind him, and then I returned to my desk to write to the coroner.

Tuesday, 14th November, 1843

Richard Field

I slept badly in the strange bed and woke before it was light, wondering for a moment where I was. I reached for Maria but of course the little space next to me was quite empty and cold.

I got out of bed slowly, cursing my aged bones, and used the pot, and then crossed to the window and looked down over the High Street, lit gloomily by the approaching dawn. Once again the day promised to be a dismal one, overcast and threatening rain.

Sparing the candle, I dressed and waited until it was light enough to see, and then I sat at the small table and wrote a letter to Maria, who was never far from my thoughts, informing her of my safe arrival and promising to return as soon as I was able. I hoped that she and the baby were both quite well, and that Annie was attending to her needs as far as it was possible to do so.

As the street outside became noisy with traders and the people of the town beginning their business, I breakfasted on bread and tea, and then made my way once again through the Market Place and out of town, towards the Cage Field and the path to Farwig. The path was dry underfoot, for which I was grateful, and with the benefit of daylight I could see the shapes of the houses a mile or so distant.

At length two women carrying baskets passed me, and I asked them if they knew of a Mrs Monckton in Farwig, and how I should know the house once I arrived at it.

'Why, sir, it has mourning above the door,' the older of the two told me. They glanced at each other, no doubt curious.

'Of course,' I said. 'I should have thought of that for myself.'

The younger woman, who might have been the daughter of the first, asked, 'Were you a friend of Miss Monckton's?'

'Indeed I was,' I said. 'I have come to pay respects to her mother. On behalf of myself and my wife.'

'Is it true what they said?'

The older woman nudged her sharply, and got a look in response.

'I heard her throat was cut so that her head was nearly clean off her shoulders.'

My mouth fell open with surprise.

'Someone said there was blood in the chapel but no blood in the privy.'

'I – I'm afraid I have no idea.'

They left me then and carried on towards the town. I heard one of them laugh. Soon after that, the path narrowed between two enclosures and came out between the houses and on to a simple track, just wide enough for a single carriage. The street was very quiet, and no more than fifteen or twenty dwellings were there, with fields beyond and a pump. To the right of me a small house had had a piece of black crêpe fabric pinned above the lintel. The shutters were drawn and no smoke issued from the chimney. To all appearances the house stood empty, but I knocked softly at the door nevertheless.

A moment later I heard the latch and the door opened. A young woman stood within, her sallow face a poorer version of Harriet's.

I removed my hat. 'Miss Monckton?'

'Who are you?' she asked.

I was momentarily taken aback. 'My name is Richard Field. I have come—'

She opened the door and stood aside to let me in. I crossed the threshold into a parlour with a range and chairs either side of it, one of which was occupied by a lady dressed entirely in black. She eyed me without any degree of expectation.

'Madam,' I said, 'I am most terribly sorry for your loss. I have come to offer you my deepest condolences, and to send you the love and warmest thoughts of my wife, Maria.'

Harriet's sister stood behind me, unspeaking. For a horrible moment we both stood there awkwardly, waiting for some reaction from the older lady and getting none. Eventually, having said what I had come to say, and thinking of no other words of comfort, I half turned to go.

'Thank you,' the lady said. I was quite shocked by her voice, having expected it to be weakened or querulous, but instead finding it firm, almost confident. 'Very kind of you, Mr Field, to come all this way.'

I bowed my head to her. 'I came as soon as I could,' I said.

'Please sit,' she said, and I glanced at Mary Ann, who with an impatient nod indicated the second chair. Once I had taken my seat she crossed the room to a bed at the other side of it and took up some needlework. The room was dark and airless for the shutters being fastened, and despite the lamp at her elbow I could not help but fear for her eyesight.

'Harriet spoke of you often,' Mrs Monckton said. 'I do know she missed you terribly when she left London.'

Her words dipped into a pit of emotion in my chest that I had struggled to suppress since that moment I had broken down in front of Maria. I felt tears start in my eyes and I swallowed, trying desperately to retain control. This lady did not need to see me make a fool of myself.

'As we missed her,' I said. 'She was a very dear friend to my wife, and to myself. Maria would be here herself, but she has been rather unwell since the birth of our child.'

'Yes,' she said, 'Harriet told us. She often read out loud your letters to her.'

I hesitated at her words, suspecting a deeper meaning, but her eyes remained calmly focused on mine. Surely Harriet would have read only some of the letters, I reasoned. Some of them she would have kept to herself.

'I understand the laying to rest has been rather delayed by the inquest,' I said.

'We are hopeful that the coroner will release her to us very soon,' she said, 'and the chapel has indicated that they will pay, so that's one worry quite taken care of.'

'I thank God for it,' I said.

'It'll be in the parish church, of course,' Mary Ann said from the corner of the room.

Mrs Monckton leaned forward. 'She doesn't hold with any of this Calvinist nonsense,' she muttered. 'And who can blame her? Look where it got Harriet.'

'You think — the chapel?'

'What do you think, Mr Field?'

'Of what?' I asked, confused.

'Of Mr Verrall, of course,' she said, fixing me with a pair of dark eyes that reminded me disconcertingly of Harriet.

I thought for a moment, and then decided to answer her honestly.

'I can't admit that I like the man very much,' I said.

'Ha.'

'We don't like him either,' Mary Ann said. 'He's a fool. And a liar.'

'Careful,' the older woman said.

'Well, he is. And you know it.'

'He serves his own ends,' Mrs Monckton said, 'and I don't believe they are holy ones.'

We sat for a moment in silence, the thought of Verrall as a liar and what that might mean hanging between us like a thundercloud. We did not speak the words but perhaps we were all thinking it: that a man of the cloth who was a liar was perhaps a very dangerous man.

I left them a short while later, promising to remain for the funeral if it were to take place within but a few days, but if it was delayed further I should return home to Maria and perhaps come back for it, if she was well enough for me to leave her untended.

On the path across the fields I noticed a man coming towards me with intent, a man who looked like a labourer crammed into a smart suit, with a tall hat thrust upon his head so hard that his ears bent outwards underneath it. I stood to one side but he blocked my path. I felt my breathing quicken, in readiness for some sort of assault.

'Mr Richard Field?' he asked.

'Yes, I am he,' I said.

'My name is Sergeant King of the Bromley police force, sir. I am tasked to give you this.'

He handed over a piece of paper. I broke the seal and read it. A letter from Charles Carttar, Esq, Her Majesty's Coroner for Kent, requesting that I attend to give my testimony at the inquest on the body of Harriet Monckton, to be held in the board room at the Bromley Union Workhouse at twelve noon on Wednesday the 15th of November, 1843.

'Well?' King asked me, when I folded up the paper once more.

'Well, what?'

'You will attend?'

'Do I have a choice?' I asked.

'Not really,' King answered.

I continued my walk a little uneasily, not sure if he meant to detain me further, but in fact he fell into step beside me and walked a little easier. I realised his entire purpose in crossing the fields to Farwig had been in search of me.

'Only, I like to ask,' King said, his tone almost genial, 'because, if I need to get firm with you, sir, then I like to build up to it. I'm not so good when taken by surprise.'

'Do people take you by surprise?' I asked.

'Sometimes,' he said. 'I don't react so well to it. I'd rather be prepared, like.'

'Can you not expect … that people will behave badly, and then be pleasantly surprised when they don't?'

'I suppose I should,' he said, 'but, when I expect people to behave badly, then they tend to be alarmed, and then sometimes they behave badly after all, when perhaps they mightn't have otherwise. So really I find it easier to ask.'

'Indeed,' I said. I rather liked him for his honesty.

'If it's all the same to you, sir,' he said, 'I should very much like to ask you a few questions. Perhaps this afternoon, if you would be so kind.'

'Very well,' I said. 'I'm staying at the White Hart.'

We parted company in the Market Place. I stopped at the bakehouse to purchase a bun, and then continued to the inn. I stood in the yard with my letter to Maria in my coat pocket, pressed against my heart, and then I returned to my room to write her another instead: I would likely be delayed some days yet. My darling Maria, I longed for her dreadfully already. I missed her sweet face and soft, gentle voice, even if her wifely attentiveness to my comfort had been somewhat diluted since the arrival of our firstborn. And in a strange sort of way I missed the squalling child almost as much.

Frances Williams

Thirty girls present at this morning's register. Betsy Burgess has ringworm; I sent her home.

From the window of the schoolroom I saw Mrs Verrall and Ruth Verrall crossing the yard; a minute later I put Lizzie Finch in charge and I went into the corridor. Mr Campling had taken them into his office. I had no desire to be caught listening at the door, tempting as it was, so instead I went to the boys' room. Will Judd had been left in charge.

'Where is Mr Campling?' I asked of him.

The entire schoolroom stared at me.

'He's been called out to a visitor, miss.'

I went to his office, then, and rapped sharply.

'What is it?' I heard him call.

Mrs Verrall was seated, Ruth standing behind her.

'My apologies, sir,' I said.

'Well?'

I had planned to ask him about the ringworm but, now I was here, I thought that a sorry excuse for interrupting. 'Just that—' I began, and stopped, and flushed, and started again. 'I wished to speak to you about the girls' reading. I shall examine them tomorrow.'

'Surely that can wait?' he said. 'As you can see, I have visitors.'

'Yes, of course,' I said.

For a moment or two I stood rooted to the very spot, staring at them. They must think me some kind of mad-woman, I thought. And Sarah Verrall smiled at me, and nodded, and somehow that released me from the spell.

As I closed the door behind me I heard the words, '... such an excellent woman, you are lucky indeed...' and, although Mrs Verrall must surely have been talking about me, I could scarce believe that she could be so very kind.

Mrs Verrall had visited the school before, of course, many times. Every year the Verralls hosted a Chapel Fair on their fields, at which a marquee was raised and the ladies of the town were tasked with baking fruit cakes and supplying cordials and various prizes. And then there was the Christmas Half Day, when the children of all the schools were provided with small gifts, and carols sung, and games played in the afternoon. Mrs Verrall was the orchestrator of these events, meeting with the directors of all the schools in the town, and marshalling a veritable army of ladies to provide the food and drink, raising funds in order that those who otherwise would have had nothing should be provided with a small present and at the very least one decent meal.

Perhaps that was why she was here now, I thought; perhaps it was nothing to do with Harriet. I had panicked; I had thought she had come to complain about my presence here, that I was corrupting the girls instead of bringing them to Christ.

I need to be careful. I will lose my head, and give myself away.

Richard Field

At two o'clock precisely there was a knock at my door. I had been lying on the bed and had half drifted off to sleep, so I was rather disorientated when I opened the door and found the large figure of Sergeant King blocking the space at the top of the stairs.

'I thought it best to come to your room,' he said, as I stood aside to let him in, 'unless of course you'd rather I spoke to you in the public bar, or perhaps at the police station.'

'Not at all,' I said.

'That's what I thought.'

He stood for a moment with his hat in his hands until I came to my senses and offered him the single chair. He placed his hat upon the table and sat, his large behind filling the seat fully and making it look rather precarious. I perched on the edge of the bed, there being nowhere else.

'You and Miss Monckton were friends, I understand,' he said.

'Yes,' I said. 'Well, she was good friends with my wife, Maria.'

Was that misleading? Of course it was. I had known Harriet for many months before I met Maria. But it was not an untruth: Harriet had indeed been Maria's friend first. They had met at the school, where Maria taught the younger girls, before Harriet introduced her to me and suggested she might join us – her own lodgings being of a poorer standard.

He made a note of this and hesitated before looking up. 'And she lived at your address, in London, I understand?'

'She lodged with me for a little over a year,' I said. 'She was employed at a school nearby. I have several lodgers,' I said, and then realising that this was untrue, I added, 'That is, I did have several lodgers. Since my marriage and the birth of my first child, there is very little room now for paying guests.'

I had said *me*. That she had lodged with *me*, not *us*. From that, were he an intelligent man, he might have deduced that Harriet had lived with me before Maria had, but it seemed that fortune was on my side, for he did not press the point further.

'Why did she leave Hackney?'

I bit at the inside of my cheek, thinking of the best way to answer him. 'She was finding the school particularly challenging,' I said. 'The board were not supportive, and she felt that her efforts were not appreciated. She was homesick, as well. I think she missed her mother.'

All of those reasons were probably true. 'While she lived at your property, were you aware of her having any connection to any particular man?'

I thought about this. 'No,' I said, staring at him.

'None at all?'

I found that my cheeks had grown hot. 'She – er – she often spoke of her cousin, George, with whom she had grown up. A sailor, I believe. But he was her cousin. And there was another man, a draper. Samuel Phipps was his name. He was friendly with her for a while – they met at my house, at a party I held for some friends. But surely...'

'Sir?'

'I mean – I feel certain that she had not seen him for some time, certainly not after she left for Bromley. It was an acquaintance, nothing more than that.'

'That's all I asked, sir. Any connections she had.'

'I can't think of anyone else.'

'This Mr Phipps, sir   do you happen to have an address for him?'

The sergeant left shortly afterwards, leaving me to kick myself for trying to be too helpful. Poor Phipps – he would no doubt get a visit from some police officer now, if not Sergeant King then some other fellow. But when put under pressure it is so much easier to answer than not to answer; the truth flows so much easier than a lie. Or, perhaps, to put it another way, one truth is easier to give up when what one really wants to do is conceal another truth, a darker one.

Phipps had been my sacrifice; he should be called to give account, and would be found entirely innocent, because he was: and his purpose had been to throw the heat away from me.

Wednesday, 15th November, 1843

Thomas Churcher

I saw the sergeant the next morning. He came to the shop and gave me a piece of paper and told me I was called to appear at the inquest. I was to present myself at the workhouse at noon sharp.

He spoke to my father, although I was present. He asked if I was going to give him any trouble. When I heard the word 'inquest' there started a roaring in my ears and I barely heard the rest.

They were talking, the sergeant and my father, and my father looked grave and was talking in a low voice and I said, 'I am a man of honour,' and both of them stopped and looked at me. I don't know why I said that. The words came from inside me without my asking.

They both stopped and looked at me.

'You can see he's not himself,' my father said

'Nonetheless, he has to attend.'

The sergeant left.

My father looked at me, standing there with an awl in my hand. He looked down at my hand and then up to my face and he said, 'Don't stand there with your mouth open, lad, get on with it.'

I went back to work but my brain was boiling. I wanted to see Mr Verrall. There was nobody else I could talk to, who would understand how I felt.

After about half an hour my hand slipped and the awl skewed through a piece of leather and tore it and my father shouted at me and I hung up my apron and left to go home. I was not ready to work. I felt unwell in my head still. I needed time.

'You make sure you are there at noon,' I heard him shout behind me, 'or you'll have me to answer to.' I did not reply.

I walked around for a bit but it felt like everyone was staring at me, so I went to the Manse, but he was not there. Mrs Verrall told me he was at the chapel. I did not want to go to the chapel, of all places, but I couldn't avoid it for ever. And I needed to see the reverend.

The gate was unlocked. I put my hand on it and it opened with a creak and I thought of that night and how Harriet had put her hand there, just there, to open the gate, and how it had made a noise. Perhaps someone had heard it, and thought that it was late for a visitor to the chapel. I had opened and closed and locked and unlocked that gate so many times, I must have heard that creak every time, and yet now it sounded loud and strange and discordant, like a note played on the organ out of tune.

Mr Verrall was in the vestry, looking through the drawers in the desk. He started when he saw me.

'Tom! Come in, do.'

'Reverend.'

He smiled but he looked odd, pale and shiny, his beard darker against his skin. His hair curled damp on his cheek. 'You are alone?' he asked me. I nodded. 'Shut the door, then.'

He sat at his desk and motioned me to take the other chair. 'Well?' he said.

'I am called to the inquest, at noon.'

'Yes, I know,' he said.

'How do you know?'

He raised an eyebrow. 'I am called too, today, although I've been following the progress of the inquest closely. I know what's going on, what the coroner is trying to prove. He means to harm the church, I am sure of it.'

'Why would he do that?'

'Because they think us radicals. You've heard me speak of it often enough. They are lazy, the High Church, full of their rituals and fat on their practices. They have no desire to see the Spirit move here in the town! They have no compulsion to bring people to God. They read the Gospel and think themselves holy; they ignore the inconvenient parts, the parts that insist we should be servants and not masters.'

He stopped talking and looked to the door. Nobody was there. The chapel was quiet, and cold.

'I cannot pray,' I said.

The reverend looked surprised. 'What?'

'It feels like nobody is listening. It feels like God has left me. There is a space in front of me, where once I felt something. Him. His presence. You know.'

'He is still there, Tom, he has not left you.'

'I cannot feel.'

There was a long moment when I could not speak. He sat and watched me. I thought he might try to pray over me, or lay hands on me, or suggest a passage for me to read from Scripture, but he sat and watched. And then when finally I composed myself enough to breathe, I wiped my face and my eyes hard and he said, 'You need to master yourself.'

'Yes,' I said.

'You did it before; you must do the same thing now. You must take a deep breath and hold it in, and keep it all in your head. You can't pray? Don't try to. Wait until this sorry mess is over with, and then God will be there waiting for you when you are ready.'

'Yes,' I said again. He was right. I took a deep breath.

'You answer their questions and you stay calm and you get through it.'

'But what if they ask me? What do I say?'

'Exactly what we agreed. You saw her on Monday night, at Miss Williams's house. You did not see her after that. You heard she was missing. You went to look. You took Sweeting with you, and he found her. It's really very simple.'

I heard him saying, *like you*, but he did not say that. I heard the words in my head.

'Tom, the Lord has chosen you to take on responsibility for this task, just as He chose Matthew and Thomas and Peter. He chose you because you are a good man, and you love the Lord and you love his church and his people. The fate of this place, and of our congregation, lies in your hands. You can save us, Tom, from the Enemies of the Cross! You can save us, if you just keep your wits about you, and don't let Satan fool you.'

He shook my hand as I left, and clapped my arm tightly. I felt differently, then. I felt braver. I knew what I had to do. I walked across the fields again, all the way to Farwig Lane, but when I got there I realised Harriet would no longer be there, in her mother's house, for the surgeon had cut her up. I had wanted to go and see her but I was too late for that.

I walked back, and by then it was nearly time to go to the workhouse.

Reverend George Verrall

As I was called as a witness, I was not permitted to listen in on the proceedings. I found this infuriating, and spoke to the high constable about it.

'I have been present at every meeting,' I said. 'Every single one. What difference does it make if I hear what is said today, when I have heard everything up to this point?'

'It's the procedure,' Joyce said. His chin thrust out at me, daring me to strike. 'Nothing to do with me.'

procedure be damned
damn you all

'I am here to defend my chapel, my congregation.'

155

He sighed. 'What do you think is going on in there? Don't go getting ahead of yourself, Reverend. It'll all come out right in the end.'

he thinks I am a troublesome child

He left me. I had forgotten that there were others, also waiting. Tom Churcher, looking as if he might vomit at any moment. Richard Field had been called, I saw. And with him a younger man, who I soon found out was Samuel Phipps, a draper and former acquaintance of Harriet's. She had never mentioned him to me.

Besides them, the surgeon, James Ilott, who was no doubt to give evidence about the smelling salts bottle that the sergeant had recovered from the night soil in the privy, something in which I had taken a keen interest. If prussic acid was a constituent of smelling salts, of any brand or variety, then surely it should remain a possibility that Harriet had taken her own life. The stain of a suicide was less permanent a mark upon the chapel than the stain of murder, and this was why I had written once again to the coroner, this time anonymously, with a view to nudging the doubt of it further into his own mind.

never mind that she died in the chapel
and there was no bottle
it is what they call a means to an end

Richard Field

I had never been inside a workhouse before, and I knew not quite what to expect. It was smaller than I thought, a long, narrow building which sat right on the road to London. I had passed it many times and had never given it so much as a glance. Moments after my arrival Samuel Phipps had entered. On the road up from the White Hart I had heard steps behind me, and guessed that whoever it was might be going to the same place as I. Not wishing to converse with anyone, I had deliberately not turned to acknowledge them, and now I saw it was Phipps and I was rather glad I had not.

We were directed upstairs by a woman in a grey flannel gown with an apron and a bonnet that was astonishingly clean and white. I had expected the building to be noisy, and smelly, but, whatever activity was taking place elsewhere, it was being undertaken silently.

The first floor extended into a long corridor with doors leading off either side; against one bare wall two long wooden benches had been placed, presumably for our use. A young man was sitting there already, smartly dressed, his legs crossed at the knee, a leather case placed at his feet. He gave us the barest of smiles, and nodded, but did not further acknowledge our presence, and we sat down next to him to wait. Further along the bench were two women, who I took to be a mother and a daughter; they were whispering together, and did not appear to even notice our arrival.

Phipps wanted to talk when we first arrived; I told him I knew as much as he did. He wanted to know who had mentioned his name, and I apologetically had to tell him it was I, in response to a direct question; he forgave me quickly, however, and for that I was grateful.

Shortly after that another young man came up the stairs to our right and sat on one of the other chairs; he was a handsome fellow, with a dark mop of curly hair and dark eyes. He looked in a state of considerable distress, his knee jerking rhythmically and his hands constantly fiddling with his hat or running through his hair or over his face. Verrall came up the stairs, then, and the young man stilled himself instantly.

The first man was called in; I did not catch the name but I heard the word 'surgeon' and I guessed he must have been the one to examine her.

Phipps muttered to me, 'We shall be here all day! I should have brought something to read.'

But in fact the surgeon was not long, perhaps ten minutes. He left the room from the door at the far end of the corridor, presumably to discourage us from engaging him in conversation. I saw then that there was another set of stairs at the other end of the corridor, and thus we could give our testimonies and leave without meeting the eyes of those who were left waiting.

Moments later the high constable was called, and after he left the door opened and the usher – or whatever he was – said, 'Mr Richard Field?'

Thomas Churcher

I was made to wait in the corridor outside the board room. Someone had put benches in a row, making the corridor narrow and small. I sat in silence and tried to keep my breathing calm, and my face empty of expression, just as I had done on Tuesday. It was difficult; at the back of my head a voice said, *you cannot do this*, and another voice reminded me of the way I had felt afterwards, how hard it was and how my head felt like it would explode with the pressure of keeping myself calm.

The surgeon went first and he was in the room for a time, and Mr Verrall stood by the door and tried to hear what was going on inside, and made us all be silent in case he could hear. I could not hear anything. The surgeon was a quiet man. I liked him, better than his father, whom I had thought very stern. He had been kind to us when my mother was ill, and charged us for one visit when by the end he had made three. And she died, but he had not been able to do anything to help her, even though he tried.

The surgeon left by the door at the end of the corridor; we did not speak to him. Then Mr Joyce went in, and then two men who had been talking together but I did not know either of them; they were not from Bromley. A young man and an older man. I notice people's shoes, because I make them. I stared at their shoes and tried to guess their occupations. The younger man had poor shoes, resoled, simply made with the stitching wide and the leather marked, but he had a good suit, although it was plain; so perhaps he was a draper, or a tailor, or an apprentice; for he looked too young to have styled it himself. And the older man, dressed in a pale tweed jacket, his shoes were good; well made, with a cutwork detail and the stitching invisible. The leather was plain and they had been resoled perhaps twice; not very expensive, but well-made. His profession was a mystery, but he seemed as though he might have been artistic. They were both from London. I could tell.

Richard Field

The room was large, and stuffy, and full of people. Directly in front of me, under the high windows, sat the jury: two rows of men, slouched and looking bored. To the left, half of the room was given over to the audience, contained behind a rope strung across the room, attached to the back of a chair at either wall. Seats had been provided for the smartest of them, whilst at the very back a general rabble was busy gossiping and chattering.

The usher gave me a Bible and very quickly got me to swear, and at that point the coroner spoke, in a voice loud enough to bring the room to an immediate silence.

'Please tell the court your name, address, and occupation.'

'My name is Richard Field,' I said, 'of Fieldgate Street, London. I am employed as a manufacturer of varnishes.'

'And you were acquainted with the deceased?'

'Indeed. We were good friends.'

Now the matter was under way I felt rather better; it felt more like a business meeting, face to face, than a schoolroom.

I stood up straighter.

'Please tell the court when you last saw the deceased alive.'

'It was some time in the month of August last, at my own house in London.'

'And when did you last hear from her?'

'On Tuesday – that is, the 7th of November – a letter was delivered by the postman, addressed to my wife, from the deceased.'

'You recognised the handwriting?'

'Yes. And Maria showed it to me. To have reached me on the Tuesday it must have been posted on Monday the 6th of November, in Bromley. It bears the Bromley postmark.'

There was a murmur from the crowd behind me. I was struck then with a sense of us being on a sort of stage, acting our parts, being judged by the good people of Bromley town as well as by the gentlemen – using the term very loosely – of the jury. It took me out of myself to think of it thus, as a performance, and it gave me a jolt of confidence.

I took the letter from my pocket and approached the table. The usher moved to intercept me, took the letter from me and passed it to the coroner with a look that suggested I had broken a rule. I returned to the single chair, although I did not sit down. The coroner read through the letter in silence and then passed it to his colleague, sitting to his right. The sallow-faced man read it through and passed it back to the coroner, who proceeded to read aloud:

My dear Maria,

I received yours on Saturday and was a little surprised not expecting to hear from you so soon. I am however much obliged by your kindness. I showed it to Mr Verrall and he said it was a very nice note. I cannot come to Town this week as I am attending to Miss Williams's school, she being very ill herself, but on

Wednesday next I shall hope to see you – and the dear baby – once more. I am rather unsettled and hope you will excuse this short note. I shall hope to see you if I am spared – my dear Maria, I often remember your words: 'All things work together for good'. I trust this will be, but I must say adieu. My mother and sister desire their kind respects to Mr Field and thyself.

Ever yours most affectionately,

Harriet

P.S. A kiss for baby – I long to see him. I have a great deal to tell you when I see you. Goodbye.

The crowd at the back of the room could barely contain themselves, and the resulting noise caused the coroner to bang upon the table with the flat of his hand. I heard words passing between them like *spared* and *if I am spared* and *what must she have wished to say* and *Verrall*.

'Please, quiet! Else I shall have the room cleared!'

Reluctantly, the noise subsided. All things work together for good, I thought. She used to write letters like that to me, before she brought Maria into our lives but afterwards, too. Only very recently had the tone of them changed. I still had those letters, of course; although I would not be sharing them with the court.

'Mr Field,' the coroner continued, 'to what was the deceased referring, when she said she would see your wife on Wednesday next?'

'I expected her at my house on Wednesday last. I know that she had obtained a situation at Arundel, at which she was much pleased. Her visit to Town was preparatory to her going to Arundel.'

Here the coroner turned to his assistant and murmured something. A piece of paper was produced, which the coroner examined, then returned.

'You may have learned, Mr Field, that the deceased was found by the surgeon to be around five to six months pregnant. Were you aware of her pregnancy?'

'I was not at all aware, until after her death. I am surprised to hear it.'

'Did you know of any attachment that she had to any man?'

'At the time she was staying at my house I believe she was much enamoured of a person by the name of Samuel Phipps whom she met there, but she was told that he was engaged to another lady.'

A further murmured discussion took place at this; the sallow man made a note.

'Can you tell us, Mr Field, how you came to hear about the death of the deceased?'

'I heard of it by letter, sir: I received word from the Reverend Mr Verrall, minister of the chapel at Bromley.'

Again, a note was made. I wondered at the careful notation of my words, which surely had very little bearing on the case. My feet were beginning to protest at so long standing in one spot, and I wished now that I had sat down from the start; if I were to sit, now, it would look like weakness.

'You mentioned a Mr Phipps – were there any others to whom the deceased appeared to form any sort of attachment, whilst she was in London?'

'She had frequently met at my house several gentlemen students of Hackney College – my wife and I like to host suppers and social gatherings – but I never heard of her being intimate or attached to either of them.'

'Do you visit Bromley frequently, Mr Field?'

'Not recently, sir. I have not been in Bromley before today for some months.'

'It has been suggested to us that the deceased may have taken her own life. What is your opinion of this suggestion, Mr Field?'

'I never saw anything in her conduct or manner or disposition to lead me to think she was likely or capable of committing self-destruction.'

Further mutterings between them, papers passed between them across the table. The delay lasted long enough for the rabble at the back to resume their conversations. At last, the coroner said, 'Thank you, Mr Field, you are excused.' And to my very great surprise I found myself escorted by the usher to the back of the room. I felt all eyes upon me as I passed, and for some reason – perhaps relief at being thus dismissed – I smiled and nodded to all those who caught my eye, which brought a few muttered *well, reallys* and *did you evers*.

I cared not a jot for them. I had escaped, with but one little lie. Only one, in all of those questions. I felt that I had come out of it rather well.

Thomas Churcher

When the older man went in, I stared at the younger man, who did not lift his head lest he should make eye contact with anyone present, although Elizabeth Hopperton, bored with her mother's conversation, kept trying to pass the time of day with him. Who was he? Who was he to her? Had she walked out with him? Had he known her, as I had known her? I stared and stared at him, his pale hair cut short, and badly, his whiskers pale.

The older man came out of the other door, and nodded to the younger man, who was called inside. Then I was left with Elizabeth Hopperton and her mother, and the reverend.

The younger man came out quickly. Then Mr Taylor came to our door and called for me.

Despite the season, and the single high window that was open, the room was as hot as high summer. There were too many people, there was too much noise, the smell of too many bodies pressed in a confined space and my nerves, ringing like bells.

'Tom.' Mr Taylor put his hand on my elbow and indicated that I should take a seat in the single chair, my back to the crowd. I took a breath and another, and I swallowed, and closed off the panic as best I could.

'Can you please tell us your name, your address, and your occupation?'

I stared at him. He knew my name, for he had called me, and my occupation was known to almost everyone in the room. But he waited for me to reply nonetheless. I said, 'My name is Thomas Blackstone Churcher, I live in the Market Place, and I am a shoemaker.'

The man sitting by the side of the coroner was making notes on a large sheet of paper. I fancied he was writing everything down, for his script was swift. He barely paused, and the dipping of his pen in the ink was a matter of but a moment, before his nib found the paper once again.

'You knew the deceased?'

'Yes.'

'Please tell the jury the circumstances in which you last saw her.'

The jury? The men by the side of the court. I looked at them, glanced down the rows at the faces. All of them staring at me. Some of them I knew, but I drew no comfort from that. Their eyes were like the eyes of the people in the Market Place, watching me and Emma arguing.

I swallowed. 'I went to Miss Williams's house on Monday evening, the 6th of November. The deceased was there, staying with Miss Williams; she – Miss Williams – had sent for my sister to go and take supper with her, and I accompanied her there and stayed for supper also.'

'And you saw the deceased? How did she appear to you?'

I stared. 'She appeared well, and in good spirits.'

'You spoke to her, then? What did she say?'

'She told me that she was going in a few days to take charge of an infant school at Arundel in Sussex, and she was happy to have obtained the situation.'

All of that was true. *Tell the truth, Tom, don't lie, Tom, all of it is true.*

'And can you tell the jury how it is that you know the deceased?'

'I belong to the chapel. She attends the chapel. I saw her there on Sunday evening, during service.'

'Now, you went to the chapel on Sunday, but you also went there on Monday, is that the case?'

'Yes. I went to the chapel on Monday afternoon between four and five o'clock for the purpose of packing up and putting away the music used at the services on Sunday – it is my usual custom.'

'The gate to the chapel, was it open?'

'No, sir. I took the keys of the outer gate and chapel with me and I unlocked them. The outer gate in the iron railing in front I unlocked. After passing through the gate I could get to the privy without going down the passage by the side of the chapel by going into the front door of the chapel and passing through it and out the back door of it – the back door is within a few feet of the privy door – the back yard is very narrow. I remained at the chapel a very few minutes.'

'And then you locked the gate behind you, when you left?'

Don't lie Tom don't lie do not lie ...

'I am not sure, sir. I believe I did.'

'The gate is usually kept locked?'

'Yes.'

'And so the privy is not in use by passers-by?'

'No, sir. The privy is not used except during service; there was no service or meeting at the chapel on Monday night.'

'Thank you. Let us now turn to the events of Tuesday. When did you first learn of the deceased being missed from home?'

165

'I heard of the deceased being absent on Tuesday morning and I, with Mr Sweeting, agreed to go in the evening in search of her.'

'Yes, yes, but who was it told you that she was absent?'

'I had seen Mr Verrall during that day and had talked with him about her absence. Mr Verrall said he was afraid she was in the Bishop's Pond.'

'And you resolved to search for her?'

'After seeing the police about five o'clock who told us they had not succeeded in finding her, although they had searched all the ponds and woods about, Mr Sweeting and I left to make further enquiries of her friends. As we passed the chapel we tried the outer gate, which was shut to, but found it unlocked and we went in and round to the yard behind, where we found the deceased lying on the floor in the privy – dead. I did not touch her, but returned and called for the police and alarmed the neighbours. I returned with the police – the body was not disturbed until Mr Ilott came.'

'When you were at the privy, either the first time with Mr Sweeting, or afterwards when you returned with Mr Ilott the surgeon, did you see any sort of bottle, or vessel, close to the body?'

'No, sir. I saw no bottle.'

'You may have heard, Mr Churcher, that the deceased was found to be somewhere around five months advanced in pregnancy. Were you aware of this, before her death?'

Nothing
No
Nothing
I cannot
I cannot speak
Breathe
What hell
What hell

'Mr Churcher?'

Swallow
Breathe
Think, think, focus
'Mr Churcher?'
Breathe
'No, sir, I was not aware.'
'She had not spoken to you of it.'
'No.'

A consultation with the man beside him, and the crowd behind me and the jury to the left of me – I had forgotten them, they were still there, murmuring and the sound rising like the swell of a wave. My neck grew hot as if their collective breath was warming my skin. I could feel their eyes upon me, and those of the jurymen, and their judgement upon me.

'Quiet please, gentlemen!'
Breathe
Breathe
Better
'You said, Mr Churcher, that you visited Miss Williams on Monday night at about six o'clock. How long did you remain there?'

'About three-quarters of an hour,' I said.

'And Miss Monckton was in good spirits, you say?'

'Excellent spirits.'

'You saw nothing in her demeanour to suggest that she might have been contemplating taking her own life?'

No
No
No
I saw nothing
Nothing like that
She was happy
Dear God she was smiling and laughing and lovely, lovely with her smile and her eyes on me

'I saw nothing to suggest that.'

167

'Thank you, Mr Churcher. Is there anything you wish to add, for the benefit of the jury?'

She had gone to post a letter
I waited outside the Beezleys'
And Miss Williams said she had gone to post a letter
And she would not let me wait
She was already
gone

I stared at the man and the other man and then the murmuring started, and I glanced across to the jury and even though there were men of the chapel seated there, staring, there were also men who did not attend chapel, and I thought of what they knew and what they could not know, and before I could stop them the words were out.

'She was very intimate with Mr Verrall.'

And the room broke into uproar, like at Mr Baxter's auction house that my father took me to once, when I was younger and sick with the crowds and the noise; and I ran out through the wrong door, the door I had used to enter the room, and I ran past Mr Verrall and down the stairs and out into the street, and I ran all the way home and pulled open the door and slammed it behind me.

Frances Williams

Twenty-eight girls in attendance today. The Harris boys are back, but the girls have been sent to Miss Lamb's school, I hear. Alice Harvey wishes to be considered for pupil teacher, but there is not enough for her to do at present. Lizzie Finch is to be sent to complete her education at a school in London, as her uncle has offered to pay, but even so I cannot justify replacing her, with numbers being so depleted. At least the tide of girls leaving my charge has abated; if they were going to leave, they would surely have done so by now.

I wonder every day if I should resign. I feel the weight of suspicion on me very heavily, as if they know I am lying. By now you might think that the gossips would have found another source of amusement, but it seems they have not. Instead of hearing the whispers as I pass, now I hear them shouting after me, that I should have known. That I should be ashamed of myself. That I am as bad as she was.

I know not what source of inner strength I have found that has kept me going in the face of such vitriol; only, perhaps, that to leave Bromley would be to run away, and that should surely increase the suspicion levelled at me and not diminish it.

Curiosity took me to the workhouse when the school day was done.

I should have thought that the inquest must be over by now, that there could be nobody in the town with an opinion who had not already expressed it before the coroner and his assistant, and yet they were still at their business when I arrived late in the afternoon. James Older, the coachman, was being examined, and his testimony was a short one. He had not brought any parcels from London, or anywhere else, for Miss Monckton or anyone of that name. I asked Jane Cooper what the purpose of that enquiry had been, as I had missed the start of it. She told me they were trying to find the way in which the poison had got to Harriet.

James Older was quickly dismissed, and George Verrall called. He was dressed in a black coat and trousers, but without his hat or his silk gown that he was known to wear, perhaps to suggest a humility for which he was not generally known.

'You know the deceased, Mr Verrall?' asked the coroner.

'Indeed, sir, I knew the deceased very well. I have been in the habit of seeing her frequently but from some cause or other she has seldom visited me much of late.'

'When did you last see her?'

'At the evening service at the chapel on Sunday, the 5th of November.'

'And did you speak to her?'

'I did not. I saw her from the pulpit.'

'What were your observations as to her temperament?'

'I have observed nothing particular about her lately in her manner but she has frequently been subject to excitement. I have observed great excitability about her. She had formerly the management of a school at Hackney and she applied to the committee there for testimonials as to her character and conduct for the purpose of enabling her to obtain a similar appointment at St Albans. I saw the testimonials they sent – she showed them to me – they were very satisfactory in all respects excepting that at the conclusion it stated that there was a great want of humility and energy about her. This affected her very much and preyed on her mind – she often spoke to me about it.'

'It has been said, Mr Verrall, that the deceased was regularly seen in your company; is that the case?'

'Her visits have not been frequent to me of late.'

The coroner paused, then, and consulted with his colleague, who was noting everything carefully. Then he asked, 'I understand that you have had cause to ask questions of the jury, Mr Verrall, by passing a note to my assistant, Mr Gregg. Is that true?'

'I gave two questions on a piece of paper to one of the jurymen to ask the medical witness – Mr Ilott – whilst under examination. The first question was, whether she might not have taken the poison herself to procure abortion. The second was, whether from her position her death might not have been caused by suffocation.'

'What provoked you to ask these questions, Mr Verrall?'

A small, tight smile fixed itself upon his lips, and he licked them before answering.

'My own curiosity, sir, nothing more.'

'You say you saw the deceased in chapel on the evening of the 5th of November, but you did not speak to her. When was the last time you spoke to her?'

'Earlier on the very same day – Sunday. After the morning service, in the vestry room of my chapel. She came in to speak to me of her own accord.'

'You were alone with her, on that occasion?'

'I was. No other person was there at the time.'

'What was the nature of your conversation?'

'She conversed with me about the school she was going to at Arundel. She wished the school to be put off. She expressed a desire to postpone going at present, in fact not to enter upon her engagement until some time after the New Year. She asked me to apply to the committee for her and I told her I would write.'

'And what was your action in regard to that request?'

'I did not write the letter, although I promised that I would. I wished first to find the opportunity to counsel her to reconsider. It was my view that by postponing going she ran the risk of losing the appointment altogether.'

'Did she give a reason for her request?'

'She said she was desirous of going to stay with her friends in London before she went down there; that was her only reason to me.'

'How long were you in your vestry together, discussing the matter?'

'About seven or eight minutes.'

'And did you see her after that?'

'I did not see her again.'

'How did you come to hear of her absence?'

'I heard she was missing on Tuesday morning. I made enquiries of several people about her during the morning. In the afternoon I went to the police station and asked them what was best to be done.'

'What did you surmise had happened to her?'

'I said I feared she had destroyed herself. I said to them, search the Bishop's Pond.'

'And when did you hear that she was found?'

'Between five and six o'clock I heard that she was found in the privy behind my chapel.'

'She was a regular attendant at the chapel?'

'She was indeed, and a consistent member of the Church under my care.'

'Thank you, Mr Verrall.'

This last from the coroner was, most likely, intended to be a dismissal or a preface to that, but the reverend was not ready to step down. His head held high, he turned to the jury and addressed them directly.

'I believe from what I have heard in evidence the deceased to have taken that which is said to have killed her with the object of procuring abortion.'

This roused the gossips and a buzz of excitement went around the room, so that the coroner had to raise his voice to say, once more, 'Thank you, Mr Verrall. You are excused.'

He made a great show of bowing to the desk, and to the jury, and I half thought he should turn to the audience and bow to them, but he did not. Instead, he stepped down and walked towards the back of the room, to the door through which James Older had been dismissed. But, instead of leaving, he took a place amongst the crowd of onlookers, standing just to my right. I felt my skin prickle at the proximity of him.

I had thought the business of the day must surely be concluded, then, but one last witness was called: Elizabeth Hopperton, peevish at being made to wait for hours, out in the corridor. And her evidence was very brief: that she had seen Harriet walking towards the chapel at about eight o'clock on the night of her death. With that, she was dismissed, and the business of the day was concluded.

Only as I left the workhouse did I notice a man walking alone, back towards the town. There was something familiar about him, and yet I knew I had never seen him before; perhaps it was the cut of his coat, or the look of him, but I risked the embarrassment of being wrong, and caught up with him.

'Sir, I beg your pardon.'

He stopped walking and turned to me, and smiled warmly. 'Yes?'

'Are you Richard Field?' I asked.

'I am indeed.' He removed his hat and bowed slightly. 'And you are ... ?'

'My name is Williams. I was a friend of Harriet's. As, I believe, were you yourself.'

I thought, perhaps, that he might have been weeping. In any case, his eyes were watery, his skin blotchy. We were none of us unchanged, I thought – all of us, those who loved her and those who did not. She had left none of us untouched by her presence among us.

'Miss Williams,' he said, 'I wish we could meet under happier circumstances.'

I stared at him. He was of my height. We met, eye to eye. 'Indeed.'

'How do you do?' he asked, and the look on his face was one of genuine concern. 'Are you well?'

'I am quite well,' I replied, feeling a tightness in my throat, and remembering that Harriet might well have written to him of my illness, which had kept her in Bromley. 'As well as can be expected. How is your wife?'

'She is in reasonable health, thank you.'

'And the child?'

Finally, he managed a smile. 'My son ... yes, he is very well.'

As we were walking in the same direction, we fell into step beside each other. My mind was itchy with it, the idea that this man, of all men, might be thought the one most

173

likely to have taken Harriet's life. Why had the police not arrested him? It seemed to me that he should have been questioned, at the very least. And yet, here he was, all tears and smiles, a very model of the dear, distant friend.

I asked him if he intended to remain in Bromley for long.

'I believe the funeral is to take place tomorrow, now that the surgeon's business is concluded,' he said. 'I should like to see the verdict, but I fear it might be some time yet.'

'What makes you think so?'

'The coroner is a very thorough man,' he said, 'and no satisfactory explanation has yet been reached.'

'But surely,' I said, 'if there is no further evidence to be found, then the matter must be closed?'

Field looked up at the figure of the Reverend Verrall, who was striding ahead of us, head held high. 'There is your trouble,' he said.

'The reverend?'

'He gives the appearance of trying to help, to bring the inquest to a speedy end, and yet what he is doing is complicating the matter, and slowing it down. Forgive me for speaking frankly, Miss Williams, but I wonder if he really is as clever as he tries to appear.'

He tried to divert my attention and my suspicions to the reverend, but I do think Field is the one on whom suspicion must most likely fall. Mr Verrall is, for all his vehemence and silks, a respected member of the community here; his wife is universally loved for her good works. They will never convict him, no matter the gossips. If someone is to be made to pay for Harriet's death, then it should be Field; for, from the things Harriet had said to me about her life in London, he was the one that had started it all.

Thursday, 16th November, 1843

Thomas Churcher

I was in the back bedroom with the curtains drawn when Father came in.

'What are you doing down there, lad?' was the first thing he asked me, and that was because I was sitting on the floor in the space between the bed and the wall, the place I used to hide when I was a boy, only now I'm too big to hide there and there isn't any point in doing it, but it was somehow the place that I ended up.

'I don't know,' I said to him.

'Come out and sit down,' he said. 'Or are you going to stay there the whole day, and miss the funeral?'

For a moment I stayed where I was because I did not want to talk to him. Despite my thoughtless words at the inquest the reverend had sent a note this morning to ask if I would bear the coffin with some of the other chapel members. He said he thought of me especially because I was Harriet's friend.

I wanted my father to go away and leave me in peace, but he sat down on James's bed and waited and I realised he was going to stay there forever unless I moved, so I got up from my hiding place and sat on my bed opposite him. I could see his knees almost touching mine. I did not want to look at his face. At last he reached out and put his hand on to my knee. His hand was old and gnarled like a tree root, calloused and lumpy. One day my hands would be like his.

'Why did no one think to tell me?' I asked.

He sighed. 'I think, son, we did not realise you didn't already know.'

'I don't listen to gossip,' I said. 'I don't listen.'

'No, Tom. That is very true. You're a good lad, a kind lad.'

He patted my knee and withdrew his hand.

'Now I have been made a fool of, again,' I said.

He didn't deny it. I noticed that, and I felt glad of it.

From the kitchen I heard the sounds of Clara singing as she worked. I could smell the food she was cooking for our breakfast and my stomach gurgled in spite of me.

'You really did not know that Harriet was with child?' he asked.

'No,' I said.

'You spent a lot of time with her, walking her home from chapel and so on.'

I nodded. 'But I can't say that,' I said. 'I can't tell them, or they will think I harmed her, and I did not. I couldn't harm her.'

He breathed in, and out, and he was quiet for a bit and I thought he was thinking of something else to say. For the first time, I raised my head and looked at him, just a very quick glance, and he was studying my face so carefully, frowning, looking sad, as if I had disappointed him terribly and he was trying to find a way to say it.

'Don't tell them, then,' he said. 'Just say very little, and, if you need me to talk to them in your place, I will.'

I hated it, I hated the lies. Mr Verrall had asked me if I had hurt her, and I said I hadn't, and he said he believed me, although I could see in his face that he wasn't sure. I asked him the same question and he said he hadn't, and I didn't know whether I believed him or not because there she was, dead, and if she had done it herself or if someone else had done it the fact was that she was dead in the chapel and the town would think badly of us all, and the name of the chapel would be dragged into the mud and the chapel might have to close for good, and then the town would end up at the Gates of Hell and it would be our fault for not defending it against the Enemies of the Cross.

He said she had done it herself, because she was sad and unhappy, and sometimes people did that when they thought they had no other means of escaping from their troubles. But I knew that wasn't true. I held my tongue because she wasn't there to tell him herself, and perhaps I had been wrong, but she hadn't been sad and unhappy, she had been afraid. Which might be the same as troubled, but I wasn't sure. Perhaps people hurt themselves when they were afraid, and troubled; I didn't know.

'I wish it would stop,' I said. 'I wish they would all go away and leave us be.'

'I know, son. I wish that too. We just have to get through it as best we can.'

The reverend had said the same thing. He said we just had to hold on for a little while and defend the chapel, and all would be well in the end, for the Lord was on our side and the Lord would prevail.

'You know I have to ask you this,' Father said.

'What? Ask me what?'

He didn't say anything for a minute and I thought that he couldn't find the right words, and then I thought perhaps he felt ashamed of me or that he thought me a fool after all. Then he put his hand on my knee again.

'Did you do it, son? Was it you that put the child in her?'

The odd thing was that I hadn't even thought of this. And then straight away I remembered what Emma had said to me in the field, almost exactly the same thing, 'Did you do it?', and I'd thought that she was asking if I'd killed her, and all the time she probably hadn't been asking that at all. She knew me, she knew I wouldn't harm anyone, or anything, I couldn't. So she wasn't asking if I had killed Harriet at all, she was asking if I had put her in the family way. That was what she thought.

Frances Williams

Twenty-one girls in attendance today. A small boy called Peter Voakes fell down in the playground this morning and cut his head quite badly. It was an accident and none of the other boys was to blame. I examined the girls this morning and there has been a great improvement in reading generally. I shall be sorry to lose Lizzie Finch, as she has worked hard in helping the less able girls with their reading. Alice Harvey was absent. The excuse given was 'indisposition'.

The boys' room is still as full as it ever was, leaving me in no doubt that the girls are being kept away because of me. I cannot allow this to continue, but I do not know what is to be done to mend it. I hope that once the inquest is complete, and some man has been arrested and charged for Harriet's death, all will return to normal. If that does not happen, I shall have to leave Bromley and find employment in a fresh town.

I sought permission from Mr Campling to close the girls' room an hour early, to allow me to attend Harriet's funeral. He snorted, and waited, perhaps for me to withdraw my request. I stared him full in the face. Damn the man, he would not see me cry. I looked down on him, resolute. Despite his violence to the boys and the shouting, he did not intimidate me, not ever.

'Very well,' he said, at last. 'But the girls will be examined again at the end of the month, and I shall be taking into consideration the disruption caused by all this...this... matter.'

'The girls have been considerably distressed by it,' I told him. 'Miss Monckton spent a good deal of time with them, especially the younger ones. They admired her very much.'

'That is as may be,' he said, 'but the business of the school is to learn, and the girls need a moral and spiritual education more than they ever did.'

He walked off towards the boys' entrance. Bandy-legged, funny little sort he was. In any other man I should have thought him somewhat to be pitied, but he was a good teacher, and, even if I believed his method to be rather brutal, I could not discount his forbearance in keeping me on.

The girls were noticeably quieter in the afternoon, for which I was grateful. The younger ones had been crying; one of them would start and then they'd all be off, weeping and wailing. I had to get Lizzie to take them outside to practise drills. They don't do drills very well, they are too young, but it gave them some fresh air and something to concentrate on. The older girls didn't quite know how to behave. They were wary, expecting a reaction from me, and I found this troubling. And I was trying to be as normal as possible, keeping my voice light, remembering to smile when such a thing was required; but my eyes were on the clock above the mantel, the slow tick tick as the afternoon dragged on into the gloom.

At half-past two, I dismissed them. They left quietly, remembering my instruction not to disturb the lesson continuing next door. Lizzie helped me to tidy the books away and thus was I able to lock the door at a quarter to three, and make my way up to the church.

There was already quite a gathering. Harriet's mother, Mary Ann supporting her; Clara Churcher was there. Sweeting and his wife, and his eldest two daughters; the Milsteads, all of them, including Emma, who was holding her youngest sister by the hand. Reverend George Verrall, waiting stiffly in the porch with the vicar beside him, the latter in his cassock, the former in that curious robe he wears to preach in the Market Place, black silk, moving in the breeze. Behind them, Sarah Verrall, the reverend's wife, and the younger two of their three sons. The reverend's sister was with them, holding both the boys by the hands. All of them looked very smart and clean, and solemn. The eldest boy,

Robert, was still away. Harriet had told me he had been sent for a preparatory visit to a dissenting academy in Highbury, the same one the reverend had attended.

I went to stand with Clara. She gave me a brief smile, and looked to the lychgate, where the coffin was borne through the parting crowds by Harriet's brother, and her brother-in-law, and by Tom Churcher, and by three of the chapel deacons.

Tom looked very ill. His face was white beneath his dark beard; he looked as if he had neither eaten nor slept for a week. As the coffin approached I heard some women weeping; some of them crossed themselves. The men removed their hats and stood with their heads bowed. But beyond them, those few, far more of them were looking, whispering and judging us, those of us who stood and loved her.

I felt for Tom. He stooped to accommodate the other pallbearers, who were much shorter than he; but even so, he would not lift his head and look at anyone. Not even Emma Milstead. She had not taken her eyes from his face, and her look was difficult to discern.

We all followed the coffin inside. The church was, perhaps, a quarter full, and cold, and full of echoes. Clara, sitting next to me, took my arm and squeezed it.

The vicar gave the welcome, and then allowed Verrall to continue. I had never been to a Congregational funeral, still less one taking place within the restrictions of the parish church, but after a short while I stopped paying attention to the words anyway. I felt sick with it; being here, in this vast, cold building with statues staring down at us from every corner. I would not sing. I would not pray. I would sit here and count the minutes until this would be over, and I could pay my respects to her mother and go home and cry.

Reverend George Verrall

The Reverend Mr Newell, whom I have always privately despised, allowed me to conduct the funeral service according to our ways and means, remaining within the restrictions of the Anglican rituals as dictated by the Book of Common Prayer. Nevertheless, being in the parish church made me uncomfortable. The family wanted it; a compromise, of sorts. I should be grateful for Harriet's sake that her mother at least allowed me to officiate. We could have held the service in the chapel, and conducted the coffin here for an interment. But to parade her through the streets, under the circumstances, felt imprudent.

The shame of it, of course, was that even with the situation as it was, we should have at least half-filled the chapel with mourners. Here it felt but a few, a paltry number, the family gathered in the first two pews and the rest of them scattered in the vast space so as to make it appear fuller, and in fact doing the precise opposite.

'...happy are those who die in the Lord...'

That there should be so very few present! I would have said that Harriet was a popular girl, that she was well-liked; but here was the evidence of it. Just a small number of people here to remember her, and that number included my wife and two of my sons, and my sister, who to my knowledge had spoken to Harriet but once or twice.

'...he will swallow up death in victory; and the Lord God will wipe away tears from off all faces; and the rebuke of his people shall he take away from off all the earth: for the Lord hath spoken it...'

And of all of them perhaps I should be mourning Harriet the most. I knew her better than anyone here: her mother, her sister; that sour-faced old maid Miss Williams; even Tom Churcher.

Harriet on her knees before me

you repent, do you?
do you?
the curls of hair at the nape of her neck
the bruise on her throat

'...into your hands, O merciful Saviour, we commend your servant...'

She never once thanked me for my attentions to her, as I recall. Never said that what I did to her was good.

not like the others
Phoebe said it was good
and Anna

Had she done so, perhaps I would have been content with her, and perhaps everything would have been different. But she spoiled it, spoiled everything.

Newell pronounced his rituals over the coffin as I looked on. In the congregation, Harriet's sister wept.

Thomas Churcher

I thought to unravel it. That would be my salvation. The Lord had left me, I knew that for a fact, for I was sure I felt something before and I did not feel it now; the same with her. When she was in the room, there was something – a thrum in the air, like a bee in a garden, you cannot see it but you knew it was there and you knew when it had gone. Harriet had gone, and she had taken my faith with her.

My life was fine, before.

It was fine.

I always tried to be holy. I always tried to do the right thing. But sometimes Satan caught me out.

This church was not my church. This church was dry and cold, and even though I knew the voice of Mr Verrall, closing my eyes and pretending I was in the chapel did not help. The chapel was tainted and Mr Verrall was tainted and all of it, all of it felt broken and dirty and destroyed because of what had happened to Harriet. The whole town was cracking and twisting and falling into shreds, all because of her.

The coffin at the front looked too small.

And yet it had felt heavy, on my shoulder, as if weighted with rocks and not with the body I had once held against me. That time I lifted her and she was easy to lift, light, her arms around my neck, laughing and saying she was afraid I would drop her, and saying no, no, put me down and yet holding herself tightly and tucking her head under my chin. Why did it take six of us to carry her into the church, each of us burdened with the weight? It did not make sense. None of it.

I felt the warmth of someone's eyes upon me, and I glanced to my right, and she was looking at me. Emma.

I didn't love Emma, first off. I started walking out with her after Harriet left for London, because Joe told me I should, so I walked her home from chapel, first of all with all of them, all the Milsteads, and then later she would hang back and wait for me to pack up the music and the books, and she would walk back with me. It was nothing, just a friendship. But after some time if you had asked me, of all the girls in the town, I should have said I liked her the best. That was why one Sunday I told her I should like to come and visit her father.

She smiled at this, for she knew what I meant.

'Would you like that, Emma?' I asked.

'Not this week,' she said, lifting her chin. 'I should like to think about it for a while.'

'Of course,' I said.

I almost flew home, so happy was I. It had taken hard courage to ask her even that question; how I should then summon up the further courage required to ask her father for her hand in marriage, I have no idea. But even that small thing – *not this week* – felt like a good thing, then, and not a dismissal. Or perhaps was playing with me, making me wait for her answer.

Of course, I did not get to ask her father the week after, because something happened. Something put my feelings for Emma in the shade, and that something was Harriet Monckton.

Frances Williams

Harriet was to be buried at the back of the churchyard, next to the place where her father had been interred some years before. There was no headstone for the father, and I doubted there would be one for Harriet. I expect none of the family could afford to have one made, although perhaps the chapel might put together some funds to help.

I doubted they would. She would be forgotten, in a very short while, by all except a very few of us: her mother, her sister; Clara, Tom, and I. And perhaps even Tom would be able to put his thoughts of Harriet aside, and make a life with Emma Milstead.

That night, how he came to my door, asking for Harriet. And at that time I was not even worried about her. She had gone to post a letter, and perhaps she had gone for a stroll, for it was a fine evening.

So, he came to my door. I forced myself to remember it. We had all been talking with Clara, laughing and joking. I was tired, and I felt ill. And Tom at the door.

'Harriet is not here, Tom. She has gone to post a letter.'

He had wanted to come in and wait for her. Why did he want to do that? He must surely have known that I had no desire to sit there with him, waiting for Harriet to come back.

Perhaps he wished me to vouch for him? Perhaps because he knew Harriet was dead. Perhaps because he had followed her, and murdered her, and he wished me to provide him with some sort of defence.

He was stooping, now, lowering the coffin on a rope. Stephen Monckton had the other side of it, frowning at the effort. The coffin jerked, and disappeared from view. I felt myself overcome, a shuddering breath taking me almost by surprise.

Tom stepped back, stumbled a little on the turned earth, then stood with his chin on his chest, bare-headed. His dark curls moved in the breeze, as Verrall said something about the Resurrection. He looked up into the cloudy sky and then down into the grave. It is all an act, a show, a sham. Nobody says what they really think, or what they really mean. There is no honesty to it, no objective proof.

Verrall said something and the mourners began to disperse. Almost immediately I heard a woman laugh, perhaps at the relief of it, but I looked around none the less. Susannah Garn was there, all smiles, her hand tucked under the arm of Joseph Milstead, Emma's elder brother. Tom Churcher's best friend.

Something made me stay. I watched them all walking away. I could see the edge of the grave, the black space into which Harriet had been lowered. I forced myself to go closer, to stand at the edge.

I did not want to leave her here, all alone.

'I'm sorry,' I whispered. 'I'm sorry I got things so wrong. I hope you know how much I loved you.'

There were no flowers in her grave, just a scattering of mud across the bare wood. A simple coffin, barely hammered together. The cheapest wood, the roughest nails, in a grave barely deep enough to cover her. All expense had been spared when it came to the funeral of the girl I loved.

Some movement caught my eye. To my right, half concealed by an ancient fir tree, a man was turning to leave. I recognised him from the cut of his coat, the length of his hair, curling over his collar under his black topper. It was Richard Field.

I hurried to catch up with him, lifting my skirts and tripping between the gravestones. 'Mr Field! A moment, please!'

He stopped. Behind us, the sound of the gravedigger shovelling earth on to the coffin.

'Miss Williams,' he said, turning to me and lifting his hat. His eyes and his nose were pink. He had been weeping, and he did not want me to see.

'Why did you not attend at church?'

'Ah, but I did. I was right at the very back. Out of the way. I did pay my respects to her mother, briefly.'

'I am sure your presence was a great comfort to her, Mr Field.'

'Perhaps,' he said.

I could not quite bring myself to smile. 'Harriet would have been happy that you were here, I am sure.'

I fancied I saw tears start in his eyes once more, and he went to turn away from me. 'At least you and I were present, Miss Williams. The two of us who cared for her the best.'

I followed him down the path towards the High Street, but his pace was too rapid for me to keep up. I thought of Harriet's journal, of the descriptions in it I had seen of Richard, of his vitality and his energy, and how little resemblance they bore to the older man I saw walking away from me then. We had so much in common and yet much to separate us. What had he thought of me? What had Harriet told him of me? I wondered at it, what she might have said to him.

I had a sudden desperate urge to run after him, to ask him, to beg him to show me her letters so that I could hear her voice once more. But my feet faltered. I saw him go into the White Hart, no doubt to wait for the London coach. I wondered if he would continue to attend the inquest, to its conclusion, or if we should never see him in Bromley again. I would not blame him if he never returned.

Tom Churcher was in the shadows of the alley beside his father's shop, watching something. I followed the line of his gaze. In the Market Place stood the Verralls, conversing with Harriet's mother and sister; or at least, Sarah Verrall was conversing with Mrs Monckton. The reverend stood back, impatient, the two fidgeting boys holding each of his hands, whilst his wife in her silk crinoline held the hand of Mrs Monckton and spoke to her earnestly. Ruth was next to her, her face a very picture of that beatific mask that they all wore – deepest sympathies – whilst she moved her weight from foot to foot, like one whose boots are pinching. I watched as Sarah Verrall took a lace-edged handkerchief from her pocket and passed it to Mrs Monckton.

Although even from this distance, I could see her eyes were dry.

Tom straightened as I approached, and took off his hat. 'Miss Williams,' he said. His hands were shaking.

'You did well, Tom,' I said, 'bearing her to the church as you did. Harriet would have been proud of you.'

A muscle clenched in his jaw as he tried to smile. I turned to go, but he touched my arm.

'I've been thinking,' he said, hesitating over his words. 'That night. I mean, the afternoon. Harriet was at the chapel. You sent her on an errand, and I was there putting away the music. She mentioned it, you remember, that evening.'

Reminded of it thus, I could call it immediately to mind: Harriet, laughing, saying that she had taken Tom by surprise, that the noise of the door opening had caused him to drop all his books on the floor.

'What of it?' I asked.

'Just if people ask,' he said, 'if anyone should ask. I wouldn't like people to know. That I was there with her, alone, on that last day. You know people like to talk. It's not fair, the things they have been saying about her. She was a good girl. You know she was, don't you?'

'Yes, of course.'

'So if they should ask you …'

'I'll say nothing about it, Tom. It's nobody's business.'

I thought, afterwards, that perhaps it was a foolish thing to promise. But, whatever had transpired between them in the chapel that afternoon, I had seen Harriet alive and well – more than that: happy – afterwards. So it clearly had nothing to do with her murder, and everything to do with her reputation, and that was something I would protect with all my heart.

Thomas Churcher

It was dark when I called at the Milsteads'. Joe answered the door and he looked at me strangely, like he was angry with me but he couldn't remember why, and then he said, 'What do you want?' and I told him I wanted to see Emma. He said Emma was busy but a moment after that she came to the door and she already had her shawl and her bonnet and then she was out of the door and shutting it behind her.

Without saying anything we walked up to the High Street away from the Market Place. There were still people around but the town was not busy; the coach was about to depart from the White Hart so it must have been near six o'clock, and a few people had gathered to wave it off. We walked past it and up towards the workhouse for somewhere to go.

'I thought you were asking me one thing but now I think you were asking me another,' I said.

'What?'

'You said, "Did you do it, Tom?", and I thought you meant did I kill her? And it upset me, because you know me well enough to know that I couldn't harm another person.'

She took hold of my hand. Nobody was there, then, the street was quiet and dark and nobody was there to see. 'Of course I know that. I know you couldn't hurt her, no matter how much she ruined you.'

I looked at her, but her face was shadowed by the bonnet. 'She did not ruin me, Emma.'

'Aye, she did. She fooled you good and proper, and you can't even see it, but I'll not go on about that now. The girl's dead, for all of her sins. Talking about it won't bring her back.'

'You were asking something else, weren't you?'

She didn't answer for a while. I thought she was angry; she felt angry, stiff and hot.

'I was asking if you'd done it with her,' she said.

I didn't like her being angry. 'What if I had?' I said.

She dropped my hand quickly, like I had burned her. 'Did you?'

'If I did or I didn't, it's no concern of yours,' I said. 'You and I weren't promised. You said you needed time to think. You're acting like I betrayed you by talking to Harriet but I did not. And then just last month I told you that whatever we had was finished. Remember? I told you that.'

She stopped walking and turned to look at me. We were out in the country by this time and the moon was waning and I could just see her knitted brows and her dark, angry eyes.

'Weren't any of your business,' I said.

'Why did you call for me, Tom?' she asked. 'Did you get me out of the house just so you could insult me all over again?'

I didn't answer because I didn't know. I hadn't wanted to insult her, but she had insulted Harriet and I couldn't take that, not yet. Harriet was dead and perhaps there might be a time when I would forget about her, or not mind if Emma wanted to talk badly of her, but she had only been gone just a very few days and only laid in the ground just a few hours, and I could still feel her in my heart, I could still hear her voice and her laugh and feel her mouth on mine and her breath on my cheek. I wanted to keep her close and safe and I hadn't protected her the night she died but God knew I would protect her memory if I could, for as long as I could.

'You're crying,' she said.

I pushed her hand away.

'It wasn't my baby,' I said. 'I didn't know anything about it.'

'Oh, Tom.'

Her voice had softened and she felt sorry for me, or something like it, and this time when she put her hand up to my face I let her do it. And then her arm around my shoulder and then the other one and I put my arms around her waist and held her close and for a moment it felt better.

'I do love you, Tom Churcher,' she said, 'though I've tried so hard not to.'

I let her hold me, because it made me feel better. But all the time she did I was thinking about Harriet, my poor, dead Harriet, in the cold ground of the churchyard that wasn't her home.

Friday, 17th November, 1843

Reverend George Verrall

According to the *London Medical Gazette*, the general opinion of the medical gentlemen is that, in suitably diluted quantities, prussic acid can be used medicinally with beneficial results on such conditions as phthisis and other coughs of a spasmodic nature, melancholia and acute mania, gastralgia, headache and nervous pain, and skin diseases of various types.

Perhaps most usefully, the correct dose of prussic acid is known to be fatal to roundworm.

that I never had but I believe the boys did
nasty little buggers

The problem is the dose: that the pharmacist making up the medicine must needs dilute the acid from a full-strength solution to one at a therapeutic level, a task fraught with danger. Esteemed physicians would complain that patients had most likely been dispatched by an incautious pharmacist, and as a result only used the acid as a medicine when they had mixed it themselves; others had patients who had taken it upon themselves to improve the dosage recommended to them, and thus had unintentionally brought their sufferings to a fatal conclusion.

The possibility remained, therefore, that the dose taken by Harriet had been unintentionally strong, or that it had been taken by her mistakenly, thinking perhaps that it was something else; or, at the very least, that she had taken it herself intending to take her own life.

although you know well enough that none of those things happened, George

you are not looking for the truth

you are looking for an excuse

The bottle found by the sergeant in the night soil remained the most likely source of the substance she had taken, and, if there was even the remotest possibility that it might have contained prussic acid, then there could be no verdict of murder brought by the jury.

I spent many hours last night poring over the medical texts, and could find no mention of prussic acid being used as a constituent part in any smelling salts, but that did not mean it had never happened. Chemists mixed all manner of compounds these days – that was the very nature of their profession, to experiment and find new uses for things. Surely some chemist, somewhere, had prepared a new type of smelling salts, to revive the most desperate of hysterics, and it had contained a tiny part of prussic acid? Or Scheele's Acid, to give it a proprietary name? Or, indeed, hydrocyanic acid, for that was the same substance. How the coroner should think to make sense of all this, and convey it to the jury, was really a matter of some concern.

that it did not happen is neither here nor there

it could have happened and that is all they need to know

The notable fact about the presence of prussic acid appeared to be the smell; all the physicians commented upon it. There would invariably be a strong, sweetish smell of almonds; during one of Mr Thomas's experiments, in which he administered thirty drops of Scheele's Acid to a parrot, the resulting smell was so powerful that three ladies were forced to run from the room, before they were overcome by it. Surely, then, the acid could be used effectively as a smelling salt?

I took up my pen and, writing in a slanted hand pleasingly dissimilar to my own, I wrote:

To Mr Carttar
Coroner for Kent

Sir,

You will I am sure excuse my recommending to you to direct the phial containing what is called (in the Times *of the 16th Article Bromley Inquest) sal ammoniac to be carefully examined by some competent chemist using only half the quantity which may be contained in it. There are salts which under certain circumstances smell strongly of ammonia and which contain prussic acid but it would be very unwise to publish the particulars as they may be used for bad purposes.*

Yours resp'y
Chemicus

I thought about the best way to address the letter, and decided that the best course of action would be to address it to the coroner, care of the Reverend Dr Scott, the magistrate. He should be able to pass it on, with no thought or interest concerning the origins of it.

I called into the kitchen to ask Mrs Burton for a stamp, but only Sarah was there. She, however, knew where Mrs Burton kept the postage.

'What's this?' she asked, turning the letter over in her hands.

'Insurance,' I said to her.

Wednesday, 6th December, 1843

Thomas Churcher

My memories of her were blurring. I tried to hold on to them, but we had such a short time after that first kiss, just three weeks. Already a month had passed since she died. How would it be in a year, or two years? I wanted to remember her, I wanted to remember everything. And not just the tender kisses, and the smiles, but also the moments when she felt fragile, the moments when I thought I was too strong for her, too rough.

That particular late afternoon, I had called for Harriet at Miss Williams's lodgings. The air was warm and still. We headed for the riverbank. There were still people out; Charles Davies the blacksmith, and his wife, passed us, and James Dow, who tipped his cap to Harriet. She was walking ahead of me, almost as if we were not together. I watched her neck, her shoulders, shadowy in what was left of the light, her skirts swishing against the bare earth.

And then all was quiet. Nobody else was in sight.

We talked, a little. Then she stopped suddenly, and lifted her hand to her eyes. The sun, setting in the west, was just at the horizon, and all was red and gold and darkness beneath it. Her face, turned to the sun, and her eyes closed. A tear spilled from beneath her eyelashes. Her lip was trembling.

'What's wrong?' I asked.

She shook her head, and brushed her tears away. 'Nothing, nothing,' she said.

I took her face in my hands. I wanted her to open her eyes but she did not. I thought she would pull away from me, but she did not do that, either. I kissed her hard, because she was not Emma and she did not shrink away, or cry out. She pushed her tongue against mine and her arm around my neck and I could feel the heat of her against me. I heard her make a sound, like a gasp.

I thought: *What am I doing? What am I doing?* It felt like something over which I had no control. It was happening anyway, whether I willed it or not. And the kiss was fierce, hard; it felt like I was biting her and she me; we devoured each other and I clutched at her and she grabbed her bonnet as it slipped. I turned her to the bank at the edge of the path and we half sat, half fell against it. I moved on top of her and pressed myself against her, pinning her there, hard, like prey.

But she bit back.

And then – after seconds, maybe, or minutes – I pulled back and we sat there close together, breathing hard and staring. Her eyes, feverish, almost angry. Mine, afraid. I had been too rough with her, too fierce. I remember thinking I had nearly forced myself upon her and, if I did that, I would surely lose her.

It was getting dark.

She hitched her skirts up. My hand moved under them until I found bare skin above her knee. She put her hand over mine and held it tightly. I stared at her, kissed her again. She made a sound and shook her head, and I stopped.

Then she pushed me away and got to her feet.

Without another word she began walking again. I followed her. I did not know what else to do. We walked on in silence until we got to the path at the end that leads to Farwig Lane. By then it was too dark to see anything clearly. She moved closer to me again and I felt her mouth against mine. A gentler kiss this time.

Then she turned and walked away.

I had spoken not a word to her since her tears. I had no knowledge or understanding of what had passed between us, only that my feelings for Emma were like water, like muddy water, and my feelings for Harriet were like dark blood, hot blood, flowing, pulsing. I felt like a man, properly, for the first time. My heart beat hard and fast in my chest.

I felt alive.

Frances Williams

The average attendance in the girls' room for the month of November was the lowest since I took over, in fact I believe it is the lowest attendance since the girls' room was first opened. Lizzie Finch has finally left to continue her education in London, and I have permission from Mr Campling to replace her with Alice Harvey. The girl is keen but lacks authority; she will need to learn to keep the attention of the younger girls, or she will not do. I shall put her on a one month trial, and examine her at the end to ensure her own learning does not suffer.

At the beginning of December many children were absent, some of them for want of boots. There was a further outbreak of scarlatina; two of the younger boys died and their siblings were absent for weeks. Today Annie Taylor was sent home by Mr Campling with a message that she was not to attend until she brought her pence. Her father came to the school within the hour and argued with Mr Campling in the yard. I thought it might descend into a brawl. The children left their desks and crowded about the windows to watch, despite my attempts to regain order. The boys' room was in uproar, and when Mr Campling came back inside, red about the face, the door was slammed behind him. Minutes later we heard the swish of his cane and the yelp of some boy who suffered the consequences of their misbehaviour. The rest of that day was conducted in silence.

This morning I woke up from a dream about Harriet, poor Harriet, lost and looking for me. And I was there next to her, the whole time. I do not believe, as some do, in spirits; I do not believe in the afterlife, or heaven, but I sometimes wish I did. I can see the benefits of it. When you lose someone you love, there is comfort to be had in the thought that they have just crossed from one path and on to another. Not dead. Not ascended. Just, perhaps, transformed into something we cannot quite see, cannot quite hear.

I lay in bed in the darkness thinking of her face. Every morning I did this, while I made tea and ate bread and butter, while I walked to the school. Every moment of the morning before I spoke to another soul I thought of her face, committed it to memory; her hair, her eyes, the dimples in her cheeks when she smiled; the small brown mole at the side of her neck, under her ear.

Already she was fading. I wished I had an image of her. I wished I could draw, or paint, and I should perhaps have made one for myself. I could have done it while she slept.

The weather had broken, at last. So many days of grey, mild days, mixing in together one after the other. The day of Harriet's funeral was the last of it. As if, perhaps, she had been sent away somewhere and now the sun could show his face and we were supposed to carry on.

The inquest met again on the 6th of December. I did not attend. I walked up to the workhouse at the end of school, and found myself next to George Verrall just as he turned away from a conversation with the high constable, Mr Joyce.

He raised his hat to me, unable to avoid acknowledging me as I was standing in front of him.

'Miss Williams. You are well, I trust?'

'Quite well, Mr Verrall.' Then curiosity overcame me. 'Has progress been made?' I asked.

He looked down at me, clearly in a state of some agitation. 'Alas not. The coroner has adjourned once again, pending further evidence being brought to light.'

'What evidence?'

'Nobody seems to know.'

'But surely the purpose of an inquest is merely to ascertain a cause of death? Is that not already done?'

He ran a hand wearily over his face. 'I believe it is.'

I did not like the man. There was something odd about him, something that went beyond the evangelistic fervour that I customarily abhorred. He had a way of looking through you, as if he could see something in you that nobody else could, something earthly.

'Poor Harriet,' I said, staring into his eyes.

'Our poor departed sister,' he said. 'I pray for her daily.'

He wanted to say something else – that she had gone to a better place, perhaps, or that she was now seated at the right hand, or she was with the angels – but he thought the better of it. *Perhaps you're the one who sent her on her way*, I wanted to say. For all his piety and his showy good works, he was still a man. He was just as capable of harming a woman as any other.

'I was interested to hear that you spent time alone with her on that last Sunday,' I said challengingly, perhaps to gauge his reaction.

He drew himself up to his full height. 'What of it?'

'What did you discuss?'

'Exactly as I told the jury. She asked me to write to the school, to delay her appointment.'

'But you did not do so.'

'I did not; as you know, she was missed on the Tuesday. I did not have the opportunity.'

Liar, I thought. 'You knew she was pregnant,' I said. 'The coroner asked every single witness if they knew she was in the family way, except for you. Every one.'

'The coroner must have suspected that Harriet had confided in me, as indeed she had.'

'Then you must also know the identity of the man in question.'

'That, sadly, I do not. And, if I did, I should likely not say, for judgement is the Lord's, not mine, and not yours.'

I frowned at him. It could be him, of course. He would not admit to it; and saying that Harriet had confided in him as a pastor was a convenient way to excuse their meetings, their – what was it Tom Churcher had said, in court? – their intimacy. And yet, I could not imagine it: Harriet, with this man. She was not a foolish girl, to be taken advantage of by an older man in a position of authority. She had not fallen for him. I would have seen it.

'I thought if anyone would know, it would be you, Miss Williams.'

'I? How should I know?'

He smiled. 'Were you not also in her confidence? Surely more so than I? And yet, you profess not to know that she had found herself...in difficulties.'

Damn the man! 'She did not share everything with me, Mr Verrall. And, unlike some other people, I do not lie in court, even when my testimony might be surprising or inconvenient to other people.'

I could not admit to him that I had wondered the same thing, many times. Why had she not told me? She knew I did not share her faith. I would not have judged her unfairly. I might have been able to help, in some way, had I known. Perhaps she thought I would not have understood her situation; or that I might have liked her a little less, to have had such evidence that her affections clearly lay elsewhere.

She wanted so badly to be loved, I thought. She wanted so badly for me to love her!

I did not tarry in the town but went back to the Beezleys early, closing the curtains against the early dark. Lying in bed with the covers up to my chin I could hear the Beezleys in their own bedroom. Did they not realise that I could hear every word? Had they heard me, too, when Harriet was here? Had they heard us laughing, and talking, and making fun of Mr Campling? Lottie Beezley wanted me out. She thought me responsible for Harriet's death. She had not said that aloud, and certainly not to my face, but other things suggested it.

'The whole town is seething,' she said.

'What do you expect me to do about it?' Beezley responded.

'When there's an infection,' Lottie said mysteriously, 'you clean out your house. You scrub it from top to bottom, and whatever vermin has caused the stink, you get rid of it along with all the other rats and spiders and whatnot. We need a clean house, Ben, or we shall soon lose customers. And if you shan't do it, then I will take up the broom.'

She got louder and louder as she said it, as if she wanted me to hear.

I sleep badly these days. I fancy that I hear them coming for me, the people of the town; that they suspect me because I was not born here, and all was well enough before I came. Before Harriet made me her friend. Every knock and bump in the darkness jolts me to wakefulness, and I lie there listening out for the sound of boots on the stairs outside, thinking that at any moment the sergeant will come and take me. Or Ann Metcalf, or Sarah Jessops, or any one of those women who think me unsuited to teaching their girls. What do they think? That I gave her the poison? That I tried to help her to rid herself of her troubles? Do they suppose that I am, then, a danger to the children in my care?

Why do they not look more closely at Richard Field, who likely got her in that predicament in the first place?

In the bedroom next door, Beezley began to snore. I listened to it and tried to sleep, and thought of Harriet again, and still I could not. I did not consider myself the sort of person to run away, and yet I had no wish to remain in a town so blind to its own faults and inadequacies!

It felt that the world was twisted, and that the town was mired with guilt and suspicion and hatred. This was not the Bromley I knew. Even Clara had little time for me now, although she was caring for her brothers and for her father. She did not suspect me at first, but I thought she had listened to the gossips and had now altered her opinion of me. She was too close to the chapel to see it for what it was; she thought too highly of the reverend. One day she might see what he is like. One day the sergeant might come for him, instead of me, and a curious sort of justice that should be!

Reverend George Verrall

The inquest has been delayed for some months, for no apparent reason. None in the town has heard word from the coroner, and there is no sign of a new meeting, or any progress towards a verdict.For the most part, I was busy, as I always am, with Christmas, although I cannot admit that my heart was full of good cheer. The chapel was perhaps half full on Christmas Day. The numbers attending had fallen off since November, despite my best efforts in paying calls on some of those who had been missing.

Andrew Griffins had been unwell, and had been attending at the parish church which was not quite so far to walk. When his foot healed, he said, he would be back at chapel with his family.

be ye steadfast, immovable

forasmuch as ye know that your labour is not in vain in the Lord

At least Mary Costin was more honest. She told me that she didn't like to come, not 'with all of that bad business'. I told her the bad business was unfortunate, but it had nothing to do with the chapel, and very little to do with me, other than that I felt I had failed the girl by not being a better friend to her.

'But who did it, Reverend?' she said. 'That's what we are all wondering.'

'Who knows, indeed,' I responded. 'It is a matter for the coroner, after all. All we can do is pray for our dear sister's soul, and guard each other closely, and take care of God's children and trust that He will keep us safe from the wolves that surround us at every turn.'

'T'weren't you, then?' she cackled, showing me her remaining three teeth.

I did not dignify her joke with a response. If she had even half a notion to believe her pastor guilty, I thought, then perhaps the Lord was leading her to worship with a different congregation, and that was not a bad thing. Let her infect another flock with her vitriol; I wanted none of it for my sheep.

That Sunday I put aside the sermon I had prepared on the Lord's Last Supper, and instead took as my text the first verses of James, Chapter One. *My brethren, count it all joy when ye fall into divers temptations; knowing this, that the trying of your faith worketh patience.*

I stared out at the congregation – a number I could have counted out within the space of a minute – and at the faces before me. Some of them expectant, waiting for the blessing of God's Holy Word. Some of them curious, perhaps expecting me to say something else – a confession, perhaps. And still others scowling or looking at their feet or hands or each other, or whispering, or smirking, or nudging each other and pointing.

Do you not see, I told them, that we are being tested? That the enemies of the church are all around us, waiting for us to tear ourselves asunder. That just as St Paul feared the Corinthians would fall to envyings, wraths, strifes, backbitings and whisperings, so should they. Is not the reward of Heaven great enough to keep them from harming each other? Is the Lord Himself not enough for them?

I said all of these things and I found my voice growing louder as my anger grew. But I had not prepared the sermon, and I found myself straying from the sanctity of the text and into my own, desperate fury. The whispering and the pointing stopped, but in its place I saw the shock on their faces, and the fear in some of them, and I thought to myself *yes* and *you may well look pale* and I shouted to them that the Lord sees what is in their hearts, and may they all be sorry for it and repent, for the truth will out.

how dare they?

how dare they challenge?

when the Lord comes again you shall be humbled before Him

And the Word of the Lord flowed through my vitriol and left them all afraid for their very souls, which is, indeed, as it should be. Looking out across the rows of faces, I chanced upon Sarah's. Her eyes were closed and the smile on her face was serene. She knows, I thought, she understands the price of it. That their ignorance and their lack of faith will bring them to Satan and carry them off to their own destruction.

Afterwards, she said she thought I spoke well.

We sat at dinner and I was somewhat morose, as I often am after a sermon of that nature. 'But they will not listen,' I said. 'I pray for their souls constantly, and yet they cannot see the danger that lies all around. That we should be the very models of steadfastness and virtue, and instead they are shrinking from the task.'

'There is much work to be done,' she said, calm as always, 'and you are as much guilty of excitement as they.'

Afterwards, my mood low, I took tea in the study and thought of Harriet. She had been the source of so much trouble, and yet she had proved to be a source of rich inspiration, too. In such things I see the Hand of God, leading me forward as He always has.

I prayed for guidance and opened my Bible, and chanced upon Proverbs: *He that covereth his sins shall not prosper: but whoso confesseth and forsaketh them shall have mercy.*

Should I, then, confess?

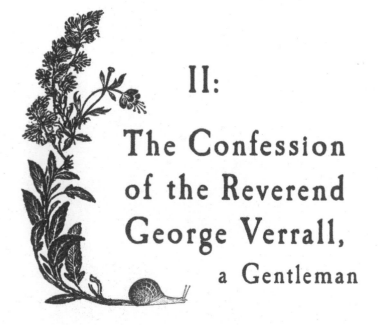

II:

The Confession of the Reverend George Verrall, a Gentleman

Covering Letter

The White House
Widmore Lane
Bromley

Mr William Rose
Messrs Rippingham and Rose, Solicitors
17, Great Prescot Street
London

15th January, 1844

Dear William,

Pursuant to the recent events here in the town, I
have decided it would be prudent to describe in detail
the facts of the case as I see them, as they relate to me.
I would ask you to leave the enclosed document sealed,
and perhaps bring it to light only in the event of my
arrest for the murder of Harriet Monckton.

I am, of course, hopeful that such a circumstance
would never arise, and in that case, and in the event of
my predeceasing Sarah, perhaps you would undertake to
destroy the document and leave it forever unread.

As for the rest, make of it what you will.

I shall look forward to seeing you in Town in the
near future, and until that happy occasion I remain,
Yours most sincerely,
Geo. Verrall

Confess your faults one to another, and pray one for another, that ye may be healed. The effectual fervent prayer of a righteous man availeth much.

James, Chapter Five, Verse 17

What good will it do, to confess? Will it change anything? Will it bring back the keenness of my younger years in the ministry, set alight my words and cause the good people of Bromley to turn from their sin, from their doubt? All I know is that everything has changed, here. All I know is that what was light is now grown dim; what was fellowship has become suspicion. There is a murderer among us, I hear them say, and they look to their neighbours and friends, and to me, and nobody trusts anyone any more.

What, then, must be done here? I have prayed hour after hour until my knees are chafed. I have walked the streets, and counselled my flock, and prayed with them; I have begged them to think to the future and trust in the Lord. But still the doubts remain.

And there is a nagging sense that I am the cause of all this, that I am to blame. For if these dark times began with the murder of Harriet Monckton, then surely the dreadful history of that girl is threaded through with my own, and the mistakes I made are what led directly to her death.

So, then, I have decided to confess. To you, William Rose, my solicitor, for you are as good as anyone. Can I trust you not to reveal this terrible tale? For it is not yet ended; there is still no verdict, and who knows when the inquest shall resume, and what condition the town will be in when it does.

Are you paying attention? Are you comfortable, and warm? For it may take me some time. Perhaps I should make this confession brief and to the point, and yet in order to understand what happened with Harriet Monckton it is necessary to go further back. In the event of this account being needed to provide evidence in my defence, then perhaps you can decide what is relevant and what is not.

And so, Rose, I shall start at the very beginning.

Before I was called, I had ownership of a small tallow chandlery business in Peckham, and through the course of that occupation I became friends with a man named Stephen Halley, who owned a stables in Woolwich. His brother, Robert, was a teacher of Classics at the Highbury College, the renowned dissenting academy, and, knowing that I had a great deal of interest in the Scripture, and esoteric matters, he called upon me regularly to dine with his brother.

On one fine Saturday evening, I was invited to dine at the college with Robert Halley, and Stephen, and some other gentlemen. One of these was John Caney, a man of religious habits who divided his time between London and Yorkshire, where he owned a fine house and some three hundred acres. He seemed to be impressed by me in some way. Over the course of the evening, we had some intense discussion relating to the Book of Revelation, and how we as good servants of Christ should interpret it.

One would think, perhaps, that John Caney would have felt in some way intimidated by the presence of so many religious men. However, I believe rather that he was enjoying the discussion, exploring his own beliefs and improving his knowledge of the doctrines of the faith. At the end of the evening he asked me to dine at his house in Chelsea on the following weekend, it occurred to me that he perceived me as some sort of personal spiritual guide.

Over post-dinner cigars, Mr Halley told me that John Caney was a man of some considerable independent wealth; a week later I was nonetheless taken aback by the grandeur of his London abode. To my pleasure and surprise, I was the only dinner guest. I dined with the family, which consisted of John Caney himself, his wife Mary, their three daughters, and John's elder sister. There was, on that evening, some talk of religion, but far less than I had supposed. I had been seated next to John Caney's eldest daughter, whose name was Sarah. She was three years older than me, that is to say, twenty-six years old. She was, sadly, not what you might describe as a beauty, for her complexion was a little sallow and her eyes widely spaced, but they were the same bright blue as those of her father, and whenever we had the chance to converse, she fixed me with rapt attention.

There have, even, been times in the years since when I have wondered if John Caney had seen some potential in me at our first meeting and had effected that intention swiftly, before I had a chance to realise what was happening.

For I thought myself in love, that very evening. No conversation passed between us that anyone could describe as indelicate; no words of affection, no promises, no sighs. But I left the house a little before midnight and danced all the way back to Peckham. It was almost daylight by the time I arrived, and my sister, Ruth – who lived with me and acted as my housekeeper – had been almost beside herself with worry at my absence.

I wrote to John Caney immediately and thanked him for his most excellent hospitality, and apologised that my own abode was too humble to permit me to offer an invitation in return without considerable embarrassment. I told him that I should be happy to meet him, perhaps, in a coffee house or hostelry in town, and continue our religious discussions.

He took pity on me and invited me once more for dinner. As I had hoped, again I was seated next to Sarah.

This time, our conversation was more personal. She spoke of her own religious feeling, how she had longed since a young age to be married to a good Christian man, and to perhaps one day fulfil her own religious desires by becoming a vicar's wife.

It was very soon after that evening that I received my own calling into leadership. A cynical man might say that the two events were connected; for my own part, I remember the evening at the chapel I attended, a Lutheran chapel in Peckham, and feeling a burning within my own chest as the minister preached about being compelled to serve. In fact he was talking about serving the Lord in whatever work we undertook, but it felt as though he was speaking to me, and me alone. I had been sitting there thinking about Sarah – she was, then, never far from my thoughts – and then I had the clearest awareness of what I had to do.

At the end of the sermon, the minister said that he had a strong sensation that someone in the chapel had received a message from the Holy Spirit, asking them to make a change in their lives, and to accept Christ as their saviour, and that that person should make themselves known to him.

In fact he said this at the end of almost every sermon. Most weeks, some poor soul got to their feet and came to the front of the chapel. I myself had scoffed, albeit internally, wondering if the Holy Spirit was called to the Lutheran Church in Peckham every Sunday at a quarter to noon, and if He was getting a little bored of it.

And then, that day, it stunned me. Perhaps something similar happened to St Paul on the Damascus road, although I saw no blinding light. The minister was looking at me. I raised my head and I said, 'Sir, I have been a believer and saved from a very young age. I believe the Holy Spirit is calling me to the ministry.'

And with those words I fell into a kind of glorious faint, and when I came to myself the minister and all the deacons were kneeling over my body and hands were all over me, and someone was singing Alleluia.

I resolved myself that I would enrol at Highbury College and nowhere else. There was, however, the small matter of the fees. I applied for scholarships and honoraria, to no avail.

I prayed and prayed for guidance, suspecting it to be personal vanity that drew me to that particular establishment; and yet my resolution to study there did not diminish. This continued for two years, whilst I laboured as a lay preacher at the Lutheran chapel and several others, and visited the Caney household occasionally to continue my conversations with Sarah.

Finally, in the spring of 1825, the solution to both problems presented itself, and I asked John Caney for permission to marry his daughter, and he accepted.

It began somewhere, I suppose, in the way all matters of the faith do. It might be considered unconventional, and I daresay many of my peers would believe it to be sinful, but I earnestly believed that what happened to me was something given to me by the Lord. A gift, if you will, in the manner of the gifts of prophecy and of tongues, and interpretation: my gift was that of preaching the Word, and it was fuelled by physical exertion, and, eventually, a very specific activity.

But I must not get ahead of myself; for the way the gift revealed itself to me was very gradual, or else I should have thought it foolish, or an attack by Satan himself.

After our marriage I remained at the house in Chelsea. John Caney, recognising my own straitened circumstances, conferred upon me an annual income which was more than sufficient to keep Sarah in the manner to which she was accustomed, and also, finally, to permit me to enrol at Highbury College and commence my studies for the ministry, with his full support. To this end, I took rooms at the college and returned to Chelsea some weekends.

I suppose it is fair to say I enjoyed the student life to its fullest. I had become close friends with a Welshman named Richard Jones, a man whose religious fervour was matched only by his abhorrence for drink. It was he who set me upon a path of abstinence. As well as Richard, I enjoyed the company of brothers called Charles and Henry Drewitt, from Marlow in Buckinghamshire. We four became fast friends, and on the weekends we stayed at the college we spent the days preaching in town, or discussing theology long into the night. You may determine from this information that my habits at the time were very pious.

And yet something happened to set me upon a course of what some might regard as moral duplicity. Or moral duality, perhaps, is a better way of describing it. It was as if, in one very minor aspect of my life, I had discovered a quite separate path from that traditionally followed by those training for the ministry.

The college employed servants to tend to our baser needs whilst we concentrated upon our studies. Each wing of bedrooms was in the charge of a manservant, who sent away our laundry, replaced our linens, and set the fires in our rooms each day. Since we spent most of the day attending lectures, or prayer meetings, or Bible study, we naturally came to the conclusion that the manservant performed these tasks alone.

It was only one day, when I found myself indisposed with a bad head cold, and remained in bed, that I discovered the truth. The wing might well have been managed by Mr Wilkins, but he had at his disposal an army of women who performed all the menial tasks. Having spent the night tossing and turning, I pushed a note under Richard's door, asking him to forward my apologies to the tutor for my failure to attend classes that day, and that I would pay my dues on the morrow. (The regulations at the time stated that a failure to attend any class would result in a fine of twopence, that was to be payable along with a detailed explanation as to the nature of the absence, on returning to class.) That task done, I fell into a fitful sleep, accompanied by the sorts of dreams one only experiences when suffering from a high fever.

At some late hour of the morning I awoke in my bed, my nightclothes damp with perspiration. I sat up, and was shocked to see a young female with my chamber pot in her hand, a cloth over it. She was staring at me. I thought I might still be dreaming, and asked her if she was real.

'Begging your pardon, sir, I thought you was unwell.'

'I am unwell,' I replied. 'Who are you?'

'My name is Betsy, sir.'

'What are you doing in my room?'

'Cleaning it, sir.'

'Where is Mr Wilkins?'

Something in her face hardened. Perhaps she thought I was going to report her for some misdemeanour. 'In the scullery, sir, I expect. Shall I fetch him for you?'

'No,' I said.

She made a half-hearted curtsey and made to leave the room.

'Wait,' I said. 'I didn't mean to alarm you. Do you visit every day?'

'Yes, sir.'

I thought of my room, how I regularly left it in disarray, with my undergarments placed over the chair, thinking that only Mr Wilkins should ever see or touch them. The thought of Betsy taking them away, laundering them and bringing them back again made something very strange stir within me.

'Always my room?'

'I've never taken nothing, sir.'

'I didn't mean to imply that. I am missing nothing at all. I was only curious.'

'Yours, and all the others on this floor, sir.'

'You do it, and not Mr Wilkins?'

'He checks to see I've done it proper, sir.'

'Very well,' I said. 'You do a most excellent job, Betsy.' And I smiled at her, and coughed.

'You're not well, sir.'

'Indeed I am not.'

'Shall I fetch you some water, sir?'

All the sirring was beginning to grate upon my poor fevered brain. She disappeared and returned some minutes later with a glass, and an earthenware jug. By then I had almost drifted off to sleep again, and the chink of the jug against the glass startled me back to wakefulness.

'Thank you.'

'I should be most obliged if you would not mention this to Mr Wilkins,' she said. 'I should have left your room untended, once I realised you was in it.'

'Of course,' I said.

She nodded, and left, closing the door softly behind her.

I liked her. You might assume from this tale of our encounter that I took advantage of her. That at some point I began to make excuses to absent myself from classes, or to return early and unexpectedly in the hope of catching Betsy in the privacy of my rooms.

It was not a deliberate thing, I will say that. Purely by chance, having collected a parcel one morning from the porter's lodge and returned to my room to leave it there, I intercepted Betsy. She was coming out of the Drewitts' room. She saw me and stopped dead, and then calmed herself, because it was me.

No words passed between us. I approached her. She did not move; she did not back away. I put Sarah's parcel on the table in the hallway. Still she watched me, uncertain. I put out a hand towards her, and she stepped forward. Close enough that I could feel the warmth of her body. Her eyes were entirely focused upon mine; I felt her hand touch me intimately. I flinched at it and she removed her hand, but then I did not move further, and after a moment she tried again.

She would have found that my body had responded to her of its own volition. You understand my meaning, of course. Her eyes flicked behind me to the door of my bedroom and back to my face. I nodded. In my head, I was thinking, no I cannot do this, I will not do it, at the very same moment as I was walking into my room and my hand was closing the door behind us. I unbuttoned my breeches. She lay upon the bed and lifted her skirts around her waist. Her legs were creamy white, and bare, and at the top of them a thick dark pad of hair.

You may well raise your eyebrows. What is the point of confessing, if I do not tell you the details? Do not pretend to be shocked. You know how these things are.

The sight of her, the servant girl, raised me up to a strength I had never yet encountered. I felt a surge of supreme power, enlightenment, that felt every bit as wonderful and glorious as the moment of my own conversion, and greater still than the moment of my calling.

So, yes. I fucked her. There is no better word to describe it, for all your sensibilities. She welcomed me into her body and into her arms, and she kissed me upon my mouth, and curled her fingers into my hair with a passion. She wrapped her legs around my back, and held me inside her after I had finished. I did not move until I weakened and my body slipped away from hers, and then, coming to a sudden awareness, I stood up and turned from her, dressing myself quickly.

When I looked back at her, she was standing, her skirts once again decorously to the floor. She was straightening the bedclothes swiftly and expertly. A mere moment later it would have been impossible to tell that we had disturbed them.

She spoke not a word to me. She left the room, and closed the door quietly behind her. When I went out into the corridor, she was nowhere to be seen.

You may have expected, afterwards, that I should be soused with guilt, with a horror at what I had done. But in fact I felt thrilled by it, warmed, energised. Blessed. It was so very close to the sensation I received in church, receiving the grace of the Holy Spirit, that in a very short time my mind formed a fixed association between the two conditions, and saw them as one and the same.

A sin? Yes, I am no fool. I know now, as I knew then, that what I had done amounted to adultery. Yes, that is my confession, Rose, in a nutshell. But there is more to come.

My friends noticed a change in me. I did less carousing with them; I spent longer in private prayer. Jones asked me many times what had happened, and he came very quickly to his own conclusion: that I had been touched by the Holy Spirit. I did not put him straight – yes, I can almost hear you say it, Rose, because I was ashamed. But at the time I kept my counsel because, as I have said, the two experiences felt very similar; who was to say that he was not telling the absolute truth? For the more I contemplated, the more I prayed, the conclusion I came to was just that. Betsy had been sent by God, to draw me closer to Him. Betsy had not been sent to tempt me; she had been sent to me as a form of relief. I could clear my head, and see the glory of God and His intentions for me and for his people, only if this basest form of my physical need had been relieved.

After that first encounter, we met often. I would leave her a note, slipped inside my pillowcase, arranging to meet her at night, in some back street of the town, or at the park gates at an appointed hour. I could not continue to miss classes, and at the weekends I would often travel back to town and spend them with Sarah in Chelsea.

So, on a Friday evening I would spend inside my wife, having the previous night fucked Betsy against a wall.

And my spiritual life thrived on it.

At the end of my second term at the college, a terrible tragedy befell our family. Sarah's mother fell seriously ill, and, shortly after her, the two younger girls. John Caney, who had been at Chelsea with us, returned to Yorkshire to comfort them, and fell sick himself. He died first. Sarah wanted to go too, but I prevented her; it was too dangerous. A week later, her youngest sister succumbed to death, and then her mother, and finally her last remaining sister. Sarah wailed that she had gone from being part of a good family to being all alone in a matter of just a few short weeks. I reassured her, of course, that she was not alone. She had me.

She suffered greatly with the loss of them, and retreated to her room for some weeks, often not even getting up. I stayed with her for a while, sending letters of apology to the college, but eventually I had to return, for fear of losing my place. I wrote to Sarah every day, but her replies to me were brief. She was feeling a little recovered; then she relapsed. She had received a visitor; then she found herself in the depths of darkness once more. She never once requested that I should return to comfort her; in fact, when I suggested that I should be back at the weekend to tend to her, she wrote and asked that I should stay at the college and use the time to further my studies. She was relying on me, she said. I was all she had.

It was at that time that I struck upon the idea of asking my sister Ruth to stay, ostensibly to keep Sarah company until my studies were completed and I could return home. In fact, Ruth never left. I should like to say that they became firm friends, but in fact Sarah treated Ruth as one might a companion. Ruth did not seem to mind.

I met with Betsy with decreasing frequency, for she had been assigned to another lodging, and so it was harder for us to arrange our meetings. The result of this was that my spiritual life deteriorated. I found it difficult to pray; my sermons lacked fluency, and inspiration. I resorted to self-abuse, but this made no difference to my spiritual wellbeing, and I quickly tired of it.

Between Betsy and my first ministry in Bromley, there came first Anna, then Charlotte, then there was Hester, and then it was Phoebe.

Anna was the daughter of the postmistress in town, who flirted with the young men of the college as if she was on a personal mission to lead them into sin. One summer evening I found the porter's lodge was locked shut, and so I went out to purchase a postage stamp, to send a letter to Sarah. Anna was alone in the shop. She followed me out.

'Does she miss you very much, your wife?'

We walked side by side for a little while.

'She does.'

'What does she think of you, being away from home so much?'

'You should ask her,' I said.

We walked up the hill, so fast that I became breathless with the exertion of it. She matched me step for step, and the thoughts that filled my head were all concerned with the strength of her body, and how that would manifest itself in the carnal act.

In the end she followed me into an alleyway in a part of town I had seldom visited, behind a public house. I went in, and asked for a room, and handed over a shilling. Anna was beside me all the while, watching and listening. I went up the stairs after the landlord, who showed me a room bare of all except a bed and a chair. No sign of Anna. I thought I had wasted a shilling, but a few minutes later there came a tap at the door; when I opened it, she stood there shyly.

'I thought you meant to be rid of me,' she said, a little sadness in her voice that increased my ardour more than anything she had yet done.

'On the contrary,' I said. 'I mean to fuck some sense into you. If you do not desire that, then please leave immediately and do not trouble me again.'

She did not answer. Instead she came into the room and I closed the door behind her. She took off her dress and unfastened her stays, while I unbuttoned my trousers. I thought she would lie on the bed and present herself to me as Betsy had done so many times, but rather she came to me and unbuttoned my coat and my waistcoat, pulled them off me, and my trousers too.

Anna was the first, then, that I saw completely naked. There was an even deeper spirituality to this encounter, because of it. I felt like Adam to her Eve, before the Fall. We had no shame, either of us; even still with the evening sun setting through the small window, the breeze blowing the loose curtain and sighing over our heated skin like a balm. She pushed me gently on to the bed and straddled me, and so my member was lost inside her body, melted into her and we became one flesh.

Anna was very different from Betsy, and as unlike Sarah as anything it was possible to imagine. If Sarah was chaste, and Betsy was pure, Anna was full of Holy Fire. Our fucking was fierce, and prolonged; every time I thought I should spend, she stopped and allowed my ardour to subside, before resuming and taking me to a spiritual plane higher than the last, until I thought I should die with it. When, finally, I thrust inside her and reached my peak, I saw God and the angels beside him, singing His praises and worshipping Him in Glory.

Afterwards, she wiped herself on her skirts, and said I was a trickster.

'How am I a trickster?' I asked. I was barely awake, still floating on a glorious cloud somewhere above the earth.

'You made me believe you didn't like me,' she pouted, and then laughed.

I did not answer. Let her think what she would. I had her, and I knew I could have her again, and at any time of my choosing. Liking her did not come into it.

I fucked her many times after that, often several times a week. My sermons were written quickly and were much praised for their fluency and zeal. My prayers during the prayer meeting were well received. The minister told me

I might well graduate from the college with the highest of honours, now that I had finally taken my studies seriously and was clearly devoting so much time to my spiritual well-being.

I agreed with him.

Once you have sinned, my dear Rose, it is easier to keep sinning than to turn back. Such is the very nature of it, and the problem. There is a choice to be made at every moment: to turn back, or to press on. And in pressing on, one must deny the sin in some way. One must find a way to justify it. And the devil is very clever at revealing to you that way, whilst keeping himself hidden in the shadows.

One Sunday at the end of term, I was invited to Berkshire to hear Henry Drewitt preach. He was destined for this parish, as his father had previously held it, and the parishioners had a subscription to help pay his college fees. Charles, meanwhile, had set his heart upon missionary work.

I had asked Sarah to accompany me, but she was still not quite herself, and so I found myself in the care of Charlotte Swift, a young woman of a gentle disposition, who had taken it upon herself to ensure I was not left without a guide and companion. She was gentle, but there was something keen about her, some warmth. After my previous encounters, I felt I was developing a sense of awareness of those women with whom I could seek spiritual succour. I would get a certain tightening in my chest; that feeling that something was about to happen, some circumstance that would carry me inevitably into a sexual encounter.

I felt that with Charlotte. And yet, here I was, in the Lord's house, listening to my friend preach about the blessings of a pure heart.

Whatever; my heart was pure enough.

And afterwards, as the congregation filed out to congratulate Henry on his sermon, I took Charlotte to the vestry. She came willingly, as if understanding my intent, and yet when the door was closed behind us she dropped to her knees in front of me. The shock of it! I thought she meant for us to pray together. And yet a further shock was to come, for before I could join her in kneeling before the Lord she reached for me and undid my breeches and pulled my member clear of my clothes. I was breathless, and speechless, and when she took me in her mouth I let out a gasp of surprise.

At some point during the next few minutes I looked down. I had my hand upon her straw bonnet, and I could not see her face; just her hand gripping me and her bonnet moving backwards and forwards with some vigour. The sensation was very different from fucking; the intensity of her efforts concentrated just upon my sex, coupled with her being on her knees in front of me, as if in supplication, as if in prayer ... I found myself muttering some words out loud: 'Lord grant me ... in Thy Holy Name ... lead us into Thy Light ...' and that too seemed to amplify the sensations.

The Lord was with me. The Lord had sent me another, to teach me His Way. That a woman on her knees could bring me to Christ, could anoint me with the Spirit and take me into His Glory ...

At my peak I called out, 'Praise be!' and spent into her mouth.

At any moment someone could have come in; indeed, a few moments after my crisis, when Charlotte had arranged herself and straightened her bonnet and let herself out, Henry himself came in to collect his coat and hat.

'My dear chap,' I said to him. 'That was a most excellent sermon; your best yet, I fancy.'

He shook my hand and thanked me very much for my supportive presence. He said he had felt the Lord had moved in the room. I agreed; I said the Holy Spirit had undoubtedly been present.

Of course, you may already have followed the progress of this story and surmised what happened next; for over dinner at Henry's father's house, I was introduced to a young lady by the name of Charlotte Swift, who curtseyed to me most prettily and thanked me for my kindness to her fiancé. She said Henry spoke of me often; that he saw me as a man of the world as well as a man of God. That he looked to me as an example of how to perform the Lord's work on earth whilst still looking to Heaven.

We parted company a couple of hours later when I went to catch the coach. She visited Henry at the college on a few occasions before we all completed our studies and dispersed; each time, somehow, we found a moment for her to drop to her knees before me, to the glory of God, the Father, the Son and the Holy Spirit.

There were times, of course, when I thought that really I should be able to achieve my spiritual peak with my own wife, instead of seeking out other women. But, in truth, that was one part of our lives together that seemed lacking. Despite my every effort to initiate some sort of pleasure in the procedure, Sarah perceived of coitus as something that was done for the sole purpose of producing children, and once a pregnancy was achieved, and for some length of time after each, Sarah would not suffer me to approach.

Her first pregnancy, very soon after our wedding, ended in miscarriage in the fifth month, when I was away at Highbury College. I was made to wait a considerable length of time for marital relations to resume, and it was only having had a doctor to the house to examine her, and reassure her that there was no reason why she could not bear a healthy child, that she permitted me access once more. She told me she prayed for a son every night; it began to consume her. Our couplings were perfunctory and, for a few years, frequent. They were pleasurable as far as they went, but they resulted in no rapture. No enlightenment. Robert was born three years into our marriage, by which time I was engaged as an itinerant preacher in London, working for three or four dissenting chapels as required, which enabled me to spend time at home with Sarah and our son. He was always a robust, healthy child, for which I thank God, and his presence went some way to healing the wounds Sarah had suffered through her losses. George was born four years later, and William just two years after that. We had three healthy sons, and I thanked God for them every day. Through all of this my accomplishments as a preacher were becoming well known in south London; congregations were expanding in the chapels where I had preached, and people travelled some distance from their homes to hear me speak.

During this time my need for Holy Fire was fulfilled by the wife of a minister at one of the chapels I had been called to serve. He had been laid low with an illness and was regularly indisposed. He was not inclined to temperance and I assumed from the mutterings in the church and the occasional word from his wife that his bouts of fever were brought about through overindulgence with spirits. The minister's wife, whom I shall call Hester, though that is not her real name, worked hard for the benefit of the community, spending her evenings on visits to the poor and the sick, sharing everything she had, and never turning away anyone who was in need. I admired her very much, and told her so, and after a while we found ourselves drawn together. Thus we formed an attachment, which culminated in moments of intense passion in those times we found ourselves alone.

Hester had no children, and told me it was because the Lord was angry with her husband, and would not bless the marriage. She believed that what we were doing was sinful, but she wanted a child so desperately. We corresponded regularly when I was away from home, and when I was back in Chelsea with Sarah the correspondence continued.

Our letters were entirely innocent in nature; I wrote to her with advice on chapel matters; how she should secure funding from local well-wishers to facilitate her work with the poor, for example. Despite our regular couplings, she had not become pregnant. Perhaps that was just as well; at that time, Sarah was also pregnant once more. I told Hester the Lord needed her too much; for she was a minister in the truest sense of the word, performing the pastoral role of her husband as well as her own.

I was very fond of Hester; I should not say that I loved her, for I have only loved Sarah. But in her last letter to me Hester foolishly asked that very question, and somehow – for she was not given to snooping – Sarah found that letter, and read it. I was at home, then. I remember it clearly, finding her upstairs in a state of distress. She had the letter in her hands.

'She asks if you love her,' she said, holding out the letter with a shaking hand.

'Indeed,' I said, 'I have read it myself.'

She faltered at that, taken aback by my calm response. 'You don't deny it?'

'Deny what?' I asked.

'There has been…an association between you?'

'The woman is the wife of a minister,' I said. 'What association could there possibly be?'

'I don't want you to preach there again,' she said.

'If I am required to go, I shall go,' I said. 'It is up to the Lord where He would have me speak, Sarah, not you.'

I had not lied to her. I had not snatched the letter back, or thrown myself at her feet, or shouted that it was none of her business. I had not displayed any sort of shame, or guilt, and that was because I felt none.

As it turned out, the Lord's plans for me were already set. A few days after this discussion, our fourth son was born, a month early. He was, from the start, very sickly, and he lived for just eleven days before he was called to the Lord. Sarah descended into a grief so profound that she did not speak or eat for days; the doctor was called to sedate her. Ruth cared for the boys, whilst I prayed for my wife, and myself. The Lord told me that I should decline all invitations and remain at home in Chelsea. Some six weeks passed before there was any improvement; I had begun to consider taking the advice of the doctors, that she should be admitted to their care. An aunt of Sarah's had been similarly inflicted with melancholy, and ended up entirely mad.

It was at that point that my prayers were answered, and the Hand of the Lord was revealed in all its glory, for I was invited to take up the ministry of the independent chapel in Bromley. This news seemed to lift her spirits; she told me she was looking forward to a fresh start in a new place, and to being a proper minister's wife at last.

Phoebe was one of our maids. She came into our employment soon after we arrived in Bromley, having previously worked elsewhere with our cook, Mrs Burton, and being thus recommended by her. Mrs Burton described Phoebe as being a 'steady sort', a hard worker, and I will admit that she was that. But she was also a liar, and a thief, and much wanting in morals; she stole jewellery from my wife, money from the household purse, and silver spoons from a set we had received as a gift from a relative of Sarah's when we married.

Sarah also took a dislike to her, from the very first. Of course, we should have dismissed her, but Mrs Burton always asked us to give her another chance. Phoebe was an orphan, and, if we turned her out, she would end up in the workhouse or, worse, on the streets.

The other thing Phoebe had in support of her continued employment with us was that she knelt willingly before me and supplicated herself to the glory of God and to my tool, whenever the need arose.

The congregation had previously worshipped at the Bethel Chapel, which consisted of a few tiny rooms; having outgrown their existing accommodation, a new chapel had been built in Widmore Lane thanks to the generosity of Mr John Bromley – whose name, to my surprise, bore no relation to the town in which he resided – a local philanthropist, and one who became something of a mentor for me. The new chapel was simple in structure, and not large, but in those early days we had barely twenty or thirty people worshipping there on a Sunday. It was a dismal place to begin my ministry; and yet I set about the task with vigour, getting to know the godless souls of the town, preaching in the Market Place, exhorting my tiny flock to go out and become fishers of men.

All of this was spiritually exhausting.

Within days of our arrival, whilst Sarah was still directing my sister Ruth in the process of unpacking our belongings, Phoebe had looked at me in such a way that left little doubt of her attraction towards me, and I had felt a surge of power from it that rivalled any I had felt for a woman. On the first occasion, she fellated me on her knees in the privy. She knew what she was doing. I whispered a psalm to accompany the moment of triumph. Afterwards I told her she was a good girl; and then I changed my mind and called her wicked. She did not seem overly offended or pleased by either.

As well as the poor chapel attendance, I also had the small matter of a crippling debt to consider. John Bromley had been generous in gifting the land upon which the chapel had been built, but the construction of it and other expenses amounted to a mortgage of one thousand, one hundred and twenty pounds, to be paid back with an interest of five per cent. Despite this burden, John Bromley and I remained good friends, as I struggled to find ways of paying off the debt as quickly as possible.

Phoebe helped keep me from despair. She was, as I have said, a hot-head, unpredictable in her moods. After Sarah had gone to bed, and Mrs Burton had fallen asleep in front of the kitchen range, Phoebe would bring tea to my study. She would always begin by kneeling; the sight of her face, looking up at me, as she took me in hand, was enough to raise me up to a state of spiritual grace before she got to work. In the study, I could speak and praise freely, and I found that the act of reciting a psalm brought me to a communion with the Holy Spirit, such that my peak would sometimes cause me to see visions.

Phoebe continued to visit me, and with increasing frequency she would demand some attention after she had serviced my spiritual needs. Once, she refused to kneel and instead raised her skirts, and bent over my desk. 'Fuck me first,' she said, 'and I'll finish you with my mouth.'

Perhaps her demands should have set a warning bell clamouring in my heart, but they did not. The sexual act still gave me a vigour that I needed, and even two years after our arrival, when the congregation had grown handsomely and the debt was diminishing, my Phoebe fired my spirit like no other. The sex act was not as spiritually pure; this fact had to be admitted. I no longer achieved the same soaring lightness of spirit as I once had. That only came from standing before a kneeling girl, my member disappearing down her throat while she looked up at me, her eyes pleading for more. Or for mercy, one of the two.

At the very peak of our experimentation together, two things happened that brought matters to an unnatural close.

The first was that, one evening in the study, I said aloud, although in jest, that I wished Phoebe was my wife and that I had never met Sarah. Of course it was a joke. If I had never met Sarah, I would not have been able to afford to study; I would never have gone into the ministry, and more importantly I would never have met Phoebe. The instant the words were out of my mouth I regretted them. Phoebe's face took on a new, fervent glow.

And then the second thing happened. One evening, Phoebe brought my tea to my office as usual. My spirit lifted at seeing her, and yet she appeared troubled. After she had supplicated herself to my satisfaction, I bade her sit. She told me that she found herself with child.

I stared at her, uncertain as to how to respond. The oddest thing was that, in that moment, my need for her disappeared completely. I could not imagine kissing her, or touching her, never mind any further intimacies.

She asked for some money, so that she could go away and get rid of it.

I told her I would not, could not, facilitate such a sin.

She asked me what then she must do.

I told her I would think and pray, and speak with her further on the next evening, and she dropped an insolent little half-curtsey, and left the room.

I did think, and pray, but, whether I reached a decision or not, the matter was taken out of my hands. The following morning Mrs Burton told me that Phoebe had left the household. A note had been left on the kitchen table; an aunt had been taken seriously ill, and Phoebe was required at home to take care of her. Whether she believed it or not, Mrs Burton pretended that she did. I could have asked at what point during the night had a messenger come for her, since the house had been undisturbed since Phoebe left me my tea, until the cook went down to light the range at five; but I did not. Phoebe was gone, and in a short space of time a new maid was employed, a dark-haired, thick-waisted girl called Jessie, with red hands and dull eyes.

I was left once again with an absence of inspiration, a clouding of the senses. My sermons lacked fire; the congregation appeared apathetic, and the numbers, which had been steadily increasing, began once again to wane. The matter of the debt was, at least, somewhat easier to resolve; I had not initially considered the money at my disposal, through my wife. I prayed about the debt, and the Lord answered my prayers, and told me that I had been provided with every financial advantage, and I was expected to use these gifts and not to let them go to waste. I was indeed quite wealthy, for I had an income from the estate of Sarah's father, and now I had the proceeds of the sale of the house in Chelsea, which brought me more than ten times the cost of the house in Widmore Lane, fine as it was. Having been so directed by the Lord, I paid John Bromley the full amount owed for the building of the chapel.

Sarah, when she discovered it, was upset. I rather think that was the beginning of the coldness towards me. But it was a decision I never regretted. No, despite everything that has happened, perhaps not even now.

And so now I come to the point of this confession: to Harriet Monckton. That is what you're waiting for, I am sure. She is the cause of all this, the reason for my confession. You have been very patient, Rose, in reading all of this lengthy explanation, and now you shall hear the reason for it.

By the time Harriet came to me, my inspiration had faltered. It truly felt that she was a gift, bestowed on me in my hour of need.

She had returned to Bromley from London, where she had been teaching. Of course I remembered her from her previous attendance, but there had been a considerable change in her demeanour. She had a confidence, a quiet sort of awareness, and I daresay the difference was that she had gone away a girl and come back a woman. From the newspaper reports you will undoubtedly have read, you may have guessed: Richard Field had seduced her. She confessed as much to me soon after her return, said that she loved him, and he had dismissed her in favour of another. At our every meeting I believed I felt the hand of the Lord upon my shoulder, as if to say, *See what I have given you*. Harriet

231

was perfect for my needs in every way. She was young and unmarried, and therefore in need of a pastor's guidance as she found her place in the world. She was not so immured in the ways of the flesh so as to be hungry for it, and therefore sinful, like Phoebe and Anna; she was not so innocent as to be bruised and tarnished by it.

But despite her self-awareness Harriet was not a strong woman. She was just a girl, who had fallen into schoolteaching because she was educated and the youngest daughter in the family; and she had not, either through choice or through lack of availability, yet made a suitable match. And Richard Field had had her, and had chosen another to marry, and so that particular opportunity had most likely passed her by.

And yet she was, to all appearances, deeply spiritual. She attended chapel at every opportunity, and helped with the Sunday School, and came to the prayer meetings and stitched garments for the poor. She came with us to preach in the Market Place, handing out tracts. Often she did what the others hesitated to do: approaching people who were neither rich nor lovely, asking if they had had a meal, or if they had a room to go to, or if they needed anything. This took people by surprise. Sweeting, for one, did not like it.

'The chapel will be overrun,' he said, stopping just short of using the word *rats*. 'We do not have the space.'

'What do you think we are doing here, George?' I asked him. 'If we run out of space, we will build a new chapel.'

He muttered something like *only just paid for the old one* and something else about *that lot won't put money in the coffers* but I ignored him, watching her. And as I watched, she caught me looking and smiled.

Whether she brought anyone to Christ, I could not tell you. All that became clear to me was that she manifested her faith in action, eagerly, as if she absorbed every word I spoke from the pulpit and determined that, whatever I told her a good Christian should do, she would do it.

Perhaps that was the energy I felt from her. Perhaps it was something else entirely: diligence, or charity, or trust. Perhaps it was merely my own carnal cravings.

She asked me once if she should still be saved, even after everything that had happened. She said the devil had taken her by the hand and had at the same time obscured the path of righteousness. She said she had not fallen into sin, she had been pushed. I told her the way of the Lord was not an easy one, and that she should never have expected it to be so.

'But shall I be saved, even now?' she asked. She had tears in her eyes. I think this was just perhaps the day before she died that she asked me.

'Repent, and you shall be saved,' I told her.

She prayed with me but her heart was not in it, and I worried for her soul. Sometimes when people go so far into sin, it is more difficult for them to turn back than it is for them to continue on that path. I worried for her soul, and for the soul of Tom Churcher, who had been corrupted by his lust for her. He was being led down the same path.

She trusted me. I relished that. And I – sinner that I am – I abused it.

For if our heart condemn us, God is greater than our heart, and knoweth all things ... if our heart condemn us not, then have we confidence towards God.

My heart was sound through all of this, I assure you. From the first, I had known that the Lord had steered me on the right path, showing me the link between the physical and the spiritual, that healthy desire and action in the former led inexorably to joy and abundance in the latter.

And yet Harriet's death brought that abruptly to a halt. The death of my inspiration. My sermons were paltry and lacking; I knew not what to say to the congregation, how to lead them, how to inspire them. My heart was sore with it. My instinct was to find another to take her place, to kindle the fire within me, but for so many reasons I could not do it.

In the months that followed Harriet's decease, with all the upheaval caused by the inquest, the congregation dwindled. In the new year I redoubled my efforts, preached in the Market Place, visited all those who had left to worship elsewhere, exhorting them to return for the sake of their souls; some of them returned, but many did not. Sarah continued her visits to the sick and the poor, and, despite my requests for her to leave that side of things to me, she also visited those who had gone astray, and prayed with them.

I found out about it quite by chance, when Sarah had gone to bed early with a chill, leaving Ruth and me in the parlour.

'It is unlike her to catch cold,' I remarked, when Ruth had taken her some broth.

'Indeed,' Ruth said. 'But she has been out every day this week, and the weather has been very bad.'

I had been in town for some of the week, and visiting with Jenner and other friends. 'Out? Out where?'

'Visiting,' Ruth said, eyeing me.

'Visiting whom?'

She listed them. 'The Churchers, and the Costins; George Latter. Fanny Hemsley, the Baxters. And Emma Milstead — we have visited her several times.'

I ignored mention of the Costins and the Baxters, both families that I had expressly asked Sarah to leave in peace. They were at a delicate stage, all of them God-fearing Christians, who had felt tainted by the inquest in some strange fashion. I should speak to her of it later.

'What's she doing with Emma Milstead, of all people?'

'You know she is promised to marry Tom Churcher?'

'What of it?'

'Mrs Verrall is determined that the match should happen. She says it is quite the best thing for both of them.'

I barked a laugh at the thought of my wife playing match-maker in the town. It was like a sport for her, I thought, bestowing her good wishes on those less fortunate. I thought of Tom Churcher and how he had been with Harriet, and perhaps in this instance if none other my wife was right. Emma would certainly keep him in line.

At the time I thought it a fine idea and allowed my wife her meddling; it was only afterwards, perhaps a year later, when the congregation was slowly beginning to build again – although without the younger Churchers, or most of the Milsteads – that I thought again about it.

They had married in the July, in the parish church, with Emma's mother and brother as witnesses. I heard that Clara Churcher did not attend. When I saw Tom Churcher in the town, he bowed his head and would not look at me. They had taken a house in Beckenham Lane, although with what money I cannot say, for neither the Churchers nor the Milsteads had ever had very much to spare. He had been such a kind, gentle young man, but the circumstances of Harriet's death had quite changed him. Now he appeared to all as surly and bad-tempered, mixing very little with his former friends and instead keeping to his own business.

Such things can only be expected for those who turn away from the true path.

The Lord did not send me a replacement for Harriet, nor did I seek one out. Perhaps I realised, then, that I had been as mired in sin as any; my sin was pride. I believed that certain verses of the Lord's Holy Book did not apply to me, or that I should interpret them in my own way. *Thou shalt not commit adultery*. It is as clear as clear can be. It is not open to interpretation.

I confess I sinned against them all: against Phoebe, Anna, Betsy, Charlotte, Hester, and Harriet. And Sarah. Perhaps Sarah most of all. I used them to slake my lust. And I used my own relationship with the Lord to justify my actions! I am shamed by it, now.

I wrote my sermons, and prayed for the forgiveness of my sins and for the Lord to bless the people of the town, and for us all to be spared, and they were passable sermons. And the summer turned to autumn once more, and the inquest remained adjourned, and then a full year had passed since that terrible night. Harriet's name had not been spoken in the chapel for some months, and I fully expected to never hear her mentioned again. But, of course, there was no verdict. And such matters cannot ever be left to rest.

I expect, my dear Rose, that you anticipated my confession to be this: that I am a murderer. That I used her for my lust, yes, I freely admit it – and for my inspiration, that, too. But that I took her life when she grew difficult?

I did not.

I did not kill her.

On my honour, I did not kill her.

Do you believe I am forgiven? Hours I have spent on my knees, I tell you. Do you think the Lord will save me and raise me up on the last day? Or shall I be cast down for everything I have done?

Really, it matters not. I ask that you consider these words as the basis for such defence as may be offered for my soul, should I be taken by the constables. I realise that my behaviour warrants punishment, and I trust that the Lord will carry this out in whatever way He deems fitting. For the rest, Rose, I leave it up to you.

Recorded as a true testimony in my own hand,

> *Geo. Verrall, Gentleman*
> *Bromley,*
> *15th January, 1844*

III:
1846

Tuesday, 3rd February 1846

Thomas Churcher

They told me I was the first to know, because of the police.

Sergeant King came to see me, to tell me that the coroner had been pressed into opening the inquest again. Emma was out the back in the kitchen and she heard, and came through, wiping her hands on her apron. Her stomach was vast and round, and she had started walking with it sticking out even more, as if she wanted people to see it. 'What's all this?' she asked, looking from me to the sergeant and back again.

'The inquest,' Mr King said. 'They're to reopen it. Next week.'

'Whatever for?' she asked. 'That's all dead and done with. It's been over two years.'

'They never reached a verdict,' I said.

She looked at me with one eyebrow arched, for she had been addressing the sergeant and not me, but he seemed too nervous all of a sudden to answer her. I knew how he felt.

'Well, that's their fault, not ours,' she said. 'All those weeks and weeks of talk, talk, talk and nothing to show for it. Ridiculous, I call it. And now the town is all settled once again and her name is mentioned and everything's to be brought up all over again? What a show.'

'Let's trust that it will be a formality,' King said to me. 'Perhaps it'll all be done with in a day. Nobody wants it all dredged up again.'

I felt an odd feeling in my insides at the thought of it, a sour apple on an empty stomach. When Emma had gone back to the kitchen, Mr King tugged at my sleeve and took me outside.

'Look here,' he said, 'they're sending detectives from London. I thought you should know.'

'Why?' I asked him.

He stared. 'No particular reason. Just being neighbourly, like. You being a friend, and all. It's out of my hands.'

I wouldn't have described him as a friend but it was good of him to think of me. But it was out of my hands too, and Emma's, and my father's, and everyone else's.

In the Market Place the next day or the day after that, everyone was talking of it. They had heard from Richard Hodges, the hairdresser, known around the town as Barbarossa for his red hair and beard, that he had written to some person in London to try to get the coroner to bring the inquest to an end, one way or another. So I thought it was his fault, and that otherwise all would have been left to lie and be forgotten about; but then some other person told me about letters in the newspapers and how things like this could not be left, they had to be finished one way or another and the only way to do that was to get the inquest reopened and dealt with for once and for all.

I don't listen to gossip. There's no point to it. They talk themselves round and round in circles and, when I said that Sergeant King had already told me, they rounded on me like dogs, wanting to know this and that and the other. Why did he tell me, they wanted to know, in advance of everyone else? I had nothing to say, and it made me nervous to have them all asking.

And then I got to thinking, and I went to my father's shop. I shut the door behind me and he could see through the shop window all of them out there, nudging each other and pointing and waiting for me to come out again. I sat down on the bench seat beside the counter and rested my head in my hands and groaned.

He stopped what he was doing and came out from behind the workbench, shaking off his apron. 'What's the to-do?' he asked.

I could not speak for a moment and I shook my head. He placed his hand on my shoulder and said, 'What's she done now?'

'Not Emma,' I said at last.

'Well, that makes a change,' he said, but then he saw my face and he sat down next to me and sighed. 'Harriet, then.'

And then I could nod. She might have been dead for over two years but she was still there, right there, in my heart, and he knew it.

Nobody else did. I made my face hard and cold like stone, and if I heard her name mentioned I would turn around and walk away so that they all saw I had had my fill of it, the suspicion and the accusations. None of it was doing any good. None of it would bring her back. Let them think what they liked; my face was set, and they would not be able to tell anything of my true feelings if they only had my face to judge.

'Well?' he asked.

'The sergeant came. They want to start the inquest again. He said there are detectives coming.'

'Detectives?'

'From London.'

'What for?'

I shrugged. He looked at my face and breathed out hard, through his nose. 'Was Emma there? When he said it?'

I thought back, and remembered him taking me outside. 'Not then. She heard about the inquest, though. She wasn't happy.'

'Is she ever?'

I thought and thought back and I ended up right back at our wedding day, and I thought then that she smiled a lot. On that day, and on the day she realised she was expecting our first child. 'Sometimes she is,' I said.

'She'll be fine,' he said, 'once the baby's born. It's difficult for women, especially for the first. They don't know what to expect, despite all their brothers and sisters and nieces and nephews.'

'Will you be there?'

'What, when the child comes? No, son. You have to manage that all on your own.'

'No – when the detectives are here. If they want to talk to me.'

He patted my shoulder. 'They *will* want to talk to you, you know that. And here you are, a man grown, and you still want me there to hold your hand?'

I got to my feet quickly.

'Steady,' he said. 'I'm just teasing.'

'Well, don't. I don't like it.'

'Sit down.'

I sat once again, still fidgety and tied up inside. 'It was years ago, Father – how am I supposed to remember it all now? What I said and when?'

'All right, if you want me there, I'll be there. Don't you worry.'

'Emma will be cross about it,' I said.

'Let her be cross. You do what you need to do. Right?'

'Right.'

I didn't like to say to him that it was all still in my head, bright and coloured and clear as day. Everything that happened, every word that she spoke to me on that last day she was alive. How she was happy and excited and scared all at the same time. How she held my hand and told me I was a good man, a kind man, and she trusted me. And then, how I failed her so badly that she died.

I can't tell them about that. I have to stick to the things I told them in the beginning.

Trouble is, the truth is plain and easy to remember. Lies, though, that's different. You lie once, you have to remember the lie, and truth doesn't fade when time passes, but a lie does.

Reverend George Verrall

I had hoped the day would never come. They are to return to the case after more than two years' peace, resurrecting the filth of it for all to see.

At the deacons' meeting yesterday night, two of the deacons who had served on the jury, Thomas Parry and James Sherver, let it be known that they have both received letters from the coroner asking them to attend on Wednesday. On that particular night Robert Cooper was away on business, otherwise he should most likely have told the same story. The venue is to be the Swan, since the workhouse is now gone. I thought back to those days I had spent in that stuffy boardroom upstairs, staring at the jowly man at the table at the front, praying and willing him to see sense and direct the jury to the most appropriate verdict.

Sweeting told me that the fat barber had written letters prompting the coroner to finish the case and release them all from their obligation; he had been boasting to all his customers, and anyone who would stand still in the market and hear him, that his letter had been forwarded to the Home Secretary, no less, and that he had received word that his careful diligence had been noted and appreciated by the most senior lawgivers in the land. And now, thanks to him, the coroner is to return, and dredge it all up again.

I was dreading it. Chapel attendance was back to how it had been; the pews were full every Sunday. The Sunday School had had such good attendances that there was talk of erecting a new building at the back of the chapel purely for the purposes of ministering to the children. There was even discussion with John Bromley to purchase the land upon which his house stood, so that the chapel could be rebuilt to even grander proportions, to house the growing flock.

And yet, and yet.

Harriet

I had deliberately not spoken her name, or thought about her, for many months. I had put the events of that dreadful night to the back of my mind, lest it send me mad. For months following the last inquest I had expected at every moment to receive a summons to attend a further hearing, or even that the police might take things further still and arrest me – although for what, and upon what evidence, my fevered mind could never quite decide. It took a long time for the terror of that to fade, and, for the bad dreams to reduce in frequency, longer still.

Harriet

Even now I could see her face quite clearly; pale skin, dark hair, those dark, dark eyes. In years past, she might have been thought a witch. Some might say she bewitched me, even, as she had young Tom Churcher – that I was in thrall to her. But of course that was not the case. I used her for my own ends, that is the truth of it. I used her for inspiration, and when the time came I had no choice but to deny her.

At the deacons' meeting I watched and listened, and answered their questions, and revisited the subject of the sermons and the question of monies to be sent to missionaries; I read a report from my own son Robert, who was away at school and very much in need of prayers for the Godless boys in the supposedly Christian establishment to which I sent an astonishing fee every term. I listened as Mr Darnley read aloud from correspondence he had received in relation to the situation in Ireland, and we agreed to send chapel funds for the relief effort.

I listened and watched, and all the time I thought of her and saw her eyes and memories of that night came back to me, swelling up inside me like a fountain: her bonnet, pulled forward over her eyes; the weight of her in the darkness. The dark blood between her lips. The shock of it all, the horror.

Harriet

Frances Williams

A sharp drop in attendance today, owing to the fair coming to Shifnal. Miss Barclay suggested that tomorrow we should call a half-day holiday, as the fair begins properly, but Mr Jarrow has refused. Agnes Smart was sent home today with a rash upon her face. The measles is still rife in the town. I trust the parents will have the good sense to not send their offspring to the school if there is a chance of infection.

I have written to the Shifnal school board this morning to ask for funds to purchase a wall chart showing the countries of the world. I should like to add Geography to the lessons, as Jane Harris has an older brother who has gone to sea, and Lottie Adamson asks me all the time where is America, and where is Ireland, and are they the same thing? I have shown her in the atlas I keep behind my desk, but a wall chart would be so much easier to use.

The letter was waiting for me, lying on the table in the kitchen. Emily was already home, heating soup for us to have for our supper. The letter bore a Bromley postmark, and if she had noticed this she did not remark upon it.

I greeted her and asked after her day. She is engaged as a governess for a wealthy family in Telford, but they have recently begun an extended visit to family in Scotland, and they are unlikely to return for some weeks. She was asked to go with them, but she refused, and it seems that they value her skills enough to keep her on, paying her a fee to retain her connection to them whilst they are away. She is not expecting to sit idle, however, but to write. She is a fine poet, and wishes to compile a collection of her work for publication. She told me that she had written a great deal, although most of it would necessarily be discarded.

I opened the letter, then, to see that the inquest is to be resumed into Harriet's death. I am only surprised that it has taken them so long. What is more troubling is that the coroner requests my attendance on Wednesday next and that I should repeat my testimony, given that a considerable amount of time has elapsed, to refresh the minds of the jury and to enable them to reach a final verdict.

'What is it?' Emily asked, seeing my face.

'The coroner has called me to Bromley, on Wednesday,' I said. 'They are resuming the inquest.'

She knows, of course, about Harriet. I told her early in our friendship, for in those days the loss of Harriet was something I felt acutely, like a rent in the fabric of my soul. She listened, as a friend might, and at some point in the listening and the telling of the story I told her that I loved Harriet, and she told me that she understood. I recalled the look on her face, and how the hand which had been holding mine moved to my cheek, and stroked it, and how I shivered. Was that the first time we kissed? Perhaps it was.

She looked at me, and immediately said, 'We can inform Mr Jarrow that I will stand as your replacement.'

'But you are to go to Northumberland,' I protested. She had been hoping to visit her sister, who is expecting her first child.

'This is more important,' she said. 'My sister will have the baby whether I am present or no.'

'But I don't wish to go.'

She saw my face, and came to me to kiss me. 'It will be over with soon enough,' she said, 'and finally then you will be free of it.'

'I cannot go back there again, Emily. I swear that town will break me.'

She made me look into her cool blue eyes, so wise and comforting. What ill could possibly befall me in Bromley, when I had Emily here awaiting my return?

'All will be well,' she said. 'And besides, how should it look if you failed to attend?'

'They all think me guilty anyway.'

'I am very sure they do not. From what you told me, that town is full of men who had good reason to harm her. You should be the very least suspected!'

'And yet, they all thought me guilty. The school—'

'Did you not think that the mothers kept their daughters away not because of you, but for another reason? That they did not want them walking to school and back when there was a murderer abroad? Or perhaps they suspected Mr Campling, or one of the older boys?'

I smiled at her. 'You're very kind, but you weren't there. You did not see them, gathered like rooks in the Market Place, gossiping and murmuring.'

'Nevertheless,' she said, 'you must attend. Shall I be obliged to escort you there myself?'

I thought of Emily in that place, and how they should stare, and comment, and I couldn't bear it. 'I'll go,' I said. 'As long as you're here, waiting for me, I'll go.'

'That's better,' she said, and took the letter from my hands, and kissed me.

Reverend George Verrall

'You would do well to keep out of it,' Sarah said.

We were having luncheon together, seated at opposite ends of the dining table, with Ruth in the middle, and Jessie had just brought through dishes of chops with boiled potatoes and cabbage. Everything doused in a watery gravy. I looked at it with dismay.

'We ask you dear Father to bless this food that has been brought to us through your bountiful mercy,' I said. 'Amen.'

'Amen,' said Ruth.

'Amen,' said Sarah. 'The Lord Himself knows what trouble it caused us last time.'

'I shall involve myself only as far as my Heavenly Father requires me so to do,' I said. This was an expression I used often; it seemed to work.

Sarah ate her food with a sour expression on her face. We had not dined together for some time, I realised; often I was late back for luncheon and had to be satisfied with a cold plate, served to me without ceremony. Sarah and Ruth ate at one o'clock promptly whether I was there or not. This insistence on her part to eat without me felt like rudeness; I had many times wished to admonish her for it, or to at least request that she would wait if I were to be, say, a half-hour delayed.

'You may do as you please,' she said to me then, a small, tight smile upon her face. 'I shall eat at the same time every day, for routines are needed in a household such as this, no matter how busy its occupants.'

She often spoke as if Ruth were not there, I noticed.

It wasn't as if we had the boys any more to keep us to the routines; all three of them were now away at school. If this made Sarah sad, she did not say. Ruth, I knew, missed them terribly. But Sarah kept her occupied in the household and sent her on errands, and Ruth, perhaps fearful of being sent away, her usefulness expired, said not a word against it.

At least she ate heartily, clearing her plate before either of us had so much as tackled a chop. I turned to her.

'And how do you do, Ruth? What news from the parish?'

'But little,' she said. 'Annie Storer has had her baby, a little boy.'

'Thanks be to God! And mother and child are both well?'

'I believe so, yes. Richard Humphrey asked me to call upon his father. He has been unwell in the colder weather; I said I would take him some broth.'

Sarah made some noise and I looked at her sharply. I met her eyes and looked away.

'You are fond of the Humphreys, Ruth?'

'They have not had an easy time of it,' she said. But she was looking at Sarah, not at me. 'Since Mrs Humphrey was taken to Glory, the family has found it very difficult to manage ...' Her voice trailed off.

I returned to the chop.

'We are all of us quite changed,' Sarah said, 'by the events that surround us.'

It was such an odd thing to say. I stopped eating again and regarded her, but having uttered those words she had set herself to the task of eating, and did not apparently wish to speak further.

Wednesday, 4th February, 1846

Reverend George Verrall

The door knocker rapped after supper. Sarah and I were in the drawing room. Ruth had already retired. We were sitting in quiet companionship, with no need for conversation; I was reading from a book of sermons, Sarah was at her mending.

Mrs Burton answered, and told me Thomas Parry was asking for me.

I rose to my feet. 'Show him into the study, Mrs Burton, I shall be there presently.'

The study was warm and stuffy, for the fire had been lit earlier in the evening, and I considered opening a window. Parry was standing by the bookcase, twisting his hat in his hands.

'Well,' I said. 'Sit down, man.'

He sat, perched on the edge of the hard seat as though not wishing to taint the wood with the unworthiness of his behind.

'Let us begin with a prayer, shall we? I feel the nature of our discussion is likely to be a serious one, and I wish to make sure that we hold the Lord himself close to our hearts whilst we talk.'

His eyes widened, but then he closed them and bowed his head.

'Heavenly Father,' I began, 'I ask you to bless Thomas, and keep him close to you; and honour him for his work in Your Name to keep your people safe from the enemies of the Cross; we ask you now, Holy Spirit, to descend upon us and guide our discussion, for the sake of Your Son Jesus Christ, in whose name we pray, amen.'

'Amen,' he said, and coughed.

I spread my hands upon the desk in front of me. 'What news, Mr Parry?'

'Well, sir. The coroner called us all in, and we held a meeting upstairs at the Swan.'

I knew this. If he meant to tell me every detail, we should be here hours. 'And?'

'Four hours, we was in there. Hodges was talking and talking, and then Barrett pipes up, and you'd think he was an expert on it to hear him go on...not meaning any disrespect, sir, but I found it tiresome.'

'And what of the business of the meeting?'

'The coroner, he apologised for its going on so long, and said he had been very busy, but that that was not an excuse. He said he had been hoping all along for the police investigation to reveal the person that had done the deed, but that the police had been working on other matters, and there had been very little progress.'

very little progress

He paused and turned his hat a full circle in his hands, and I thought to myself that perhaps he was the wrong person to ask. But he was a true friend of the chapel, at least, and I trusted him to keep my questioning of him private.

'And what of his intentions, Mr Parry? Did he indicate what he required of the jury?'

'He said they would go over the evidence, to refresh our minds of the case, given that so much time has passed since our last meeting, and that he should call the witnesses once more to give their testimony.'

'What, all over again?'

'He said it was important that we did not miss any detail. Barrett said that it was a waste of our time, that we had heard it all before, and what purpose should be served by beginning

251

all over again. And the coroner said that we had sworn an oath of diligence, and what man among us could recite the testimonies of the witnesses word for word, and that if any man could not do that, then it was his duty to ensure that we were all familiar with the circumstances, given that it was a difficult case the like of which he had never seen.'

the man does not know what he is doing

'It will be weeks, then, no doubt about it,' I said. 'And presumably the matter will be open to public scrutiny?'

'I don't know that, sir, only I think it should be. He said the first sitting will be next Wednesday, the eleventh. A week today. He asked us all to make sure we were free to attend.'

'At the Swan?'

'I believe so, sir, yes, sir.'

'And what of Mr Churcher?'

'Mr Churcher?'

'Thomas. Was he mentioned?'

he's squirming in his seat

that means he was

'I couldn't say, sir, not that I recall.'

'There was no mention of the police's suspicions in that regard?'

'I'm not sure I understand you, sir,' Parry said, flustered.

'It doesn't matter, Mr Parry. It's just that I am aware that our own Mr Churcher was – and is – the man suspected by the police. I don't think it does any harm to say it, just amongst ourselves. We *believe*, of course, that he is innocent of such a charge – but I feel it can only help us to know which way the coroner's mind is inclined ... '

'Oh, I see. Yes.'

'So his name was not mentioned?'

'Not that I noticed, sir, no, not, as you said, sir, in that regard.' He coughed, and then continued, 'I think his name was mentioned in respect of his being called as a witness, sir. That, only.'

'Ah. And the other witnesses, were they as before? Nobody else is to be called, whom we have not yet seen?'

'I couldn't say, sir.'

'Very well, Mr Parry. Thank you for your diligence. You are a true friend to Jesus.'

'I hope I am, sir.'

'You understand, of course, that we must keep this discussion to ourselves, for the time being?'

'I do, sir, yes, sir.'

I showed Parry out myself. The lane was dark, a wind blowing from the west. I offered him the loan of a lantern but he said he knew the lane as well as he knew his own face, and that he should find his way well enough.

The drawing room was empty. I considered writing letters in my study, but I felt tired and my mind was turning over the conversation with Parry, and I knew I should not concentrate. Thinking of the inquest made me think of Harriet, and the thoughts of her made me restless. I went upstairs to find Sarah already in bed, her back turned to the door.

'Are you awake?' I asked, loudly enough to ensure she was.

She ignored me, but when I got into bed beside her and blew out the candle she acquiesced to me in the end. I went at it hard, thinking of Harriet, and I made her gasp with the force of my body. Her hands were fists, resting on my shoulders. I spent in her quickly, feeling little but disappointment.

I hoped, as I always do, for a surge of inspiration or for the warmth of the Spirit, but there was only exhaustion, and Sarah turning her back on me once more.

Thomas Churcher

'I just do not understand,' I said to my father, 'why they want to see me again.'

'Because it's been years, Tom,' he said. 'The coroner wants the jury to have the case fresh in their minds.'

'Then the man should read it all aloud to them,' I said. 'The man who wrote it all down. What did he write it down for, if not to refresh all their minds?'

Father shrugged. 'It is what it is. You have to attend, and make the best of it.'

Emma was not pleased. I had work to do, she said; did the coroner think we were all sitting idle? I hung my head and said it was nothing to do with me.

She stood watching me for a moment and then she came to me and put her arms around me, and I felt the hardness of her belly pressing into me. She pushed her hand through my hair and cupped my cheek and pulled me to her mouth so that she could kiss me. I had forgotten the sweetness of her kisses, when she chose to bestow them.

'Don't fret, Tom,' she said, after a while. 'It will all be over with soon enough.'

'But what shall I say?' I said. 'I have forgotten it all. I have put it to the back of my mind, as you told me to, and now I can scarce remember what I did or said and why.'

She knitted her brows and held my hands in hers. 'It'll all come right,' she said. 'When you're in there, you just say what you can remember and tell them if you've forgotten. They can't expect you to have kept it all fresh in your mind, can they?'

I thought about it at supper and later that night, in bed with Emma beside me, snoring because now she had to lie on her back, so that some nights I lay there for hours listening to her, and sometimes I went down the stairs and slept in the chair by the stove. But those nights I made sure to wake early and pretend that I had only just got up.

I can't have kept it all fresh in my mind, she said. But that was not true. Some of it was fresh, but not the right parts. The day after the last inquest I promised myself I would not think of that night again. But of Harriet herself I thought more and more. I remembered her face, turned to mine, half of it in shadow, and her smiling at me and looking at me in that way she did just before she kissed me. I remembered her pressing her hand to my heart and feeling the beat of it, and taking my hand, and pressing it to her breast, so that I should feel hers.

I remember her solitude. That, even when she was with other people – with me – she always seemed to be alone. That she seemed to desire me, as I did her, but that she had strength and virtue and honour, no matter what they said about her at the inquest.

Sometimes I look at Emma and her swelling belly and I think of what Harriet might have looked like, had she lived. I think of her child that never had a chance at life and my heart hurts.

I should have liked her baby to have been mine. Then things might have been very different. But the truth of it was, she gave me so much of herself, but not enough for me to hold on to. Not enough for me to keep.

Wednesday, 11th February, 1846

Thomas Churcher

The two London detectives came to the workshop when my father was absent. I don't know if they did that on purpose, so that I should not be embarrassed, but for me it was not convenient, and I told them so.

The older one – a Mr Pearce – looked about him in a dramatic fashion, as if to point out that there were no customers present and so I was clearly not occupied in serving anybody.

'My father is out on business,' I said.

'It's not your father we've come to see,' he said.

'You'll have to come back,' I said. 'Maybe this afternoon.'

The other policeman, Mr Meadows, who was round in the face and the body, held up his hands. 'Now, then,' he said, 'you know you're due at the inquest this afternoon, and it will only take a moment or two. Just a few questions. You know why we're here, don't you?'

They would not leave, and I stood there with my head down while they interrogated me. They asked me endless questions, and I simply repeated the same words over and over: that I had already said everything I had to say at the first inquest.

Mr Pearce then asked me if I had walked out with Harriet.

'Once or twice I walked her home,' I said. 'But it was Emma I was walking out with at the time.'

'Did Harriet Monckton know this?'

'Yes.'

The shop door opened then, and it was Emma. I was relieved to see her and scared to see her at the same time, for she looked at the men standing there and at me, and back to them, and said, 'What's all this?'

Mr Meadows looked at me, and said that would be all for today but that I should expect to see them again, and they nodded to Emma, and left.

She waited until the door closed behind them, and went to the window to see them walking away. Then she turned back to me. 'Well?'

'They're the detectives from London, Emma. They just asked me some questions,' I said.

'And you answered?'

'Of course I did,' I said, not wanting to admit to her that I had requested for them to wait for my father to return and had answered hardly anything at all.

'So why did they say they were going to come back? What do they want with you?'

'I don't know!' I said, and I didn't, but my voice rose, and sounded guilty even to me.

She took off her bonnet and put on her apron, scowling. 'I once believed it was a good thing, that Harriet was gone,' she said. 'I never expected the whole town to be still talking about it two years later.'

Frances Williams

Returning to Bromley has been a very odd business, after so long out of it. The place was instantly familiar and also very strange. The sense of unease increased as we passed places I recognised. At Beckenham the foreboding manifested itself as an uncomfortable twist in my stomach.

The coach brought us down the High Street and I saw that the workhouse has been completely demolished; in its place a row of houses is being built. I wondered where the poor of the town were to go for relief.

I had written ahead to the Bell Inn for a room, which in my day had always been the most comfortable and reasonably priced establishment. I had addressed my letter to Mr Davis, the landlord of the Bell, but it was his daughter who had replied. She told me that her father had passed away not long after I had left the town, but she had taken over the business and would be very pleased to welcome me back and offer me her best room. I was glad of her kind words, and wrote to accept.

The White Hart profited from its position as the town's main coaching inn, and the unwary traveller stepped off the coach and straight across its threshold, not bothering to look elsewhere; but the Bell was across the other side of the Market Place. Thus, when I dismounted the coach, my limbs and back stiff from hours in the jolting carriage, my clothes creased, I had to walk a little way before I reached my accommodation.

Little had changed in the town itself. There was the Market Place, with the fine market building at its centre; there was Mr Storer's confectionery shop, renowned for its fine gingerbread; here the ironmonger's, there Cooper's yard; Isard's butcher's shop, and Harvey's sheds and yards, the stables and the paddock behind. In the market itself the costermongers and barrow boys were selling fruit and loaves and oysters and flowers of every possible variety. The town was alive with it.

This place where I had been so happy, and so very troubled.

As I walked on, I found my eyes drawn to those businesses whose owners had had a direct bearing upon the matter which brought me back to this place. Sweeting's house, from which he ran his plumbing business; Joseph Milstead's, carpenter and upholsterer, who had provided Harriet's coffin which Tom Churcher had carried to the church. As if the thought of that man could conjure him up, I noticed his father's shop, the sign over the door that said CHURCHER AND SON and, below it, in smaller letters, BOOT AND SHOEMAKER.

I should have gone inside, but as I crossed the square I saw Emma Milstead come out, rub at a spot on the window, and go back in again. As she turned I saw her swollen belly. Tom Churcher must have married her after all.

I checked my watch and saw that, after all, there was but little time to spare. I carried on to the Bell and, having been shown to a room that was plain and yet warm and comfortable, I changed my dress and went out again, to the Swan Inn, and to the inquest.

Richard Field

I was called to Bromley again in the early part of the year, for the resumption of the inquest. I had thought the whole business done with, concluded without me somehow, unreported in the newspapers, when in fact the business was resurrected unexpectedly with the arrival of the coroner's letter.

Maria, pregnant with our second child, had been strangely unconcerned when I told her I had to return to give evidence a second time. She merely sighed and said if I had to go, then that was that. Thus released from my marital responsibilities, I wrote to book a room at the White Hart again, and took the coach down to Bromley.

The room where the second inquest was to be held was part of the Swan Inn, and was a low-roofed building which rambled on as far as the corner of the Beckenham Lane. The inn itself stood back from the road to allow the carts and carriages to pass freely around the sharp bend and onwards to London. I had spent some time walking up and down the High Street looking for it, for the coroner's letter had directed me to the Swan and Mitre. But this had to be the place, for half the town's population seemed to be heading through a door in the single-storey extension at the far end.

I joined them, and found myself in a room packed full of people all talking at once. The noise was overwhelming, and the aroma of bodies and clothes and malt and hops over-powering, for this had until recently been a brewing room. The innkeeper, whose name I learned was Matthews, was engaged with two or three members of his staff in setting out chairs at the back of the room, whilst at the same time trying to dissuade those canny members of the townsfolk from helping themselves to chairs from the store room. 'Only for the gentlefolk!' he repeated. 'Hold off, there! Chairs for the gentlefolk – you can stand, right enough, Robert Cooper!'

The coroner's assistant, a young man with a fair complexion and pink-cheeked with his own importance, was directing the operation from behind the table at the front. The jury had been seated on low benches to the side, and they were talking amongst themselves and watching the chaos. 'Mr Matthews!' called the young man. 'Matthews, I say! We shall have to close the doors. There simply isn't the room!'

Eventually the door closed and those who remained outside were forced to listen at the window, which thankfully remained wide open. Every opportunity for fresh air in this enclosed, darkened space, was much appreciated by those within it.

The coroner arrived moments later. Without his even speaking, an expectant hush spread through the assembled crowd. I looked about the crowd and saw faces I recognised; Verrall, taller than the rest, bare-headed, wearing his black gown, setting himself apart from the rest of them; Frances Williams was there, too, and several of those I had seen at the previous inquest.

'Gentlemen,' the coroner began, addressing the jury, 'your attendance upon this sorry occasion is, again, appreciated. We are resuming the inquest into the body of the deceased

Harriet Monckton, who was found in the privy behind Bromley Chapel on the seventh of November, 1843. You are aware, I am sure, of the circumstances of this tragic affair, and yet it would be remiss of me not to ensure that the evidence as presented at the last meeting is presented to you once more. You may expect to see many of the same witnesses who spoke before you in 1843. It may be helpful, therefore, to treat this inquest as a completely fresh start. Thus, the verdict reached by the jury will be an honest, true and fair one, based solely on evidence and not upon any supposition, gossip or act of imagination that might have taken place in the intervening period.

'Mr Leadbeater, our first witness, please.'

The young man stood, and called for Sarah Monckton.

Harriet's mother came forward then, attired in a green serge gown, her bonnet trimmed with black velvet. Her testimony was brief, and the coroner was about to dismiss her, when someone immediately to my left spoke up.

'A question for the jury, sir.'

The coroner looked peevish at the interruption, and then, upon seeing that it came from Reverend Verrall, he set his mouth in a line. 'What is it, Mr Verrall?'

'It should be asked perhaps whether the estimable lady is aware of any illness in her daughter, in the months leading up to her death? I should have thought that a relevant question, sir, as we are keeping an open mind as to the cause of it.'

The coroner paused, perhaps considering whether to allow the question to stand, and then he turned to the witness and repeated it.

Mrs Monckton added that Harriet had been very poorly about a month before her death, and had been unable to attend the Sunday School because of it, but that she had recovered well enough the following day.

That said, the witness was excused, and almost immediately was called the next: Joseph Milstead, carpenter and undertaker to the town of Bromley, who testified that he had buried the deceased, and was still owed the sum of three pounds and eighteen shillings for it. After Milstead, the postmaster, Mr Acton, was called. There was some talk of an anonymous letter addressed to the coroner, but posted to some other person; Mr Acton asserted that the letter had not passed through the hands of the Bromley postal service and must, despite the postmark upon it, have been delivered in person.

Then George Sweeting was called. He looked at the very same time both uncomfortable and pleased, dressed in a tweed jacket which might, perhaps, have been a good fit in his younger days. He was first asked about the night when Harriet was found, emphasising that it was Churcher, not he, who had suggested that the chapel should be searched, and Churcher who had tried the chapel gate and found it unlocked. There was a murmur amongst the crowd and I judged from the comments that his testimony had changed in that regard. He was asked about his connection with the chapel, and at that he puffed out his chest and said he was superintendent of the Sunday Schools, and was at present also a deacon.

The coroner then sought to dismiss Sweeting from the inquest but he raised his hand to indicate he had something further to say.

'Yes?'

'My opinion, sir, is that the deceased took the poison of her own accord.'

The coroner looked as if he might question the witness further, but then seemed to think the better of it, thanked him, and told him once again that he was dismissed.

Mrs Monckton was then recalled. She then volunteered said that Mr Sweeting's opinion of her daughter was not what she would consider to be a very Christian one, but that she expected nothing less from a chapel that followed what she called 'unusual practices'. From the back of the room, Sweeting gave out a 'Well, I never!' and some other shout, and Verrall pushed through the crowd and hushed him, and for a moment they stood toe to toe, and I thought a fight might break out; I glanced back to the front of the room and saw a curious sort of smile cross the face of Mrs Monckton, and then the coroner called for order, and dismissed the witness for the second time.

My feet were beginning to ache from standing, and I shifted a little to relieve them. I considered going outside for a walk, as others were doing in the minutes between the calling of witnesses, but then Thomas Churcher was called and I stayed in my place.

Churcher repeated his testimony, saying that he was with Sweeting when the body was found. He was asked who had a key for the chapel gate; he replied that the keys were kept by Mr Beezley, that he used this set and returned them whenever he needed to enter the chapel to return his music. He said anyone might obtain the keys from Mr Beezley without his knowledge as they were hung up in his shop.

The most natural witness to be called after that was Beezley himself. He was asked first about Miss Williams, and he stated that the deceased had a habit of visiting Miss Williams, who took rooms at the upstairs of his house. He last saw Harriet during the afternoon of the day she went missing. He said she was in his bakehouse, looking out of the window, and then eventually went up to Miss Williams's room.

I heard a stir behind me at that moment and I looked back to see that Miss Williams herself was standing beside me. She met my glance for a moment and nodded a greeting. I nodded in reply.

The coroner asked Beezley what his connection was with the chapel.

'I am clerk and deacon,' he answered.

'And you keep a set of keys?'

'Yes, sir. And, whatever Tom Churcher thinks, they are never out of my possession, unless some legitimate person has had cause to use them.'

'Whom would you determine to be a legitimate person, Mr Beezley?'

'Why, Mr Verrall, of course; Mr Sweeting, Tom Churcher, or the woman who cleans.'

He was then asked whether he had cause to use prussic acid or essential oil of almonds in his business. He replied that he did not, nor did he use volatile salts. And with that, he, too, was dismissed.

Once again my desire for fresh air was thwarted by my own curiosity, for next was called Miss Williams. I regarded her, how she held herself – very erect, for a woman who was as tall as many men – and how she looked. Her hair was impeccably neat, with no stray strands or curls visible under her bonnet. She was not what one might describe as handsome, but she had fine, clear eyes, and a steady sort of defiance that might, at first, appear to indicate a prickly nature. But Harriet had been fond of her. Perhaps she was the sort of woman who only revealed her true nature to her closest friends.

'Miss Williams, you have heard the previous witness saying that you lodged at his address. Is that true?'

'Yes, indeed.'

'And how did you come to know the deceased?'

'I was schoolmistress at Mr Campling's school. Miss Monckton assisted me there at times, particularly when I was unwell or indisposed, as she was a capable and talented teacher herself.'

'Please tell us what you remember from the night the deceased went missing.'

'Harriet was to stay with me that night, as I was ill. She left to post a letter, and I expected her back within the hour.'

'Can you remember anything of your conversations that evening?'

Miss Williams hesitated then, as if struggling to recall, then said, 'I believe we spoke about the previous day's sermons.'

'Did she seem in any way troubled?'

'On the contrary,' Miss Williams said, and glanced purposefully around the room as she did so, fixing all of us with a look so certain we had no choice but to believe it. 'She appeared in good health and in excellent spirits.'

'Miss Williams, you mentioned the deceased had left you to post a letter. Was she in the habit of corresponding regularly?'

'She was a frequent correspondent, yes.'

'And was there anybody with whom the deceased corresponded particularly frequently?'

'Several, sir.'

'Do you know the names of those people?'

Miss Williams hesitated, then, with an expression fixed on her face that indicated she believed it was none of the court's business and that she had little time to spare for producing a pointless list. Nevertheless, after a moment's reflection, she continued, 'Richard Field, and his wife; her brother and sister that lived outside of the town; and Mr Carter.'

'Did the deceased show you any of their letters to her?'

'Many of them, yes.'

'And did any of them seem particularly curious, or concerning, in the light of what we now know of the deceased's unfortunate fate?'

In the stifling room, my breath seemed to falter, and my heart with it. I should have taken the chance for fresh air before now, I thought, hoping that I should not faint or be otherwise overcome.

I breathed through my nose and swallowed, straining to hear Miss Williams's reply.

She hesitated again, but this time appeared troubled, as if unsure how to proceed. 'There was one matter of concern. Mr Carter's letters. I thought him quite improper in his tone.'

I felt the weight of it fall from my shoulders. She had spared me!

'You thought his letters improper?'

'I did not say that. I had no concerns over his writing to her. But his tone was very free.'

The coroner conferred for a moment with his assistant, and then said, 'Are you aware of the circumstances under which the deceased came to know Mr Carter?'

'He has preached at Mr Verrall's chapel. I assume that is where they met.'

'You know Mr Carter yourself?'

'Only through his acquaintance with my friend. I met him in person only once, after a tea meeting Harriet had attended at Mr Verrall's. I encountered her in the fields as she was on her way back to her mother's, and he was accompanying her. She introduced me and they went on their way.'

'What did Mr Verrall make of that acquaintance?'

'I have no idea. You must ask him yourself.'

The coroner set his face against her, then, perhaps thinking her impertinent, for all his stupid questions. He dismissed Miss Williams and called the next witness, Mary Ann Monckton. I felt certain that she would have little to add to her previous testimony, so I took the opportunity to vacate the room along with a half-dozen others, including Miss Williams herself.

She made to walk away, but I called her back.

'Forgive me,' I said, 'I should stay close, as I believe I am to be called.'

'I wish you luck with their pointless questions,' she said, under her breath.

'They were, rather, weren't they?' I said, smiling.

Her face almost cracked with the effort of returning my smile. I thought perhaps she did not smile often, which was rather a shame, as it improved her countenance considerably.

'Thank you,' I said.

She knew what I meant, although for a moment she looked surprised. In reply to me, all she did was nod.

'I should like to return the favour,' I said to her, 'if the situation ever presents itself.'

Her brows furrowed; she did not understand. Never mind. At that moment we were interrupted by a shout from the door.

'Mr Field is called!'

I returned to the room, and walked straight past the crowd to the front, to the chair in front of the coroner. As before, I was handed a Bible and swore an oath as directed, and then I was permitted to sit.

'Mr Field, your wife has also been summoned to attend, but I understand that she is currently indisposed. Is that the case?'

'Yes, sir. I have a letter from her physician.' I took the letter from my jacket pocket and approached the table with it, passing it to the coroner. I thought for a moment he might read it aloud, but he merely perused it and passed it to his assistant.

Maria hoped – indeed, we both did – that the doctor's insistence in writing that she could not attend without a conveyance being provided for her would result in her summons being revoked. Surely, she had said to me, her attendance at the inquest was not necessary? What could she say, that I could not say on her behalf? The coroner, however, seemed keen to hear her testimony, and told me that he would arrange for a conveyance, as neither he nor anyone else would wish to place the life of a witness in jeopardy. With that arranged, he expected to see my wife present at the next meeting of the jury. My heart sank a little, but there was no time to consider it further, for the questions then began in earnest.

'Please tell the jury how you came to know the deceased, Mr Field.'

I told them that Harriet was intimate friends with my wife, and that she had last stayed with us in August of 1843.

'And I understand you were frequently in correspondence with the deceased?'

'I was, and my wife also. Sometimes we wrote together, and she replied to us jointly.'

'Can you tell us, please, of the very last letter you received from the deceased?'

I took a deep breath and removed another letter from my pocket, and passed it to the coroner. 'This was posted, according to the mark, on the 6th of November, 1843, and it was in answer to one I had written to her on the 4th.'

'Can you recall the contents of your letter, Mr Field?'

'Mr Edwards, of Trinity Square, Tower Hill — a mutual acquaintance of ours — had obtained for her a situation at Arundel, and in my letter I informed her that he was requesting that she settle about going down as soon as possible.'

'And how did you come to learn of the death of Miss Monckton?'

'By letter again, sir, this time from Mr Verrall.'

The coroner conferred with his assistant. I thought for a moment he should ask to see that letter, as well, or ask me about Harriet's demeanour in London in August, or about her baby. He did none of those things.

Moments later, the coroner said, 'Thank you, Mr Field, that will be all. We should like to see you and your wife at the next meeting, please.'

I was released. I heard the crowd begin the muttering that punctuated the space between each witness, and I walked past them all, feeling their eyes upon me and no longer caring. I left the brewhouse and, believing it unlikely that any other witness would have some testimony that required my further examination, I walked down to the Market Place and purchased a pie and an apple. From there I strolled back to the White Hart, and sat by the fireplace with my pie and a glass of their own beer. I thought it odd how all of the witnesses had given testimonies that were at once the same as, and yet in marked ways different from, those they had given previously. It also seemed we all felt the need to add some comment, or some jibe, whether directed at the coroner or some other person involved in the case. Everyone was looking for someone to blame; not just for Harriet's death, but for the delay in reaching a verdict, which meant all of our lives were in effect frozen, leaves suspended in an icy pond.

I retired to my room after an hour or perhaps more, having had just enough ale to know that I should leave the bar before I started calling for spirits. I lay, clothed, on my bed for quite some time, thinking of all that had transpired today, and, all thoughts fresh and ordered in my mind, I rose and sat at the table for a while, composing a letter to my beloved Maria.

Frances Williams

After my testimony I returned to the Bell, and rested for a while on the bed, but I found it impossible to settle. I sent for tea, and, thus restored, I went out for a walk and some fresh air. My feet took me back to the Swan, and to its brewhouse at the corner of Beckenham Lane. The door was propped open to allow air into the room, and the crowd had much reduced in number since my own testimony that afternoon. I was surprised to see that the session was still in progress, and took it as a sign that the coroner had every intention of bringing matters to a swift but thorough conclusion.

I went inside and made my way to a position where I could see the person currently testifying, but by then I had already recognised the deep, melodious tones of the Reverend George Verrall. Yet again he was stating that he had suggested searching the Bishop's Park, the ponds, for he felt certain that Harriet might have chosen to do herself some harm. The price he had to pay for this dogged insistence as to Harriet's state of mind, when everyone else who knew her had testified that she was not the sort of person who would consider self-destruction, was that it had become very clear that he alone, of all of us, had known the truth about her condition. I thought him very clever, for that. For who could argue with him? Indeed one might believe that he knew of her pregnancy because it was he who had impregnated her; but it might equally be that he knew of it because she saw him as a trustworthy confidant and had shared her worries with him. Who could question him for that? He would answer that his stance could be seen as a foolish one, for he made himself appear, sometimes, quite guilty, and why should he do that, if he were not entirely innocent?

It took a moment to realise that Mary Ann Monckton was standing beside me. She nudged me and murmured, 'He's been going for a full twenty minutes.'

'On what subject?' I asked, my voice low.

'Calvinist nonsense,' said Jane Humphrey, who had attended chapel when she had taken a liking to Joe Milstead, but Clara told me she had not bothered since.

Verrall was good at that, I thought. He made you think he was clever, whilst all the time he was dancing around you, a trickster in a black silk gown.

'What can you tell me of this Mr Carter, who was mentioned earlier this afternoon, Mr Verrall?'

My ears pricked up at this; for it was my own testimony that had brought that name to light. Really, I had mentioned Carter only in passing. I should instead have mentioned

Richard Field, and I had not. I was not quite sure why; for I had seen enough of his letters in Harriet's hands. I had seen declarations of affection from him, reminiscences of their time in London, strong assurances of how much they both missed her. I had not said anything critical of their relationship to Harriet. But at some point during the autumn she had stopped sharing his letters with me. What was it in those later letters, that Harriet had not wanted me to see? At the time, still wary of my own true self, I had thought perhaps that she had written unkindly about me to her friends, making sport at my nature, and he had replied in kind. But now, I thought that perhaps she had confided in Richard as well as Verrall; and perhaps her reasons for doing so were very different.

If that was the case, though, Richard Field had lied under oath before the inquest, and that painted him in a very different light.

'I knew a person named Carter,' Verrall was saying. 'He lived in Deptford, and had been to preach for us once or twice.'

'Do you recollect a tea party at which the deceased and Mr Carter were both present?'

'I have held a number of tea parties, and I believe I have, on occasion, had cause to reprove some persons as to their conduct. Mr Carter was certainly present at one of these parties, but whether he was one of those I reproved, I cannot recollect.'

'Whether you reproved him for it or not, did Mr Carter pay close attention to the deceased at that tea party?'

There was a hesitation, then. I noticed that he did not like questions regarding matters of his personal judgement. 'Not that I recall,' he said.

The coroner made a note and moved on. 'Did you ever say, Mr Verrall, that after the jury had given their decision you would be prepared to give yours?'

'Yes, I stated so publicly, and my reason was this. The Thursday after the deceased died was a lecture night, and on that night I took occasion to say that I would endeavour to improve the event by preaching a sermon on the following Sunday. When I found that the jury had not arrived at a conclusion, I at once saw the impropriety of my entering upon the subject, and I forbore to do so. I gave public notice that, as soon as the jury delivered their verdict, I would give mine, and by that I meant that I would improve the event.'

Jane Humphrey sighed and pulled a face, and whispered to me, 'Why can't he just say yes and let us all get on with it? He likes the sound of his own voice too much.'

The coroner continued, 'Have you not expressed a desire that this inquiry should be closed, that you might leave Bromley?'

A murmuring went through the crowd at this.

'Yes, I have been very anxious on that subject. I did not wish the jury to come to a verdict without sufficient evidence, but I had hoped that they would have returned an open verdict. I am of the opinion that the deceased took the draught intending to terminate her unfortunate condition; and it is not quite clear to me that you have gone far enough, in not having examined the chemists and chemists' wives in this town. It was not impossible that the deceased might have applied for some medicine to procure abortion, and have been served with prussic acid instead.'

The murmurs grew louder. It was difficult to tell whether the crowd liked the fact that Verrall was strongly against the coroner's line of questioning; *he* seemed, in any case, to be enjoying himself. The sight of it sickened me.

The coroner said, 'I have here a number of letters, addressed to both myself and members of the jury.'

The assistant got to his feet and took a sheaf of papers to Verrall, who glanced through them and passed them immediately back to the assistant.

'Are these letters written by you, Mr Verrall?'

'They are in my hand, yes.'

'You wrote them?'

After a moment, he answered, 'Yes.'

'Did you also write to Mr Ilott, the surgeon, regarding the case?'

'I did so, yes. I wished to enquire as to his previous experiences with poisons, and their effects. I received an adequate reply.'

The coroner thanked Verrall and dismissed him. Whatever those letters contained, we were not to hear of it.

Mr Ilott was then called, and asked simply whether he entertained the same opinion now as he had formerly expressed. He replied, 'I do, most undoubtedly,' and added that he had the results of his analysis to hand, which should be sufficient to satisfy any chemist.

With that, the coroner checked his pocket watch, thanked the jury for their close attention and adjourned, stating that they would meet again in two days' time, in the hope that further important witnesses would then be able to attend. The jury got to their feet and stretched; the rest of us turned to go. I saw Verrall once again approach the table and address the coroner; the look of annoyance on the latter's face was clear to see. But Verrall spoke with him only a moment, and then turned his attention to the jury, shaking hands and smiling, although they all looked weary to a man.

I walked back to the Market Place with Jane Humphrey, who spoke the whole way of Harriet and the horror that had befallen her, and how desperate she must have been. I had heard this opinion before, and I disliked it, for it reminded me that I had thought myself such a very good friend of hers and yet she had found me not trustworthy enough to be drawn into her confidence. Why would she talk to Verrall, of all people, instead of to me? Even after all this time, the pinch of it upon my conscience was sore.

273

'You believe Verrall, then?' I asked her. 'That she took the draught herself?'

'Oh, no,' she answered. 'I mean, I can't imagine how it happened. Perhaps she took her own life, perhaps someone helped her. All I'm saying is, to find yourself in that condition – and her such a pious girl ... she must have been absolutely terrified of it. I've been wondering about that situation she had, in Arundel.'

'What of it?' I asked.

'Whether it was true. I thought perhaps she was going somewhere, to have the baby, and here we would all be thinking her away at a school.'

That thought had crossed my mind, too, but the situation had been arranged for her by Mr Edwards, and Mr Field, and surely they would not go along with such a ruse on her behalf? In fact it was more likely that she had obtained the situation and only then, afterwards, realised that she was with child. And Jane was right: how desperate, then, must she have been? I thought of Tom Churcher, who had thrown aside his sweetheart to pay his attentions to Harriet instead, and I wondered at the origins of their association. It had happened quite quickly. I thought back to that summer, so much of it spent with her crying over Richard and Maria, and then, quite suddenly, by autumn Tom Churcher was calling for her and walking her home and accompanying her to chapel. By then, judging by the surgeon's testimony, she must already have been pregnant; possibly already aware of it, or at least feeling that something was not quite right.

'Who do you think it was?' Jane said then, nudging me. 'I don't mean who killed her. Who do you think got her in the family way?'

'I couldn't say,' I replied.

'I wondered whether she was forced,' said Jane. 'Terrible thing, but it happens. When it's someone like that – someone gentle, and good; makes you wonder, don't it?'

A little way ahead of us, Tom Churcher was walking towards the Market Place with Emma. She had her arm through his, gripping him tightly, and his head was down.

I thought of Harriet all evening, as I ate my supper, as I read a novel, as I prepared for bed. I wrote a letter to Emily, entreating her to manage without me for a little while longer, as the inquest was to continue on Friday, and I could not return to Shropshire until it was over, lest I should be recalled. It seemed unlikely that I should be, but the important witness who might attend in two days' time could be Maria Field and my curiosity burned for a glimpse of her, this woman who was more to Richard Field than Harriet had been. I wanted to see her. I wanted to hear her speak.

Harriet. I had thought, privately, that the father of her child must be Richard, for she had clearly loved him, and had left London only when his affection for Maria had appeared to grow stronger than his feelings for my friend. But, in that case, why not confront Richard with it? Why not ask for his help?

Perhaps she had, and he had refused her. What would she have done, then? Turn to Verrall, to ask for his advice? Look for someone else to marry?

And there it was.

Poor Tom.

Friday, 13th February, 1846

Thomas Churcher

In the morning, Mr Verrall called at the workshop and spoke to Father. I was in the back, working on a pair of silk slippers for Miss Holgate, and I could not hear what was said between them, but a moment later I was called to the shop.

'The reverend wants to ask you something, Tom,' my father said.

I had not spoken to him for a good while. I had given up the music at the chapel before my wedding, claiming to be too busy to do it. Alfred Elliott had taken responsibility for it, at first just as a temporary measure, and then I simply didn't go back. At the time I worried and fretted and lost sleep over it, thinking that the reverend would come to me and say that I was shirking, and accuse me of backsliding, following the Devil's path, and would demand that I pray with him.

But time passed and he did not come; and Elliott did not come either, and Emma and I missed a week at chapel, to visit her sister in Nottinghamshire, and then we missed another, because Emma was ill, and then the following week we went to the parish church to hear Miss Charlotte Birch, the renowned soprano, and after that we simply did not go back. It was before Christmas. We worshipped at the parish church when we could; sometimes Emma did not feel like it, or she had too much to do at home, or else she demanded that I spend the day working on the house, with her supervising so I did not make a mess. We were not heathens; we were just occupied.

I had worried about it, and then as time passed I worried less and less. But now Mr Verrall was there, and I was there, and the fear of it leapt to my throat like a fish in a stream.

'Tom,' he said.

I wanted to tell him that I was *Mr Churcher*, that I was an adult, with a wife, and a child nearly born, but I held my tongue.

The reverend glanced towards my father – who continued to worship at the chapel, although he was no longer deacon, and yet had never once commented on my dwindling attendance – and he excused himself, and went to the workshop and out the back, into the store room. That served to increase my nausea.

'Yes?' I asked.

'I should like you to do something for me,' he said. He was holding his hat in his hands, and I wondered if he had removed his hat in here before, or if he had kept it on his head. I did not remember.

If he was expecting me to agree without his explaining what he wanted, he was to be thwarted. I waited for him to continue, and that look appeared upon his face, the one that made me think of an adult disappointed in a disobedient child.

'The inquest resumes today,' he said. 'I find that I am unable to attend, due to another more pressing engagement.'

I stared at him.

'I wondered if you would be so kind as to attend,' he said, 'on behalf of the chapel.'

I wanted to say many things to him, things like *why should I do that* and *I do not represent the chapel or you* and *why are you here.*

What I actually said was, 'I have work to do.'

He said, 'Ah, Tom, but you do not. I spoke to your father; he has released you for the rest of the day.'

I could have argued with him; I could have told him that I would not be bullied by him any more, and neither would my father follow his instructions for no better reason than that he called himself a reverend.

Instead, I nodded.

'Perhaps you will come to my house this evening? You shall have supper with me,' he said.

It was not a request.

With that, he placed his hat upon his head once more and bade me good day. As if he had been listening for the shop bell to ring, Father came from the store room at that moment.

'Well, Tom,' he said, 'you'd best go. Don't want to miss anything.'

I was half angry to be so used, but, as I walked up the High Street to the Swan, part of me was also pleased to have a day out of the shop. And all I had to do, after all, was listen.

When I arrived, the lane outside was full of people, the door to the brewhouse being firmly closed. The rising din sent my mind into swirls and knots. I stepped away from them and sat under a chestnut tree on the other side of the road and waited. Joe Milstead came across and sat down next to me; I had not seen him in the crowd.

'There's a delay,' he said, taking out his pipe and filling it from a leather pouch that I had made for him. 'Didn't expect to see you.'

I shrugged, not wanting him to know that I had been sent. 'What delay?'

'The coroner is talking to the jury in private,' he said. 'We are to be called in when they are finished.'

He puffed on his pipe and we sat there for a while. A weak sun was trying to shine through the clouds, and it felt almost warm.

'How does my sister?' Joe asked.

'Well enough,' I said. 'Getting big.'

He laughed at that. He had married Susannah Garn six months before I married Emma; their first child had arrived

278

less than a year after that. Every experience in my life, Joseph Milstead had done it before. I often felt myself dragged along in his wake, a frayed bit of rope, snagged by a keel.

We talked about nothing for a while, and then eventually the door opened and the coroner's assistant propped it open, and was almost pushed aside as the gathered throng jostled to get a good viewing position. Joe and I joined them. I saw Mr Beezley there, and Miss Williams, who I had not seen for a long, long time. Clara told me she had moved away, to be a teacher somewhere in the north. I should have liked to speak to her, but the coroner was already at his desk.

The two London detectives were there, at the side of the room, and they both looked at me as I found my place. I did my best to ignore them but I felt the discomfort of their gaze upon me.

Sergeant King was the first one called.

'Did you ever see the deceased in the company of a man, in the weeks and months leading up to her death?'

Sergeant King cleared his throat, and cast his eyes about the room, and alighted on me. He held my gaze for what felt like a very long time, then he looked back to the coroner and said: 'I saw the deceased frequently walking in the town, and on a Sunday evening shortly before her death I saw her walking with a man.'

I felt queer all of a sudden, hot and cold at the same moment, and I thought I might be ill.

'Who was that man, Sergeant King?'

'I am afraid, sir, I cannot identify that person.'

And with that, Sergeant King was dismissed. The coroner said that there would be a delay, as the next witness had been held up, and the jury were allowed to get up and walk around. Most of the spectators left the brewhouse to wait outside in the fresh air, or go to the market or home for some dinner. I saw Inspector Meadows and the other one, Pearce, approach the coroner and speak to him, and I fancied they were telling him something about me. They had called again, once when I had been out with Father, and once again that evening. I had insisted I had nothing further to say, even with Emma standing at my shoulder. I had managed to remain calm, but only just.

I looked back at the coroner just as I was about to leave the room and I saw Meadows point to me. That was enough. I walked back to the shop, thinking about what it was Mr Verrall had asked me to do and whether he had sent me there on purpose, to remind the coroner and the detectives that I had been in Harriet's company that day.

By the time I reached the shop I had made a decision, and I walked on to the corner and on to Widmore Lane. I tried the chapel gate, but found it locked, and so carried on the half-mile to the Reverend Verrall's house.

I had run this way on the night Harriet died. I barely remembered that part of it: the desperation, my feet flying on the gravel, my lungs aching with the effort of it.

I should not think of that; it was not helpful.

I rang the bell and the maid answered, showing me into the study and saying that she would see if her master was at home. He was an ordinary man and an extraordinary man, all at the same time. He spoke like us, he knew what it was like to live as a plain person, and yet he lived in a great big white-painted house with a drawing room as well as a parlour and a study and who knew what besides, and he had a maid and a cook and probably someone else to clean his boots for him. He told me once that it was as well he did have a good house, for all the people who needed it; he meant visitors, men who came to preach, but I always thought that there were people in greater need of a warm bed and they were never to be found inside its walls.

For all that the house was fine and well-appointed, he kept the study plain: the walls were lined with bookcases, and he had a good oak desk, but beyond that, and a plain, threadbare couch, and a worn rug before the fire, there was little in the way of decoration.

'Thomas?' the reverend said, coming into the room and closing the door behind him. 'What is it? I expected you for supper, as we agreed. You are very early.'

'The inquest is adjourned,' I said, although I wasn't sure if that was the right word to use to describe the delay. 'They are waiting for the next witness.'

'Who is that, do you know?'

I shrugged.

'Whose testimony did you hear, then?'

He had not offered me a seat, but he had taken his, behind his desk; I stood before him, my hat in my hands, and I felt like a schoolboy waiting to be caned.

'Just Sergeant King's,' I said.

'And what did the good sergeant say?'

'He said he had seen Harriet walking out with a man one evening, but he could not say whom.'

He waited. 'Well, go on,' he said. 'What else?'

'Nothing else. Sergeant King was stood down. Then I came here. I am otherwise engaged for supper,' I said, haughtily.

'Tom,' he said.

I waited for him to continue.

'We used to be fine friends, Tom, you and I.'

I stared at him for a moment, not trusting myself to reply, and then I bade him good day, and went back to work.

Frances Williams

Having delayed for the arrival of the next witness, only the very curious, or those who could afford to be absent from their labours for a full afternoon, were in attendance at the later session of the inquest. The Reverend Mr Verrall, who to my knowledge had been in attendance at every meeting of the jury, was conspicuous by his absence. As well as myself, Jane Humphrey, Lottie Beezley and a few others I did not know, there were some I thought to be newspapermen, taking notes, no doubt to satisfy themselves with the filthy sensationalism brought about by the death of a young woman.

I shan't say innocent, for she was not. The space between losing her and where I now stood had widened like a chasm; the Harriet on the other side was scarcely recognisable to me, now. She had courted Tom Churcher, or, more precisely, she had allowed him to pay court to her, knowing that she was in a desperate situation and that he, a single man, could help her out of it. Had she even thought about Emma Milstead? Had she thought about me?

As the jury arranged themselves and the bodies in front of me cleared I noticed that a woman was already sitting on the seat in front of the coroner's table, and there, standing close by, was Richard Field. This, then, must be Maria. She was dressed in a blue silk gown, with a dark wool coat over it, and a straw bonnet tied with a black velvet ribbon. From my position I could see but little of her, just a pale cheek and a small, sharp nose, but then she turned to a noise behind her and I caught a glimpse of a frightened little face, with pale eyes that were perhaps blue, or grey. She seemed very young. She did not look unwell, I thought, given the extraordinary efforts it had taken to bring her here. But then I caught something in the stiffness of her movements and I realised that her coat served to disguise what must surely be a pregnancy.

She was not asked to stand for her oath, but allowed to take it sitting down, which she did in a voice that began timidly and grew only a little in strength. She gave her name as Mrs Maria Field, and her address as King Street, London.

'Please tell us how you knew the deceased,' began the coroner; his usual opening for every new witness. He barely looked up as he said it.

'We taught at the same school, in Hackney,' Maria said. 'We became fast friends almost straight away, and remained so.'

'And she also formed a friendship with your husband, is that correct?'

Maria hesitated. I saw the bonnet move to show that she glanced to her right, to Richard, and his mouth twitched in the briefest of smiles. 'Indeed. We lodged together with my husband before our marriage, and afterwards she was a regular visitor at our house in London.'

'Were you at all aware of the deceased's pregnancy?'

'I was not aware. I noticed that over the course of the latter part of the year she appeared to increase in size, but I had not the least suspicion that she was with child.'

'Did you ever have any indication of there being any intimacy between her and any young man?'

Maria Field replied that she had not.

'Can you tell us how you were made aware of the death of your friend?'

At this, Richard Field stepped forward and produced a letter, which he handed to the coroner, who cast his eyes over it for a moment. It was from Mr Verrall, and Field said he had received it on the 9th of November, three days after Harriet's death. The letter was read out to the court.

There was no disputing it had been written by Verrall; full of pomposity and religious rhetoric, the effect of it was to inform the Fields that Harriet had been found dead, and therefore would not be visiting them in London after all, prior to her onward journey to Arundel. He had clearly felt compelled to elucidate his theory that Harriet's death did not involve a third party but was caused, of all things, by *excitement* at having obtained the situation at Arundel, having been so long without.

Was I the only person in the room who thought this utterly preposterous? That someone should fall down and die, because they were happy, and looking forward to the future? And at the same moment he seemed already to be entertaining his later theory – at odds with the first – that Harriet was unhappy and swallowed poison to end her own life. What was she, Mr Verrall? Was she happy, or unhappy? Or perhaps she had no expectation at all that she was about to meet such a horrific end. Such desperation in the man, to distract minds away from the word *murder* and away from the place where Harriet was found … and to place the blame at Harriet's own feet, rather than looking elsewhere for it!

Harriet. Her name was so seldom spoken in that room. Instead, she was 'the deceased', as if her whole life had been reduced to nothing so interesting as the method of her leaving it. But she had been young, happy, intelligent, brave, always as willing to learn as she was to teach. She had had everything to look forward to, and then a man had caused her to fall, and a man had killed her for it. What else was there to discuss?

Wednesday, 18th February, 1846

Reverend George Verrall

William Rose, solicitor, arrived at a quarter to two, just moments after Jessie had cleared away the luncheon plates. I excused myself from Sarah, and retired to the study to receive my visitor.

'Good God, man,' he said, 'you look quite dreadful.'

Unlike many, Mr Rose has never felt the need to moderate his language when I am with him. That directness is, at least in part, why I felt able to trust him with the lengthy document that he now had presumably stored in a safe place, pending my need for it. I did not ask after it on this occasion. If the Lord should will it, perhaps we should never need to speak of it again.

'I am quite well, thank you,' I said.

'You look as though you have wrestled with the very Devil himself half the night.'

He was almost correct: at some dark hour, Sarah had shaken me to wakefulness.

What? What is it?

You were shouting, she said. *Again.*

Not I, I denied, but the tangled bedsheets and the perspiration that soaked me were testament to the nightmare that had disturbed me. I had lain there awhile longer, hearing Sarah's breathing deepen, and then I'd got up and dressed in the dark. As I did so, the clock in the hallway chimed for five. I had gone down to the study where the grate was still barely warm, lit the lamps and sat at my desk, listening out for Mrs

Burton and Jessie, beginning their day in the kitchen. As always, I had been almost surprised to find my study as I had left it, for it had been the same dream that haunted me: men, searching; throwing my papers around, destroying books, turning over the desk, emptying drawers, and all the while the bottle marked POISON on the mantelpiece, growing bigger each time I saw it.

'Shall we?'

Rose, treating my study as his study, had seated himself on the sofa and withdrawn a notebook and a silver pencil from his case. I sat at my desk and prepared my own notebook.

'Carttar arrived at eleven o'clock,' Rose said, 'and he remained closeted with the jury for upwards of an hour. Upon the room being opened, I made myself known to him and told him that I was a solicitor, and I was here to represent your interests and those of the chapel. I said that you considered that the newspaper reports had placed an improper interpretation upon your words, previously uttered before the inquest, to suggest that you had intended to leave Bromley as soon as the enquiry was over. Such was not the fact, I said. You merely meant that you had no intention of departing Bromley to another part of the country whilst the investigation was still under way, in case your assistance should be required for it. I said that you had been excluded from the room and the assumption made by other parties as a result of this was that you were a party to the death of a young woman.'

'What said he to that?'

'He said that I was assuming a point they had not yet arrived at, and your exclusion from the room was only in common with all the other witnesses.' He paused, and a strange sort of a smile played about his lips before he added, 'As well you know.'

'But he allowed you to remain, as my representative?'

Rose reclined further in his seat and crossed his legs.

'He said I was as free to listen as any other member of the public. He even offered me a seat.'

the man is the very devil
I am certain of it

'Well, then,' I said, 'tell me of the proceedings.'

'The first witness was a ...' he consulted his notes ' ... Dr Leeson, who declared himself a physician at St Thomas's Hospital, and a lecturer on chemistry and forensic medicine. He deposed that he had conducted an independent analysis on the remainder of the stomach contents handed to him by the surgeon, Mr James Ilott, and that he had similarly conducted experiments on the bottle found in the night soil, to ascertain whether it had ever contained prussic acid.'

'And?'

'I will not trouble you with the details, fascinating as they are. Suffice to say that the stomach contained in the region of thirty-five grains of prussic acid, around three-quarters of a grain being sufficient to kill an adult. She would have died almost instantaneously. Certainly within seconds.'

'And the phial?'

'Now,' Rose said, uncrossing his legs and leaning forward, 'that is also very interesting. It turns out that the phial contained sal ammoniac, dried up: common smelling salts, discarded by their owner when the efficacy of the preparation ceased for want of lime water. Definitely no prussic acid.'

'We knew that from Ilott,' I said.

'Ah, but Dr Leeson had an interesting point to add, in that the salts found in the phial would react *with* prussic acid, and render that substance inert. In other words, the phial could not have contained prussic acid, for, if it had, the poison would have had no, or at least little, ill effect upon the person taking it.'

I found my mind was whirling with this news, considering whether it might be plausible that Harriet had intended to drink the poison and then revive herself with an antidote but found it dried up … but no. She could not have had such rare scientific knowledge. The phial's being found in the night soil was nothing more than a dreadful coincidence.

'But you should not trouble yourself with that, Verrall. The next witness, however, was of rather greater concern.'

'Who was it?' I asked.

Rose went back to his notebook. 'One Martha Coote. Do you know her?'

I shook my head. I had heard the name previously – she lives in Widmore, I believe – but I had not made her acquaintance.

'She declared she was coming to Bromley on the night of the 6th, in the company of her brother-in-law, to fetch her husband from his club. She cannot be sure of the time, so many months having now elapsed. As she reached Widmore Lane, just before the chapel, she saw a man running down the middle of the lane very fast.'

'From the chapel?'

'From the direction of the chapel, although she did not see exactly where he came from. Just that he was running in the middle of the lane, away from the town. Towards, in fact, this very house.'

'And others besides,' I said.

'Not very many others at all,' he said.

what are you driving at, man?

'It could have been any man,' I said. 'She could have made it up, for the sensation of it.'

'Indeed.' He steepled his fingers, regarding me with a steady gaze.

'Did she recognise the man?'

'She did not, but the brother-in-law, apparently, thought it was a man named Wilson. However …' he consulted his notes once more ' …the witness enquired of Wilson's wife the next day, only to be told that Wilson had not been out.'

she saw me

or perhaps she saw Tom Churcher running for me

'There we are; probably it's a dispute between them. An opportunity for a score to be settled.'

Rose nodded slowly, looking doubtful. I breathed out heavily, wondering if I needed to remind Rose that I was paying him handsomely for this; he should reserve his opinions for his private moments.

'Finally there came James Churcher,' he said.

'Senior?'

'No – the son. Tom Churcher's brother.'

'What on earth did he have to do with anything?'

'He deposed that his brother Thomas was at home on the Monday night, ill, and was in bed at nine o'clock...'

that is a lie

'...and that he has no recollection of having seen Mr Verrall on that day, and that they all have a clear conscience, and can answer any questions.'

'The coroner asked him if he had seen me?'

'He did.'

'You see what I mean, Rose? The man has me at the very head of his list of suspects. Why else should he ask that, of a witness who had no interaction with Harriet before her death, nor any part in the finding of her? To ask whether he had seen *me* that day – why? What is he getting at?'

'Calm yourself, man,' he said, perfectly reasonably.

I sat for a moment, checking myself, allowing the fire to dissipate. Eventually, I said, 'What else?'

'That is all,' he said. 'They adjourned for dinner. They meet again at four; I assume you wish me to be there?'

'I shall attend in person,' I said, determined.

'George, I must advise...'

'What? That I should sit back and let the coroner blacken my name?'

'I am sure he has no such intention.'

289

'On the contrary: he seems determined to find my hand in every small detail of the case. The testimonial, for example ...'

'Ah,' said Rose. 'I wondered when you would come to that.'

'They are suggesting that I wrote to the board recommending Harriet for the position at Arundel, and I did not.'

'Really, George, that is such a trifle. As you said, a small detail. Why should it matter if you did or you did not?'

I pointed my pen at him. 'Because it is impugning my reputation, Rose. He wishes to prove that I knew Harriet was with child; that is fair enough, for she confided in me, and I counselled her as a true Christian and a shepherd would; but to then suggest that I wrote a letter recommending her – a single woman, with child – for a position as a teacher! It is unthinkable!'

At last Rose seemed to see the truth of it, for the half-smile dropped from his face.

'Well, perhaps you should make that point,' he said, after a moment, 'if it will satisfy your conscience.'

my conscience damn you

it is the truth

I breathed hard, staring at Rose and thinking him a smug bastard and wishing in that moment that I had never thought to employ him. I stared and waited, and after a moment I stood.

'Will you accompany me?' I asked.

Frances Williams

Outside the Swan's brewhouse, I saw Richard Field standing on his own, smoking a pipe. He was causing something of a stir amongst the others waiting, all of them standing in groups and gossiping, occasionally glancing across at him.

Let them gossip, I thought, and approached him.

'Miss Williams,' he said. 'Are you well?'

'Very well, Mr Field. I am surprised to see you still in Bromley. Unless you are called once more?'

He knocked his pipe out against the wall of the inn, stamping on the embers. 'I have resolved to attend until the verdict,' he said.

'Indeed? And Mrs Field?'

'Ah. You may have noticed she is near her confinement.'

'I believe I did notice,' I replied. 'My congratulations to you both.'

'Our second child,' he said.

'Yes.' The first, of course, had been born not long before Harriet's death. I had heard all about that child, after all.

'Maria has returned to London,' he said. 'But she is just as keen to hear the results of this miserable business. We are hopeful that the police will be able to uncover the guilty party.'

I stood for a moment with him, looking at a group of three young women who were standing close by, heads together. I recognised the tallest of them: Millicent Judds. I had taught her, and Mr Campling her four brothers, all of them difficult to manage. Millie once threw her slate at another girl, and had to be caned.

'I wish I had your optimism, Mr Field,' I said.

'You do not share my opinion?'

'I fear the police have made up their minds,' I said.

At that very moment Tom Churcher appeared, with his brother and his father flanking him. The attention of the assembled townspeople turned from myself and Field to them, for they looked purposeful and determined. Tom looked white-faced and wild, as if he was minded to fly at someone's throat.

The door opened, and the assistant called for the public to be admitted. We filed in.

'Do you think we shall have a verdict today?' I asked Richard Field, who had accompanied me to the side of the room.

'Who knows?' he replied.

The coroner called for order. Verrall was summoned to repeat his oath. I had not noticed him in the crowd, which caused me to think that, perhaps, he had been inside the room all along, speaking to the coroner in private. I found that thought disturbing.

'Mr Verrall,' said the coroner, with a voice that suggested great forbearance.

'I had wished to clarify a point made at an earlier sitting of the jury,' he said, looking towards the men seated under the window, and showing them his teeth in an approximation of a smile.

'Very well,' the coroner said, looking over the notes upon the table.

'I have been giving the matter careful thought, and I have no recollection of giving Harriet Monckton a testimonial for the Arundel school.'

The coroner referred to the assistant, who shuffled through the papers and produced a document, which the coroner then read aloud.

'*Bromley, Kent. To the Committee of the Arundel Infant School. Miss Harriet Monckton, who is a candidate for the office of teacher, has been a member of the church under my pastoral care since August 1836 and has conducted herself with great propriety. I beg to recommend her to your confidence as one fully adapted to fill so important a station. Wishing you God speed in your laudable endeavours to train up the little ones to be useful members of society and to share at length as heirs of immortality, I am, yours truly, George Verrall, Pastor of the Independent Church assembling in Bromley Chapel.*' He looked up. 'This is the testimonial to which you refer?'

'Indeed,' said Verrall.

'This was found by Inspector Meadows in the deceased's box, and in the deceased's handwriting, as if she had made a copy of it before posting.'

Verrall appeared not to have heard him. His cheek was pale, the sheen of perspiration visible on his forehead even from my position some distance away. He continued, 'I have no recollection of having written such a document to the committee of the Arundel school. Although the letter is in my style, and indeed I recall having written a similar letter to the promoters of a school at St Albans, where the deceased was formerly engaged.'

There were murmurings in the room, as the assembled audience considered this.

'Did you send your testimonial directly to the St Albans school, Mr Verrall?'

'I did.'

I frowned. I had seen the document myself in Harriet's hand, before she sent it to the school. Why should he lie? Perhaps it was not the proper thing to do, to give a character directly to the person to whom it related. Proper behaviour was certainly something the Reverend George Verrall would be concerned about.

'How, then, could the deceased have obtained it?'

His eyes widened slightly. He looked trapped.

'I do not know. Perhaps she requested it to be forwarded on to her, to use again.'

The coroner stared at him for a moment, then asked if he had anything further to add. Verrall did not, and he was dismissed. I thought then Carttar would move to adjourn the proceedings, for he examined his pocket watch and turned to his assistant, but at that moment Tom Churcher stepped forward.

'Mr Churcher?' said the coroner. 'You have something to say?'

'If I am permitted,' he said.

'You are free to speak,' the coroner said.

For a moment he stood and I fancied he was trembling with some great inner turmoil. Like Verrall, he looked pale, and thinner than I had seen him. For a dreadful moment I thought he was about to confess to it. He had that look about him: a man who had had his life wrenched asunder and wished only to be done with it.

'I have had a very painful charge made against me, sir,' he said. His voice was low, and unsteady.

'By whom?'

'By Inspector Meadows and Superintendent Pearce. I wish to inform you, sir, and the jury, that I have been charged with attempting to frustrate the ends of justice.'

The coroner said he had heard nothing of any charge.

'Certain officers have been sent down by the government to investigate the affair, and asked me for information. I refused to speak to them, sir, for I have answered all questions to you, sir, and to the jury directly, and I have spoken to Sergeant King, and I ... have had ... enough of it ...' His voice did not rise or fall, but remained on a level, as if he was desperately trying to keep control of his emotions. 'As would I daresay you, or the jury, or any man in this room, if they had been ... if they had been *pursued* ... to this degree.'

The coroner looked at a man standing at the side of the room, whom I recognised as one of the London police detectives. 'Inspector?'

The man stepped forward and stood by the side of Tom, who would not raise his head or turn to look at him.

'I regret to say, sir,' said the inspector, 'that Mr Churcher has been most reluctant to afford information.'

Before the coroner could speak, Tom looked at the inspector for the first time and burst out, 'You are no gentleman, sir! You are no gentleman! I am willing to state all I know.'

'Mr Churcher, please,' said the coroner.

Tom contained himself and spoke, his voice now shaking with the effort. 'I have been shamefully treated. And the reason I declined to give information was that I have already done so, as I said, to Sergeant King, and to the inquest. And because the London policemen would not allow my father to be present at the interview ...'

'You are a grown man, sir – why should you need your father there?' The coroner spoke harshly, I thought, as a man who did not know Tom Churcher; if he had known him as we all did, he should have been more understanding.

Tom looked sulky now, his head down. 'Because I know well enough that all men are not honest men,' he said, 'and my father is better at telling them apart than I.'

Perhaps this statement struck the coroner as a true one, for he appeared to soften. He told Tom that his concerns had been noted, and that he was free to step down.

At that, he was about to clear the room, but of course Verrall had not yet been permitted to have the final word, and he raised his hand.

'Mr Verrall?' the coroner asked, with a heavy sigh.

Verrall stepped forward once more. He looked composed this time; the desperation of his earlier statement had dissipated.

'Just to add, sir, that on reflection I feel certain that the testimonial referred to is the one I addressed to St Albans, which must somehow have been obtained by the deceased, and copied.'

He did not wait to be dismissed, but bowed his head to the coroner and returned to his place at the back of the room, with all eyes upon him. The coroner addressed the jury, thanked them for their forbearance, and asked for some time alone with them prior to an adjournment.

'This will be a long adjournment,' Richard Field said, as we walked back towards the town.

'You are certain of that?' I asked. 'How so?'

295

'If it is to be a matter of days, he tells the court when they will next assemble,' he said. 'I have noticed this. I feel certain it will be a few weeks.'

I did not respond, thinking of Emily, and going home to Shifnal. 'We may then not see the verdict delivered after all,' I said.

'On the contrary,' he said. 'I will return whenever they next meet. I have to see this dreadful business to its conclusion. For Harriet.'

For Harriet. 'What of Maria?' I asked. 'What if your child comes?'

He breathed deeply. 'Well, then I shall have to forgo the hearing. God willing, the conclusion will be soon.'

We had reached the White Hart, where we would part company. I felt ambivalent towards him now. At first I had thought him a vile man for his treatment of my dear friend. Now, I thought of Harriet as someone who had allowed circumstances to overtake her, and afterwards had made things worse by using other people. Perhaps Richard, too, had been similarly used.

'Harriet spoke of you often,' I said.

Something crossed his face, a ghost of an expression. Fear? Or was it loss, hearing her name spoken?

'She wrote to me of you, too,' he said, smiling, the momentary lapse of control passed. 'And I find you are quite as she described. What was it she called you? Her warrior? I feel she was right; an apt description.' He offered me his hand, and I took it. 'Goodbye, Miss Williams.'

'Goodbye, Mr Field. No doubt we will meet again soon enough,' I said. 'My best wishes to Mrs Field.'

He went into the hotel and I stood there for a moment, feeling an inexplicable unease. Then I returned to the Bell, and enquired of Miss Davis whether she could send a boy to ask for a seat upon the last London coach.

Saturday, 21st February, 1846

Thomas Churcher

The fat detective called at our house again in the evening, when Emma was in the parlour. I told him at the door that I still had nothing to say.

'I regret that we are obliged to persist with our enquiries,' he said, or something like that, not smiling.

'I shall answer no more questions,' I said. 'I have spoken to the coroner about the way you have hounded and persecuted me, and I shall talk to you no further.'

'Thing is, Mr Churcher,' he said, 'Mr Pearce and myself, we weren't fortunate enough to be present at the first inquest, and I just wish to be satisfied on one or two points.'

'I have satisfied the coroner,' I said, 'and his man wrote everything down. You should go and ask to read it.'

I was about to shut the door in his face when Emma came through into the hallway, her face white apart from two high spots of colour on her cheeks. 'Tom. Ask the man inside. I will not have our business discussed on the doorstep.'

I stared at him so he should know that I was unhappy about the invitation, but I opened the door wide and let him in. Emma took him into the parlour and bade him be seated, and I stood in the doorway until she said, 'Sit down and answer the man's questions, for pity's sake, Tom, so that we can all be done with it.'

I sat, and looked at him. Emma went back to the kitchen.

'What time did you leave the chapel that night?' he asked.

I breathed in. 'About a quarter past five o'clock,' I said. 'I had been there to put up my music, and then I took the keys to Beezley's, and then I went to my grandmother's.'

'And you went to Miss Williams's house later on?'

'With my sister. I have said all this.'

'What time did you go there?'

'I shall not repeat myself again,' I said, getting to my feet. Truth was, I could not for the life of me remember the exact timings of that night nor what I had said over two years ago.

He grumbled something about co-operation and taking care of matters properly but our evening and our house had been disturbed enough by his intrusion. I could feel my hands curling themselves into fists. I stood close behind him, ushering him to the door.

I could hear Emma banging and crashing in the kitchen, scraping the chairs on the tiled floor and slamming drawers closed in the dresser. I waited outside until my breathing had returned to normal before I went in. She would not speak to me at first, and I thought she was angry at him, the detective, but it turned out I was wrong.

'You pathetic little fellow,' she said. 'I'm so ashamed of you! How should you not just answer his questions? Why can you not just tell him what he needs to know? Tell him the truth and be done with it!'

I did not respond, but stood there waiting for it to be over.

She pointed a shaking finger at my face. 'Or is the truth not something you can tell? What *is* the truth, Tom Churcher? Can you even tell me? I don't believe you killed her, so help me, because you're too afraid of your own shadow to do anything like that to anybody, but you were up to something that night, I know it. *I know it!* You did something that you won't tell me, and for all you said that baby wasn't yours I don't believe you didn't have your hands up that girl's skirts because I saw the way you looked at her. You – you just about drooled over her when she came back from London! You couldn't leave her alone, and all the while you said you were in love with me?'

I looked at her face, twisted with rage, spittle on her lower lip.

'You had better think of something to say, Tom, to satisfy those detectives, because they can see right through you and so can I and we all know you're hiding something. I'm sick of trying to protect you when you won't even help yourself, you cowering excuse for a man! Heaven help this babe of mine, with you for a father.'

She carried on for a while, slamming and shouting. I listened but did not listen. It would not last forever. In the morning she would be sorry. She always was.

Thursday, 5th March, 1846

Richard Field

Contrary to her previous assertion, Frances Williams was not present at the next meeting of the jury.

I had been warned of the meeting by William Pawley, landlord at the White Hart, who had promised to inform me of any developments in the case after my return to London. I wondered if Miss Williams lacked a similar source of information in the town.

The first witness called was Clara Churcher. I could not recall having heard her testimony before, and I hoped she had something worthwhile to say. She appeared in a plain dress of a dark green fabric, with a dark satin sash about her waist, and a bonnet lined with green silk. The effect of it, against her hair, was really rather beautiful.

She was first sworn, and then asked about her family. She stated that her family consisted of herself, a sister, and four brothers, John, Henry, Thomas, and James. The two former had not lived at home for some years, and Tom had left home upon his marriage, a year and a half ago.

'Please tell us how you knew the deceased,' asked the coroner.

'I have known Harriet for many years, but I came to know her better recently, as she helped me with the Sunday School at the chapel, when she was between situations.'

'And what do you recall about the circumstances of her death?'

'The last time I saw her alive was on Monday, the day before

300

her body was discovered. I saw her in Miss Williams's apartments around six o'clock that evening. Miss Williams was ill, and there was very little conversation about anything but her illness.'

Here Clara Churcher looked about the room, as if she was expecting to see Frances Williams there, and was almost relieved that she was not.

'Please continue,' the coroner said.

'I left Harriet with Miss Williams, and promised to return, to bring her some spirits, to relieve the spasms under which she was suffering. But at home I felt suddenly unwell myself, and so I sent my brother to take the spirits in my stead.'

'Your brother Tom?'

'Yes. He had come to Miss Williams's room to walk me home, and after that he took back the spirits.'

'Were you aware of any attachment the deceased had with another person?'

'I was not.'

'Not even your brother Tom?'

She hesitated, then, and appeared to summon up some inner reserve to enable her to continue. 'Tom is a kind man. He walks home with anyone who asks him. Nothing is meant by it, no matter what the people of the town might say.'

'You do not believe he was courting her?'

'No, sir, I do not. On the contrary, Tom was promised to another, who is now his wife. Everyone knew it. Harriet knew it. And besides ... '

She hesitated, and the coroner pressed her to continue.

'I merely wished to say, sir, that Harriet used to speak as if there was nobody in Bromley good enough for her.'

I felt my heart twist a little, at that. It reminded me of something Harriet had said to me once. That she should not meet anyone she loved as well as me. But that was the old Harriet, of course. The good, kind Harriet. Not the hypocrite, the harlot, the betrayer.

'Miss Churcher, could we please now turn to the events of Monday evening? After you returned home, did your brother follow soon after, having delivered the spirits to Miss Williams?'

'Indeed, sir. My father and all the family were in bed by nine o'clock. Tom came back about half-past eight, and did not go out after.'

'And how can you be certain that he did not leave the house after you all retired?'

She hesitated, again, and then told a most curious tale.

'We all slept, and then, in the middle of the night, I was awoken by a noise, which I fancied was the gate at the back of the house moving. And I was frightened, and went into my father's room, where Tom and my brother James also slept. I called for my father, and told him of my alarm, but he said it was nonsense as the house had been properly secured, and the wind must have shook the gate. I went back to bed, sir, but could not settle, and so I caused him, my father that is, to go downstairs with Tom, and I got a candle and lit them down; everything was safe.'

'You are quite certain,' the coroner asked, 'that Tom was asleep in the room when you first went in?'

'Yes, sir.'

The room was silent, holding its collective breath. To me, despite her assertion, the explanation was clear: Tom Churcher had gone out, when the whole family was asleep, and upon returning to the house had made a noise which had disturbed his sister.

And then she turned that theory quite on its head.

'The following day my alarm was much on my mind, and I spoke of it to Mrs Allen, our neighbour in the house next door to ours. Mrs Allen said that I should not be alarmed, for her husband was in the habit of getting up in the night and making a noise.'

The coroner made a note.

'And your brother Tom: what is the nature of his association with Mr Verrall?'

'They are very intimate friends,' she said, and looked to say more, but stopped herself.

'What have you heard Mr Verrall say on the subject?'

'Only that he wished it could be found out,' Clara said, 'as do we all.'

At this the coroner considered his notes once more, and finding nothing further to ask, dismissed Clara Churcher. The next to be called was her father, James Churcher. I had seen him regularly about the town; a handsome man, in his senior years now beginning to stoop, which gave him a deferential appearance. His voice, however, was strong and resonant, and the people gathered were quiet when he spoke. His testimony, however, was but brief: he replied to the coroner that his daughter had been entirely correct. All the family were in bed, asleep, by nine o'clock on the night Harriet died, and to the best of his knowledge, other than checking the door was secure, they had all remained in their beds.

Next called was Mary Ann Hopperton, whose daughter Elizabeth had spoken at the workhouse on the same day I gave my testimony, about having seen Harriet pass by that evening. On this occasion the mother was examined, and said that her daughter's previous deposition had been incomplete.

'In what regard?' asked the coroner.

'Elizabeth neglected to state that she had also seen young Tom Churcher pass our house two or three times on that night, the last time being about a quarter of an hour after the deceased had passed towards the chapel.'

'Why did she not say this when she was called to appear?' asked the coroner.

'For fear that it might bring Tom Churcher into trouble, and if innocent that she should be blamed, sir.'

'It is the business of the jury to decide the relevance of any facts, Mrs Hopperton. All that is required of the witness

– as stated in the oath – is that you should tell the truth, and omit nothing.'

'She's very sorry about it now, sir.'

'Did she tell anyone else about seeing Mr Churcher on the night of the 6th?'

'Only Mr Sweeting, sir. She had mentioned it at an early stage of the investigation, and some conversation took place between them.'

'What conversation?'

'You should need to ask her, sir.'

'Or, indeed, Mr Sweeting, whom I see is in the room. Thank you, Mrs Hopperton, unless you have any further revelations, you may step down.'

Accordingly, Sweeting was called.

The coroner reprimanded him for not stating the circumstance at the time, and asked if he had anything further to add to Mrs Hopperton's testimony as regards his conversation with her daughter. He said that he remembered the conversation but indistinctly, and thought that he had said to her to pay it no mind. He said if he should have the same conversation with her today, perhaps he should direct her rather differently.

The coroner asked him what he meant by that.

Sweeting replied, 'When first questioned, sir, about the finding of the body, I was in a state of some distress, as I am sure you can imagine. The searching for Miss Monckton and the finding of her is, or should I say was, rather confused in my mind. But now, sir, having had a proper time to reflect upon it, I thought that it was rather strange, that Tom Churcher should suggest the chapel as a place to look for her.'

'Why should that be strange?'

'Well, sir, because all day people had been searching. The chapel should really have been one of the first places, as the deceased was accustomed to going there. One would assume, sir, that it was as searched as searched could be. And yet

Tom Churcher led me in that direction, and told me that we should look, and he tested the gate, and to my surprise – and apparently his surprise too, although I can't rightly be certain as he was surprised at all, come to think of it – the gate was open and he let me go first down the passage, and so I was the first to find the body.'

He gave a dramatic shudder and raised his eyes to the ceiling, as if some sort of relief from his distress might be found there.

'You think Tom Churcher intended you to find the body?'

'The more I think of it, sir, the more certain I am that he knew what was to be found there, and didn't want to be the one to find it, lest suspicion should fall on him. Far rather it should fall on me, a respectable married man, and a deacon of the chapel! I cannot speak to him, or any of his family.'

The coroner breathed a heavy sigh. He asked if Sweeting had anything further to add that was of a factual nature and not supposition, and Sweeting said he had not, at present.

The business thus completed, the coroner adjourned the jury for a further fortnight, and I was about in time to catch the last coach to London.

Wedged between two ladies and their voluminous skirts, I had plenty of time during that dark journey to think about the course of events, and I found my thoughts tending to Miss Williams. What would she have made of it all? I wondered whether she might appreciate a letter from me, but then I realised that I had no address to which I could send such a letter. Perhaps I could send it care of the school, at Shifnal? How many schools could there be in a small Shropshire town? And then I thought that such a personal letter was probably not to be entrusted to a vague address. And perhaps the next meeting would, after all, be the last; it felt to me that the business of the jury had descended into gossip and supposition, and could not possibly be helpful to the outcome.

Thursday, 19th March, 1846

Richard Field

With each sitting of the jury, having to leave Maria grew harder and harder. She was not alone; she had a nurse with her permanently now, both to keep the boy occupied and to assist his mother, now that the second child was expected. God willing, there should still be a few weeks before the birth of our second child might trouble us, but the sooner the jury were directed to reach a verdict, the better.

'Must you go, Richard?' she had asked, her eyes pleading.

'It should not be too much longer. Perhaps this next sitting will produce the verdict,' I said, kissing the top of her head.

'You have said that each time,' she said. 'And still nothing. Perhaps there will never be one.'

I assured her that there had to be a verdict, as the government had insisted that one should be brought, and that the coroner was only exercising diligence, and for that we should at least be grateful. Whatever had happened to her, Harriet deserved to have her story told.

'But that's just it,' she said. 'It's *not* Harriet, is it? Not our Harriet. It's some manufactured creature, that exists only for this blessed inquest: something to be summoned up like a spirit, to be examined and pored over, to be sneered at and judged. Harriet deserves to be remembered as she was to us, not picked at like carrion.'

She apologised a minute later, but it was too late. All the way to Bromley I had that image in my mind, of our Harriet, being consumed by the vicious vultures of the town. Perhaps Maria was right: she deserved to be remembered, as she was, loved by us both, once upon a time; and not as she had been latterly.

To banish the distressing thoughts from my head, I gazed out of the coach window as the dawn began to brighten the sky, and allowed myself a brief reminiscence: Harriet in my bed. Maria – she was not my wife then – had gone out, taking the maid with her, to see her dressmaker about a new gown. It was the cook's half-day. Harriet had come to my study, and, wordlessly, had placed her arms about my neck, and kissed my cheek.

I think I said her name. I did not ask her to desist; on the contrary. I turned to face her and placed my hands upon her bodice, and she stopped me and asked me to take her to bed.

She had been distant with me, and a little sad, and there were days that she seemed to avoid our company, allowing us to be alone, even knowing, perhaps, what that would mean. I might have assumed that she had found another lover, but I knew that was not the case, for I am certain she would have told me.

So. Maria was at the dressmakers, and not expected back for an hour or more. We took full advantage of the empty house. She was intoxicating to me in a way that she had never been during our previous times together. She was glorious, and colourful, her skin so lustrous it glowed in the bright, hot light of the bedroom. Her hair, loosened, was shining and soft in my hands. Her eyes, her white teeth, her cheeks – I could go on. Harriet had never been plain, but on that one occasion she was a siren, a temptress; utterly irresistible.

Afterwards we lay beside each other and talked, and I confess it crossed my mind briefly that I had fallen in love with the wrong girl. I had thought Maria was the only woman to marry, and now here was Harriet, who had been such a joy, such an intelligent, kind, thoughtful friend, as well as a generous lover – why had I never thought to make her my wife? I had nearly admitted this very curious thought to her, aloud. I am glad I did not. Perhaps she knew my affection towards her had changed; perhaps this was the moment she decided to quit London and return to the town of her birth, for I remember her face darkening just as a cloud passed over the sun, outside. She said, 'We must dress, for Maria will be home sooner than we think,' and we washed, and dressed, and Harriet went to the kitchen to prepare some supper for us all, and then Maria was home, and no further connection passed between us. A day or so later, with very little discussion between us, she moved back to Bromley, and in doing so she gave me unspoken permission to pursue Maria, and make her mine.

The Swan was as busy as ever when I arrived, and as usual we were made to wait outside the brewhouse door whilst the coroner remained in consultation with the two London police detectives. Outside, there was much discussion about what this might mean; that perhaps an arrest was imminent. Clara Churcher was there, waiting, with a young man who looked so much like Tom Churcher that he was likely to be the brother. Of Tom Churcher himself, there was no sign.

We were called in, and to begin proceedings Clara Churcher was called. She said that she wished to make some corrections in her former evidence as to her knowledge of the deceased having any particular attachment. With that, she cast a glance nervously about the room, fixed her eyes upon me for a second, and then returned her attention to the coroner. This, of course, gave me due warning as to what she was about to say.

'I recall the deceased once told me that she had a letter from Mr Richard Field, inviting her to lodge at his house when she took up her position at the school upon whose board he was a governor. She showed me the letter; I thought his tone was very free. I told her I thought it was wrong, that she had better remain at home and assist her mother. I asked her if Mr Field was a married man.'

The coroner looked up, at this, and glanced about the room. His eyes, like the witnesses, alighted on me. I wondered with some degree of foreboding if I was about to be recalled.

'Go on, Miss Churcher,' he said.

'Harriet – sorry, sir, the deceased – she said with a jolly laugh that this Richard Field might well try to seduce her, but that he was as old as her father.'

That sounded very much like Harriet, to me. Those assembled in the room whispered and shuffled, and I felt eyes upon me. Clara was thanked, and dismissed, and as she walked past me her cheeks were flushed. She did not look at me.

I understood. At the last inquest, the tide had turned against her brother, and this was her defence of him: to implicate another, as best she could, within the boundaries of truth. She had not lied; but the testimony did not add anything to the evidence; it was hearsay as much as the rest of it. They had no proof – of anything – and at some point the coroner was going to have to make exactly that point to his poor beleaguered jury.

I should report the rest of the day's proceedings, but after Clara's declaration a kind of despondency came over me. I listened, and watched, and it seemed to me that a succession of witnesses were called forth to state that they had now remembered that they had seen Harriet in the company of Tom Churcher on the night of her death. A woman named Elliott had stated that her husband had told her that Churcher had been in the chapel in the afternoon, and that Harriet had also been there, on some spurious errand. Elliott himself, for some reason, was not called to confirm this story. In any case, it was scarcely relevant. I wondered if the coroner, or perhaps more significantly the jury, were at all convinced by what was, surely, mere speculation. Why should they only recall now, more than two years after the night in question, something so apparently memorable, given the circumstances? Two possibilities presented themselves: either they had, at the time, been so convinced that Tom Churcher could not possibly be the guilty party that they had utterly discounted the significance of his being in Harriet's company during the afternoon, and more importantly that night; or someone had convinced them to speak up against Tom Churcher now, perhaps at the very least to encourage the inquest to a final conclusion.

The Reverend Mr George Verrall, who struck me as the sort of man always to wish to have the final word, was called to the stand as the last witness of the day. A letter was produced; it had been addressed to the coroner. The contents of the letter, which were read aloud, were suggesting that the phial found in the night soil must surely have contained prussic acid, and suggesting that 'a competent chemist' should be directed to conduct an examination of it. The letter was signed 'Chemicus'.

A murmur went around the room, and eyes turned towards Verrall, as the assistant passed the letter to him. We all knew his opinions and his manner of phrasing well enough by now to know that he had written it. I fancied his usually pale complexion had darkened a little at hearing his words read aloud in front of the people of the town.

'Is this your handwriting, Mr Verrall?' asked the coroner.

Through his teeth, Verrall answered, 'It is not.'

'Then,' said the coroner, clearly enjoying his sport, 'if any person were to say that it is like your handwriting, and that the ink is such as you are in the habit of writing with, that would be false?'

'If a thousand persons were to say so, it would be false,' Verrall said, slightly raising his voice. 'There is no similarity to my handwriting.'

The coroner gave the tiniest of smiles, and whispered something to his assistant, who duly made a note.

Then Verrall was dismissed, and the room was cleared. We waited outside for upwards of an hour, and then the assistant came out to announce that the inquest was again adjourned. I went back to London, and to Maria, too tired to think about Harriet, and that long May afternoon.

Wednesday, 22nd April, 1846

Reverend George Verrall

Thomas Carter sent me a letter, stating that he had been called to attend an inquest in Bromley, and should be obliged for me to receive him for an hour or so prior to that event, to provide such explanation as I was able. Reluctantly, I agreed. I had been unwell for a week or more, a nasty rash creeping from my throat up to my face, causing my cheeks to appear reddened and sore. It was not a pleasant sight to behold, and yet it occurred to me that I could invite Carter to preach on Sunday, so that I should be able to remain at home and recover.

He duly arrived at the house, and his first comment upon seeing me was that I looked very ill, as though I had been happily unaware of the condition of my face. Before he even sat down, he told me that he had a prior engagement for the Sabbath and so he would be unable to preach at the chapel, although seeing me now he was sorry for it.

Peevish at having to appear before the congregation thus, I offered a quick prayer once more for healing and bade him sit.

'What's this all about, Verrall?' he asked, and his manner vexed me further.

I told him of the inquest and the prolonged delays with it, although he had been following the case closely in the newspapers. I told him that the reports I read were scant in their accuracy, as I had attended all sessions but one and had found the accounts of them to be very misleading. He knew why he had been called, of course: the testimony of Miss Williams, and her description of his 'free' manner with Harriet at the tea party.

I remembered the occasion much better now I had had time to give it careful thought. It had been my intention to hold a prayer meeting at my house, and I had invited a few carefully selected members of the congregation – Harriet, of course, was one – to meet and converse with Mr Carter in an atmosphere of prayer and contemplation. Tea was to be served, and cake. From the very beginning, Carter had sought her out. So vigorous was his pursuit of her, I wondered if she had somehow said something to him, about my own friendship with her; or if he had heard something odd in the way I had spoken to her. Anyway, she had him spellbound: within just a very few minutes they were fast friends, speaking to no one but each other. After the prayers, and a talk, they took tea and disappeared. I sought them out, and found them in the garden, walking on the path to the gate.

I should not like to think about that any more.

I walked with Carter to the Swan, and, as we arrived, in full hearing of those townsfolk crowded at the door, he said he thought it was a very poor little establishment, and was there really nowhere more suitable?

I did not answer. We waited inside as the jury settled in their seats and the coroner took his place. I thought momentarily back to that first inquest, and how I thought him then rather efficient, if a little pedestrian in his methods, and how much my opinion had altered since then. I loathed the man, absolutely abhorred him. I repented, and the Lord forgave, and yet at each sitting of the jury I found I hated him still a little bit more. In the end, I gave up the repenting, deciding to save it all until the verdict.

Carter was called to the stand, and sworn, and asked to state his name, address, and occupation.

'My name is Thomas Carter,' he said, 'and I reside at Fenny Stratford, Buckinghamshire, and I am a Baptist minister.'

'And did you reside there in 1843?'

'No, in 1843 I was living at Letton, in Somersetshire.'

'Prior to this afternoon, when did you last visit Bromley?'

'My last visit to Bromley was in August of that year, to see friends who are residing here. I came about four o'clock in the evening, and left about seven.'

'Who are these friends you mention?'

'I saw Mr Verrall, the family of the Churchers, Harriet Monckton, and many others.'

'How long had you been acquainted with the deceased in particular, and how did you become familiar to her?'

'As with my other acquaintances in this town, through the circumstance of my occasionally supplying the chapel. I had known Miss Monckton for some time before her death. I was in the occasional habit of corresponding with her.'

'Mr Carter, what was the nature of your correspondence?'

I saw him fluster a little, but he recovered quickly and replied, 'The correspondence I used to have with her was generally of a religious character, and, on occasion, about her changing her situation. I believe her to have been of a very religious character.'

'On your visit in August, where did you see her?'

'It was at her mother's house. Her sister was present all the time.'

'Thank you, Mr Carter. Were you aware that she was with child?'

'I was not,' he said, as if the very suggestion of it was an improper one. 'Nor did I suspect such a thing. She made no communication to me on the subject.'

'And prior to that August? You will have heard, Mr Carter, that the jury has been told of a tea meeting that took place at the Reverend George Verrall's home, several months before the deceased's death. Your presence there was noted.'

'Yes, I recall the tea meeting, and conversing there with the deceased,' he said.

'You are a married man, I believe. Was your wife present at this tea party?'

'She was not present. But my behaviour towards the young lady was, I assure you, beyond reproof.'

The coroner noted this. 'You will recall, Mr Carter, that in my letter inviting you to attend the inquest today I asked you to bring any copies of your correspondence with the deceased; have you done so?'

Carter duly handed a letter to the assistant, which was passed to the hands of the coroner.

'Is this the manner in which you were generally accustomed to address this young woman?'

Carter fumbled. 'Possibly it might be,' he said.

The coroner then read aloud the letter. It began, '*My dear girl*', and went on to describe how he proposed '*to myself the pleasure of a scant half-hour of your company*'. It was a foolish letter, overbearing, pompous and repetitive, and it met with more than one snigger from the witnesses present.

'And your visit to Bromley today, Mr Carter. Have you paid a call to anyone in the town, before attending the inquest?'

'I arrived in London from Fenny Stratford last night, and came here this morning, direct; I have not called upon anyone since I came here.'

The coroner dismissed Carter, who came straight to me at the back of the room, the fool, all smiles. Superintendent Pearce then said he had wished to bring forward Miss Williams, who was at present at Shifnal, in Shropshire, again, but she had not appeared; and so the inquest was once more adjourned, the room was cleared, and we all trooped out to the darkening sky. Carter was anxious to catch the London coach, and so he left immediately; I waited for half an hour, and then, asking Beezley to send for me if anything further transpired, I made my own way home.

Sarah was waiting for me, in the drawing room.

'Where is Ruth?' I asked.

'She has retired already, complaining of a headache,' she said. For a moment she carried on with her work, and then she placed it in her lap and said, 'Will there ever be a conclusion to this dreadful matter?'

I said I hoped there would, and I prayed that the day would come very soon indeed.

'And shall we then be free of her?'

She meant Harriet. I did not answer.

'Then let us hope that no more harm shall be done by her, or any other godless women,' she said, picking up her embroidery once more. 'Praise the Lord!'

Frances Williams

Over the course of the week, three letters had arrived at my house. The first was from Verrall, forwarded by Miss Davis, landlady at the Bell Inn. It was full of his usual religious tripe, praising the Lord for this and that and promising hellfire and damnation to the enemies of the cross. He asked if I was expecting to visit Bromley again, and requested that I should be so kind as to call upon him if I did so. I decided immediately that I would do no such thing; I did not either like the man nor trust him, and so no reason why we should have any private discourse.

The second letter was from Richard Field, again forwarded by Miss Davis. He said that he had missed me at the two last sittings of the inquest, and that the proceedings appeared now to have reached the very dregs of opinion, with most witnesses stepping up to recount nothing but hearsay and speculation. He said that the tone of it had changed since my last attendance, and that now it seemed likely that Tom Churcher might be the guilty party.

I put the letter down.

'What is it?' Emily asked. She was at the table with her own correspondence, a letter from her sister, from which she occasionally read aloud. The joy and humour in her letter, compared to the ill tidings in mine, was remarkable.

'I fear someone is to be made a scapegoat,' I said, and explained to her how Tom Churcher, a man ill equipped to defend himself, was being singled out as the guilty party.

'What makes you so sure he is innocent?' Emily asked. 'Surely they would not accuse an innocent man.'

I sighed, and considered it. 'You have to understand how desperately Harriet's death has affected the town. Or perhaps not her death but this Godforsaken inquest. It drags on and on, and no conclusion is reached; they are now resorting to gossip and presenting it to the jury as evidence. The whole matter is a farce.'

'But the purpose of an inquest, surely, is merely to determine the cause of death? Not to find the murderer.'

'Exactly,' I said, 'and yet it seems that the coroner is driven to do exactly that, and he will destroy the community by doing so.'

Today a third letter arrived, and I received it upon my return from the school. This one was addressed to me directly, and yet it had been delayed where the other two had not. It was from the coroner, requesting my attendance at a further meeting of the jury. He apologised for calling me once more from the country, but said that he was very close to the conclusion of the evidence and he asked me to indulge him with my presence one final time. The letter was dated Wednesday, 15th April, and it had taken a whole week to reach me.

The date of the inquest was today, Wednesday the 22nd, and I had missed it.

Wednesday, 6th May, 1846

Thomas Churcher

Emma's confinement drew near, and the hot weather made her bad-tempered. She bade me do chores, and then complained I did them poorly, and finally threw me out of the house. I had nowhere to go and so I sat on the wall outside, picking at the moss that grew in the crevices, thinking of the things that usually occupied my thoughts when Emma was out of them.

When I went back to the house she was crying. I stood in the doorway, not sure what to do. Her hands were clasped over her belly and she rocked herself, wailing.

'What is it?' I asked. 'Shall I fetch your mother?'

She shook her head and held out her hand, and I sat beside her with my arm about her shoulders, and comforted her as best I could.

'I want to be a good wife,' she sobbed. 'I've tried, I've tried so hard.'

'I know you have,' I said, 'and all I want is to be a good husband to you.'

She seemed a little calmed by that, although I wondered what I had done to provoke her thus. At length she reassured me that the baby was not coming, and told me to fetch the clean linen from her sister's house, and I went off again a little relieved to be outside in the fresh air.

I walked the long way, up towards the White Hart, and past it and down across the meadow towards the river. The brewhouse at the Swan was being made ready, for there

318

was to be another meeting of the inquest. This time I would keep myself away from it, lest the police find further reason to question me and accuse me of not co-operating. Besides, what happened inside the inn had very little to do with Harriet any longer. It was the town, the town tearing itself into pieces, and pulling those pieces into shreds. No longer were the women muttering about murderers in their midst and which of them might be next; now they wanted it over, forgotten, buried. Never mind the chapel; that had been torn asunder long ago. Now the reverend was doing his best to cling to those who were left behind – the foolish, the God-blind, the resolutely faithful, who had their eyes closed to the hypocrisy and the shame.

He would do it, for he always did. If the chapel could survive the murder of a young woman, it would survive anything. All he had to do was stay where he was and preach, whilst his wife crept around the town in supposed secret, bringing gifts and bestowing money to those who needed it but did not ask. She never gave so much as a farthing to those who asked. Thus were the people of Bromley obliged to her, and to him, and those on the receiving end of the largesse found it convenient to forget whatever scandal might have been laid at the reverend's door. He attended every inquest, not for the reason he gave – to look out for the interests of the chapel and its congregation – but to look out for himself; so that he should know immediately if he was accused. Thus he allayed suspicions before they had a chance to develop, and all the while he appeared to be representing those who were too poor or weak, or too ignorant, to represent themselves.

But he never represented me.

They might yet come for me. I kept myself ready at all times, thinking that they should arrest me and take me to jail. And there I should rot for want of a lawyer, or probably hang for my own lack of clever conversation. Perhaps it might be something of a relief.

I had found my way, as was often the case, to that hidden spot on the riverbank where I kissed my Harriet for the first time. I remembered it so well, taking her hand to help her down the rutted bank. And all that time she was already pregnant, with the child growing inside her. I should have held on to her hand for good, and then I might have kept her, but instead I let it go, and in the darkness of that November night she slipped away.

What if she had told me she was pregnant? She might have expected that I would have run, perhaps, or called her a whore. I have thought so long about that situation and what I might have done, and I cannot imagine turning away from her. But she did not know that, just as I did not know her secret in time.

And why did she not wait for me, that last night, as we agreed? Did we miss each other in the darkness, or did she decide that she was better off without me, after all? Did she think that I might defend her, and in so doing injure Mr Verrall, or he me? Did she think that he might have told me of her condition, before she had the chance to tell me herself? I think, now, that she intended to tell me, some time that night, before or after she met with Mr Verrall. That she liked and trusted me enough to share that desperate secret.

I think I shall be haunted forever, by those things she did not say.

Frances Williams

The day was bright and clear, and the sun shining in a cloudless sky. I had caught the early coach from London, leaving the boarding house in Southwark at dawn, and speaking to nobody on board as far as Beckenham. At that point they all seemed to wake up, and the coach was full of lively conversation about where we were all going and why.

I lied, and told them I was visiting a dear friend. As I left the coach at the White Hart, the elderly lady who had been seated opposite me caught my arm and wished me every happiness.

The simplicity of her remark made tears start in my eyes, although she did not see. I wondered if today would be the start of that, true happiness, which I had craved for so long, and missed. Perhaps it was this, or perhaps the sunshine, that made Bromley seem so very much brighter; or maybe I remembered that Mary Ann Monckton and Jane Humphrey had both remembered me on my last visit, and spoken to me; but I felt less trepidation this time.

The inquest began at half-past ten, and the room was as crowded as I had ever seen it. Richard Field was already inside, and I took a moment to thank him for his letter, and ask after his wife. He said she did well, although the child was due imminently.

'You have surely not left her alone?' I asked.

'She has a maid with her, to tend to the boy.'

'Do you think we shall see a verdict today?'

'I do hope so, Miss Williams,' he said. 'And you must also hope, as do I, that we shall see Harriet brought justice after all.'

I told him he was mistaking the office of the inquest if he thought he should see justice. All we might hope for was a verdict of murder, by persons unknown. For surely there was no way a verdict of suicide could be returned, with all the evidence to the contrary.

I was called, then, and re-sworn. The coroner made me repeat my evidence for the benefit of the jury, and for perhaps the third or fourth time I recounted to those poor, bored faces the story of my illness and Harriet's letter, and Tom Churcher bringing gin. That Tom had not waited for Harriet to return, and had left the bottle of spirits sent by his sister, and had gone out into the night.

I had said the same thing, with very similar words, so many times that I believed it myself. There were omissions, yes, of course there were, but they were not relevant ones. Did the jury need to know that, in fact, I had made my illness appear worse because I was so desperate to keep Harriet for a day or two longer? Of course not. That was my business, my shame. Did they need to know that Tom Churcher had tarried on my doorstop for several minutes, begging to wait for Harriet? No. Did they need to hear of the desperation in his face, that made him run out to the town again, to look for her? No. For I believed his desperation was born of a desire to love her, to protect her, not to harm her.

Besides, they had not asked me a direct question.

The coroner asked me if I had been asked by Tom Churcher to conceal his name at any point, for any purpose.

I said I had not. Then, quite suddenly, I remembered. I said, 'Yes, on one occasion Tom suggested it was not necessary for me to mention his name. Harriet was in the habit of going to the Sunday School room to take back the books. I acted as the school's librarian, and was therefore obliged to keep account of them. On the Monday, Harriet returned the books for me as I was unwell, and that evening Tom said that he had seen her there. If I had thought Tom Churcher might have been in the chapel in the afternoon, I would not have sent Harriet with the books.'

'Why not?'

'Because the people in Bromley, as they always do, would have talked about it.'

'Why did you withhold this information on your former examination?' asked the coroner.

'Because I agreed with Tom's opinion that it was not necessary to state it. I saw Harriet alive and well later in the day than that, after all, therefore no suspicion could be attached to such a chance encounter.'

'You may have heard, Miss Williams, that another witness has stated that she saw Mr Churcher and the deceased several times that evening, after the time you assert she left to post the letter. How do you respond to that?'

'If you are talking of the testimony of Mrs Hopperton and her daughter, I would say that I disbelieve their evidence.'

'Why?'

'Because I know that they have both, in too many instances, stated that which is quite untrue.'

One of the jurymen – the barber, Richard Hodges – raised his hand and addressed me.

'Miss Williams,' he said, 'I urge you on behalf of the jury to tell all you know, else it might be necessary to send for you from the country a second time.'

I replied, 'Many of the new enquiries seem to be suggested by the tattle of the town of Bromley. If I were to reply to all the observations made, I should probably detain the jury some three days or above.'

I heard laughter from the crowd behind me. How could they find it so amusing? I wanted to shake sense into them all, to remind them that Harriet was dead, in the foulest possible way, and yet her murderer was walking unfettered, and untroubled by these proceedings.

Whether he thought me impudent or had merely reached the end of his questions, the coroner dismissed me then. There followed some discussion with Inspector Meadows, and the high constable, Mr Joyce, as well as Superintendent Pearce. None of them had any further comment to make at that time. No new evidence had come to light; the case stood as presented.

I had returned to the crowd and found myself standing next to Richard Field. He nudged me. 'Here we go,' he said. 'The end of it, at last.'

The coroner declared the evidence closed. He read through a sheaf of notes passed to him by his assistant, and said there was nothing in the evidence to justify their coming to a positive conclusion with respect to any person, and so they would therefore, having fully recapitulated the evidence, leave the matter in the hands of the jury.

'Thank God for that,' said someone behind me, and we all left the room and went out into the bright sunshine, to allow the jury to deliberate. James Humphrey began passing through the dissolute crowd, taking bets as to how long the jury would take, but the wager was almost immediately voided, as the door opened and we were permitted back in. It had been less than five minutes.

Hodges, who had been appointed foreman, was on his feet as we all filed in. He waited respectfully for everyone to enter and be still, and then announced that he and his brother jurors had unanimously agreed to the following verdict: 'That Harriet Monckton was wilfully murdered by some person or persons unknown.'

Despite this being the only possible verdict, considering the evidence, the room erupted into uproar. There was even cheering. I felt overwhelmed with it, breathless, tears rolling down my face, and I could not have explained why. I felt Richard Field take my arm, and I realised I must have stumbled. I held on to him gratefully, whilst, just barely audible above the din, Hodges continued, eulogising about the exemplary efforts of the coroner and the London detectives in bringing the matter to a conclusion. Nobody was listening.

We were free.

Richard and I walked together, as we had on those previous occasions.

'Now you can return to your wife,' I said.

'And you,' he said, 'can return to Shifnal, and be a warrior for your girls once more.'

I thanked him, and shook his hand, and we parted company.

For hours afterwards, sitting on the coach, a strange griping sensation bothered me. It had something to do with Richard Field, for it had first troubled me the previous time I had seen him, and now it nagged at me again today. It was only as the coach reached Southwark that I had it, with a sudden shock. It had taken me all this time, the distraction of the inquest and the verdict preventing my mind from unravelling the mystery of it.

Warrior, he had called me.

He'd said that Harriet had told him that she called me by that name, but it was a lie; or perhaps, to give him the benefit of the doubt, he was confused.

Harriet had not told him. *Our secret*, she had said; *my word for you*. She would not have written it in a letter. But I knew exactly where he had learned of it: Harriet's diary.

He had read Harriet's diary, the lost journal I had searched, and searched for.

He had read it, and the only possible occasion on which he could have obtained it was the night she died.

The coach arrived at London in the early evening. I took recommendations from the coachman as to a boarding house for the night, and it was pleasant enough, providing me with a room that was small but clean, a bed that was comfortable but not enough to make me wish to stay longer.

I lay for a while upon the bed, still dressed, my mind full of the inquest and of Harriet. My mind felt like a fly, buzzing from topic to topic without ever resting long enough to consider it properly. Firstly I thought of Verrall and Churcher, and how the suspicion had appeared to fly from one of them to the other; how the questions posed on one day seemed to fall against the minister, and his letters, and then at the next meeting the talk was all of Harriet being seen in Tom's company. I supposed, now the verdict had been reached, the police would investigate further and arrest one or other of them, and then there would be a trial. For all the jovial spirit at the close of the proceedings today, the matter was far from over.

I thought of Emily, and Shifnal, and how I might see her the next day, if I could get a coach to take me all the way. Then I thought of Richard Field, returning to Maria. Perhaps he was not yet home; I had expected to see him on the London coach, but he might have taken the coach that went via Beckenham instead, or caught a later one.

I looked through the small window at the darkening sky, and got up, and found my boots and a shawl. I knew I should not sleep, not without asking that question.

I found a hansom cab to take me to King Street, and I enquired of a flower-seller which house might be occupied by Richard and Maria Field. She did not know, but suggested I speak to Mrs Lewis at the Three Bucks, around the corner in Gresham Street, which I did, and was told that the Fields lived at number eleven.

By that time it was nearly nine o'clock — really, far too late to pay a social call. And yet I had come all this way, and I fancied Richard was perhaps the type of man who stayed up late, reading or conversing or writing letters. And besides, as I stood outside it, the house was brightly lit, upstairs and down.

It was a plain house, the middle of a row, with a flight of three steps up to a painted front door. It was like all the others in the row, neatly kept, with a small paved yard to the front and a young oak tree growing forlornly from the middle of it.

I thought of Harriet, but of course she had never been to this house. The Fields had moved from Fieldgate Street, where Harriet had lived before Maria arrived and for a while after, in between the first inquest and the second. Perhaps Maria had felt the ghost of her at Fieldgate Street; perhaps she had wanted a fresh start.

I climbed the steps and pulled the bell. I heard it ringing inside the house, and expected to hear sounds, perhaps footsteps, from within; but at first there was only silence. I heard laughter coming from an upstairs room in a house further along the row. Someone out on the street behind me was singing There was the rumble of conversation and a clink of glasses from the open door of the public house on the corner.

I rang the bell again, and looked at the door. It was not fastened. In fact it was slightly ajar. Still nobody came.

Then, from inside, quite faint, I heard a cry.

I looked behind me, but the street was empty. Not even a carriage on the street. I pushed at the door, and it swung wide on to a dim hallway, the tiled floor showing the staircase on the right, a door – closed – to the left. At the end of the hallway, another door was ajar. That, surely, must be the kitchen. 'Hello?' I called.

From upstairs I heard a wail, and a shout. 'Richard! Is that you?'

I went inside and closed the door, and made my way up the stairs. 'Mrs Field? Mrs Field, are you well?'

'Help me, help me!'

I hurried, then, and found the door to the bedroom open, the lamps lit. Maria Field was lying upon the bed in a nightgown, her hands clutching her swollen belly. Her face was white as chalk and shiny with perspiration, her hair loose and spread over the pillow, a dark tangle.

'Mrs Field?'

When she saw me she held out her hand to me, breathing hard. 'Who's that? Did Richard send you?'

'It's Miss Williams, Mrs Field. I haven't seen your husband. Is he not here?'

'He went to ask for the doctor,' she said. 'The baby – oh!'

Her hand gripped mine so hard I felt the bones should break. The baby was coming, and I was the worst possible person to help her. I had never had anything to do with babies – the whole idea of it terrified me. Maria was overcome with some immense pain, her head lifting from the pillow with the force of it, her eyes closed, her teeth gritted.

A minute later, the pain eased and she released my hand. 'Sorry,' she gasped. 'I'm so sorry.' She had no idea who I was, but in that moment she seemed relieved that she was no longer alone.

'Where is your son, Mrs Field?'

'He is asleep,' she said, 'thank God! If I have not woken him with my cries.'

'Shall I see?'

She nodded, and I left her for a moment. There were two further rooms on this floor, but neither of them held a sleeping child. I took the stairs to the second floor, and there I found the nursery, and a small boy fast asleep on his back, his thumb half in his mouth.

I closed the door as another cry came from his mother, and returned to her.

I wetted a cloth on the washstand, and used it to mop her brow as she was racked with pain once more. Her belly rose next to me and I tried not to look at it; it looked almost obscene, a horrid thing, like a deformity.

'Oh,' she said, resting onto the pillow once more. 'Where is Richard? Why is he taking so long?'

'It is late, Mrs Field. Perhaps he cannot find the house. Where is your maid?'

'It's her ... half-day ...'

I wiped her face. She seemed a little calmer, and then her face creased. 'It did not hurt like this, last time. There must be something wrong.'

'I am sure you are quite fine,' I said, although I had no basis for this assumption. 'What about your neighbours? Is there someone else I can call upon for you?'

'Them?' she said. 'Not likely.'

328

And then the pains came again, and for a few minutes more my hand was crushed and all I could do was hold the cloth to her hot, creased face, and wait for it to pass.

This time she looked at me closely. 'Who did you say you were? I am so sorry. I feel I should know.'

'Miss Williams,' I said. 'I was – a friend of Harriet's, in Bromley.'

'Oh!' she said. 'You were at the inquest!'

'I was.'

'And what are you doing here?'

'I was returning to Shropshire, where I live now. The verdict was today; perhaps Mr Field did not have a chance to tell you. I wanted to speak to you, and Mr Field, about something, and—'

Her eyes closed and she gasped, and held her breath; this time she threw her head back on the pillow as if in a fit, and let out a sound from her throat, guttural, almost a growl. It seemed to me to last longer, this time, and the pain was so intense that when her eyes opened they were glassy, unfocused.

'Mrs Field?'

'Maria. For God's sake.'

'Maria. My name is Frances. What can I do? Fetch you something? Brandy?'

'Brandy, yes. Downstairs, in Richard's study. Quickly.'

I ran down the stairs, grateful for something to do. The study was lit with lamps and the fire was burning low, as if Richard's evening had been interrupted. A fine mahogany cabinet stood against the wall, a decanter and glasses on a tray. I sniffed at the brown liquid inside, determined it to be brandy, and poured a generous measure.

At the door, I stopped. I heard the cry from upstairs, a wail, turning into a moan. I had the drink in my hand. Richard was not here. Maria was not going to get up from the bed. I looked around the room. Harriet's diary might be in here, somewhere – perhaps concealed, or perhaps not, for there would be no need to hide it; I was not expected here.

I walked back to the desk, which was littered with papers and books and other objects: an inkwell, dried and empty, on its side; an apple, on a plate, uneaten; a small pile of farthings and pennies. I longed to sort through everything and put it into order; I could not imagine the type of mind which could work and concentrate amid such chaos. I lifted papers and books, but the journal – bound in green leather, with creamy paper – was not in plain view. I opened drawers, and shuffled through the contents.

From upstairs came another cry. I ignored it, thinking that Maria was so distracted she could have no clear idea of how long I had been gone. Drawer after drawer. More papers. Pens, ink, tobacco, a silk handkerchief, crumpled; letters, notes, a notebook, with nothing in it.

I gave up.

The back wall of the study was filled with bookshelves, and books. I looked, vainly, for a moment, but I could see nothing that looked like Harriet's journal.

A quavering call came from upstairs. 'Oh! Miss Williams? Frances!'

I left the study and took the brandy upstairs to her. She sipped it, and pulled a face, and lay back on the pillow with a sigh. 'Thank you,' she said. 'Thank you, thank you. Oh, why does Richard take so long?'

'He will be back soon,' I said, soothingly. 'How do you do?'

'Ill, I think. The pain is very bad.'

'Try not to worry, Maria. It will make things worse, I am sure.'

She gave me a flash of a smile, and then her mouth opened again in a soundless scream. She clutched at the covers, looking for my hand. I gave it to her and winced as my knuckles cracked. Her fingernails dug into my skin.

'There,' I said, 'It will be over soon. Try to breathe.'

Minutes passed. She writhed, and moaned, and then her voice rose into a wail so loud I thought she would waken the child upstairs. A clock, somewhere in the house, chimed ten times. I had been here with her for an hour, and there was still no sign of her husband.

The pain left her once again, and she lay at peace, breathing hard, her eyes closed. 'Do not ever marry, Frances,' she said, but with it she smiled.

'I have no plans to,' I said, and patted her hand.

'You are a friend of Harriet's,' she said. 'Did she ever … speak of us?'

'Often,' I said, for it was the truth. 'She thought of you as a very dear friend.'

'She left us,' Maria said. 'She left me with Richard.'

'Maria,' I said, determined to broach the subject at last, 'Harriet had a journal. You know of it?'

Her eyes opened and looked at me, alarmed. In such a vulnerable state, she was unable to disguise her reaction. And then, just as quickly, she denied it. 'No,' and then added, 'That is, she never kept a journal whilst she was with us, I am sure …'

And then the pain returned, conveniently, and this time she doubled up and turned on to her side, her knees drawn up around her stomach, her arms around her belly as if to protect it. 'This one …' she gasped ' … will kill me.'

'No,' I said. 'Not while I am here.'

It was a mistake to say so, I thought. For all I knew, the birth would be a violent one and she might well die from it. Perhaps the baby was too big – I could well believe it, from the size of her belly in comparison to her slight frame – or perhaps she would bleed to death. But it could not possibly help her to consider those things, and so I consoled her and told her she was quite well, and her child would be born safe and well too.

When she could next speak, she said, 'Did you know Richard loved her, first? Before me?'

I nodded.

'She stopped writing to me,' she said. 'I wrote her letters, but she only ever wrote to Richard, or to us both. Until that last time.'

'The last time?'

'The night she died,' she said, and this time she sobbed. 'I cannot continue,' she said, weeping. 'Oh, where is Richard, where is he?'

I thought of Richard returning, and how the situation might then change. I had to insist. 'Maria,' I said, 'there *is* a journal, and your husband has it. Do you know where it is?'

Her eyes opened and she regarded me, her lips dry and bloodless. 'Walk,' she said, as if she had not heard. 'I need to walk. Help me.'

I let her put her arms about my shoulders and I helped her get to her feet. Under the nightdress I could feel her bones, fragile, like a bird. I supported her and we walked about the bedroom, this way and that, until the pain took her and I tried to get her back to the bed, but she would not move. Her arms about my neck, she swayed and stood, her head damp upon my shoulder, moaning.

'Better,' she said, at last. 'God help me, it hurts.'

I did not mention the diary again. Whether she had heard me, I could not say.

We stayed upright for a while, walking when we could, and I taking her weight when she could not. Eventually she tired of that and I took her back to the bed. I turned her pillows and wiped her face once more.

'Thank you,' she said. 'You have been so very kind.'

'I am no nurse,' I said. 'I only wish I knew what to do.'

'You stayed with me,' she said, and closed her eyes.

I fancied she snatched a moment of sleep, for her breathing deepened, but doing so appeared to have affected her adversely, for just a few short minutes later she began to fidget and her mouth opened in a desperate scream of agony. 'Oh! I shall be torn in two!'

The screaming masked the sound of the front door opening. I heard steps outside the bedroom and Richard calling, 'Maria! Maria, I am here!'

He opened the door a moment later and saw me, sitting on the side of the bed with Maria's hand gripping mine, my hand with the cloth wiping her brow. He was shocked but did not comment. I stood, but Maria would not let go of my hand until the pain had eased again; and then I was free, and went to the window.

'You're here,' she said, smiling at Richard.

He kissed her hand and stroked her cheek. 'The doctor is coming,' he said. 'He will be here presently.'

'Thank you,' she said, 'oh, thank you.'

'Miss Williams,' he said, at last, turning to me. 'I do not understand how you come to be in my wife's bedroom, but I find myself grateful for it nonetheless.'

I turned to look at him.

'Now you are here, Mr Field, I shall leave you both in peace.'

I got to the door when I heard him say, 'Please, Miss Williams. Will you wait in the kitchen? It's warm in there. I shall come when the doctor is here.'

I said I would, and went to the kitchen. It was indeed warm, and I filled the kettle and set it upon the stove, for I thought they should surely not object to my making tea. I searched for the tea caddy, and cups, and saucers, and by the time I had filled the pot I heard a knocking at the door, and I went to let the doctor in.

'Upstairs?' he asked of me, and I nodded, and he handed me his coat and hat.

A few minutes later Richard came down and into the kitchen, wiping a weary hand over his face. He collapsed into the chair and groaned. 'I fear for her,' he said. 'This is so much worse than it was for the first.'

'They are all very different, so I've heard.' I was not sure if I had indeed heard that, or whether I had by now grown accustomed to uttering platitudes.

'You made tea,' he said, 'good, good. Thank you.'

I poured him a cup of tea and he drank a gulp, then got to his feet and left the room, returning a moment later with the decanter of brandy from the study, tipping a generous measure into his cup and offering it to me.

I felt similarly in need of fortitude, and nodded. We sat in silence for a moment, soothed by the brandy and the tea. Upstairs, Maria let out a wail.

'I should go to her,' he said, but in that moment we heard the doctor coming down the stairs. I got to my feet, thinking I should absent myself, but the doctor spoke to us both without giving me time to depart.

'She'll have a tough time of it,' he said. 'The baby is facing the wrong way.'

'What does that mean?' Richard asked.

'Just that. All should be well, but it will be a hard job. I can send a woman to help you,' he said, looking at me, 'if you need one.'

'Are you not able to stay?' I asked, my eyes widening.

The doctor laughed at this. He was a young man, handsome. I wondered how many babies he had delivered; how many women he had saved. Richard looked at me and then back to the doctor and said, 'Thank you. If you could send a woman, that would be greatly appreciated. As soon as possible.'

'Oh, your wife will be labouring a good while yet,' he said. 'Pray she does not get too tired.'

And he took his coat, and hat, and Richard saw him out. I thought he should go straight upstairs again, but for the moment all was quiet. I wondered if the doctor had given

Maria something to calm her and she was able to sleep. I checked my pocket-watch and saw that it was a quarter to eleven; the doors at the boarding house would be locked tight.

Richard came back to the kitchen and stood in the doorway.

'Why are you here?' he asked, as if only now had he recalled that my presence was unexpected.

'You have Harriet's journal,' I said.

He frowned. 'What on earth...? Why should I have Harriet's journal, of all things?'

Years of dealing with poorly behaved children meant I could always spot a liar. I rose from my seat and crossed the room so that I was facing him. He was just a little taller than me. I raised my chin.

'I do not know why you should have it, only that you do. I should like to see it.'

'I do not, I tell you,' he said. 'And, Miss Williams, this is not exactly a convenient moment...'

A sound came from upstairs, just a whimper. I glanced at the door. He exhaled sharply and left the room, going up the stairs to Maria. I looked about the kitchen, in case I should see the journal lying around, discarded, but of course it was not. I sat for a while in the chair and drank the tea, which was dark and strong and bitter, and then I closed my eyes to think, and must have fallen asleep for a very short while, for I awoke to a knock at the door.

Dazed, I went to answer it. The light from the hallway illuminated the top step, and standing upon it was a woman of middling years, with a wide, smiling mouth and deep-set eyes. 'Doctor sent me,' she said, and I stood aside to let her in. 'Not you, then, requiring my services?' she said, looking me up and down. I must have looked startled, for she winked.

'She is upstairs,' I said.

She did not give me her coat, or her bonnet, or ask me for anything further, but went upstairs and I heard her voice as she entered the bedroom. 'Here we are, is it? There, there. I've come to see your baby safely out of you ... '

Her choice of words made me shudder. I could not imagine anything quite so horrific. I went back to my seat and settled down, hoping that the stove would stay alight and warm long enough to let me sleep again, but a few moments later I heard steps and I thought I was about to be pressed into assisting again. It was Richard.

'I have been sent out,' he said.

For a moment he stood there, dazed, like a man who had walked into a room and forgotten what it was he came in for.

'If you're going to sleep,' he said, 'better do it in the drawing room. I'll light the fire.'

I followed him through the door to the right of the staircase. Alhough he called it a drawing room, it was merely a small front parlour, with a bay window that overlooked the street. Richard lit the lamps and I pulled the shutters and drew the heavy curtains against the chill. With the curtains closed the room looked even smaller, but it did have two upholstered chairs either side of the fireplace that looked comfortable. He crouched in front of the fireplace and piled up the coal, then lit the fire with a spill from the mantelpiece. It did not take, at first, and he placed the curved firescreen around it and covered that with a large sheet of newspaper, to draw the fire out. Soon it was roaring, and he removed the paper, and refolded it.

I yawned, and hid my yawn behind my hand. Fortunately he did not see, for he might have changed his mind about his next words, if he had.

'Why did you ask about the journal?'

He indicated with a gesture that I should sit. He remained standing, his back to the fire, as if warming himself, but his eyes were alert.

I thought carefully about my response, and then decided to tell the truth. At least, the part of it that would be most likely to gain a positive result.

'I am a teacher, Mr Field, as I'm sure you know. Harriet wrote in her journal regularly, and she wrote about me. She saw her journal as a …a place she could write freely. As I am sure you will appreciate, the contents of that journal might prove very damaging to me, and to my reputation, if someone might read it who did not understand the nature of our friendship. That is why I want to ensure it is kept safe.'

'I can assure you it is safe.'

That was it: he had admitted it. He had the journal.

'That is as may be: but as Harriet's friend perhaps you can appreciate that I should like to see it for myself.'

I stopped speaking. He left the room, then, and I thought he had gone back upstairs, but a few moments later he returned with the brandy decanter and two glasses. He poured one for me without asking, but I did not refuse it. It occurred to me that his aim might be to render me insensible, so I should sleep, and forget all about my request.

'The journal was sent to Maria,' he said.

'Sent? To your wife?'

'The night she died, Harriet sent us the letter which I read out in court. But she also sent a parcel, addressed to Maria. It was posted the same night, but wrapped separately. It seemed she wanted to appraise my wife of the Bromley news, which she was always seeking.'

I frowned. Why would she send her own diary, if she had been planning to visit the Fields just a day or so later? It made no sense to me.

He took a long draught of his brandy and grimaced. 'I can judge your thoughts, Miss Williams, from your expression. I wondered the same thing. Why send it? I thought, perhaps, she had changed her mind about taking the situation at Arundel. When I learned of her condition, that seemed to make more sense. She could not have hoped to keep that a secret very much longer.'

'I should like to read it,' I said again.

'I believe Maria has destroyed it,' he said, quite calmly.

I did not believe him. He was still hiding something from me, and the journal itself was only part of that. I got to my feet.

'Where are you going?' he said, alarmed.

'To ask her, of course,' I said. 'She will tell me that she has destroyed it, and I will know if that is the truth.'

But he was quick on his feet for an older man, and he reached the doorway before I did. 'Don't,' he said.

'Why not?'

'Good God, woman! My wife is labouring, in great pain! You wish to interrogate her, now?'

I sighed. He was right, of course. 'Then I shall remain here until she is ready to speak to me,' I said.

He waited until I took my seat again before he moved. 'You are a stubborn woman, Miss Williams.'

'And you, Mr Field, are not a very accomplished liar.'

He sat down once more but with a heavy sigh, and rested his head in his hands. 'We both have secrets, Miss Williams, and, if you don't mind me saying so, neither of us is very good at keeping them.'

'Why did she send the journal to Maria?' I asked again.

He sighed.

'Because she wanted to tell her about me.'

'About you?'

He filled the brandy glass once more and drank it almost dry. Then he reached into his jacket pocket, and withdrew something from it. The journal! He placed it upon his knee and stroked the leather gently, reverently. I wanted to reach across and snatch it from him, to take it and run.

'It's like hearing her speak again,' he said. 'When you read it, you can almost hear her voice. Most extraordinary.'

'She was a fine storyteller,' I said.

'Do you still miss her?' he asked me.

I thought for a moment, wondering whether I should tell him of my suspicions regarding the manner in which she had treated Tom Churcher, the manner in which she had treated me, and others in the town. But then I changed my mind, and said, simply, 'Every day.'

He placed his hand over the book and held it still, as a diviner might try to sense a spirit vibration, perhaps to try and catch a whisper of Harriet's ghost.

'I don't believe she meant any harm by it,' he said. 'You'll see for yourself.'

He intended to let me have it! I took a sharp breath in, and held it, scarcely daring to believe it. I had thought that at any moment he might toss it upon the flames, and that his reverent caresses were his way of saying goodbye to it. I leaned forward in my seat, and his hand gripped it harder.

'An agreement, Miss Williams. Between us?'

'What agreement?'

'That you may read it, all of it, here in the parlour. That you will not steal it, or cause it to come to any harm, and when you have read it you will restore it to my possession, and allow me to explain. You have my oath that nothing contained within its pages regarding yourself will be made public in any way, if you agree that you will also keep its contents to yourself.'

'I agree,' I said.

He passed me the journal, and held it still so that it hung suspended in the air, gripped by us both, as if he had still not quite decided that he could trust me.

'You will be my secret-keeper, Miss Williams,' he said, 'and I shall be yours.'

He let go. The diary felt uneven in the middle, thicker, and the pages fell open to reveal three pressed flowers. I lifted one of them, a cyclamen, fragile, and still with the faintest hint of the delicate pink of the bloom. I replaced it and closed the book, and held it to my face, trying to find a scent of her, a trace. I scarcely noticed when Richard Field got to his feet, and left the room.

IV:

The Diary

Thursday, 1st June

I miss him so very much, and it has been just a little less than a week. I felt it was the right thing to do, to leave. But the right thing for whom? Certainly not for me. Maria is so much more worthy of him than I, so very good and clever and kind. They will be very happy together, and I wish them well.

And now I am home, although that word does not seem to fit the way once it did, and I miss both of them so fiercely I feel my heart should break in two. My mother was pleased to see me, at first; but since then she has fallen into silence and sulks, and my sister is at times openly hostile. She is cross because she no longer has the bedroom to herself, and must share with me again. I think she should go and find herself a husband, and then she will have a whole house.

Still. This is a fresh beginning, and I have begun a new journal to mark the occasion. It is one he gave me, a fine leather-bound volume, with creamy pages. I was saving it for a special time, but I am not sure there can ever be such a thing and so I am beginning it now. Perhaps it will bring me good cheer to see it every day.

Friday, 2nd June

The town has changed so little. I cannot say what I was expecting to find, after eighteen months – a period during which I visited, perhaps, three times? – but everything is just as it was. The Market Place is the same, the fields, the houses and the people within them. The coach still thunders through, and shudders to a halt in front of the White Hart. The post comes, and goes.

I returned to Bromley the week after the fair and all the talk in the Market Place was of the stalls and the sights, Mr

Storer's gingerbread shapes, the tightrope that had been strung up from Isard's yard to a scaffold pole across the way. Joe Milstead fell from it and broke his arm, or that's what he would have us believe. I have found nobody who saw it happen. I believe he fell off a horse and is trying to make the story more exciting.

Joe Milstead is walking out with Susannah Garn. This is quite a surprise, as he was expressing intent towards Jane Humphrey when I was last here. Jane is looking sour about it, I saw her in the butcher's. I think the arrangement is quite new. Clara Churcher says that Jane was crying outside the chapel just last week.

Wednesday, 7th June

My mother wishes me to visit Mr Campling, to enquire about a position at the National School. I told her I would do so, were it not for Mrs Campling, who is the very worst kind of woman, sly and bad-tempered. I do not trust her at all, and I could not bring myself to work in the same room with her. Clara says she is there but little, now, for she has been unwell since the birth of her last. Nine children, and the youngest is very frail. I told Clara I would only work there if I could have charge of the girls' room, but she laughed and said working in Town had quite gone to my head; and in any case they have had a new teacher for eighteen months now, who is showing herself to be very capable. I smiled but I was a little offended; I had sole charge of the class in Hackney, and my girls thrived under my care. If I can manage a class in Hackney, I can certainly do the same in Bromley!

Friday, 9th June

Oh, my poor heart! I thought by now I should begin to feel better, but I cannot. I think of him in the house with Maria, how quickly everything changed. I told him, before I left, that he should marry her. In my heart I hoped he would deny it, perhaps laugh at my foolish suggestion, but all he said was, 'She would not have me.' I think, perhaps, she will. Especially now. All he needs do is ask.

Monday, 12th June

The sun is shining once more, after a week of cloud and rain. It feels as if a heavy curtain has been lifted from the town. Underneath it all, everything is in its place. Everything is exactly as it was.

It reminds me of playing that old game, called Memory, with my father – he would fetch a tea tray and a selection of objects, and place my mother's silk shawl over it. Then he would tell me to close my eyes tightly, and he would remove something from under the scarf, and hide it; and my task would be to remember what had been there, and decide which of the items was missing. I even remember the objects he used: my sister's thimble, a candle stub, a pencil, a spoon, a walnut, a skein of Berlin-wool; once he chose a small wooden animal that my brother had whittled. I got to be very good at it, finding different ways to remember what was there. I remember once he tried to fool me by adding an object – a daisy – instead of taking something away. I saw it at once, of course. And I remember afterwards thinking how very strange it was that he should have had a daisy in his pocket, not knowing that I would call upon him that very afternoon to play our game.

I always meant to ask him about it, and I never did, and now of course I never shall. I think of him every day. I wonder what he would have thought of Richard, should he have had the opportunity to meet him. Really Richard was not my father's sort of man at all; and yet I like to imagine they might have been friends.

Saturday, 17th June

It seems something has been added to the tray, after all!

Clara invited me to tea, and introduced me to the new teacher at the National School. Although she has been there for some time now, the whole time I was in London, so she is not really new at all. Perhaps it is I who am new, and not her.

Her name is Frances Williams, and she seems a very capable sort: tall and quite stern-looking, with her hair very neat under her bonnet, and yet friendly enough. She was interested to hear of my experiences in Hackney. I told her about my girls, about how well they had been progressing, and how my own confidence had grown along with theirs; then of course she asked me why I left. I had been smiling up to that point, but that question, of all the questions she could have posed, quite undid me. I felt the emotion of it rise up to strangle me, and I swallowed some tea and breathed and waited until it passed. I have no doubt at all that she noticed, but she said nothing of it, and when I felt quite better she asked me if I liked to watch the cricket, and whether I should join her on the White Hart Field on Sunday afternoon, before the weather turns. I thought her very kind, and I accepted. Perhaps we will be friends.

Saturday, 24th June

A happy occasion today: my brother's child, Elizabeth, a fine, bonny girl, was baptised at the parish church. Their fourth child, and first daughter. My first niece. His wife, also Elizabeth, looked well and hearty, although the baby screamed for the duration of the service. It seems to be the custom to name your children after yourself, these days, and I cannot comprehend it. It feels like a vanity, to me. If I am ever blessed with a child, I shall choose a name that nobody else has. Something that will sound intriguing, that will make people want to meet him, or her. And there is nothing intriguing about Harriet!

Afterwards, the Reverend Mr Newell asked me how long I had been back in the town. 'But a little while,' I reassured him. He asked why he had not seen me until now, rather oddly I felt, as I had never been a regular attender, preferring to worship at the chapel, as he well knew. I could not find the words to reply, so I smiled and turned away from him. The infant was still squalling, affronted at the wetting of its head and the ancient family Christening gown into which it had been stuffed. And, no doubt, being saddled with the same name as its mother.

And then, at home, a letter from Richard. As if he could see my distress from Fieldgate Street and had taken pity on me, at last. I took the letter out with me, and walked through the fields. Perhaps an hour passed before I could bring myself to read it; and, after all that, it said nothing of any consequence. If he knows, he would surely have said something, so I can only assume that Maria has not told him yet. Or perhaps something has happened. But then surely she would write to me, and she has not.

It is strange to read Richard's handwriting once more. He wrote me so many letters, and notes, in the time that I lived in his house. You would think it a foolish thing, since we saw each other every day, but he was – he is – a man who expresses himself best by the written word. In London I treasured every note he wrote me, keeping them wrapped in a parcel in my trunk. On my last night in London I burned them all in the fireplace, and I regret my hasty actions bitterly. How I would love to read those letters now! But to do so would only prolong the sadness, and really I must not spend the rest of my life sobbing over what might have become of us. I need to put it behind me and try to find happiness here in Bromley.

I have not burned this letter, of course. I shall keep it here, tucked inside my journal, where it will be safe.

Sunday, 25th June

In an effort to avoid the vicar, and to annoy my mother and my sister, I did manage to go to chapel this morning. I went with Clara Churcher, who leads the Sunday School. The building is quite new, being constructed there only a few years ago. It is much smaller than the parish church inside and out, which makes for a congenial atmosphere. I am pleased to report that the congregation has grown in number since my last visit. I found the service refreshing and very jolly. There are many things different: no catechism, no book of Common Prayer; members of the congregation take turns to read from the Gospel, and there are many hymns, prayers, again, led by members of the congregation of both sexes. The minister there, Mr Verrall, is just as I remember him: an excellent preacher, inspiring and inspired. The atmosphere was a happy one – not for them the sombre filing out of the faithful. In fact they seemed all quite disinclined to depart for their homes!

Thomas Churcher was there, Clara's brother. I see that now he plays the organ in the services, and is quite grown-up. Before I left for London he had been in the habit of accompanying me across the fields after chapel meetings. He immediately offered to do the same today, and it felt quite natural to accept, as I knew from before that we would do so in peaceful silence and my thoughts would not be intruded upon.

At the door, we paused and Clara took great delight in reintroducing me to the reverend. He smiled and told me that of course he remembered me from my previous visits. I shook his hand, rather in awe of him, for he is a handsome man, with fine dark hair and whiskers, and bright blue eyes. He was very interested to hear that I had recently returned from Hackney; he himself had resided in Peckham until five years ago, when he was called to the ministry in Bromley. He told me that there is to be a tea party at his house in a fortnight, and has asked me to attend. There now, I have two invitations already!

Saturday, 1st July

This afternoon I took tea with Miss Williams, the new teacher at the National School. She has a room upstairs at the Beezleys', directly above the bakehouse, although I think she wishes she had found somewhere more amenable. She did not complain of it but I understand that the walls are thin enough to hear Lottie Beezley cough, and Mr Beezley has already asked her whether she says her prayers regularly, as he has not heard her. She told him that she prays quietly, as the Lord can hear her perfectly well, but from her expression I judged that she prays when she feels the need, and otherwise not at all, and does not take kindly to others paying such close attention to her activities.

Before she took the room at the Beezleys', she resided at Mason's Hill with the Misses Mercier, and she asked if I was acquainted with them. I told her that they were stalwarts of the parish church, and I fancy that is almost all I needed to say. I explained to Miss Williams that my own preference was to worship at the Congregational chapel, and how very engaging the services were, and that Clara Churcher − her good friend − also attended; I told her I hoped I might persuade her to join us there one Sunday.

She told me she would consider it. I rather think she will not; I judge from our conversation that she is not an ardent churchgoer, and yet I find I like her a little more for it, instead of a little less.

Friday, 7th July

My sister seems to have taken exception to my attendance at the chapel. All week there has been a difficult atmosphere at home, with her hardly being able to speak to me in a civil fashion. After supper I told her I was going to attend the women's prayer meeting and she boiled over in rage! She called me a heathen, said that I should think of our mother and everything she has been through, exclaimed how all that she has left is her reputation and how she would not stand by to see me ruin even that … and she said far worse things besides. Things that led me to believe she has intruded on my privacy in the worst possible way. I am ashamed to say I raged back at her, called her a sneak and a hypocrite, and then I left. My mother is growing deaf but even she must have heard us, for as I put on my bonnet and my shawl she looked at me in a way that suggested her sympathies lay with Mary Ann, and not with me.

I need to find somewhere secure, where I can keep this journal without its being discovered; and perhaps I need to be more discreet about certain matters in London, just in case she should decide to intrude again. Perhaps I shall just carry it with me at all times, and sleep with it under my pillow. In fact I care little for Mary Ann's opinions of me, but I promised faithfully to keep certain matters secret, and to reveal them, even accidentally, to my hot-headed sister would be just awful.

I walked across the fields and into town, and made my way directly to the chapel. Clara was not there – I still do not know why – but Susannah Garn was, and Jane Humphrey, and they both saw I was upset and made to comfort me. When the prayers commenced, the two of them prayed for my family to have wisdom, and to be forgiven for their harshness, and for me to be blessed with the Grace of the Holy Spirit and to know I was loved. I was touched by their sensitivity and kindness towards me, and the emotion of it all spilled out. I think it was many things: the argument at home, the letter from Richard, and the constant, nagging ache in my heart of missing someone I loved dearly – all of that came out and I cried and sobbed. Susannah Garn put her arm about my shoulders and Jane prayed, and some of the other women prayed too, quietly, allowing me to be overcome and not judging me for it.

Afterwards, I walked back to the Market Place with Susannah and I asked her how the chapel could be so very different from the parish church and still be in the service of the Lord. She told me I should visit the reverend, and ask for his opinion, for he was very vocal on the ways the High Church kept God separated from His people.

She left me at the pump to go to her home, and I, disinclined to return to the house, paid a call on Miss Williams, who fortunately was at home and seemed pleased to see me. I told her that I had had a disagreement with my sister, and she told me I was welcome to sleep with her, but I knew my mother would worry if I did not come home, even if my sister did not.

Still, Miss Williams – Frances – made me tea and I felt all the better for it. I stayed late talking about the school, and there is some honesty about conversations had late into the evening, even if they are conducted in a whisper, lest the Beezleys should overhear.

Her opinion of Mrs Campling is very similar to mine, and yet she has learned to better Mr Campling when his wife is not present, just by standing up to him and not capitulating. She says she learned this from Mrs Campling herself, from observing how she behaved with her husband, and by copying her tone and stance. She says Mr Campling is as much in fear of his wife as everyone else is, and he disguises this by being angry and violent when crossed, but he is a bully and all bullies are by nature afraid. Thus far Mr Campling has shouted at her and threatened her with dismissal, but has never yet taken it further. She says she rather enjoys it when he is angry, for he reminds her of a stove that has overheated and is about to blow.

She told me all this, whispering and giggling quietly, and I felt so very encouraged by it; not so much by her bravery, although I admired her very much for that, but because I truly felt that in her I had found a friend.

Saturday, 8th July

Another letter from Richard. The letter I had been expecting but dreading. He tells me he and Maria are to be married, quietly, on Tuesday next. A simple ceremony with just a few witnesses present. He thanks me for introducing him to my friend, and says that it has changed his life completely. He says he is so sorry that I felt I needed to leave the household, as it had been filled with such happiness with me in it, and that it is very much quieter without me.

What did he expect? That I could continue to live with them both, once they had fallen in love? Once everything changed? That I should perhaps be a sort of – whatever the correct word is – a concubine for him? He has always surrounded himself with young women, he himself said as much – that he drew life and energy and enthusiasm from having pretty girls to admire; perhaps he meant us to be some sort of harem, such as the Arabs have! I knew I would never be the only girl he admired, but at least in my time with him he did not favour anyone over me. He was generous and loving and kind to all, and discreet. The jealous Harriet thinks now that he probably had several girls to entertain him while I lived in his house, but if he did I never saw evidence of them. When I was with him, at first he focused all of his attention, his love, his favour, on me. It's quite a dazzling thing, to be so admired. Small wonder I fell in love with him.

And Maria – perhaps, now some time has passed, I feel the loss of her even more than I feel the loss of him. We were such very dear friends, from the very start. She had been so very kind to me when I started at the school and was homesick; it had been the most natural thing to suggest to Richard that she should move from Philpott Street to lodge with us, instead. And, after everything that happened, I had thought that by leaving London I might be able, at least, to assure her continued friendship, even if I had lost Richard. But that was naïve.

I remember that night so clearly: Richard at his club, and Maria sobbing, sobbing; and how I held her for hours and told her everything would be all right, that she was safe, that nothing bad would happen, that Richard loved her so much more than he loved me.

And the next morning I told her I would leave; and she wept again with what must have been relief, and she apologised and thanked me. She did not tell me not to be foolish; she did not beg me to stay. She said she should miss me and wondered however was she to manage without her best friend, and said that I should come to visit whenever I wanted, at least once a month or more. Only hours later, when I was packing my books into the bottom of the trunk, did she come to me and stand in the doorway and ask about the school, and what she should say to the girls. I replied that I would hand in my notice the next day, and that I should need to stay until the end of the week at least, and I would tell the girls myself.

She said nothing and left the room. I believe she had thought I was planning to leave there and then, maybe without even saying goodbye to Richard. But I was not going to just run away, as though I had committed some sort of crime.

After that there was an uneasy atmosphere in the house. I told Richard I was leaving; I did not tell him why. That is, I told him I was needed at home. Whether he believed it or not, he said but little. He was sullen and withdrawn, and kept to his study.

Maria stayed away from me. Perhaps she was afraid I might change my mind. It had been a hasty decision, and I had the whole of that week to regret it; but lying awake in my small attic bed I thought and thought and could see no other solution. Richard loved Maria. He did not look at me in the same way; he did not love me as fiercely as he loved her. How could I stay, and watch that love deepen? It would surely destroy me.

I think now that perhaps Maria was not quite the friend I thought she was. I introduced her to Richard because she was still so much the way I had been, on first arriving in London: dazed by it all, by the noise and the busyness and the people. Richard had such a calming, positive way about him, and he knew so many good people. He could help her, I thought, as he had helped me. How naïve I was! And, perhaps, how foolish of me not to fight for him. I never told Maria that I was sweet on Richard, because I thought she might judge me unkindly. And then she told me she loved him, and of course I didn't judge her for that at all.

And she has not written to me, not once. Perhaps she does not know what to say to me.

So Richard and Maria are to be married, and they have not even invited me to attend their wedding. I see Richard's hand in that decision. He does not want to risk changing his mind.

Saturday, 8th July

I had not the heart for it, but I had less inclination to stay at home, so this afternoon I went to Mr Verrall's tea party. He lives with his family in a fine white stucco house a half-mile or so out along Widmore Lane, quite a way from the town. The house is beautiful and very grand for a reverend of such a small chapel. I was quite taken aback when I saw it, and wondered if I should call at the back door instead of the front. But then a maid admitted me and I was shown into a drawing room.

I expected Clara to be there, or Jane, or some friend for me to converse with, but in fact it was mainly the men of the chapel and some others who I believe were associates of the reverend's. It seemed that it was intended for it to be a rather formal affair, with prayers and quiet reflection, and yet by the time I arrived some people were already playing games, and one of the young ladies was playing parlour music on the piano.

I found myself helping Ruth Verrall, the reverend's sister, in her efforts to direct the servants in bringing out the tea and cake and making sure everyone had what they needed. Mrs Verrall was there too, surrounded by ladies wearing fine dresses. Ruth told me, when I enquired, that they were ladies from the Bromley College, widows of clergymen who were entitled to reside there securely into their old age. Some of them were rather young, still, and I felt sorry for them, but I suppose they have a comfortable life.

'I have never visited the college,' I told her.

'Nor I,' she said. 'I hear the rooms are well appointed. Mrs Verrall visits regularly, and takes tea there.'

'Do you call her Mrs Verrall when it is just the two of you?' I asked her with a smile, but her face turned stony and I thought I had been too familiar.

The reverend saw me, then, and perhaps saw my discomfort, for he took me by the elbow and steered me to the doors which were open on to the paving behind the house. It was a fine day, with a cool breeze. He introduced me to a Mr Jenner and his wife, and there was Mr Carter, a lay preacher who lives in London and is to preach at chapel tomorrow morning. I had met him before at the chapel once. I recall feeling quite moved by the sermon he gave. Mr Carter was most interested to hear that I had taught at Hackney, and we found that we had some acquaintances in common in the area. He has heard of Richard through his philanthropic efforts, but has not had the pleasure of meeting him.

I had not planned to stay long, for Richard and Maria were never far from my thoughts, and it was driving me to melancholy. I made my way to the kitchen, taking a pair of teacups with me, and to my surprise Mr Carter followed me in there, talking more of Hackney and looking at my shoulders instead of into my face. I went back to the drawing room and he followed me there, too; I told Mr Verrall that I had a headache and I should like to go home, but I was grateful for the invitation, and Mr Carter offered to walk me. I told him I could manage perfectly well, but he absolutely insisted, saying that if I was feeling unwell I should not attempt the walk unaccompanied, lest I be overcome and faint upon the path. I was not afraid, although perhaps I should have been − reverends are, after all, just men, dressed in black − but he was slight and weaselly and I had no doubt that I could push him away and run faster than he, should he attempt an assault on my person.

I believe I sighed and said I could not prevent him, and he followed me out eagerly. At least it should all soon be over, for he could not very well have followed me into my mother's house! At the stile to the second field he offered me his hand to help me up, and I ignored it, hoping that he would discern from it my reluctance to have him in my company. All the way he was full of flattery and attention and telling me the town needed more pious, quiet young women to be brought to the Lord ...

And then in the second field I saw Miss Williams, across on the other path. I called out to her and she came to us.

She seemed most curious − and a little disapproving − to see me alone in a man's company. I tried by the expression on my face to communicate that I would have appreciated her company far more readily, but she did not appear to notice, or perhaps she was in a hurry. I introduced her to Mr Carter, and she looked from him to me, and said that she was pleased to meet him, and did not return his bow; but asked us to excuse her, and hurried back to her path. It was no matter. A few short minutes later we had arrived at Farwig, and I wished him a good day, and shut the door fast behind me. Mary Ann wanted to know who was the man standing on the doorstep, hat in hand, as if he expected to be admitted? I pressed my finger to my lips to shush her, and eventually he went away.

Hours later, it is a subject of some amusement to me, but at the time it was a little alarming.

Monday, 10th July

I told Frances about Richard, and Maria. Earlier, while we were walking back from the school, with leisurely steps and uninterrupted by anyone else, we had talked about the school, about how the fundamental principle of the National School is to instil Christian morals into the poor, rather than teaching them to read and write. Frances disagrees with it. I believe that the two aims are not incompatible; that it's possible to use the Bible to teach reading and writing, and why not, after all? No harm can come to the children from such a method. We had quite a lively discussion without any animosity arising between us, although I do not believe I convinced her of my holy justification! I admire her honesty about her lack of faith, and I like her for allowing me to see this part of her, which is by necessity a very private one. I asked her how she coped with teaching something she did not herself believe in. She told me that she loves her girls, genuinely loves them, even the naughty ones, and, if being permitted to teach them means she must sacrifice some of her principles to do it, then it is a small price to pay. She said, 'One day all men and women will be free to believe anything they choose, without judgement from others,' and she was so earnest about it I almost wanted to laugh. Not at her fervour, but in delight at the strength of her conviction. She makes me feel that anything is possible.

I admire her very much. I wish I could be more like her — braver. I told her so, and she took my hand and smiled at me.

Much later, as we had supper, she asked me why I appeared troubled. I had tried so hard to hide it, and it was easy to do that in her presence, but still she recognised the sadness in my heart, I think. So I told her about Richard, the man I love, and how he is to marry one of my dearest friends. The wedding is tomorrow, in fact. She listened and listened as it all poured out of me, out of my poor broken heart, and at the end of it to my very great surprise I felt a little less sad.

She thinks what I did was a very noble act. But then, I did not tell her the whole of it, as I am still bound by my oath. She does not know that in fact I had very little choice.

And now, I am writing this in the bedroom at home with my sister and my mother in the parlour, and I feel better still. I think perhaps I will look for another position, somewhere far away from here, and from Hackney — somewhere I have never been. A fresh beginning for me, and who knows what might lie ahead?

Monday, 10th July, evening

After much thought and prayer, I wrote to Richard and Maria, congratulating them most sincerely on their engagement and marriage. I wished them every happiness and blessing for their future lives together. I read the letter twice before posting it, anxious that there should not be any evidence at all of my jealousy or the pain that their union had caused me. I want them to be happy, because I genuinely love them both. Frances said to me that Richard was not the right person for me, and yet my time with him had taught me valuable lessons and so I should not see it as something to be regretted. I believe this is a fine sentiment, and I told her that what she actually meant was Richard was not right for me because it was not God's will. She looked at me and raised her eyebrow and we both laughed. I told her I was too old to make a match now; that I would end my days like my sister, a spinster. Frances is thirty-seven years old, although she does not look so much older than I. She says being with her girls keeps her young; marriage and childbirth are the conditions that age people. She says she has no wish to marry, but I did once believe all women say that who have not found a suitable husband. She, at least, would rather be happy on her own than subjugate herself to another: and for that I admire her even more. If I could be Frances Williams, and yet be married to Richard Field, surely I should be the happiest of women!

Sunday, 16th July

At chapel this morning the reverend preached a sermon on a verse from James: *For whosoever shall keep the whole law, and yet offend in one point, he is guilty of all. For he that said, Do not commit adultery, said also, Do not kill. Now if thou commit no adultery, yet if thou kill, thou art become a transgressor of the law.*

I noted it down. I have taken to writing notes during his sermons, for I feel that he says so many important and wise things, and by the time I am home I have forgotten them. I noticed sometimes Clara takes notes, so I took her as my example.

I watched him as he spoke, listened to his every word, and thought what a very godly man he was. He talked about those who follow God's teaching in one respect, and think themselves pious, and yet in other areas of their lives they are sorely lacking. Should we call ourselves good Christians, if we follow the Commandments and yet do not help the poor? Or if we give alms, but do not at the same time bear witness to the Glory of God? To sin just a little bit, he said, is still a sin.

After the service I got up the courage to go and speak to him, in the vestry. I asked if I was disturbing him, and he said not at all, and I told him I had enjoyed his sermon. He smiled at me and asked me if I was innocent of sin. I answered, 'Of course not.' He said that as long as I confessed my sins to the Lord, and was sorry for them, everything could be forgiven. Everything.

I thought he might have meant something by it, and I blushed crimson, which made me look even more guilty. I told him I was truly sorry for my sins, I repented every day, the big sins and the small ones. He said he thought it unlikely that I was guilty of big sins.

He said, and I thought it sounded strange, the way he said it, 'Come now, Harriet: you're not guilty of murder, or adultery, are you?'

I replied that, according to the Word of the Lord, the big sins are the same as the little ones – surely that was what we were to understand of his sermon?

I also thought it was odd that he called me Harriet. I know we had been formally introduced, but it felt a little overfamiliar to me. Perhaps a little paternalistic. And really I didn't see him in the same sort of way. Perhaps as a teacher, as a good man – rather like Richard, in fact.

Then he said that if the small sins were as bad as the big sins, then also the big sins were no worse than the small ones. And how incredible was it that God forgives everything, if only we are sorry, and we ask. I said that it was truly a wonderful thing.

We talked a little about other things – about the weather, which has grown warmer again, and about the town and how I was liking it now I had been back a while. He walked me out to the porch and by then the chapel was entirely empty. It was just he and I, and I felt very special, to have his singular attention, all upon me. He said he was very glad I had chosen to return to the chapel as it was blessed greatly by my presence in it. I laughed then, for what a thing to say! And he said he would pray for me, and asked if I would also pray for him? And I said I would. As I left, he reminded me that I was invited to take tea at his house, and said that if I wished to come during the week I would be most welcome. I said I could come on Tuesday, and he said that would be agreeable and so we fixed upon it for me to visit at three o'clock on Tuesday.

Of course, not everyone had gone home, for Thomas Churcher was waiting in the lane for me. He asked if he could walk me back to Farwig. He was always a harmless, kind boy, very quiet. On the way home we talked but little, and at the gate he nodded and said goodbye, and went back the way we had come with no further word.

I am looking forward to taking tea with the reverend greatly; and tomorrow I am having supper with Frances. Two very good excuses to be out of the house, and away from my miserable sister!

Monday, 17th July

I told my mother and my sister that I might stay with Frances, and not to wait up for me. They said nothing about it, but I think Mary Ann at least was pleased. How sad it is, to not feel welcome in your own home!

But, for all that, I had a wonderful evening with my friends. Clara was there for supper and she brought cake and gin, and I looked at her and thought perhaps she should be setting a good example – after all, the reverend preaches temperance – but then we had some gin anyway and soon it did not matter. Frances and Clara talked of the Sunday School, of George Sweeting the superintendent and what a boorish oaf the man is – full of worthy suggestions that he fails to bring to fruition, always expecting someone else to act in his stead. Clara calls him the worst kind of hypocrite. Frances knows him because he regularly attends the National School to hear the boys' recitation, as though he is a subscriber, but he isn't. He says he is there to check on the standard of moral education. And Mr Campling, who is High Church and proud of it, puffs up his chest like a pigeon at the mere thought of a man from a dissenting chapel standing in judgement over his interpretation of the Holy Scripture.

And then after a while Clara said she should go home, and asked me if I should like to walk with her as far as the field, but I said I would stay a little longer, and that I did not wish to walk across the fields in the dark; and Clara said she could ask Thomas to walk with me if I wished it. And I said that I should sooner stay here the night with Frances, if she would permit me to. And Clara smiled and left us to it.

We went to bed soon after that, for Frances has to rise early for school, and she thought that if Mr Campling smelt gin on her breath he should have some sort of a fit and dismiss her on the spot.

I was so tired that I fell asleep almost straight away; in the night I woke to find Frances's arm around my waist. I was warm and comfortable in bed with her but feeling her arm around me like that caused me to remember Richard, and then I could not fall asleep again. I sat in the chair for a while beside the stove, although it was all but out, thinking of Richard and the last time I was with him in particular. I thought about the big sins and the little sins, and how they were one and the same, and that God forgave us no matter what, as long as we were truly sorry.

It is difficult to decide what is a sin and what isn't, when you do not feel guilty about it. I do not feel sorry that we fell in love. I do not feel sorry that we had an intimacy; in fact, the only regret I have is that very last time. We had shared so many private moments, but in that last week, when I had determined to leave, nothing had transpired between us. Not until that very last day. I know, in my heart, that to love him in that way must be a sin. We were not — are not — married, in the sight of God or indeed in any moral sense. We had the deepest affection for each other, it was so simple and yet so difficult, all at the same time. And for all I was in love with Richard, he was in love with Maria, and so there must have been some sin in his heart for him to lie with me, when he wanted to lie with her. And marry her, as it turns out.

Is it adulterous, to lie with someone when you are not married? Surely it must be something else, some different sin: lust, perhaps, or covetousness, for I know I did covet him and by that time he belonged to Maria. And yet, why should it be a sin to love someone, and to want to demonstrate that love in the physical act?

I tried to repent, I tried hard to be sorry for it, but I could not. I prayed, and begged for forgiveness, but then I kept hearing the reverend's voice in my head, saying that the Lord forgives us only if we are truly sorry. Just asking for forgiveness does not work, for how then shall we learn? Eventually the tears began to fall, and I bit my handkerchief to stop myself making any noise and waking Frances. She looked so peaceful, and with her hair down she looks quite, quite young, and serene. She is so deserving of love, perhaps more than most people I know, and yet here she is, making her own way, so brave and proud. A warrior against the world and its vices.

Thinking of Frances made me stronger, and after a while I got back into bed beside her. All thoughts of Richard and Maria were temporarily banished from my mind, and at last I managed to fall asleep once more.

Tuesday, 18th July

I attended the reverend's house at three o'clock promptly. Mrs Verrall was seemingly not at home. For a while, I was entertained by Ruth Verrall, and had more of an opportunity to converse with her. She lives in the household and I understand that she acts as a sort of nurse or perhaps a governess to the Verralls' three sons, although they will all soon be sent away to school. The eldest is twelve years old, a fine tall boy who is handsome like his father, and confident in his manner. Ruth Verrall is a few years older than me, and softly spoken, although it is easy to see that she is very proud of her brother. When, at length, the man himself entered the drawing room, she looked upon him with open adoration.

He apologised for keeping me waiting; he had had pressing matters to attend to in the town. Ruth was sent to the kitchen to fetch more tea – although she could have rung the bell for it – and I surmised that perhaps he wished to ask me something confidential whilst Ruth was out of the room. He did look a little uncomfortable, leaning forward in his chair and looking at me most earnestly, as if he was expecting me to consult him on some private matter.

He asked, then, if I had had any further thoughts upon his sermon? I told him I had indeed been thinking about it at great length. I felt that he had somewhat put me on the spot, and before I knew it I found myself asking if there could be such a sin as adultery when neither party was married. I felt myself quite shocked by my boldness, although I had not named either myself or Richard as being the subject in question.

He asked me why I had thought to ask that question, given that I was not married myself.

I could not think of a way to answer, and I thought it would be better to change the subject, but at that moment there was a knock at the door and Ruth brought in a tray. The three of us had tea, and cake, and the atmosphere was quite jolly. Ruth and I talked, mainly, and the reverend sat still and watched, as if he was observing me, until I began to feel uncomfortable about it.

As the tea party came to an end, the reverend himself showed me out, while Ruth took the tray back to the kitchen. At the door he put his hand upon my back. He said nothing of any consequence as he did so, just that he hoped I would have a pleasant evening and he looked forward to seeing me on Sunday. I felt a strange, not altogether unpleasant, physical reaction to the touch of his hand. I wished that I had been able to stay longer, to talk more to him, and only him, even though that conversation might have been awkward. It was almost as if I had a need to confess.

But this evening I am much vexed by it. Being touched, even just in a familiar manner, by a man – it reminds me of Richard. I still miss him so very much. I know I should forget him, but how? He occupies my every waking thought.

Monday, 24th July

This morning I received another letter from Richard, written in haste. He has heard of a position at a school in St Albans, and suggests I might consider writing to the board. He asks if I have received a character from the Hackney school yet, and that reminded me that I have not. I have written to them to ask.

> *My dear Harriet,*
>
> *I hope this letter finds you well. Your presence here is very much missed. A new mistress has been appointed to take the girls' room at the school, although we both feel sure she could not possibly undertake the task as well as you. I heard very recently of a situation at a school at St Albans. Mr Edwards is acquainted with a member of the board there, and he asks whether you might consider leaving your home once more for a teaching position? If you are amenable, please reply quickly, or perhaps*

write to Mr Edwards directly, if you prefer. He is happy to write you a character but you will need at least one other. Maria sends her very best regards, and I remain, affectionately,

> *your*
> *Richard Field*

Even if the job in St Albans is unsuited, I will need a character for my next employment, and so the sooner they send it, the better.

In the afternoon I walked to the school and met Frances just as she was finishing lessons. She dismissed her two pupil teachers and I helped tidy up the girls' room with her, although we could not talk freely for Mr Campling was in the room adjacent, separated from us only by a wooden wall. We could hear him admonishing some poor boy for having mud upon his shoes; the unfortunate recipient of his ire was set to work sweeping the floor of the schoolroom on his hands and knees.

I told Frances of Richard's letter, and asked her for her opinion. She was a little cool in her initial response, but then she softened and said she thinks I should be very capable at any school that would have me, and offered to have me take some lessons with her girls if I should wish to; helping Clara with the Sunday School is all very well, but she feels I am missing what she calls 'proper teaching'. She thinks it will help me get up the nerve to write to Mr Edwards. I told her I should be happy to, as I have heard many in the town say what an excellent teacher Miss Williams is, and that, if these reports are even half true, her girls should be delightfully mannered and well behaved.

She said she would miss me, were I to go.

I felt quite sad at the thought, for I realised she is a true friend, to think so much of me after only such a very short time. I told her I was glad Clara had introduced us, and that I hoped if I were to leave town once again that we should write to each other regularly and maintain our friendship thus. She said she would write to me every week, and smiled and held me tightly by the hand for a moment.

When the room was quite clean and ready for the next day's lessons, we walked back to the Beezleys' and I took tea with her. She asked me about Richard and Maria, and whether I felt better about their marriage now that it has taken place. I replied that I had honestly given it less thought since then, and that without doubt her kindnesses to me had lessened the sting of it. She said she thought that Richard must be a fool to have chosen another over me, and that perhaps, in common with so many other men, he 'desired a woman who would simply knit and sew, and run the household and bear him children without giving any further thought to her own life and intellect'. Those were her precise words. I was rather shocked by them; not for the vehemence with which she said them, but rather because in that moment I realised that what she said was absolutely true. As dear a friend as Maria is to me, she is every inch the perfect wife in waiting; she taught at the school only whilst waiting for a husband, not because she particularly enjoyed it, or because she wanted to educate her charges. Richard must have seen that, her readiness to be a wife, and perhaps that is what he fell in love with after all. He would never have married me, because he could tell that such a connection would stifle me – and how foolish I have been, for I thought in all honesty that I would love to be stifled in just such a way! But Frances has shown me that such a thing would be truly dreadful, similar perhaps to an early death...although not, I think, with Richard. If I could have been the one to marry Richard, he would not stifle me thus. It's not he who has done it, it is something Maria will do to herself. She will put herself into a casket marked 'dutiful wife' and she will close the lid.

Friday, 28th July

This morning I received a letter from the board at the Hackney school, with an enclosure: the testimonial they had promised to send, two full months ago! And now I rather wish they had not bothered to send it at all, for it is really rather disappointing: they say that I am diligent and punctual, and that the standard of the lessons was satisfactory, but at the conclusion they say 'there is a great want of humility and energy' about me. I do not understand what on earth they can mean by it! The more I think about it, the more I tie myself in knots about their opinion. Surely Richard has not sanctioned such a description of me? Or perhaps he has written it himself, and had Mr Edwards copy it; perhaps he does not want me to find another situation?

In the end my confusion overcame my profound shame at being described thus, and I showed the letter to Frances. She pointed out all the encouraging things they had said, including that my pupils had responded well to my tuition and great improvements had been seen in their learning and in their behaviour. She said that schools do not like testimonials that have not a critical word to say about their subjects, that they consider such letters to be forged.

Nevertheless, the matter continued to trouble me greatly, and after the prayer meeting this evening I asked the reverend about it. He was most reassuring, and I felt better for having spoken to him.

Monday, 31st July

Last week I was very busy helping at the school, and I find it has lifted my spirits very well indeed. I worked for first one day, and then another, and then two together, and then, once, three days together, and I stayed the night with Frances to save me the trouble of walking back home only to return early the following day. I returned home only this morning to change my dress, and, there was all manner of trouble. My mother was tight-lipped and silent; Mary Ann went for me like a cat after a bird, pouncing on me the moment I stepped through the door. What meant I by it, treating their home like a common lodging house, visiting when the mood took me? Why should I work at the school for no reward, instead of looking for a position which would earn money for the benefit of my family? I was not a child any longer, I was a grown woman, and if I was not to find a husband then my role was to earn a living and support my mother into her old age, she who had given her life over to the care of her family. So it went, on and on. She barely paused for breath.

To my shame, I answered her back. I told her she was a wizened old maid who had not the intelligence nor the skill to find employment herself; if anyone was living off our mother's charity, it was she, not I.

She slapped my face, hard, for my insolence. She reminded me that she was my elder sister and I should show her respect.

I told her (but quietly, for my cheek stung) that respect had to be earned, and yelling at me like a barrow woman did not inspire me to respect her.

All the fire had gone out of her, expelled in that physical expression of violence. Our mother had watched the whole thing without any intervention. Perhaps she felt that we needed to fight every once in a while to keep us both sane. After we had finished, she looked from one of us to the other and said, 'There now. All's been said. Mary, make tea. Harriet, clear the table. We shall say no more about it.'

I brooded on the argument and thought that perhaps at the heart of it lay jealousy, that Mary Ann was jealous of my freedom and of my confidence. Perhaps I did torment her a little, with my free life, when she had little choice but to stay here and tend to the house as mother grew older and less able. I felt sorry for her, and then worried that my pity was a sign of my own pride.

Later, however, I felt stronger and angrier and I wanted to leave, there and then. My anger was cold and hard like a stone in my chest, whilst Mary Ann's own fury had burnt itself out. I cleared the plates after our dinner and washed them, and then announced that I was going to Miss Williams's house, because I had promised to help with the younger girls again on the following day.

Neither of them said a word. I took the schoolbooks and this journal – Lord knows I shall not leave it for Mary Ann to find again – and walked across the fields to the town.

But Frances was not alone; I heard voices, and laughter, as I climbed the wooden staircase that led to her door. I hesitated before knocking, thinking perhaps she would not wish to be disturbed. But then I thought of returning home to Farwig, and I knocked.

Frances opened the door and any concerns I had had disappeared immediately, for she smiled broadly at the sight of me and took my hand to draw me inside, saying, 'Harriet! What a lovely surprise, do come in.'

Clara was there, and also her brother, for she had been about to depart and he had come to see her safely home. For all his walking me back across the fields, I confess I had not paid him much attention until this evening. As a youth he had been gangly and awkward, following me around the town and watching me from the doorway of his father's shop; Mary Ann had laughed, once, and said he was sweet on me, and made fun of the whole show, but I do not think he was. I always thought he was just in need of a friend, and for some reason he had fixed upon me. But now he is a grown man, and still he is an odd, quiet sort of fellow: tall and well-built, with trimmed whiskers and fine features. He is now a bootmaker and works with his father, and yet despite the manual labour he has beautiful hands. Clara remarked upon this to Frances while I was there with them, and we all had to inspect Thomas's hands, much to his embarrassment. Perhaps it was having his hands offered to me to hold and inspect that made me look at him afresh. He seems very gentle. He is of my age and yet so quiet that people in the town say he is a little slow-witted. I have never thought this to be true. Frances told me after they had left that Thomas reads music well enough but he never learned his letters properly at school and so he has difficulties still with reading and writing. He hides it well enough and his family take care of him.

It's not right to feel sorry for people who don't feel sorry for themselves, and I do not know what led me to write of him, for the Lord knows there is nothing I can do or need to do to help him. I don't know what it is. Perhaps just that I thought it was a kind thing for him to do, to come along to a meeting of women that must surely have been dull for him, purely so that his sister would not need to walk the hundred yards or less back to their house alone.

They left perhaps a half-hour after my arrival, and soon after that Frances and I got ready for bed, for the fire had burned low and the night had turned cold. We lay there in bed talking for some time. I told her of the argument with my sister, and how I thought perhaps I had been too selfish. Frances replied that she could see fault on both sides, but for her part she was glad that I had come.

She said her heart sang when I was there with her, and she reached for my hand under the covers and held it.

I had no reply for this, for it sounded like something a lover might say. I wanted to reply with something kind, and meaningful, for it was completely true that I loved her dearly. But I realised – perhaps then, for the very first time, that Frances loved me in a different way. Not as a friend, but as a lover. As I had loved Richard. The thought was a startling one, because how could such a thing be? But the more I considered it, the more I understood that it might be true. And, while I thought of what to say, and how to say it, Frances's breathing deepened, and she was asleep, her hand still holding mine.

Wednesday, 2nd August

Maria is expecting a child.

I heard the news not from Richard, but from Maria herself; her first letter to me since I left London.

> *My dearest Harriet,*
>
> *I write to you now with the very happiest of news. Richard and I are to have a child in the autumn. I am full of nerves and anticipation, and, with the exception of a dreadful, crushing fatigue, I am quite well. The doctor says I am to rest as much as possible and dear Richard has been very attentive. Please do say you will visit us soon! We both feel your absence terribly, and I have so much to tell you. The school carries on much as it always has, although the girls miss you, and Miss Johnson begs me to send you her fondest regards. I beg you to write to me very soon with your news, and until then I remain,*
>
> *Your loving friend always,*
> *Maria*

The letter I had been anticipating was really a very bland one, no doubt because she had shared it with him before she sent it. The big secret she had put me under oath to keep was now out, and our intimate truce broken. There. I am bitter, can you tell? My heart is sore with it, for that might have been me; her life might well have been my life, had I not been so very foolish, and run away.

I wrote back almost at once, more to get the matter over and done with than because of any eagerness on my part. He will read it, of course, and so my words were carefully chosen.

My dear Maria,

I have just received your latest; such exciting news! My warmest congratulations to you both. I am so glad to hear that Richard is taking good care of you. You must, indeed, rest as much as you can; for the coming months and years will no doubt prove to be exhausting ones!

All is well here, although I do miss you both and my girls dreadfully. I long to visit and I promise I shall do so very soon. Until then, my dear friend, remember my love and that I hold you dear in this heart of mine,

Your,

Harriet

I took it straight to the post before I could think or read it over, or change my mind. An odd sort of letter. Here we continue with this merry dance: when will it end?

I have been reading some Aristotle, and thinking much on the nature of friendship. I am the sort of person who has but a few very dear friends, and all the rest are what I would consider acquaintances. I find it difficult to trust, but, once that trust has been established, I would sooner die than betray a friend. So it was with Maria, and, for all that has passed between us, I love her as much as I always did. My love for her, and now also for Frances – *philia* – is stronger than the love I feel for Richard – *eros*, as Plato defines it – although the feelings I have for them are quite distinct. How odd that the English language has just one word to describe such different emotions!

The love of a true friend surpasses all earthly affections, otherwise how should we live?

Friday, 4th August

Spending time at the school has proved a welcome distraction this week. Frances has been teaching the older girls to debate, although quietly, when I am taking the younger ones for some recitation. They sit in the corner and take a topic for discussion, and another will take the opposing view, and by so doing, Frances says, they will learn the courage of their own conviction and how best to express themselves when they find themselves challenged, later in life. Clearly Mr Campling would not approve, and she knows it, which is why she chooses the girls carefully. It is not done in secret, for I have no doubt that if Mr Campling saw and was angry then Frances would have something to say in response. She quite rules the school, without Mr Campling even knowing. I love her for that!

Meanwhile, the quieter girls are learning to speak up, and the bashful girls are finding their voice, and they are doing it all with Frances to guide them.

'Do you not worry,' I said to her, 'that these girls will find themselves dissatisfied with the life they will undoubtedly have, because you have taught them to be bold?'

I said this just after having praised her for her efforts, so she knew I was not in disagreement with her methods, just questioning of the results of it. She smiled at me and said that some of them might go on to great things, and she would not be the one to limit them. Plenty of others would try to do that, in the future, and she meant at least to give them the weapons with which to fight those injustices. What they chose to do with them was up to the girls.

Frances is the most excellent teacher I think I should ever know. She loves her girls, by which I mean she does not indulge them, but she disciplines them so well and praises them when they work hard, or try their best, that they want to improve and so work even harder for her. She knows them all as individuals, and loves them dearly, although she cannot tell them so except by giving them what they most need: the gift of an education. She defends them against Mr Campling's more vigorous complaints, and if anyone should speak ill of any of them she becomes a veritable warrior in their defence. I declare that is exactly what she is: Frances Williams, Warrior for her Girls.

I have learned so much from her, not just about teaching, but about love.

Monday, 7th August

Mary Ann has driven me from the house once more with her scolds and unkindnesses. She could see I was in distress; when I would not tell her why, she told me to stop snivelling as there was laundry to be done. I helped her for a while but I soon became exhausted with the effort of it, and Mary Ann chided me over and over. It seemed that everything I did was wrong. At last she instructed me to go, that she would manage better without me.

I walked into town and stopped at the Beezleys', but Frances was not there, of course, for it was the middle of the morning and she would have been hard at work giving lessons at the school. I wandered around the Market Place for a while but then I saw a young woman with a child in a shawl tucked under her arm. Other women were gathering round to fuss over the baby, which could not have been more than a month old.

I felt the tears start once again and the nearest place to seek refuge was in the chapel. I fully expected the gate to be locked, but at least the walk would take me out of the way of the busiest part of town, and from there I could begin the walk back across the fields. But the gate swung open when I pushed it. The main door was shut fast, but the back door was not. I called out when I entered, lest I should startle some poor person, but then immediately thought that perhaps someone might be at prayer. I was relieved to see that the chapel was apparently empty. I sat in the nearest pew and put my head in my hands and wept. All I could think of was

Richard. I had made a mistake, leaving London, I knew it surely, and now I had no way to mend what had been broken between us.

At length I grew aware that I was not alone, and with a start I realised that Mr Verrall was there beside me. I had been so overcome with my misery that I had not even noticed him approach. He asked me what was the matter. I wiped my face and got to my feet, and told him I was sorry, and I was quite well, and I should be getting along. He told me I had better take a moment to compose myself, and asked would I like some tea?

In the vestry he has a stove and a kettle, and a tin of tea, and some china cups. He told me he would make the tea strong, for fortitude, and as he made it I sat in a comfortable chair beside his desk and watched him. He asked me if he should pray for me, and I answered that he might not wish to, if he had had any awareness of what troubled me.

I should not have uttered those words, of course. He passed the cup and saucer to me, and then sat at his desk, his hands clasped in his lap, regarding me.

'You do know, Harriet, that you can speak to me freely of anything at all.'

I told him that I did know that.

'And,' he added, 'anything you do say is subject of course to the confidential obligations of my profession...'

And it was too much for me, to hold it all in; and I thought that when I had told Frances she had not judged me harshly, therefore so much the less should a minister of the Lord, and I found myself telling him the story, both what had kept me away from home so long, and what had sent me flying back here.

When I had finished he was silent, and I was grateful. He looked at me gravely and said that the Lord would judge me not by my actions alone, but by what was in my heart. And then we prayed together, and afterwards he asked if he could help me in any other way, and I said that really there was nothing to be done, and so he should not feel that he needed to trouble himself further with me.

We sat for a while and I have to admit that the tea revived me very well. He talked to me of chapel business, of the missionaries, of the church meeting and whether I should like to attend, until I felt myself again. He even made me laugh at some trivial thing: the finding of a broken coin in the offertory and who might be responsible for it, and the lengthy discussion that took place among the deacons.

'They are like a bunch of chattering monkeys sometimes,' he said. 'I do not wish to be unkind, but I just wait for them to finish and then tell them what they knew all along.'

I felt so very much better. I placed my teacup on the desk and rose. 'I should not trouble you further, Reverend,' I said.

He replied that I should feel free to visit him at any time. He said he was often in the vestry, alone, in the mornings; that he worked on his sermons and his letters here, untroubled by the interruptions he experienced at home.

I told him that he should find me interrupting him here instead, and he might regret suggesting that I visit.

He said that my visits would be a pleasure and not any trouble, and that now the idea had been presented to him he found that he was looking forward to being interrupted by me on a regular basis, although he hoped that I would come not only when I was troubled, but also the next time I felt joyful.

I shook his hand. He kissed mine. I left.

Now that I am home again, and I have redeemed myself with my sister by folding the sheets and putting everything away, and then helping her to prepare supper, I find my thoughts very much diverted by my visit to the chapel. Everything feels very different now. I have hardly thought of Richard, and Maria, since then. Even now, when I bring them to the front of my mind, rather like pressing a bruise for the sake of one's own curiosity, the pain is lessened. I can scarcely remember what it was that made me weep so much this morning.

I keep remembering the conversation, committing his words to my heart, and here on the page, as now I can hardly believe them. He is a busy man, an important man, and he knows my sins, yet he wants me to visit him again. I hope that my spirits will remain uplifted and that, when I next visit the chapel, I shall not make quite such a spectacle of myself!

Tuesday, 8th August

Of course, I should have stayed away.

However plain his invitation, I should have avoided the chapel until he had forgotten all about me once more. But Frances was busy with the school, and I wished to be away from the house. There has been no further news of Richard and Maria. I should, perhaps, have written to Richard, at the very least to let him know of my intentions regarding the school at St Albans, but I found I had no desire to contact him.

Instead I had written to Mr Edwards directly, requesting that he should speak to the board on my behalf, and that I was willing to attend at short notice, should that be required. He had replied very quickly, reminding me that they required a further character, as the policy of the school was to ask for two references, and his own alone would not suffice. Needless to say, I shall require a better testimonial than the one he has provided for me!

I thought of asking Frances but that very evening she had told me how desperately glad she was that I was here in Bromley, and how I should never leave. She meant it in jest but at that moment I could not ask her to facilitate my departure. Instead, I resolved to go to the chapel the following day to ask Mr Verrall for his assistance. That was this morning, and everything has changed, and I realise now my mistake.

It was as before: the gate was unlocked, the main door closed fast, the back door opening when I tried it. And he was there in the vestry. The stove was lit, and as it was a mild day the door was open to allow the fresh air to circulate. I say this for he saw me coming, and got to his feet, and I knew almost immediately that everything was very different, for he did not greet me as he had before. Instead he ushered me into the vestry and passed me and went to the back door and locked it from the inside with a key.

I should have spoken up. I should have voiced my request immediately, to make him realise that my intentions in visiting him here were entirely innocent, and quite business-like; but instead he made it clear, by the look on his face and by the purposeful way he passed me and went to lock the door, that my visit had become something else. Something transgressive.

He returned to the vestry and said, 'Did you close the gate?'

I told him I had.

'It would look ill, if I locked it,' he said. 'But the door is locked; if anyone should come, I shall tell them I did it without thinking.'

I did not tell him that I should prefer not to be locked inside with him; I did not tell him that I did not understand. Now, of course, I know I should have said something. I have been thinking over and over the events of the afternoon and wondering why I chose to act as I did. Or perhaps, to put it another way, why I chose to not act at all.

He was quite rough, and the deed itself was done very quickly. He did not undress. He did not look me in the eye. He kissed me, once, a dry, whiskery kiss on the mouth, firmly pressed so that I could feel his teeth behind; he was taller than Richard, and stronger, and younger, although still perhaps twenty years older than I. I observed these things as if from a distance. In my head were words like *move* and *run* and *fight* and yet I stayed motionless, like a doll.

He withdrew from my body and spent into his hand. I thought that, at the end, felt curiously like an insult. By the time he had finished I had straightened my skirt and stood upright again – for all of this had taken place, wordlessly, against the side of his desk, and the wall – and then he kept his back to me whilst he arranged himself. He turned back to face me, wiping his hand upon a handkerchief.

Afterwards he bade me sit, as if I had at that very moment walked into the vestry and found him working hard at his sermon. My bonnet was in a sorry state: the back of it had been crushed against the wall, and the ribbon half-torn off. I fingered it, avoiding his eyes. My hands were shaking. He offered me tea; I refused, saying I should rather have a glass of water.

He poured water into a glass from an earthenware bottle that he kept on the high windowsill. My throat was dry. The water tasted stale.

'Now, Harriet,' he said, 'this is a pleasant surprise. Was there a reason for your visit?'

I told him of the school in St Albans, and how they required a second character. Given what had just transpired between us, it should have been awkward for him to refuse; and yet he seemed peevish. With a cold draught of shock I realised he thought I had come with the intention of seducing him, to ask for his help, and had thought he would not have done it otherwise.

He sat and wrote it out while I watched, only in that moment beginning to realise what I had done and what he had done, and how everything between us had changed, for all that he was acting as if nothing at all had transpired. I could still feel the imprint of his body on mine. My thighs itched.

Now, hours later, I find myself wondering if it did happen, or if I simply imagined it; for everything after it was completely normal and calm. Outside the chapel, the day was grey. The town was full of people who had no knowledge of what had happened. Frances was at school; Richard was in London with Maria. None of them knew, nor will they ever know.

And the letter is here, in my hands, recommending me to the board.

TO THE COMMITTEE OF ST ALBANS SCHOOL

Miss Harriet Monckton, who is a candidate for the office of teacher, has been a member of the church under my pastoral care since August 1836, and has conducted herself with great propriety. I beg to recommend her to your confidence as one fully adapted to fill so important a station.

Wishing you God speed in your laudable endeavours to train up the little ones to be useful members of society and to share at length as heirs of immortality.

I am, yours truly,
GEORGE VERRALL
Pastor of the Independent Church,
assembling in Bromley Chapel.

I wonder at him; that he was able to write such a letter, just moments after he had committed an act with a younger woman, unmarried.

Lust. Adultery. Sin.

Wednesday, 9th August

Yesterday evening I felt numb and cold.

This morning I feel nothing but shame; I am disgusted at myself. For what took place yesterday in the vestry was an appalling lack of judgement on my part. Perhaps what I had told him about Richard Field had made him think that I would welcome his attention? But I had not. I did not invite it. I did not participate. I did not seek that out from him; on the contrary, I went to the chapel to ask for his assistance with another matter entirely. What took place was my fault in that it came from an inactivity, a passivity. *Ennui*, perhaps. Inertia.

I do not blame him. I do not think him a bad person, just really a very ordinary one. I had thought him holy, and honest, and clever; a man closer to God than I, someone who could speak the truth and bring people to the Lord. Now I see that he is, as well as those things, a human being just as I am, just as Richard is, with baser desires and a terrible lack of self-control.

A sad thing, a tragic thing, it is: such a moment, potentially a life-changing one for us both: the virtuous man and the fallen woman, the seducer and the innocent, and in fact it boils down to nothing more than two human beings crashing together and then moving apart again.

The impetuous, and the indolent. The one who cannot control his desire, meeting the one who can see tragedy approaching, but lacks the impetus to move out of the way.

I shall not go to the chapel alone again. That way, there will be no further misunderstandings.

Friday, 11th August

A letter came today, from Mr Wainwright, who is in charge of the board at the St Albans school. They are willing to employ me on a trial, for three weeks, commencing next Monday. He suggests I write for a room at an inn called the Beehive, which he recommends as being a respectable establishment. He will also enquire for suitable more permanent lodgings for me, should my performance be satisfactory.

I took the letter with me to Frances this evening. She read it carefully and said she thought it was very poor that they were not providing me with lodgings from my arrival, and that as a single woman in the employ of a school board it is the very least I should expect.

I had had lodgings in London, of course. With Richard.

She commented that I did not seem very happy about the letter, and in truth, I did not feel it. I could not say why; perhaps recent events had changed matters for me. I felt very out of sorts, distracted by it all. I told her that Mr Verrall had been kind enough to write me a good character for the position, and she responded by pulling a face.

I asked, 'Why do you dislike him so?'

She replied that she distrusted him, but she was not sure why. She said that she has a kind of sense about people, a feeling inside her, and the feeling has never yet been proved wrong.

I wanted to tell her that I disliked him too, but of course then she would want to know what had happened to change my opinion so dramatically. Besides, it was not entirely true: I did not dislike him. I just saw him, now, for what he was: a man like every other man, driven by desires that were more earthly than virtuous.

And Richard is just the same. I can only see that now: that my experience with Richard was exactly the same as that moment in the vestry, only much slower.

I decided then and there to travel to St Albans, for there was nothing else to be done. My mother and sister did not want me; the shame of what had happened was keeping me from the chapel; and if I stayed there was a chance that somehow my ill behaviour would become public, and my reputation would be ruined.

I told them over supper; they were both pleased. My mother wanted to know, where was St Albans? And my sister's face told me that she cared not if St Albans were halfway to Australia, so long as I went there and did not come back.

Saturday, 12th August

I had dinner with the Churchers, for Clara had invited me and I wished to be out of the house as much as possible. Clara had prepared a roast leg of mutton with potatoes and carrots and broad beans, and we all sat around the table in a most jolly fashion. Mr Churcher is a quiet man, but knowledgeable; as well as making shoes and boots with Thomas, he holds the weights and measures for the town and provides a service to all the shopkeepers by calibrating their scales. He says he does that more than the making of shoes these days, and that Thomas is quite capable, and in fact he has a much finer skill in leatherwork than he ever had himself.

Thomas blushed when his father said that, which I thought rather sweet. I believe he is much underestimated, for he is a deep thinker, although he expresses his thoughts but seldom. Clara talks and James talks, and often they talk for Thomas, as well, as if he were not present himself. They are so accustomed to doing so, they do not even notice they are doing it.

I found myself trying to redress this by asking him questions directly – 'What do you think, Thomas?' and 'Thomas, what music would you play in chapel, if you could choose?'

This latter question resulted in him looking up at me in surprise, and responding, 'Often I do choose. The reverend permits it.'

'Does he not match the music and the hymns to the subject of his sermons?'

'Sometimes he does, one or two, but the rest of them he leaves to me.'

'And how, then, do you choose?'

'From the season, or the festival, if there is one. Or just the hymns I like best. Or, sometimes, because we have not sung a hymn for a long time.'

He was quite pink with the effort of saying so much, in one answer. His family had stopped eating and were all looking at him in surprise.

'Emma will be pleased,' James said, and Clara admonished him for it.

'Emma?' I asked.

'Tom is betrothed to Emma Milstead,' James said.

'I am not!' Thomas exclaimed, and everyone laughed, which I thought rather unkind.

'He and Emma have been sweethearts for a long time,' Clara said to me, smiling. 'Since you left for London, in fact.'

For his part, I thought he looked uncomfortable with the idea, but had not the courage to say so.

'And James is walking out with Millie Judds,' Thomas said, as if in retaliation.

But James seemed very happy to admit it, and said, 'Indeed I am, and once I have enough money saved to get us a house I will ask her to marry me.'

'It will take a long while,' Clara said, 'since money falls through the hole in your pocket!'

We passed the dinner happily enough, and I helped Clara to clear the plates and wash them, and put them away, all the while talking of trivial things. She said she would miss me, when I went to the new school; I told her I should be back before very long if it proved to be an odd sort of place. She asked me why that should be, and I told her it was just something to say. But I was thinking that, just as Frances had an instinct about people, I have an instinct about places, and I am not sure about this. Perhaps it is because St Albans is north of London and it feels so much further away.

Not from Bromley, of course. From Hackney.

Afterwards, the whole family were going to chapel for the prayer meeting, and though I told Clara I had a slight headache, and wished to prepare for my journey, she insisted, and I relented. The chapel was almost as busy as it was on the

Sabbath, and we sat in the pews quietly whilst Tom played the Fantasia in C Major by Bach, and the reverend sat at the front, his head bowed. I looked around at them all: the Humphreys, the Milsteads, Susannah Garn and her brother Alfred; the Beezleys, the Durhams, the Robertsons; Mrs Verrall was there, with Ruth.

Emma Milstead was keeping a beady eye on the man she thinks is hers, looking daggers at me only when she could tear her gaze away from her beloved. She is a pretty girl, fair-haired, with a delicate little face. I think they shall make a handsome couple, if an unhappy one.

Prayers were said for the sick, and for the town, that it should turn from sin and come to the Lord; for the missionaries; for the Queen; for those who were suffering from want and hunger; for the poor, and the destitute, and those who had fallen into sinful practices. And I prayed, quietly, for the reverend, and for St Albans, and that I should know the correct path and have the strength to take it. A period of silent prayer gave way to those in the congregation leading us in their own prayers; Joseph Milstead prayed for his grandmother, who was poorly; Emma offered a prayer for the deacons, that their wisdom should increase. Ruth Verrall, in a timid voice, prayed for her brother, to know the love and support of his congregation, and to be steadfast in the face of temptation and the evils of the world that beset the chapel from every side. At every prayer we all said, 'Amen.' And, to finish, the reverend blessed us and this place and asked that we should all go forth as missionaries for Christ into the town, and to know that God's love carried us.

I made to go swiftly, but the reverend stopped me at the porch to talk. I lowered my eyes because I did not want to look at him, and he asked after the school at St Albans, and I told him I was to travel north tomorrow, and to begin work there on Monday. He said he was pleased but he looked flushed and his brows creased into a frown. He wished me well and asked if I required him to write to the local Congregational chapel there, to recommend me to them? I told him I was grateful for his concern but I could find my own way to the chapel and I should not wish to trouble him further. He wished me Godspeed and held out his hand for me to shake, but I hesitated.

Indeed, when I glanced behind me I saw that his wife was standing very close, and her eyes were upon us. I looked from her to the reverend and I saw from his expression that he had also only just realised how near she was, and he had been startled by it, and I thought that perhaps he had intended to kiss me. He said that he hoped to see me at chapel for the morning service before I caught the London coach.

I shook his hand, and left, and at the gate Thomas Churcher asked me if I would like him to see me safely across the fields, for it was growing dark.

I saw Emma Milstead waiting for him with her brother, and saw again the foul look she gave me, and so I told him that I was quite happy to walk by myself. He asked if I would come to chapel in the morning, and there was something about the way he asked that made me want to see him again before I left for St Albans, and so I said I would.

Wednesday, 16th August

I have been at St Albans for three days, and this is the first moment I have had the energy or the inclination to write.

The inn is perfectly reasonable, if a little noisy. I have been so very tired at the end of every day that I have fallen straight into the rough bed and been asleep almost immediately. The innkeeper's wife is a miserable woman, who keeps an orderly house above stairs, which means I am to be out of the room by eight and not return to it before six; I am to take my supper in the parlour of the inn and nowhere else, although I cannot imagine where she thinks I would go, as I am on my

own here and know no one. That said, I am to entertain no
visitors whilst I am here and I am to pay in advance.

I had thought that the school board would pay for my
accommodation for the first week or so, but they have not,
and so the little money I brought with me has almost gone. I
have kept back enough to afford a passage back to Bromley,
or at least to London, but if my wages are not to be paid
weekly then I shall have no choice but to use that money for
board and lodging.

St Albans is a miserable place, damp and grey and soot-
stained; rather smaller than Bromley, and without its warmth
and familiarity. There is a good abbey, and I am told the
market is held twice a week, on a Wednesday and a Saturday,
but otherwise there is little to recommend the town. There is
something bad in the air here, as I have not felt entirely well
since I arrived. It has rained every day.

The school itself is passable; it is smaller than the Hackney
school, and larger than Frances's National School in Bromley.
The boys have three classes, and there are two for the girls,
one for infants and one for older children. I thought from
my previous experience that I should be leading the older
girls' class, but I have been put as second teacher with the
infants, under the supervision of a Miss Mackenzie. She is
younger than I am, and very brisk in her manner. I told her I
had expected to be put in charge of the senior girls, and she
laughed at that and was quite cool with me afterwards. She
said that we must all labour for improvement, and that I took
to mean that all teachers began with the lowest position and
worked their way up.

The girls themselves are good enough, well-disciplined
if not well-taught. The youngest ones are still learning their
letters and even the oldest in this room are not reading well
when they leave it. They are taught sewing, singing, reciting
of poetry and Bible verses, some numbers although nothing
beyond addition and subtraction, and they are taken outside

388

for lengthy drills every morning, no matter the weather, boots or no boots. Several of the children are unwell with coughs and colds, and I fear that being made to perform drills in the rain cannot be good for them. Some of them are very thin. The result of the constant marching around outside is that the schoolroom floor is wet and muddy and it has been made my duty to sweep the floor and scrub it every day after school. There are two pupil teachers, and I believe one of them could do it well enough, but for some reason Miss Mackenzie has tasked me with it, whilst the pupil teachers tidy the books and count the slates and do other such duties.

Today after school I asked to speak to Mr Torrance, the headmaster. He had spoken to me briefly on my first day, but I had not seen him since then. Miss Mackenzie set her lips into a line. Perhaps she thought I intended to complain about her. Mr Torrance agreed to see me and I ventured into his office after I had cleaned the floor, and washed my face and hands.

'Well, Miss...?'

'Monckton, sir,' I said. At first I felt a little nervous, not so much a teacher as a pupil about to receive a punishment, and then I thought of Frances and her bravery and I remembered who I was, and why I was there, and I lifted my chin and smiled at him.

He did not return the smile, but I felt a little better for it. I asked him about the accommodation and the wages, and was told that payment was not made until the first of the month, and so I had almost three weeks to wait. I told him I could not afford to pay for the inn, and was there somewhere else I might find lodging? He said that was up to me, that where I chose to live was none of his business ... in summary, he was as unhelpful as it was possible to be.

I returned to the inn and took my supper of bread and cheese and a slice of cold ham, and after that I came up to my room and cried. I am so very lost, here. I have nothing, no friend, or proper place to live, or solace. I miss Richard, and now I miss Frances, and even, in a strange sort of way, I miss Thomas Churcher and the chapel and the place I was made to feel so welcome. I even think fondly of my mother and my sister and think, perhaps, that despite it all I was better off in Bromley.

Friday, 18th August

Last night I wrote a letter to Richard, asking if I could come to London for a brief visit. I did not say why, or when, but I posted the letter without further ado.

This morning I woke with a new resolve, and I packed my bag, and settled my bill, and went to the school to give my resignation to Mr Torrance. He was very angry. I went to Miss Mackenzie's room and told her that my circumstances had altered and I would not be staying, and offered my apologies to her, for she should have to manage without me. She lifted her chin and told me she had thought me rather unsuited to the position and that she hoped I should manage to find employment elsewhere. The first coach was full, and so I had to wait until the afternoon for the next with a free place, and thus it was early evening when I reached London and so too late to catch the coach for Bromley, even though that had not been my intention. I made my way to Fieldgate Street on foot, not wishing to spend the last of my coins on a cab, hoping that Richard had received my letter or at least, that Maria and he would not mind my arriving unexpectedly at their door.

In fact, they both seemed pleased to see me. They welcomed me in, and had the cook fetch me tea and a cold supper, and they sat with me in the parlour while I regaled them with my sorry tale of St Albans. Richard was very quiet, and I could scarcely look at him for fear of giving my feelings away, but Maria seemed in good spirits and enlivened by my conversation.

Maria thought it very ill of Miss Mackenzie and Mr Torrance not to make me more welcome; Richard sat and listened, and at the end said he was sorry for it; he had hoped that it would be a fresh start for me. Maria hid a yawn behind her hand, and said that she should like to retire. Her dresses no longer hide the evidence of her pregnancy, and I had not mentioned it, but Richard said to me that she has been very tired. Still she sat with us, until I realised that she did not wish to leave me alone with her husband. The thought made me sad, and I told them I should retire and leave them in peace. Richard said that the maid had made ready my old room, and now here I am, writing these sorry words in my journal and listening to the sounds of the house as it settles down to sleep.

This room at the top of the house I had once shared with Maria; it had two neat little beds, side by side, with a counterpane on each; a narrow window looking out over the street outside, with a view over the rooftops and the chimney stacks, smoke rising from each of them. On that bed I lay with Richard, more than once, on the nights he came to me. When it was first beginning.

I cannot think about him, not any more.

Saturday, 19th August

I am back in Bromley, at my mother's house. My sister has barely spoken to me, and my mother looks at me peevishly, her mouth set tight. I am a disappointment to them. If I could only be a better daughter, a better sister; if I could only have found a decent husband, or any husband, instead of entertaining such wild ideas. If only I could have been someone else.

I am sad and lonely and tired, and if it were not for the wrath of my mother and my sister I should go and visit

Frances. She, at least, will be happy to see me. I could go to the market or for a walk, but I do not wish to see anyone else, and have them all gossiping about my returning so soon. Time enough for that!

Richard was up early and away to his business yesterday morning, although I said goodbye to him it was of necessity a very brief farewell. I had breakfast with Maria, who had some milk pudding; I felt a little unwell at the thought of the rattling coach journey ahead of me, and could only eat some dry bread. I asked her how the pregnancy was progressing, and she answered that it was mostly exhausting. She feels tired all day, and has felt so from the very beginning. She says she does not feel nauseous any more. She has unexpected aches and pains, and none of her dresses fit her. She gets pains in her chest and has difficulties with digesting rich food, hence the milk pudding. She is sick of it, but eats it 'for the baby', and says she is already tired of doing things 'for the baby', and knows that the rest of her life will be thus.

I asked her if she felt the baby move, and she said she had felt it for some time, beginning as little flutters, and it grew stronger and stronger and now it sometimes kept her awake. She said it was an odd feeling, and not always a pleasant one.

I believe she was tired, but she was also ill-tempered, which I thought might be because she had slept poorly, but when I asked she said that was not the case. She said she is often disturbed by Richard, who has never slept well, and often gets up in the night to read or sit in his study.

I had been about to say that I thought he had always slept soundly, but I bit my tongue. We continued in this rather awkward fashion for a while and then she asked me how I had slept. I told her well, although it was not entirely true. I had lain awake for a long time, worrying about how it would be to go back to Bromley so very soon after leaving it.

Their latest servant, Bessie or Betty or some such name, was bustling about us and so it was difficult to speak freely. I felt sad. We had used to be such firm friends, before Richard had come between us. Even then, even during that time when he was taking turns with us, we were still kind to one another. It had been like a sort of a game to us, entertaining Richard. There had seemed to be no jealousy between Maria and me, not that I had ever discerned. We had talked about everything; until it had all come to an abrupt end that night, with Maria sobbing in my arms.

She kept her head down over her plate and made no effort to improve the conversation, and I excused myself as soon as I could, to wash my hands and gather my belongings. It was still very early, too early for the coach, but I fancied the walk would do me good. Richard had given me money for a cab, but I gave this back to Maria as I stood in the hallway, putting on my coat.

She seemed to brighten. I took her hands in mine, and smiled, and said the next time I saw her she would have a child, and how very exciting that was!

She nodded and I think she wept a little. I embraced her and said she was my very good friend, and I loved her dearly, and she wished me a safe journey home, and promised to write very soon.

I slept very ill last night, too, even though I was home safely and back in my familiar bed. I thought of Maria, and Richard, and how very badly I wanted them to be happy and yet some sinful part of me wanted them to be unhappy, too. I thought of Maria's sullenness yesterday and I wondered if she knew that my intimacy had continued with Richard until the very day that I had left, and whether she had been expecting it to happen again, perhaps while she slept. I felt very sorry for her, then, and I wondered if I should write to her, and reassure her, but perhaps that might just make everything worse?

I have the curious sensation that my life is unravelling, and I have no power to stop it.

Friday, 25th August

I have been unwell for several days since my return. A sickness kept me in my bed, and since then I have been so very weary that I have remained indoors. I think it is St Albans; that place has sickened me to the core. Mother wanted to send for the doctor, but Mary Ann stopped her, and I was glad. I knew it would pass; our mother needs to save what money she has left, to keep her. There is no money coming into the house at the moment other than the small amount Mary Ann makes by taking in dresses to be altered; my brother Stephen sends money now and again, but that is soon spent.

Frances came to see me, and Clara. Clara brought a cake and some fresh eggs, but Frances stayed and read to me, and when she was gone Mary Ann came to bed and said she thought her very high and mighty and eggs were far more useful, and I was too nauseous to even argue with her.

I am sick at the thought of seeing Mr Verrall again, at what might happen, at what he might say.

Saturday, 26th August

Mr Carter paid a visit this morning. It was a surprise, although it should not have been, for he wrote to me a while ago to say that he was coming to Bromley and should like to call in to see me. With all the confusion over St Albans, I had not replied, expecting to be away.

He has written to me several times, and I have responded in kind, but my letters have always been brief and formal. He seems to view me as some sort of friend, which is odd, given our very brief exchange at the reverend's tea party.

This morning I was called to the door by Mary Ann, and there he was. I did not want to invite him into the house, but I felt very awkward talking to him on the doorstep. In the end I told him we had all been unwell recently and I coughed loudly and that seemed to do the trick, for he backed away and hoped we would all be better soon.

Of course, Mary Ann wanted to know all about him. I told her he was an acquaintance only; she persisted and nagged, and in the end I went out to escape her.

I had supper with Frances and told her about Mr Carter's visit. She thinks it is very ill to be pursued thus; she thinks I should speak to the reverend about it. I showed her some of Mr Carter's letters, which she examined to see if I had perhaps given him a false impression. Frances said that she thought them improper in tone. I told her I had done nothing to solicit such attention, but she was comforting and suggested that men are often thus, and need to be spoken to very firmly in order to relieve them of their misapprehensions. She says she has spurned male advances vigorously in the past, and now she rarely receives any unwanted attention.

Sunday, 27th August

Clara and Thomas walked across the fields this morning to see if I was well enough to attend chapel. I was up and dressed, and, although I had not been intending to go, I felt a little guilty for not being more willing, and because they had made the effort to fetch me I put on my green shawl and bonnet and boots, and went with them.

The fresh air was invigorating, and I felt better in it, although my limbs were weak. Clara took my arm and Thomas walked ahead of us, as though we were explorers and he our guide, clearing the path and making it safe for us. I watched his back while Clara talked, for he is certainly pleasing to look at, fine and strong and tall. Emma Milstead will be lucky indeed, if he chooses to take her as his wife. The day was bright and clear and the path across the fields well trodden and not at all muddy. Clara chatted about the Sunday School and how well the little ones were doing, and of Betsy

Taylor, who had been very ill with a fever and everyone had thought her lost, until they had brought the reverend to her with some of the church members, including Clara, and they prayed over her, and now she is quite recovered.

The service was a fine one, after all my reluctance; the sermon was of kindness and forgiveness of those who injure us, and the text that Mr Verrall took as his lesson was Hosea, Chapter Two, verses 19 to 23. Emma Milstead was called to give the reading, and she read the words very sweetly:

'And I will betroth thee unto me for ever; yea, I will betroth thee unto me in righteousness, and in judgment, and in lovingkindness, and in mercies. I will even betroth thee unto me in faithfulness: and thou shalt know the Lord. And it shall come to pass in that day, I will hear, saith the Lord, I will hear the heavens, and they shall hear the earth. And the earth shall hear the corn, and the wine, and the oil; and they shall hear Jezreel. And I will sow her unto me in the earth; and I will have mercy upon her that had not obtained mercy; and I will say to them which were not my people, Thou art my people; and they shall say, Thou art my God.'

By the end of the service I felt restored, and in my heart I thanked God for it, but I felt that I should also thank the reverend, so that he should see that the awkwardness of our previous encounter was not going to keep me from my place in God's house. I waited with the other members of the congregation to shake his hand, and he was very surprised to see me. I told him the position at the St Albans school had been unsuitable, and, although I had been most grateful for his assistance, I had been led to return back to Bromley straight away. I told him I had felt the spirit move me during the service; that I felt the words of the sermon in particular had brought me closer to God and had made me feel loved.

'I thank God for it, Miss Monckton,' he said, and smiled at me warmly.

I shook his hand and walked back across the fields to Farwig — Thomas had been taken firmly by the arm by his betrothed, although I noted with a smile the wistful look he cast over his shoulder at me. The house smelled strongly of the fish stew that Mary Ann had cooked for us on Friday, the scent of it lingering in the curtains and the rug and the bedclothes, so strongly that I had to leave the house again just to breathe.

Monday, 28th August

I had a letter from Richard this morning, saying that Maria has been out of sorts since my visit; she suspected us of indulging in our previous intimacies and had been upset by the thought of it. He writes that he denied it in the strongest possible terms and assured her that, were she to ask me, I would confirm that no such transgression had taken place. He is writing to alert me, he says, that a letter from her might well be forthcoming.

I am disgusted and horrified at the very thought of it. Poor Maria! That she should suspect us now, when, of all ironies, nothing at all has happened between us! Richard goes on to state that Maria has been in a state of nervous excitement since she first admitted to him that she was pregnant. He says she has too much time on her hands, and has little to do but think and fret. He hopes that she will soon have the baby to think of, and will not trouble herself further; the baby will keep her occupied. He says that, if I should find myself in London at any time, I should alert him, and he would be happy to pay me a visit at whichever boarding house I am staying in, so as to not trouble Maria further.

Are all men like this? I am beginning to feel that they are! How foolish I have been, to not see it until now.

But this is so typical of Richard in particular: that he would fret about his beloved wife in one sentence, and almost immediately afterwards suggest that he should call upon me privately. A few weeks or months ago I might have been overjoyed to receive this letter, for it suggests that he still loves me, still desires me, and that perhaps he regrets the restrictions of a marriage covenant after all. In fact, none of these things is true. This revelation has come upon me quite suddenly, that he does not love me and probably he never did. He found me, perhaps, diverting. And with that revelation another follows fast on its heels: perhaps he finds Maria merely diverting, too. Perhaps he will find someone else more to his liking, and so it will continue.

Perhaps I am considering him unfairly; after all, he married Maria. He might have cast her aside.

Tuesday, 29th August

I planned to visit Frances this afternoon, but I arrived early and found myself at the chapel. I have decided that I shall not be afraid of the reverend, for I am certain that he must regret the event just as I do. If he should approach me again, I will decline politely and leave.

As before, I expected the gate to be locked and it was not. I should have closed the gate again and walked away, but of course I did not. I walked up the path to the side and, as before, found the back door open and apparently nobody inside.

The thought occurred to me, after my revelations about Richard Field yesterday, following his letter, that perhaps the reverend was in his vestry and perhaps he was entertaining another parishioner. Perhaps, like Richard, the reverend is a man who simply cannot decide which lover is best, and so keeps them all, until he is found out, or challenged. Men are such very odd creatures, that they do not know their own minds!

He was alone, however, and apparently pleased to see me. He made me tea. We sat and talked about his sermon, and the circumstances surrounding my return. I told him the school was lacking in facilities and was not supportive of its staff, which appeared to satisfy his curiosity.

Then he said that he hoped I had not returned on his account.

I said I did not understand what he meant, and his cheeks flushed and he replied that he hoped that I had not assumed from our previous time here in the vestry that he had developed some sort of attachment to me. I told him that I absolutely had not; that in fact the very reverse of it was true, and that we should both put it to the back of our minds, and not consider it again.

I felt stronger for having said this.

I got to my feet and made to leave, and he stood in the doorway, and apologised, and said I should not be offended, for he understood well enough that I was an intelligent woman as well as a deeply spiritual one, but that he had never thought of the indulgence of God-given desire as a sin.

I was so surprised at this remark – clearly he has thought about it in some depth, and so his intimacy with me was not, after all, a mindless capitulation to a physical need – that I took my seat once more and allowed him to continue.

He told me the most curious tale, then, about how his wife is a good woman, and a good mother to their sons, and a virtuous one besides, but how his marriage was almost entirely without the natural affection that ought to exist between a man and his wife.

I asked him why that was, and he told me that she had been delivered of a stillborn son at her first confinement and had never quite recovered, even though she had had three healthy babes since then. And then they had had a fourth child, another boy, after their youngest, but he had lived but a short while and had then been taken to the Lord, and she had quite blamed him for the death of their son.

I asked why his wife had blamed him, when such a thing, though terrible, was so very common as to affect almost every family at some time?

He said that his wife believed him to have strayed from the path of righteousness and to have been tempted into sin, and the very great fear of losing her reputation and that of her family had caused her a deal of distress, so that her pains were brought on early, and the child was born very small and weak.

'And were you?' I asked.

'Was I...?' he answered.

'Were you tempted into sin?'

He looked at me, his eyes unfocused as if his thoughts were occupied with the business of remembering that sad time; I thought he looked almost beautiful, if a man can be such a thing, with his eyes blue as the summer sky and his hair dark and curling about his ears, lost in consideration of the past. 'Of course I was,' he said.

Afterwards, in the passage at the side of the chapel I had to stop and be sick. It came upon me quite suddenly, and just as quickly was past. I wiped my mouth on my handkerchief and went on.

He thinks me, perhaps, an impressionable young girl who might feel sorry for him, this poor honest man who works so hard to bring people to the Lord and is sorely punished for having a cold wife. He thinks I should feel sorry for *him*, because his poor wife lost a child due to the pain of his infidelities! And he has unburdened himself to me, and has told me of his failings, and disguised them as triumphs. I am not entirely sure if I feel pity for him, or disgust, or something else. Perhaps I should feel a little flattered, that he revealed himself to me in that way. For he surely thinks of me as trustworthy: he knows I cannot tell anyone of our conversation, nor shall I. I have become his keeper of secrets, and in return he is my — what? What is he, to me? I cannot even think of it now without feeling unwell.

Thursday, 31st August

Sometimes situations seem quite altered when regarded afresh after a period of time. Richard is never far from my thoughts, but I have been remembering how our connection came about, the circumstances surrounding it, and it seems to me now so much less romantic than it seemed then.

That he seduced me, I now have no doubt. But it was not a seduction such as you see in a novel, with a reluctant, foolish girl being assaulted until she relents. In my case it started with conversation, and an unexpected kiss. It was not a relentless pursuit, even if the attention was unsought. I went to London that first time with no notions of love or passion, only the desire to teach and improve the lives and prospects of the girls at my school. My family released me into the care of a man thirty years my senior, recommended to them by the board as being respectable and kindly, and did not expect that I should, within the space of a few months, be sharing his bed.

It began with a kiss – on my hand, and then, on a further occasion, days afterwards, my cheek; and then my lips, when I did not turn my face away. Each of them followed by apologies for his behaviour and desperate promises not to insult me further. But in my mind he was not a wicked seducer, for I liked him; we had interesting, grown-up conversations, and he listened to me, and did not dismiss me as a foolish girl. What else should I have done? For I had nowhere else to go, and so I forgave him his indiscretions, and gradually I began to wish for them to continue.

'I fear I have developed an uncommon passion for your company, Harriet,' he said to me once. I remember it well. Afterwards he avoided me for several days, coming in late and taking his supper in his room, and breakfasting before me. In the end I was so very distracted by it that I knocked on his study door, late one evening. I told him he need not keep himself so separate on my account, that I had no desire to embarrass him in any way, and that, if he wished to avoid me, then I should perhaps seek out a new lodging.

'But this is your home,' he said. 'Do you not feel at home here?'

I said I did, I liked it very much. I had, privately, considered that my own reputation might be better served if I found lodging with a family, or perhaps a lady, but there were very few respectable houses that offered lodging in the area, and I felt myself lucky to have a room in such a fine house. Besides, were I to leave, then questions would be asked about why, and Richard's own reputation might be damaged by my departure.

'Then you must stay,' he said warmly. 'Don't mind me, my dear. You know you are safe here.'

Safe.

Such an interesting thing to consider, now. I never felt in any danger. He told me he was lonely, and sad; and that I was young, and beautiful, and intelligent. It was flattery, of course, and my soul purred like a stroked cat to hear it. I prayed for him every night, that he might feel less alone, or that he might draw comfort from the Lord. He never forced himself upon me, or subjected me to any violence, or expressed any anger when I did not comply. I never felt afraid. But does the sheep feel afraid of the wolf, the first time she meets him?

It did not feel like seduction, right up to the moment that he knocked on my bedroom door, late into the night, when I was already asleep. But that is exactly what it was.

Friday, 1st September

I have been thinking a lot about Richard, and his behaviour towards me. About Maria, and that night I held her and shushed her and told her that I would leave. She had cried all over again, with relief. Perhaps she thought my intimacy with Richard ended on that night; that she had won him, because he had seeded himself inside her. But on that hot, final day in May, my heart so desperately sad and lonely, I sought him out in his study and kissed him, and made him love me for the last time. I do not regret it, although perhaps I should. I did not promise her anything other than that I would leave, and I kept that promise.

No matter. I doubt Richard will tell her, for it puts him in a very bad light, and he shan't want that.

I had not written to Richard or Maria since his last letter, but this morning another letter arrived: perhaps with my salvation contained within it.

My dear Harriet,

I write in haste to inform you of another position that has recently been brought to my attention, that may be more to your taste: a new infant school at Arundel, in Sussex, is to be opened shortly and the board is in need of a teacher to take the management of the girls' room. The senior school is a good one, I have heard. If you should desire it, I will happily send a letter of recommendation on your behalf, and inform you in due course of their reply.

Maria wishes me to send you her love; her time is very near. I hope to write again with happy news very soon, and until then, I remain,

Your friend,

Richard Field

Your friend. He has written in sight of Maria, or perhaps he showed it to her before he sent it; there is no mention of his previous letter, sent just a few days ago. No matter: there is another position! I feel a little reluctant however, thinking that perhaps it would be wise to at least visit the school, and the town, before committing myself to another potential mistake. I wrote back to Richard immediately, asking him to please recommend me, and if he knew how soon they required the successful applicant to begin? I told him I should like to visit first, to see the school and the town and to be sure that I should be happy there.

I told Frances, of course. Once or twice I have come early to her house and brought with me food to prepare her supper, and she has been most pleased to see me when she returned, tired and hungry. We sit and eat, and she tells me all the news of the school: Mr Campling's blusterings, the progress of the senior girls; the funny little things that the smaller girls say.

I did so today: I made an oxtail stew this morning and set it on the stove to cook slowly, while I sat in her room, quietly, reading and writing here, and listening to the Beezleys bickering down in the bakehouse.

Frances watches me closely. I notice it because it is a gentle sort of watching, unobtrusive and yet strangely intimate. She watches me dress and undress; she watches me wash my body and she watches me sleep. I know she desires more from me, but I also know that she waits for me to find that same desire in myself. I do not say that I shall never find it, for I certainly feel affection towards her; I admire her very much indeed. And who knows, for certainly my heart is full of confusion for men and their ways.

Saturday, 2nd September

I woke in the darkness, needing the pot, and now I cannot sleep. I lay still for a while, listening to Frances breathing, and then I got out of bed and came to sit by the stove with my journal.

Arundel feels somehow closer to Bromley than St Albans, although it is not: this afternoon, leaving the dish of stew on the stove, I walked to the school to meet Frances and looked at the map of England that she has hanging on the wall of the girls' schoolroom. As the crow flies, it is nearer; but the roads to it look poor. It is close to the sea, however, and the air will be clear. I think I should like that very much. Above all, I should have the management of the infant school, with nobody to tell me what to do with my pupils; if I do well, in a year or two I should then have my pick of the schools in London, if I wished to return.

If I am spared, of course. It is at this time of night that I feel the most afraid; it feels that death and damnation lurk all around us, in the darkness, waiting to claim us. In the morning I shall feel foolish for these thoughts, of course, but now it seems that nothing good lies ahead for me.

Frances is stirring in the bed; she fidgets, sometimes, and talks in her sleep, just rambling nonsense, but rather sweet. She is not pretty but she is graceful, and strong, and bold. I wonder how that might feel, to love another girl; if it is different from a man. I think it should be very different, but perhaps that is a good thing. Men can be so brutal. In the act itself I find that energy rather exhilarating; but in other matters, in life and conversation, in quiet moments and in daily work, for example at the school, I find the brutality of men exhausting.

I do not know why I wrote that. I sometimes believe my honesty here is dangerous. If someone should read this! But it is the truth that resides in my heart, and this is my journal.

I am reminded of that visiting preacher — Mr Carter — who made such a point of speaking with me at that tea party and then would not leave me in peace. There was no harm in him, that I saw, just this dreadful persistence and the way he looked in my direction and yet never quite met my eyes. I sometimes believe that men can sense vulnerability the way a pony smells a pocketed apple; they seem to seek out women who are alone or friendless, and take advantage of a quiet temperament. It is a different form of brutality, I think, and just as exhausting.

I am so very tired: I shall try to sleep.

Thursday, 7th September

Maria is safely delivered of a son. I received the letter this morning. I was waiting to hear from Richard with news of the school, so when I opened his letter and saw that it contained nothing at all of Arundel, and only news of Maria, I confess I was rather disappointed.

And then I came to my senses and read the letter again, and learned that mother and child were both well, and the boy was bonny, and is to be named Richard, after his father. He actually wrote those words, 'after his father', lest I had somehow forgotten his name.

I showed the letter to Mary Ann and to mother, and then this afternoon I showed Frances.

'How do you feel about it?' she asked me, and to my very great surprise I was overcome with emotion and found myself weeping, and once I began I could not stop.

She held my hand and wiped my face, and stroked my cheek as I wept, and when I was finally still she made tea for us both. I apologised and she told me I had no need, that such feelings were best expressed, rather than left to fester. I said that they were best expressed in private, and she said that I was such a dear friend, I should have no concerns that she would tell anyone of it, or indeed of anything that I told her of myself and my feelings.

'Of all things,' I told her, with a laugh, 'I am most disappointed that the poor child is forced to live with his father's name!'

She laughed too. 'What would you have him called?'

'I don't know – something unusual, and noble. Ebenezer, perhaps, or Ephraim.'

'You have strange fancies, Harriet!'

I felt a little better for having wept, and for our conversation. We ate supper and Frances continued to suggest names for Richard's child – Elias, or Abraham, or Methuselah: fine Biblical names every one, and yet hardly seen today. We talked of children in the Bromley school and in the Hackney school, and those names we liked and those we didn't. Frances said that she had never had a child called Charlotte who was not also ill-behaved; I said I had taught three Charlottes and they had always been most troublesome. And Emilys were always sweet; Susans were often sly, but funny.

When Frances retired this evening I wrote a reply to Richard, congratulating them both on their joyous news, and wishing a long and happy life to Master Richard James Field, and hoping that I shall see them all soon, the very happy Field family. I shall pray for them, and give thanks for Maria's health.

Monday, 11th September

I believe I am in shock.

I attended chapel this evening for the prayer meeting and found but limited company there; Benjamin Beezley was the sole deacon in attendance, and Jane Humphrey, Joseph and Mary Milstead, and Jane Cooper, and just the reverend besides. It was possible to see his disappointment and displeasure at this unexpected drop in attendance, and his first prayer was for the 'ungodly' who chose to indulge their vices in the town rather than worshipping the Lord their Saviour and praying for their immortal souls.

One by one, the gathered company voiced their own prayers. Finally the reverend spoke again, and prayed for the Queen, and the wisdom of her ministers, and for those who were suffering in the world from hunger and want, and then he said an amen, and we all said amen, and then we wished each other goodnight. I do not know what it was that caused me to tarry, but I did. He invited me into the vestry. I should have said no; I should have told him that Jane was waiting for me in the lane, but I did neither of these things. I followed him into the vestry. He lit the lamp but made no attempt to light the stove.

He told me we should pray for forgiveness, and ask the Spirit to come into us and lead us closer to God. I said nothing. He bade me on to my knees and I was expecting him to pray but instead he tucked his gown behind him and unfastened his breeches and put his hand under my chin and squeezed my cheeks to force my jaws to open, much as you might do to a dog to force it to let go of something it has seized.

I believe I said no, or made some sound of protest, and he hesitated, and then pushed himself into my mouth anyway.

I could have bitten him. I could, probably, have pushed him back and away from me, and got to my feet and run. I could have screamed and shouted and called him a devil. But I did not. Instead I watched myself from a distance, as if the real Harriet were crouching in the corner of the room and the Harriet there on her knees, eyes tight shut, gagging, before the man who should be righteous and pure and instead was ugly and soiled, were some type of shadow, or spirit.

I opened my eyes and looked up to see him looking down on me with an expression of rapture; the same expression I had seen on his face during the most vehement of his sermons. If it was true, that he received the outpouring of God's Holy Spirit from such transgressive behaviour, then he was certainly receiving it right at that moment. I closed my eyes and stayed very still, made of stone, made of ice, until he had finished.

This time, he did not turn away and finish into his hand. He held my mouth closed with his fingers under my chin so that I could not deny him this final, ecstatic assault.

At last he withdrew and stepped back, and I dropped to my hands and knees and coughed and spat and tried not to vomit. By the time I had got to my feet and brushed off my skirts he had adjusted his garments and sat behind the desk. I wiped my mouth with my handkerchief.

I waited for a moment, thinking that perhaps he would say something. Instead he took up his pen and began to write. I supposed he was composing a sermon.

I walked across the fields in the dark, scarcely thinking of what had transpired between us. Thinking of it was too difficult. When I got home I changed my dress and went straight out again, telling my mother I should stay the night with Miss Williams. I gave her no further explanation, nor did she ask me for one. Mary Ann was already asleep.

Tuesday, 12th September

A damp, miserable day. I stayed with Frances last night and I have not gone home, because there are bruises upon my face, fingermarks where the reverend gripped me. Frances has noticed, and asked, and I told her that I had done them myself, when overcome with a sneezing fit. She deserves a better lie than that, but the question was unexpected and I had no quicker response. Only when I was alone again did I look at my face in the glass and see the marks. They are small ones, and if I had some powder or chalk I could cover them well enough, but Mary Ann would notice them, and she would not accept a lie as easily as Frances has done.

Frances knows I have my secrets, as she has hers; we allow each other that. It is part of the reason I love her.

Thursday, 14th September

I was reading in the parlour here when I heard the reverend's voice downstairs, talking to Mr Beezley. I heard him remark upon something and then, 'praise God for it' and 'translated into Glory'. He never stops. I heard Beezley say, 'Miss Williams is at school, but I believe she is within,' and then his tread upon the stairs, and the knock upon the door.

What should I have done? Left the door locked, and told him that I was unwell? I opened the door. He asked to come in. I told him it was not my house to invite him over the threshold, and he asked what it was I expected him to do.

I was conscious of the Beezleys, and that they must surely hear us, and I said quietly to him that he should be overheard, and he responded, 'We must be very quiet, then,' and put his hand upon the door and pushed it open.

I told him he had bruised my face. He put his hand under my chin and tilted it towards the window so that he might see, and then said he was sorry for it. 'I should not have caused you any pain.' But he said that he had experienced such intense excitement from my 'Holy prayers' that he had seen a vision of Heaven itself. He said he had written late into the night, and had written four sermons of such poetic beauty and Glory that they could only have come directly from the Holy Spirit.

'Don't do that again,' I told him. 'It leaves a mark. Someone will notice.'

He said he would not.

I asked if four sermons should not suffice, for now, as I had felt very sick afterwards and was still not fully recovered.

He was perspiring. He took out a handkerchief and patted it across his brow, then he removed his gown and hung it on the hook on the door, and sat carefully on the chair.

'Take off your dress,' he said.

'I prefer to remain clothed,' I said.

He looked at me, his face devoid of expression. I looked at him. I was perfectly calm. I would not do as he asked, not this time.

But then, 'I have something for you,' he said.

I thought perhaps he meant some sort of payment, and I was about to tell him to choke himself with it, but instead he drew from his jacket pocket a letter, which he held aloft. From my position, I could see it bore Richard's handwriting upon the envelope. I felt a jolt of fear, thinking perhaps that he had somehow entered into correspondence with Richard and they had been discussing me.

'What's that?' I asked, pretending calm.

'I called at your mother's house before coming here,' he said. 'She told me you had stayed with Miss Williams, and bade me bring you a letter that arrived this morning.'

I held out my hand for it. He did not move, or offer it to me.

'Take off your dress,' he said again.

'If I refuse?'

He nodded slowly. 'You might, of course. But you are a kind girl, Harriet. A good girl. You would not wish to deny the Lord your God, I am sure.'

'Someone might see you,' I said.

He got to his feet. 'Then we must be careful,' he said. 'Now, take off your dress, and your stays, and your boots, and your stockings.'

He allowed me to keep my chemise. His hands grasped at my breasts and squeezed them hard. He told me to kneel on the bed, at the very edge, and he mounted me from behind, like an animal. It was very painful at the end, and the act itself brought me no joy or pleasure but the word in my head, *brutality*, chanting in my head, over and over again like a psalm. I thought of the noise of him breathing, the noise of the bed shifting on the floorboards, and thought of the Beezleys downstairs, and willed someone to come and make it stop, no matter how disgusting would be the sight that greeted my rescuer and what it would do to my reputation. I thought of shouting out, calling for help, or of taking hold of the lamp beside the bed, or the poker, and hitting him with

411

it. In that moment when he grunted and held himself tense I thought of Richard and his baby son, that should have been named Ebenezer and instead was named Richard, a thought out of the air like a quiet voice calling to me, *my son, my son*, and it made me want to weep.

Afterwards he dressed, and told me I was a sweet girl, for indulging him so.

I said that I did not care for these indulgences, and I should perhaps tell someone of them.

He was not angry at me, so much as very cold, and hard, and he said that whoever I told would not believe me for why should they? I was just a girl, and a proud, excitable girl at that; and he was a minister with a large, respectable congregation, who did many good deeds in the town, to save its people.

I told him I should tell his wife, and she would believe me.

Then he said that his wife was kind and good and blameless in all of this, and to think of hurting her thus was a very wicked sin indeed; and besides, it would serve only to damage irreparably my own reputation, and what would my mother and my sister do then? I should be cast out, and friendless. Not even Miss Williams would be seen with me after that, he said, for she had her own position and reputation to consider.

He was right, of course. About all of it.

I said nothing else and when he was properly attired once more he left me alone, and I lay on the bed in my chemise until my skin dimpled with the chill of the afternoon. I got up and used the pot. There was a little blood. I found the tin basin and stood in it in the cold and scrubbed myself all over, and dressed, the clothes clinging to my damp skin. My stays would not fasten because my hand was shaking; I left them open at the bottom to allow myself to breathe. I found I was doing all of these things without thinking. Only when I had finished, and thought I should make tea, something with

412

which to fortify myself to continue, did I see that he had left Richard's letter, unopened, upon the table.

The Arundel school are willing to accept me. They require an additional character, to be sent by return of post, addressed to the superintendent of the board.

The relief of it was immediate; I will be free of this, in Arundel! And then, afterwards, the very great fear came upon me once again. For how shall I manage?

Friday, 15th September

Frances, my rock, my salvation, my Warrior, has pretended to be pleased about Arundel. I told her I cannot ask Verrall for a character and asked her if she might write one; she said she would, and did, but after she had retired I had another idea, and I copied out the letter that Verrall wrote for the school at St Albans. That was good enough, and his word as a minister will hold more weight than that of a fellow schoolmistress. It should not be thus, but unfortunately it is. It is unlikely that the school will call into question the authorship of the letter, but if they should ask him if he wrote it I think he will not deny it. He owes me that, at least.

I sent the letter immediately. I find my spirits lifted so very much by the prospect of a new beginning! Just a few weeks ago I was so desperate to return to Bromley, and now I find myself even more desperate to quit it once more.

Tuesday, 19th September

I have not written in here for three days. I am with Frances; she is asleep.

I can hardly bear to write the words, but I must. For to write them is to make them true, and this is the truth, that I can no longer deny.

I believe I must be with child.

I am so full of fear and wonder and horror at it, I scarcely know where to begin. For a long time I think I suspected, but hoped that it could not be true, and every day the suspicion grew and grew and did not diminish. Every morning I woke hoping that my visitor would return on that day, and it has not. Now I have had to loosen my laces at the bottom, as I still cannot fasten them; I have been sick, and feeling sick so regularly that it has become quite expected; and the weariness that Maria spoke of; and now, just in the last days, I have felt a sensation so curious in my belly that the only way to describe it is as if a butterfly or some other tiny, feather-light creature is trapped inside me and trying to escape.

Frances sleeps so peacefully. I have been sitting here at her table with the lamp turned low, watching her. She knows something is the matter with me, but I cannot tell her; I cannot tell anyone. I am writing this to get the words out of myself, to pull them from my head like a conjurer pulling handkerchiefs from a magical hat.

Oh, I am so afraid! What is to become of me?

My first thought was that I should go to London. I should see Richard, and tell him, and he would fold me into an embrace and reassure me. But no matter how many times I thought about it, I could not imagine what he would say. Would he leave Maria, and the baby? Of course not. But perhaps he would find me somewhere to live, nearby, but away from the school and the people who knew us. I could style myself as a widow, my husband lost at sea, perhaps, and Richard as my uncle or my guardian or some such.

And then I remembered the reverend.

I tried to think of how long it had been since I had last had my monthly visitor, but I could not. I had had some bleeding in Bromley, not long after I arrived, but it had taken me by surprise and had lasted but a day. Around that time was the first time the reverend had taken advantage of me in the vestry. Was it possible, then, that the child could be his?

Verrall, or Richard?

The more I think of it, the more confused I become and the easier it is to convince myself that it was one of them, or the other. I have been seduced by not one man, but two. And one of them has put a child inside me.

What am I to do? Whatever am I going to do?

Wednesday, 20th September

I slept in this morning and Frances had left for school when I finally woke. She left me a note, saying that I was sleeping so peacefully she had not wanted to disturb me. I think the rest has done me good, for I have woken with renewed spirit. I said my prayers, and asked the Lord for wisdom to deal with my troubles in such a way that will bring Glory and Honour to Him, and I admitted that I trusted Him and knew that he would not forsake me, for this he promised in Jesus' name. My words, whispered into the chill morning air, disappeared like vapour.

I washed and dressed, and ate some gruel that was left by Frances, and sat at the table to write a letter to Richard. I believe it is more likely that the child is his; and, of the two, I believe he is the one who will be more inclined to kindness. I have written it and rewritten it several times, but I think finally I have something that I can bring myself to send. I copy it here, for when it is sent I might misremember my words, or perhaps he might deny them, and so I will have the proof of it.

Dear Richard,

I trust this letter finds you, and Maria, and the baby, all well. I write with news of my own: I can no longer ignore the signs, and I am afraid I must inform you that I am expecting a child. I do not know when, but I can only assume that I am some months advanced already.

415

*I have told no one of my condition, and other than
some sickness and exhaustion, which may otherwise
be explained by my anxiety at being so long out of a
situation, I am quite healthy. I do feel most terribly
afraid of what might become of me, and the child, as I
am sure you can understand; and I ask you most urgently
to write to me with words of advice, for surely you are
the only person I can turn to in my troubles. I beg you
to write immediately, dear Richard, and be assured that
I am, always,*

    Your friend,
       Harriet

I tidied the parlour and the bedroom and washed the
floors, for want of something to do, and took the sheets to
the laundress on the corner who will deliver them back to us
when they are done. I took the letter to the post and suffered
only a moment's hesitation before sending it. I spent some
time preparing a supper of chops and potatoes for Frances,
and when she came in she said she thought I looked a little
brighter, although by that time I was feeling unwell once
more and went to lie down on the bed, for the smell of the
chops was making me nauseous. When she had eaten, Frances
came to the bedroom and asked me if I should like her to
send for the doctor.

'I am just a little tired,' I said, 'and anxious about Arundel.'

She stroked my cheek very softly and said, 'You know you
are welcome to stay with me for as long as you wish,' and
then she added that she could spare a few shillings a week
if I wished to send them to my mother; my company, not
to mention my diligence in tidying the rooms and cooking
her meals, required more compensation than merely her
friendship.

I told her I should not expect that of her, and thanked
her all the same, and she kissed my forehead, and told me I

was welcome to stay whenever I wished, and for as long as I wished, and that she wanted to have every minute of my time until I left for Arundel, and was vexed that she had to share me with my mother and my sister, who did not appreciate me.

Frances thinks highly of me now. She will think less of me when she knows, as she surely soon must. Spinster she may be, but she is no fool, and she knows my body well enough now to be marking the changes taking place within it.

I am mourning the loss of my friendship already, even whilst it still burns brightly in my heart, and in hers.

Friday, 22nd September

Sick into the pot this morning. Mary Ann had nothing to say other than, 'You're always sickening for something or the other,' and 'I hope you're going to clean that up yourself and not leave me to do it.'

I did, for the smell of it made everything very much worse. There seemed little point in going back to bed afterwards, as the sky was already lightening, so I swept the fire and cleaned the stove, and washed the floor in the kitchen, all the while trying not to be overcome with it. I made some tea and had some bread, and felt a little better.

Mary Ann walked to town to buy meat and eggs and flour, and a few other items, and I stayed with Mother and read to her while she sewed. The postman has brought a letter for me, from Arundel. They ask me to attend the school for the first week in November – a little over six weeks from today – and they will provide me with board and lodging with a respectable Christian family in the town, paid for at a deduction of three shillings a week directly from my wages. The letter confirms that I shall have sole charge of the new girls' infants, and I shall report directly to the board. I am permitted to appoint up to two pupil teachers from the senior girls' school, which is adjacent to but entirely separate from my own, in consultation with the senior school's headmistress, Miss Pargeter.

I never knew it was possible to feel elated and desperately miserable at the same time. Already I am thinking of the Arundel school as *my* school, as the infant girls as *my* girls; and yet, if I am right in my supposition, then it cannot be. I am with child, and my belly is already too big. Another month and surely it will be plain for all to see. Even if I were somehow to disguise it, the time will come to bring the child into the world, and what shall I do then? How shall I manage? Shall I hide the child – Richard's child, I want to believe – and send it to a woman somewhere to be cared for? Shall I take it to London and leave it in a basket on Richard's doorstep, a foundling for Maria to bring up with their own son? Shall I go somewhere else, somewhere nobody knows me, and pass myself off as a widow, and take in laundry? All of those things make me want to weep.

Perhaps I am getting ahead of myself. The Lord may yet decide to take the child from me; my sister suffered the loss of the first three of her infants, and my own mother lost a child before Mary Ann was born. It is wrong to pray for such a thing, and I shall not do it, but still I cannot assume that the child will yet live. It may be that I will be able to go to Arundel after all. So much is in the Lord's hands! He would not send me such a gift, only to wrest it out of my grasp before I have had the chance to experience it?

Wednesday, 27th September

I have been in bed for five days, with a head cold. I spent a lot of time asleep, so that Mary Ann thought me truly ill. I told her not to send for the doctor, for Mother cannot spare the money for it, and I repeated to her that it was just a chill, and I should recover well enough with rest. She brought me broth, and beef tea, and I slept, and in so doing escaped from my troubles for a short while.

Richard should have received my letter days ago, and there has been no reply. Perhaps he will never write to me again. Should I write to Maria instead? I think I should have written to her in the first place!

Frances came to visit me after school, which was very kind. She brought me apples, and a copy of Miss Edgeworth's *Helen*, and a pudding she had made, to be shared with Mother and Mary Ann, and some of Mr Storer's gingerbread, 'for fortitude'. I told her that the Arundel school required me for the first week in November, and she frowned, and said, 'If you are well enough by then.'

I assured her that I was only suffering from a little cold, and that a few days would see me back to full strength. I think perhaps she thinks me weak, after my brief sojourn in St Albans – that I cannot cope with the life of a schoolteacher after all. I wish I could tell her what truly ails me! But Verrall is right: she has a reputation to guard, and she is right to treasure it, and it would undoubtedly cost me her friendship. I value it above everything else, now. Perhaps it is all I have left.

Thursday, 28th September

A letter from Richard this morning.

> *My dear Harriet,*
>
> *Thank you for your last, although I admit I am uncertain as to how best to respond. I am sorry for your troubles, and I hope that you find a swift resolution to them. There is, as I am sure you understand, very little I can offer you in the way of assistance, as Maria and our son need all of my attention at the present time. Will you go to Arundel, as planned? Perhaps I shall see you*

in London before you continue your journey further,
although, as I am sure you will agree, it would be best
if you stay at a boarding house, rather than coming to
Fieldgate Street.

> *I remain, as ever,*
> *Your friend*
> > *Richard Field*

The letter made me very ill. He seems so cold towards me now! I suppose I should expect it, for I am no longer his Harriet, the girl he took into his care and claimed to love; I am cast aside, a woman who is threatening to bring trouble to his door.

I should have waited until I was calm, but the fresh wave of fear overcame me, and I wrote back immediately.

Dear Richard,

> *Your letter has vexed me so very much! My troubles*
> *have a cause, and you are that cause: I find myself in*
> *this desperate situation because of you, and I trust*
> *that, as my friend, if not as my love, you would offer*
> *me every possible assistance. Is there nobody of your*
> *acquaintance, who might be able to help? Or any other*
> *solution, that might be offered to a woman in such a*
> *predicament? Perhaps there is somewhere I could go, to*
> *be delivered of the child safely, and find a good person to*
> *take care of it? I am sure there are discreet establishments*
> *to help unfortunate women, and if you would only send*
> *me a little money you need not even trouble yourself to*
> *find out such a place, but I should do it myself.*

> *I find myself in this matter very much alone and*
> *friendless, and I trust that in my hour of deepest need,*
> *dear Richard, that you will be the true friend that you*
> *have always promised to be to your own,*
> > *Harriet*

Saturday, 30th September

Dear Harriet,

I found your last letter very disturbing. As you know, I have very little money to spare and what I have is spent on my wife and son, to ensure their comfort and continuing good health. You mention that there might be an establishment to which you could go, but I am certain I have no knowledge of such a thing, and to suggest that I should have is, I must say, insulting. I am sure you did not mean to imply that I have had cause to recommend such a place before?

You say in your letter that I am the cause of your trouble, and that, too, is a matter of concern to me, since, as you must well appreciate, I have only your word that I am the cause. In your letters and during your visits you made frequent mention of gentlemen friends – perhaps I should hesitate to call them that? – for example, your cousin George, and the young men at the chapel, and your very own dear friend the Reverend Mr Verrall, to name but a few. I should also perhaps remind you of Samuel Phipps, whose acquaintance you made in this very house, and with whom you displayed a very free manner more than once at dinner parties here. These aforementioned gentlemen should perhaps also be considered by yourself as worthy of approach, as you might find one of them in a better position to assist you than am I.

Richard Field

This time I have not replied immediately, but determined to wait, so as to find the most appropriate response to this foul epistle. All day I have swung between extremes of emotion, from anger, to fear, to pain, and back to anger once more. Oh, I have been most terribly wronged! I know that some fault lies with me, for I lay with him, and did not deny him what he asked; and for all that I loved him I should have seen the consequences of that love, and run from it!

That he should mention Samuel Phipps to me! I recall matters rather differently: that Richard suggested he should sit next to me at supper, and then behaved like a peevish child all evening when he found that Samuel and I were enjoying a lively conversation. Afterwards, I laughed and accused him of being jealous, and he sulked for days, only deigning to speak to me again when I had pandered to his mood and apologised.

Although the letter has brought to mind that I might also approach Mr Verrall for his help. It is, after all, also possible that he is responsible for my condition, given our association, although I expect he will deny it. He is that sort of man. Whether he believes himself responsible or no, he might still be willing to help me, given that he is a man of considerable wealth, and a Christian (I shall not say a good Christian, for I know him to be otherwise) who preaches forgiveness of sins and the helping of those unfortunate souls who have found themselves cast low. He might, indeed, have counselled other young women in my situation, if not here in Bromley, then perhaps in his previous time at Peckham.

It may be an error of judgement to approach Mr Verrall after the last time, but he has left me alone since then, and I think perhaps he has realised that he has used me ill, and has repented, and is leaving me in peace.

Monday, 2nd October

I am with Frances, and, as is always the case, I feel so much better with her than I do at home. She has such a lightness of spirit, I cannot help but be gladdened by it. For a short while I forget my troubles, and am absorbed in the news of the school, and the pupils, and Mr and Mrs Campling. But then she asks me for my opinion, or about Arundel, or chapel, and I am reminded of it all over again.

I have been hoping that some illness will befall me, that will carry the child away peacefully. I cannot pray for this, of course; even though the thought of losing the baby – Richard's baby? – fills me with a strange sort of relief, it is a child, and it is God's Holy Will that I find myself thus burdened, and I must make the very best of the matter. But how? Which avenue is the best course to take? I have followed the thread of every possible thought to its conclusion, and I am dismayed that there is none that I like better than any other.

The best way, the righteous way, is this: to write to Arundel, and offer my sincerest apologies, but inform them that my circumstances have changed and I shall not be able to take the situation after all. Then I should present myself at the nearest workhouse, or, better yet, walk to Sydenham or Brixton or somewhere even further than that, where nobody knows me, and take on a made-up name, and there go to the workhouse and ask them for help; and I shall have the child, and it will be taken from me and put with the other children, and we shall have a difficult life if we have one at all, but at least we might not starve to death on the street.

Or I could throw myself on the mercy of my family; not my mother, or Mary Ann, but perhaps my brother William and his wife Anne, who have been married a year but as yet have no child: perhaps I might stay hidden in their house until the baby comes, and then Anne could take the babe herself, and pretend it is her own? But they are not rich: Will is in service at a house in Belgravia, and Anne takes in laundry. I could promise her money from my own income to compensate them for the extra mouth to feed? Nobody need know anything about it but us. Will was always the kindest of all my siblings; surely he would take in his niece or nephew, rather than see it raised in a workhouse?

But the years would pass, and I should see my own child brought up within the family but not by me, and my heart should be broken by it; for this is my child, my own, and how should I see the dear little face and recognise it, and not love it for my own?

Tuesday, 3rd October

Today I walked through the fields, which are newly turned and muddy, and smell of rain. I think perhaps this child will kill me after all, for I cannot imagine living to see the wheat growing tall again, after this. I try hard to picture it, and the months ahead – the weather turning colder; Christmas, and the dark days and nights, and then spring – and I cannot see it. Nothing but blackness lies ahead for me.

It was thus engaged in my own bleak situation that I came across Thomas Churcher, who was on the path ahead of me beside an old, bent oak tree and had crouched to look at something in the hedge beneath it, that separated this field from the next, alongside which ran the path. He heard me approach and turned, and placed his finger upon his lips to urge me to be silent. I crept forward and reached him, and asked him what he was doing.

'Look,' he whispered, and pointed into the hawthorn, below the tree.

I followed his indication and saw a mother cat had made a nest there in the old roots of the tree, quite well hidden; and at her belly were suckling three tiny kittens. At this very little thing I found tears starting in my eyes, and I had to wipe them quickly away, lest he should see and ask me why I wept.

'I have been bringing her scraps,' he said, and brought from his pocket some pieces of meat, and a dead mouse, which he said had been in the trap this morning, and when the mother cat saw this she got to her feet and left the small blind kittens where they were, mewling. She came to Thomas and let him pet her, and rubbed up against his knee, her tail curved into a perfect arch, first this way, and then that.

'They are so very tiny!' I exclaimed.

'Would you like to hold one?' he asked.

'Will she let me?'

He nodded, and put his hand inside the hedge and brought out a kitten, while the mother cat watched the kitten and Thomas and continued to rub her body against his leg. He placed the kitten in my cupped hand, its little mouth opening and closing, its tiny pink paws splayed helplessly across my palm. I felt certain that I should drop it, or harm it, and I felt so very sorry for the mother watching me and thought that she must be terrified, so I passed it very carefully back to Thomas, and he placed the baby back in the shelter of the hedge. The cat went straight to the kittens then, and proceeded to wash them vigorously.

Thomas stood up, and offered me his hand to help me up too. I took it gratefully, and we continued walking towards the town. I stumbled a little, and he offered me his arm, and I took it. We carried on in that manner, neither of us speaking and yet with no requirement on either of us to do so. I was thinking of how very gentle he was, and kind, and how fortunate was Emma Milstead to have promised herself to a man that would take the trouble to care for a stray cat and her kittens.

We reached the end of the lane. Ahead of us sat a small, squat building rather like an outhouse, the town Cage. It is no longer used for drunks and thieves, since the police station was built, but it has been left behind as a place to store things, and because nobody is quite sure who owns it.

At the sight of the Cage, Thomas let my arm fall from his, and stood still. I turned to him.

He said, 'You won't tell anyone, will you?'

I thought he meant about taking his arm, that Emma might be jealous of it, as innocent as it was, but he added, 'About the cat.'

'No,' I said, 'of course not. I hope she is safe there until her babies are grown.'

Even though his concern had been for the cat and not for my reputation, strong emotion had overcome me, then, and I had to turn and step quickly into the lane, lest he should be seen in my company. After all, his reputation is intact; and mine, such as it is, shall soon be ruined.

In my state of distress I did not wish to venture further towards the Market Place, and the only destinations then available to me were to go further up Widmore Lane, towards the Verralls' house, or to return to the field and back home again, or to try the gate to the chapel, and go within and pray for a while, or at least sit for a moment in peace.

I did the latter. The vestry door was open, and there was no sign of the reverend, although I did not look for him. I sat at the back and prayed for my soul, and for that of my child, and for Thomas, and for the cat, and the thought of the brave mother cat bringing her kittens into the world under a hedge in the cold autumn air made me want to weep, for she might as well be me, and perhaps that same fate would befall me.

I heard the back door of the chapel open, and stayed very quiet and still, that the person who came might not notice me; but a moment later I became aware that someone stood beside me. I thought it could only be the reverend, and I steeled myself to rebuff him, to tell him that he should use me no more, for I had troubles of my own.

I opened my eyes. It was Thomas Churcher. He must have followed me in.

I looked back in my journal just now and read those words I wrote about him, after the time he took tea with Frances and Clara and myself. I wrote that people called him slow-witted, and in fact he is not. He is perfectly clever, when you get to know him, but he does not care to display it. As a result people underestimate him terribly, something I had done myself.

I ended the last entry abruptly, for Frances had called me to the table to eat with her, and now that I am alone once more I find there are more pressing things to write about. Just as we finished eating there came a knock at the door, and Frances answered; to my surprise and concern it was the reverend. He stood on the doorstep for a moment enquiring after my health, and Frances's health, and my mother and sister, all the while with Frances staring at him and trying to make him uncomfortable enough to leave; but he would not. Eventually he asked to speak to me, and Frances closed the door and asked me whether I was minded to see him, or would prefer her to send him away?

I judged that it would be easier to speak to him, and I took up my shawl and walked with him back through the Market Place and towards the chapel, where we might speak freely, without being overheard. We did this quite easily, although he had given me no indication of the nature of his enquiry, and upon reaching the chapel gate he seemed almost surprised to find where we were.

'Do you want to go inside?' he asked.

I looked about us; nobody else was within earshot. A cart laden with sacks was rumbling past, two oxen tethered behind it. 'No,' I said.

'I wished to apologise,' he said, 'for my behaviour. I feel I may have been a little harsh with you.'

'I am going to have a child,' I said. I was looking at him when I said it, and his expression showed shock, and horror, and perhaps a little fear.

'You cannot surely be suggesting——' he began, but I interrupted him.

'I need help, Reverend. I need your help.'

He put a hand on my upper arm, and opened the gate. 'Come inside,' he said. 'Let us discuss it properly, where we are not at risk of being heard.'

I followed him reluctantly, but, if my fear was the price that had to be paid for some sort of answer to my prayers, then so be it. He took me into the vestry, and I stood in the doorway while he bustled about. The sun had passed to the other side of the chapel and the room was darkening. He lit the lamp and asked if I was cold, if I wanted him to light the stove, but I could not bear to think of staying long in his company, so I shook my head.

'Very well,' he said, 'let us pray.'

He did not give me the chance to refuse, or to walk away, but bent his head and prayed, 'Heavenly Father, we commend our sister Harriet into Your loving care. Offer her guidance, and love, and comfort in her time of need, and so do not forsake her, in the name of Thy Son, Jesus Christ, who died that our sins may be forgiven, amen.'

'Amen,' I whispered.

He sat down behind his desk and leaned back in his chair. I stood before him like a penitent child, waiting to explain my misdeeds. He looked at me for a long time, his fingers steepled, until finally he said, 'Of course, you understand there is very little that can be done.'

'On the contrary, there is much that you can do,' I said.

'What is it you want?'

I hesitated. 'I thought perhaps you might know of a place I could go, where I could have the child safely, and then deliver it into the care of a kind person. With my position in Arundel, I should be able to send money, and—'

'Arundel?' he said, and he laughed. 'You believe you can still go to Arundel, in your condition?'

'Why not?' I asked, miserably.

'Do you not think they will ask you about that?' he responded, pointing with a long white finger at my stomach.

I looked down. Even I could see it now. In another month's time, how could I possibly disguise it?

'And what reason would you then give,' he went on, 'for your absence so soon after beginning your work there? Do you even know when that time might fall?'

'Then perhaps something else – something that could be done quickly, before I need to leave ...'

His face hardened. 'You do realise what you are suggesting?'

I did not reply.

'What you are suggesting, Harriet, is the most terrible of sins. A dreadful business.'

'You said once that there were no degrees of sin, that one was the same as another in God's eyes.'

'Perhaps it is unhelpful to think in terms of sin, in this instance. Perhaps, instead, we should consider it in terms of morality: corruption, profligacy, promiscuity. Do you prefer to think of it thus?'

'Not at all,' I said.

'For you are, indeed, promiscuous. Are you not?'

'Indeed I am not, sir.'

He liked to sport with me, I realised. There was some odd thing about my presence that roused him to a temper. I approached him meekly, and he saw impudence in it; I asked for help, and he relished making the matter worse.

Well, then: I had nothing further to lose in asking.

'But you could still help me,' I said, and hesitated. 'Perhaps, Reverend, if you could spare me a little money – a loan, perhaps – just enough that I could go away for a little while, and—'

'Money?'

'Yes, and—'

'You're asking me – *me* – for money?'

I lifted my head, to look him in the face. His cheeks were red, his eyes wide. Somehow this had offended him more than anything else.

'A loan,' I said.

For a moment we stared at each other. I thought of the mother cat, with her kittens, and Thomas Churcher bringing her food, and my poor broken heart shattered a little more.

'You think that I should spend my money – my wife's money, my congregation's money ... *God's money* ... to lead you even further into sin, to live your whole life telling lie upon lie? My child, you are up to your very neck in the mire of it – you are drowning in it – and I have no lifeline to throw you except to tell you to repent, and beg for mercy, and to throw yourself into the arms of Jesus, and perhaps you shall yet be saved.'

'But you could save me, and you choose not to,' I said. He was unmoved. I took a deep breath in, and turned to go.

'I shall pray for you,' I heard him say.

He did not follow me. That was a small compensation. As I left, it occurred to me that, for all his bluster, he had not actually said no. Another compensation, I realised, as I made my way to the Market Place and Frances, was that he had not suggested some other form of exchange, some tawdry payment in kind, which would worsen my predicament instead of alleviating it.

Wednesday, 4th October

I stayed with Frances and went home again the next morning to change my dress. Mary Ann had gone early into town and I had not seen her in the market, or on the path. When she came back from the town I helped her prepare dinner, but the smell of it was too much, and I ate but a very little. After that, a long afternoon of sewing and conversation stretched before me and I told them I needed fresh air.

I walked across the fields and up the lane and continued to Beckenham, and then towards Sydenham, before the long hill grew steep and my legs were tired and the weariness made me wish I had walked in circles. Now I was miles from home, and there were no carts or carriages going in the right direction, and there were but few heading for Forest Hill. I stood for a moment and pressed my hands into the small of my back, and stretched, and turned to go back the way I had come.

After a little while it began to rain, just lightly, and then it grew heavier and more persistent, and soon my dress was soaked and my bonnet too, and the water dripped from it onto the back of my neck, and I lifted my shawl to protect me and soon that was soaked, too.

I thought that perhaps this, too, was God's punishment for being so foolish; perhaps I should catch a fever and die of it.

There were things that could be done, I thought. There were medicines that could be taken, to bring the child early, too early for it to survive. I could drink gin, to dull the pain. I could throw myself under the coach. But then perhaps the coach would turn, and the horses would suffer, and those inside the carriage would likely come to harm too, and through no fault of their own. Perhaps I could take care of the matter alone, quietly, in a way that might be slower and more painful, but at least I should be in control of it, and I could keep my baby safe inside me, while I waited for the end. We should be buried together, perhaps without anyone even realising the reasons behind my actions. And perhaps God would forgive me this most terrible of sins, and on the last day we should rise together, my baby and me, and be translated into Glory. And perhaps not.

By the time I reached the beginnings of the town the rain had stopped. My shawl and my skirts were wet and filthy, and my bonnet ruined. I reached the Cage and thought of the mile I still had to walk, across the fields, which would be thick with mud now; I could continue on the road and find my way home that way, but it made one mile into four, and the road was not much more passable than the path, having had the progress of carts and carriages and horses as well as people to churn it up.

I was halfway across the field, my progress slower than usual because of my exhaustion, when I saw two people approaching. I stood aside to let them pass, but when they reached me they stopped, and I looked up to see Emma Milstead with her younger sister. I smiled and nodded, and wished them a good day despite the weather, and I had a moment to think once again that Emma Milstead was really very pretty indeed.

She bade her sister continue, and said she would catch her up; then, when the sister was a few paces away, Emma turned to me and said, 'I know what you're doing.'

'I beg your pardon?' I asked, not understanding her.

'Don't play ignorant. You were seen, walking with my Tom, chattering away to him like the slut you are.'

I frowned, and tried to think, and the only occasion I could think of was the time I met him in the field — just about there, in fact, where Emma and I currently stood, but chattering? No chattering was done, and in fact I recall that our meeting was largely conducted silently, and how very pleasant it was for that. But her tone, and her choice of words, made me indignant. That, and the fact that she stood at least a foot below me, and she was small and delicate and I could not be afraid of someone like her.

'What of it?' I said.

'He is promised to me,' she said.

'That is not what he thinks,' I answered, remembering what he had said when his brother had suggested the same thing.

Her mouth opened in a shocked little O, and she made to strike me. I caught her wrist, and squeezed.

'You are a nasty little bully,' I said. 'No wonder he wants to find someone better.'

'Better like you? I don't think so.'

'Not me, but I am sure he deserves someone kinder, and sweeter, than you are, and I hope he finds that person soon, before you spoil his life completely.'

'Let go,' she said, twisting her wrist out of my hand. 'I shall tell him you assaulted me! See what he thinks of you then!'

She did not wait for a response, but lifted her skirts out of the mud and hurried along the path after her sister, flouncing like a child in a temper.

I watched her go, and then continued in the opposite direction, looking for the place where the tree met the hedge, which should have the hollow place in the roots where the cat had her kittens. I wanted to see that she was dry in there, and safe, and that the kittens were well-fed and tended. I kept walking, and at length I saw the tree, and despite my tiredness my footsteps quickened, for I felt sorely in need of encouragement. Yes! It was the tree, and here the place that Thomas and I had crouched I bent down, my legs and my back aching dreadfully, to look.

It was the right place, for the hollow was there, but of the mother cat and her kittens there was no sign.

I am with Frances, in her rooms, and it is late: perhaps midnight, or later.

She seemed to sense my very great distress this evening, if not the cause of it. I have grown good at hiding things, even from myself. It is in the moments when I am unprepared, when I am thinking of other, innocent things, that I am struck by the remembrance of the very deepest trouble in which I find myself. Or I can be laughing, or singing, or chatting with my dear friend, and I feel the movement of the child inside me and I think of those dark moments when I have considered death over living, and I am so very sorry for it.

Frances held me in a tight embrace before bed, and said I am the kindest friend she has ever had, and how much she will miss me when I am gone. I think she knows that I will not be coming back this time, although how she can tell, I do not know. She watched me undress, and I hesitated at my chemise, turning my back to her, knowing that now my body is changing and that, surely, one day very soon, she will notice and say something and then all will be lost. How I long to tell her! For all her position, and her respectability, and her secure position with a good school, she is my very dear friend, and of all people, surely, she would help me?

In bed, she slipped her arm about my waist and pulled me close to her. Inside me, the child moved, and I thought that she must surely feel it against her hand. But if she did she gave no sign. When she fidgeted and sighed, I managed to slip free of her and came to sit in my usual place by the stove, to write in my journal.

I read back through a few of my scribblings and I noted that I never finished writing about Thomas Churcher coming to me in the chapel yesterday.

He did not ask me why I was upset, which I thought was a kindness; or perhaps he simply did not notice. He asked if I was praying, and did not wish to be disturbed, and I said I was not, and he took a seat in the pew in front of mine. He told me he had come to speak with Mr Verrall about the music for the weekend, for it was to be a service of thanksgiving and dedication, and the reverend wanted the music just so. He asked if I had seen the reverend.

I told him I had not, and said perhaps then I should go, and he replied that it was my house as much as it was his, or the reverend's, and I should stay in it as long as I wished.

I smiled at this idea, something so very pure and simple and beautiful, like Thomas himself. I said that I had errands to attend to, and I wished him good day, and he stood when I did, and made me a small bow, and I made him a small curtsey, and called him Mr Churcher, which seemed to please him very much, and we both laughed.

There. Nothing of any consequence, but Thomas Churcher being so sweet to me made the events after that – the reverend being so very callous, and Emma Milstead so threatening – seem so very much worse. They all profess to be Saved, and which of them would I most like to meet in Heaven? I think you should guess.

I wonder if he knows that the cat has gone?

Sunday, 8th October

I have been feeling better these past few days; I do not know if it is because the sickness has eased, and the weariness is not quite so dreadful, or if I have simply become accustomed to my condition and have come to accept that it is the Lord's will, and that, according to Romans, Chapter Eight, all things work together for good to those who love God. Perhaps it is merely because the grey, miserable weather has finally broken, and we have had bright, clear days with sunshine, and it is warm for October. The weather has lifted everyone's spirits, and the town is quite jolly with it.

Even Mary Ann has been better; today she wished me a good morning, and asked if I wanted to walk with her to the town, for she is going to the parish church for her weekly chanting and reading out of prayers from a book. I said I would. She had expected that I should go to the chapel, but I had not decided whether I should or no.

Of course, once we were on the path she began to talk about how she hoped I should like it in Arundel, for if I should find it not to my taste they would have to feed and clothe me once more, and our mother was not in the best of health, and so Mary Ann could not take in laundry for the damp air should affect it, so she should have to sew into the night, and her eyes were bad enough already. I said nothing and tried to think of other things, privately wishing I could tell her that Arundel was the very least of my concerns.

We passed Susannah Garn on the way, and she stopped to tell us that her aunt, who was poorly, has been made well again; she was visiting her and would miss the morning service, but she asked me to tell the reverend that she would be present this evening. She said Mrs Verrall had visited, and been very kind; and that shortly afterwards the doctor had called, and told them that payment had already been made, and they were not to concern themselves further. She believes Mrs Verrall summoned him, and she thought she should go and say thank you, but she wondered if the anonymity of the act meant that the reverend's wife wished for it not to be mentioned again? Mary Ann said she thought so, and Susannah said she agreed, but her aunt was concerned that they might appear ungrateful. I said that perhaps her aunt should write a note, privately, and have a boy take it to the house.

I went on to the service, and gave thanks for my life and the small, precious life of my child inside me, who is still a secret. The sun shone in through the windows in a shaft of light that ended where I sat, purely by chance, so the candles at the front illuminated the reverend poorly, and I had to shield my eyes to read the number of the hymn that we should sing next. I felt blessed, that God had chosen me above all the others in the congregation to experience His Divine Light; and that it was a sign, that all would be well, that a solution would be found. The baby wriggled inside me, and I had to stop myself from placing my hand upon my belly to feel it. Other women do that, I have seen them, and now I know why.

The reverend was preaching one of his sermons in a series about the Lord's Last Supper, taking his text from the Gospel of Matthew, Chapter Twenty-six, and we had reached 'betrayal'. He had spoken for a minute or two before I took out my book and tore out a page, and noted what he said, which I here transcribe:

'*And as they did eat, He said, Verily I say unto you, that one of you shall betray Me.* The Lord Jesus knew that one of them would betray Him, and He knew which of them would do it; but all the disciples gathered there all wondered who it might be. They were all afraid that it might be them, for they did not know who it was. Verse 22: *And they were exceedingly sorrowful, and each of them began to say unto Him, Lord, is it I?* These were the men who lived with the Lord Jesus Christ every day, who had heard the Word of the Lord for themselves, from his own lips, and yet each of them thought they might be capable of betraying the man they claimed to love so very much. We may find it shocking that the disciples of Christ believed they could betray their Master, and yet they knew, as we do, that when we sin against our brothers, we sin against God. First Corinthians, Chapter Eight, Verse 12: *But when ye sin so against the brethren, and wound their weak conscience, ye sin against Christ.*'

Transcribing the notes now, I am struck once again with the horror of the hypocrisy of the man preaching these words, and I wonder that clean wine can come from such a filthy vessel. But it is proof, if proof were needed, that the Lord forgives, and, if He has forgiven Verrall, then He has also forgiven me, and that, if nothing else, is a reason to be glad.

Then it was communion, and I had thought I should not take the sacrament, but had wondered whether I should be asked by someone why I had taken a blessing instead; but then I saw the reverend take it, and Emma Milstead, and I prayed, and the Lord moved me to take the bread and wine, so I did. I did not look at the reverend when he passed me the plate, and he gave no sign to me in return.

When the service was over, I saw Emma Milstead walking out with her family, glancing back at Thomas, who was tidying the music, and talking to Alfred Elliott, who has a fine tenor voice and has been asked many times by the deacons if he would form a choir for the chapel, and manage it. She dallied, and waited, and fidgeted about, and then finally was told by her father to hurry, and off she went.

I had nobody to hurry me along, and so I sat in the pew, in my shaft of bright sunlight, and waited until almost everyone had gone. I went to the porch, then, to speak to the reverend. He asked after my health, and called me Miss Monckton, and said he was pleased to see me. I told him it had been a most enlightening sermon. As I said it, Thomas Churcher hurried up to us, and shook the reverend's hand, and asked me if I should like him to see me safely across the fields to my mother's. The reverend looked at me, and looked at Thomas, and a strange sort of smile crept across his face, that I thought rather unpleasant.

I said to Thomas that there was no need, but if he was not in a hurry I should like his company very much, and we set off.

The path across the field stretched before us, the sunlight across the turned earth warm and soft and beautiful. I told him that he was very kind to walk me, but that Emma would not be happy with it, and she had already had cause to speak to me following the previous time we had walked together.

He said, with a vehemence I had not heard in him before, 'She thinks I am bound to her in some way; I tell you I am not.'

I told him he should speak plainly with her, then, for she was very much convinced of it.

He said, 'I'll not do that, I cannot.'

I replied, 'You should, Thomas, you must – for your own sanity, and for hers. If you do not care for her, set her free so that you can be free, too. You deserve happiness.'

I had said too much, for he grew quiet, then, and would not speak. It was, in truth, none of my business. Perhaps he liked her very much after all, but was one of those men who would not say it.

For a little while we walked on in silence, and then I asked after the mother cat, and said I had been very worried to see it had gone. He told me that when it rained he had brought a basket, and put food inside it, and tempted the cat within, and then brought her kittens to her, and so had taken her away from the hedge and brought her to the back room of the workshop, where at least it was warm and dry. He had left her with food and water, and the kittens were growing bigger by the day.

I was so happy to hear this, and he smiled to see that I had been concerned, and told me that I should come to see the cat whenever I wanted.

He took my hand in his, almost absent-mindedly. We walked along, and my heart was beating fast and hard. It was as if he had forgotten he was with me, and thought that he was with Emma, and had taken my hand as he might have taken hers, without thinking anything of it. I felt no artifice in him, no expectation, and that was why I carried on walking, my hand in his hand.

Now I am home and writing here, the thought of him walking home with me, when he could have hurried and walked with Emma; and the tale of the cat, who was warm and dry and safe; and Thomas taking my hand and holding it ... all of these things make my heart sing with joy. He makes me feel safe. I could be safe, with him.

If he would have me.

Monday, 9th October

This morning brought two letters. The first was addressed to my mother. It was from my brother William, who writes to inform us that his wife, Anne, is expecting their first child. They are both overjoyed to be blessed thus and ask us to pray for Anne and the child, that it should be safely delivered, God willing, in the new year.

Another door, then, that has been shut in my face; although perhaps this door was never really open to me. I am sure that God is fastening doors and windows so that I should see the correct path, and not be led to take a false one, which might yet lead me to a darker place.

The second letter was from Richard, who has been waiting in vain for me to reply to his last. He says,

Dear Harriet,

I fear you may not have received my letter to you, or perhaps you have responded and that letter has gone astray. I am certain you would not have failed to reply, as I have always known you to be a conscientious young woman, who values her friends and respects her elders. For my part, I have considered most carefully everything that you said in your last letter to me, and I think perhaps you might have believed my words to be a little harsh. I trust that the intervening days have given you time to consider your response, and your position, and that, despite the tone of your last letter and the content of mine, we are still friends? Maria has been asking after you and I hope that, perhaps, you might visit us in London after all, before you journey onward to Arundel. I hope to hear from you soon, and until then I remain, always,

Your

Richard

I cannot pretend I was not pleased to hear from him, and pleased, indeed, that he has regretted the harshness of his tone in that letter. I have read this new letter several times, in the hope of seeing something in it which might suggest that he has decided to assist me after all, but I cannot find it. However, perhaps he has spoken to Maria, and confessed his failings, and perhaps she was the one who prompted him to write – she has been asking after me, he says – and she will have thought of some possible solution that can only be spoken of in person, at their house, and that is why I should attend.

Feeling great hope in my heart, I wrote back to him immediately.

Dear Richard,

Thank you for your last letter, which was safely delivered this morning.

I did not reply to your last, as the tone of it and the content upset me greatly, and left me with nothing to say in reply that might not be considered unworthy of a Christian. I am glad you have reconsidered your choice of words, and thought them harsh, as I did too. I can also assure you that, despite your apparent belief to the contrary, I was, until you cast me aside for my friend, very much a faithful wife to you in deed, if not in name. I hope you have also reconsidered your response to my requests for help, and that you are now in a position to lend me funds, which I will return to you at the earliest possible opportunity, when I am in Arundel and earning a wage once more. Perhaps you have explained the situation to Maria, and she has been the one to urge you to change your mind? If you have not talked to her, I suggest it would be wise to do so, as she was my friend long before she was yours; she, I am sure, will want you to help me in every possible way, and if I were to ask her myself I am sure she would take my part in the matter.

I understand that my condition is far from a happy one, but I would ask nevertheless that you remember me in your prayers, as I pray for you all daily, and am, as ever,

Your own dear
Harriet

Friday, 13th October

Thomas has taken to loitering at the stile near my mother's house, so that he can walk with me across the fields towards the town. I have asked him if he does not have work to do, or errands to run, and he makes up some excuse: that his father is waiting for delivery of silks or leather, and he cannot work until the delivery is made; or that he was in Farwig to visit an uncle with a message, or, this morning's excuse, that Clara sent him to ask how I did, and if I should like to come to their house for tea.

I said yes. I might as well enjoy the time I have left in Bromley; one way or another, it will come to an end soon enough.

He has concluded the matter with Emma Milstead.

'I didn't think you would do it,' I told him.

'You asked me to,' he said, 'and I would do anything you asked. Anything at all.'

We did not walk to the town; instead, we took the path that leads to the river, and walked until there was a place on the riverbank quite hidden from the path, and without a word having passed between us in suggestion or agreement he took my hand and led me carefully through the small space between the bushes, down to the bank. There were no boats upon the river, thankfully, or we should have been clearly seen; although just there the bank was very overgrown and the river quite narrow, so perhaps it is not used by the barges.

We sat on the bank and I think I told him he had done the right thing, and asked if he felt any happier for it.

He said he did.

He was sitting very close, and once more he took my hand, which he had released when we had reached the spot, and he held it and turned it over in his hands, and looked at it, as a palmist might, or a physician. He said he thought I was very clever, to be a schoolteacher, and how I must think him very stupid and foolish. I said, on the contrary, I thought he was a truly good man, and that he played the music beautifully, and I had no skills at all to compare with his. He said he played to the Glory of God, and I agreed, and said God loved him and thought him a great man. He said he hoped it was true, but, if so, then God was the only one who thought so, as all others thought him an idiot.

I said I did not think him an idiot at all; that on the contrary I thought him very intelligent, and, whatever people thought of him, he seemed reluctant himself to disabuse them of their opinions, and perhaps that in itself showed his wisdom.

He could not look at me. His cheek was flushed. He seemed to steel himself into action, and he bent his head and kissed the inside of my wrist, lifting the sleeve of my dress an inch or so out of the way to reach it.

'There,' he said. 'I have wanted to do it, and now I have.'

He smiled at me and I smiled, too, at the innocence of him, to be so satisfied with a gentle kiss.

Friday, 20th October

I am with Frances, and almost a week has passed since I last wrote here. I think, perhaps, I only write when I am afraid, or desperate, and that this journal is my solace; it serves me well, for telling a blank page of my worries is my only escape from them. So you may determine that my sojourn in the real world has been a happy one; and that is thanks to Thomas.

I have told no one of our friendship, and I believe neither has he. Frances suspects, for he calls for me at her lodging, with some excuse or other, and, as hard as I try to keep the smile from my face when he does so, she must surely have seen that my demeanour has brightened considerably in recent days.

This evening Thomas called for me as Frances and I were reading. It was barely dusk, a still evening at the end of what had been a beautiful autumn day. I told Frances I would walk as far as the chapel and then come back, that I should not be gone long. In the Market Place we saw Emma's sister, and I should have dodged her and gone into Isard's yard but Thomas held my arm and steered me into the open. We walked together in silence until the narrow opening to Widmore Lane.

Thomas said that the reverend had asked after me; that he had seen us walking together and had enquired if he had broken off with Emma.

'What did you say?' I asked.

'I told him that Emma and I were never promised in the first place, and that I had told her plainly of it.'

'What did he say to that?'

'He said he thought it was a pity, and he asked if I was now promised to you instead.'

'And what did you say?'

'Nothing,' he answered. 'None of his business what I do, is it?'

'Indeed it is not.'

I was pleased at this, and that Thomas is a man of discretion, for heaven knows he will need it if he is to continue to associate with me.

Then he said that he wanted to tell someone, and of all people perhaps it should be the reverend, who knew us both so well. I asked what he should tell him, and Thomas flushed, and shuffled his feet, as he does when I have challenged him in some way, and then he said he wanted to shout it from the Market Place to everyone that he and I were walking out together.

'Is that what we are doing?' I said, and I was teasing him.

'You know we are,' he said.

'Tell anyone you like, then,' I said, '*except* for him.'

That was the wrong thing for me to say, for then he would not let it rest. Why did I not want him to know? Did

I not like him? Did I not trust him, who was appointed our Shepherd? I made it even worse then, for I said I was a little afraid of him.

He said, 'Why? He is a godly man.'

I tried to make light of it, and said that I thought he was a man, who thought himself godly and tried hard to be so, but fell a little short. He said in reply that we all fall short of that, and I knew he was right. We had reached the path to the riverbank, and we took it, even though it was almost dark. There was a half-moon, enough to see by, but not enough to encourage the whole town to be out and walking. When we reached the space in the bushes, he took my hand and led me carefully over the rough ground, until we found our usual spot, and then he asked me if Verrall had ever hurt me.

What could I reply? I said he should not think badly of him; that he is Thomas's pastor, and will be here long after I am gone.

He pressed the matter, and pressed it, and asked again and again, until finally I said that I had told the reverend something once, in confidence, and that I thought now that it had been a mistake to do so. It was not an untruth; perhaps, at worst, a half-truth. Thomas wanted to know more, and my heart wanted to tell him all, there and then, because it was dark enough for him not to see my face clearly and for me not to see his; telling stories that are as miserable as mine is becomes a little easier when you do not have to see the pain in the eyes of the person you are telling. But I stopped myself in time, for selfish reasons. I wanted to enjoy Thomas just for a little while longer, to enjoy the feeling of being liked and admired, for certainly when he learns about Richard and Maria, and the reverend, and, worst of all, that I am carrying another man's child, surely he will not want anything further to do with me.

We kissed, a little. He stroked my cheek, and kissed my neck, and my throat, and my wrist, and then my fingers, and then my mouth again. He kisses well, and is gentle, but strong. His arms hold, but do not grip. He is full of desire, and yet also full of self-control. This I know to be rare, in a man. I felt a rush of longing. How I wish I had more time! How I wish I had taken more notice of him before Richard, that I might have chosen differently!

'I should like to marry,' I said impulsively. 'I should like to promise to love one man above all others. And to be loved in return.'

Thomas looked as if he was about to speak but did not dare, and I am glad of it. However he sees me, and however safe I feel with him, however hopeful, I am broken, tarnished, used, and forsaken. He deserves better than Emma Milstead, but, if that is true, then how much more so is it that he deserves better than me.

Monday, 23rd October

Another letter from Richard.

> *Harriet,*
> *Your letter to me sounded, again, rather threatening. Was this your intention? That if I do not tell Maria of our most recent association, then you will do it yourself? Do you not think it possible that I can intercept such a letter, if it arrives here, and if you mean to tell her in person do you not think of how very hurt she will be by it? Do you think so little of her, your very dear former friend, that you would destroy her thus? She has, as you know, been unwell and is still very fragile after her confinement. I do not exaggerate to suggest that such a shock might kill her. Therefore I trust you will think carefully before such an act, and consider the consequences of your actions, and your behaviour.*
> *Richard*

If he thinks of Maria as weak, he is mistaken; she is stronger and wiser and bolder than she looks, and if he is taken in by her feminine manner then more fool him. With her having been pregnant herself I would not be at all surprised if she already knows, and perhaps that is what lay behind the awkwardness of our conversation on my last visit to London. Men underestimate women all the time, and, whatever pains we take to enlighten them, they never quite seem to realise the truth: that we are every bit as intelligent and strong as they are. It is only the demands of society that separate us.

Nevertheless, he is right that she will be hurt by the news, for all the truth that she is married to Richard and I am not; and I should do anything to avoid hurting her, for I still consider her my friend. I am under no illusion that Richard would leave her to be with me, nor do I have any desire for that. What is it that I do want from him, deep within my soul? I am not sure. I think perhaps I have been entertaining the idea that we might all live together in the house in Fieldgate Street, as once we did: one man, one wife, one lodger, and two children. Perhaps I could be their governess, and bring up Richard's two children together? Stranger family arrangements have been known.

But no, the man is a callous fool, and both Maria and I deserve to be treated better than this.

I still have no solution to my problem. For the past two weeks I had thought my best chance of salvation seemed to lie with Thomas. And indeed if Thomas would come with me, away from Bromley, we could be married elsewhere; in a strange place, who would know the child not to be his? But my foolish sudden lightening of heart, of hope, has been all too quickly driven away by my conscience. To use him in this way would surely make me no better a person than Richard Field.

And so I cannot go to Arundel, unless I can delay the position until after the child is born, and can also secure some funds or support to keep me somewhere apart from Bromley until then, when I have had the child, and might yet perhaps find a place for it in a loving household. Perhaps, after that, Thomas could come with me to Arundel and we could begin a courtship afresh, without the eyes of the town upon us, and be legitimately and honestly married.

If he would have me. If, indeed, he would want me; for he shall know the truth one way or another. I will have to tell him.

Frances asked me this evening if Thomas's intentions towards me are honourable ones. I told her that he is honest, and kind, and I like him very much. I believe she thinks I am hesitating because I do not consider him my intellectual equal. If only she knew the truth! He is a better person than I, on every count.

Oh, how I hate keeping secrets!

Next week I should leave for Arundel. Whatever decisions I make, I must make them soon. The fear has come upon me once again, of what will happen to me, and to my baby. I shall be cut from society, but that I can bear. I shall lose my friends, but perhaps I can bear that too. I shall be cast out from the chapel, but God does not reside in that place, He resides in the hearts of those who believe, and I do believe God at least will not forsake me. I only hope that I can survive this, somehow, and that there might be happiness on the other side of it.

Thursday, 2nd November

Frances is very sick, with a fever and a violent cough, which she believes she caught from Annie Slow, who has never been taught to use a handkerchief.

I promised to stay with her, although that serves me as well as it does her; I have no desire to stay in Farwig. Mary Ann is vexatious once more. She is not happy with me at home, nor is she happy with me quitting it, for now she says I should help her more with the household chores, and how shall she manage when I have 'trotted off to Arundel' and left her with all the work?

Staying at the Beezleys' makes it easier to see Thomas.

I spent an hour with him after prayers at the chapel this evening, in one of our secret places: the narrow strip of grass that lies behind the chapel, close against the fence which borders Cooper's yard. Nobody goes there at all; in fact, it has become a place for discarded items to be left out of sight. There is a pew there, the end of it broken off; the old gate, rusted to pieces; some broken bricks. We sit on the pew, in the gathering darkness of the evening, quite sheltered, and whisper together, and sometimes he kisses me, and sometimes holds my hand.

I have resolved that I shall tell him the truth, and ask him, if he still likes me enough, whether he will take me away and look after me, even if he does not want to have me or the child afterwards. And, if he cannot do that, I shall ask if he could please keep my secret, until I am safely away, and after that he can tell anyone, for my reputation will be soiled by Verrall in any case. Every day I think to myself, one more day, with Thomas thinking me good, with Frances loving me as she does, without expectation, and then I shall tell them the truth and throw myself on their mercy.

In the meantime, though, another hope has presented itself, from a most unexpected source.

I went to Mason's Hill with a note for Mr Campling, to tell him that I am to take Miss Williams's classes for a day or two, until she is recovered, and walked back across the Bishop's Park to Widmore Lane. It was not a shorter way, but a scenic one, and I was visiting familiar places in the town thinking I should say goodbye to them, for once Frances is better, one way or another, I shall leave Bromley for good. The Bishop's Park is beautiful, with a fine view into the

449

valley, and a spring, said to have healing properties thanks to St Blaise. Mr Verrall does not believe in the saints, but my sister does, and my mother, and I am open to other people's beliefs even if he is not.

The path took me to the far edge of Widmore Lane, and I found myself standing outside the beautiful white house occupied by Mr Verrall. I thought perhaps to try again to throw myself upon his mercy and hope that the Lord, finally, would speak to him and ask him to do the right thing.

The door was opened by Ruth, Mr Verrall's sister, and she told me that her brother was not at home, but if I wished to wait for him he should not be long. I wanted to get back to Frances, but my limbs were tired from the long walk back across the park, and my back ached terribly, so I said I would wait.

She showed me into the drawing room, and asked if I should like to have some tea. I said I could not stay very long, but perhaps she might permit me a glass of water instead, and she left to fetch it.

The drawing room was not empty. Mrs Verrall was there, at her sewing, beside the window. She looked surprised to see me, but then she smiled and bade me come to sit beside her. She apologised that her husband was not at home, but I assured her I was not expected, and I did not wish to trouble the household with my presence so I would not stay.

Then Ruth brought me a cup of water, and left again.

I sat beside Mrs Verrall, and asked after her health, and that of her sons. She said the boys were very well, and then she asked if I should like to talk to her of my troubles, instead of the reverend, as she thought herself a good listener.

Of all the things! But I found myself sharing them none the less, for what else should I do? I told her I was in trouble, and that I had been wronged by a dear friend, and now my reputation would be torn apart just when I needed it most. I shared none of the details of it. I did not tell her that her husband, while perhaps not the cause of my problems, had certainly done nothing to make them any better. She smiled, and looked at me gently, and patted my arm, and asked if I should like her to pray for me.

And that simple kindness caused me to weep, where I had been so strong for such a long time.

She offered me her handkerchief, and took my hand, and to my surprise told me that men were dangerous creatures because of their own stupidity, which leads them into sin; and they do it all without a care for the persons who shall suffer because of it. Her hand gripped mine, and it felt very strong. She said all things come to good in the end, because women look after each other, where men fail to look to anyone but themselves.

Neither of us had mentioned a name, and yet I had the strangest feeling that she was speaking about the reverend. Perhaps he had told her everything? Why should he not do so? He was bound by a moral obligation to keep my confidence about Richard Field, but as for the rest...if his own conscience was resolved by telling his wife what had happened, then that was his concern. She appeared to have cast no judgement upon me, and for that I was profoundly grateful.

Then she asked me what help I needed.

'Pray for me,' I said, for I could not ask her for anything else.

'Do you need money?' she asked.

I gazed at her, and her eyes looked calmly back into mine. 'I cannot ask—' I began, but she interrupted.

'You have not asked. I am asking you: do you need money?'

'It would help me enormously,' I said, 'but the reverend said—' And I stopped short, because I realised that I had brought him into it, named him, even as a person with whom the details of the matter had been discussed. It felt as though I had torn a spider's web, and broken a spell.

Her expression did not change. 'He will not offer you money willingly,' she said, 'but that does not mean I cannot see that you receive some. It may take a few days. And you should, perhaps, keep this discussion between ourselves.'

'Of course,' I said, weeping afresh, 'thank you. Oh, thank you.' At last some understanding; a real offer of help! She comforted me, and I leaned against her, and the child inside me danced with joy. I wanted to take her hand and press it to my belly, so she could feel the relief and what it had caused: but in that moment the door opened, and the reverend came in.

He saw me sitting next to his wife, and saw that she was holding my hand; and I saw his expression, but not hers; he looked enraged by it, but then some look passed between them, and he calmed himself. He asked if I was quite well, and I answered that I had been walking outside and had felt unwell, and had asked for a drink of water, and his sister and his wife had been so very kind, but that I now felt quite recovered and should be on my way.

He said he would show me out, and I turned to Mrs Verrall and made her a curtsey, and thanked her for her kindness; and in return she offered me a small smile, and wished me a good day.

At the doorstep, the reverend asked what I thought I was doing.

I said, 'I have told you the truth: all I did was accept a glass of water. Your wife, Reverend, is a kind and gentle lady, and I am most grateful to her.'

I said no more, but left him standing there, no doubt wondering if I had confessed everything!

Sunday, 5th November

The service this morning was bright, and cheerful, and I took communion as I did last week. The reverend preached on the

Last Supper, again, and his sermon concerned *He that eateth and drinketh unworthily, eateth and drinketh damnation to himself.* I thought perhaps the message was directed at me, although it could just as well apply to the man himself.

At the porch he asked me quietly to wait behind, for there was something he wished to say to me in private. I was anxious to get back to Frances, but I stayed, hoping that perhaps Mrs Verrall had spoken to him, and that had prevailed upon him to help me.

Thomas watched him, and me, dark-eyed: and I saw that he took his time clearing up the music and even helped to pile up the hymn books with Elliott. When the congregation had departed, all aside from the two of them, the reverend led me into the vestry. I glanced behind me and met Thomas's gaze, and then the reverend closed the door.

He bade me sit down. I told him I preferred to stand.

'Very well,' he said, and took off his silk gown, that he liked to wear in the pulpit, and hung it behind the door. My heart beat a little faster, for I thought this might be a prelude to some physical assault, but then he crossed to his desk and sat behind it.

'You and Tom Churcher are very close friends now,' he remarked.

'What of it?' I asked. There was no point in denying it; we had been seen walking out by all manner of people, chapel members and townsfolk alike.

'Does he know of your condition?'

I felt a twist of fear in my stomach, and the child inside me moved. 'He does not.'

'Do you not think he has a right to know?'

'As you observed, Mr Verrall, we are friends. Nothing more. He is a good man.'

'Am I not also a good man?' he said, and I did not respond. He knew and understood far more about this than he had any right to, I thought. How I wish I had not shared my burden with him! For I had expected comfort, and help, and instead I have more troubles than I ever had before.

'You mean to use him, Harriet? To press him into marriage, when he does not know that you are far from the virtuous girl you present yourself to be?'

I gritted my teeth at this, and said nothing other than, 'The Gospel of Matthew, Chapter Seven, Verse 5: you are familiar with the text, Reverend, I am sure?'

'Impudent girl,' he said, but he smiled. 'You believe yourself to be so very clever.'

'On the contrary, sir, I am alone, and afraid, and I have, as you have told me, very few friends. Whenever I throw myself on the mercy of some person who is supposed to be good, my condition appears to worsen still further. You will forgive me if I have grown cynical.'

He took a long breath in, and exhaled it in a sigh.

'I do not mean to use Tom,' I said, in response to his earlier question. 'I mean to be honest with him, when the time is right to do so. I would ask you that you allow me to do that, for his sake as much as for my own. I should like him to be able to decide his opinion of me himself. Perhaps you owe me that courtesy.'

'Perhaps I owe you nothing at all,' he said.

If I had nursed any vain hopes that his wife had interceded on my behalf, in that moment I was certain that she had not. As always, I must argue for myself. I said, 'If you should prefer it that I leave Bromley completely, and leave Thomas Churcher behind, then I will do it, if you will only help me.'

'Money, again?'

'I do need money, but not only that. I need time, to resolve the issue. Perhaps you might also write to the school at Arundel, and ask them to delay my appointment there? I would leave as expected next week, and go somewhere else until the child is born and I can find some loving home where it can be raised in safety, and then journey on to Arundel as planned.'

He stared at me, as if considering my proposal.

'It is really such a very small thing to ask.'

'And if the school should ask me why?'

'Tell them that I am tending to a sick friend. It is partly the truth: Miss Williams is very poorly. I am to take her lessons tomorrow, and until she is better.'

'It is still a lie,' he said. 'And I shall be called upon to lie further, when people ask me if you are gone to Arundel and I know you have gone somewhere else entirely. You would have me tell falsehoods for you, on top of every other sin you have caused me to commit?'

I looked him in the eye, and answered, 'Yes.'

He answered, 'Well, Harriet, I shall not do that.'

There was to be no answer, no easy solution. His pride and his stubbornness came before everything else, from my wellbeing and that of my child, to Thomas Churcher and his reputation, which would be dragged down along with my own.

Monday, 6th November

I have spent the day at the school again, in Frances's place.

She seemed a little better this morning, although all night she was feverish, and I spent much of it pressing a cool cloth to her head, and listening to her breathing coming ragged and gasping. She has been thus all weekend. Her chest is raw with coughing. This morning, when I went home to change my dress, Mary Ann said that she thought Miss Williams not at all unwell, that she was merely pretending, so that I should stay longer with her and not go to Arundel after all. She had a sly smile on her face when she said it, and I longed to slap it off. I told her she should think more charitably of a woman who was decent and kind, and that if Miss Williams needed me to stay, then I would stay as long as possible.

I have not written to Arundel myself; I am expected there in two days' time.

The girls at the school have been very good, and well-behaved, performing the tasks that Frances set for them admirably. I told the girls that I would report favourably on their behaviour to Miss Williams, who should be pleased to hear it. Amelia Taylor said they wished their teacher a swift recovery, and asked that their good wishes should be sent back to Miss Williams, which I promised to do. The younger children have all written letters to her to wish her well. During their sewing lesson this afternoon we could hear Mr Campling whipping one of the boys; Jenny Taylor said she thought it must be their brother, Albert. I told them they should keep their opinions to themselves, as the boys' room was none of their concern, and after that they kept very quiet, perhaps fearing that I should call Mr Campling in to see them.

I walked back from Mason's Hill by the main road, but as I was passing the Rising Sun I saw Mr Verrall cross the road to meet me. 'Miss Monckton,' he said, tipping his hat to me.

'Reverend,' I said, for I could not very well ignore him.

'I should like to ask you to meet me in the chapel this evening,' he said, lowering his voice, lest anyone should think his request an inappropriate one.

'To what end?'

'I wish to speak to you, in private.'

'Surely all's been said,' I answered.

His face was white, but there was a sheen of perspiration upon his brow. 'On the contrary,' he said. 'It is something that might be advantageous to you.'

I felt a sudden leap of hope, then, that his wife must have spoken with him at last, and had persuaded him to offer me a small amount of money after all. I could think of no other reason for him to ask to meet me, now, after all that had been said yesterday.

'This evening?'

'At eight, perhaps. There is no meeting in the chapel, but I have pastoral visits to attend to first.'

I thought about it, and about leaving Frances, who needed my care. 'Very well,' I said. 'Although I cannot stay long.'

'I assure you, it will be worth your while,' he said, and bared his teeth, again.

I watched him cross the road to the gate that leads across Abraham Nettlefold's paddock, and from there to the Bishop's Park. He was heading for home, then. I continued walking into the Market Place. Thomas was standing in the doorway of his father's shop, talking to Clara, but looking at me. Clara turned to see who had caught her brother's eye, and smiled at me. 'How does Frances?' she asked.

'A little better, I think,' I told her. 'Although her cough troubles her dreadfully.'

'Should I call on her?' she asked.

'I think she would like that very much,' I said. 'Come this evening? Though first I have to return some books for her, to the chapel for the Sunday School.'

All through this exchange I could feel Thomas's eyes on mine. I told Clara she should come to us at around six, and she agreed and said she would bring cake.

When I got in Frances was awake, though still in bed. I prepared some soup and put it on to simmer, and she said that she was feeling quite well enough to eat a little and to get up and dressed for Clara's visit, while I took back the books.

Mr Verrall's request has been much on my mind. He had made his position quite clear to me, and yet he says that our meeting should be to my advantage? I do not trust him, and yet what can I do? If his wife has chosen to convey money to me through her husband, then I would fall to my knees in relief and gratitude.

As soon as I entered the chapel, I looked about for Thomas, for I knew he would be there. Out of sight of the gossips and in the dark, cool quiet of the empty space, he put his hand up to my cheek and kissed me. My breath was quite stolen by it.

'I should like to be with you all the time,' he said, 'and not in secret.'

I said that I should tell him something that would make him change his mind about me. He said nothing I could say would do that, and I felt my eyes fill with tears at the thought of it.

'You cannot say that,' I said, 'until you know.'

'Tell me, then,' he said.

There was a noise outside at just that moment, and we shrank back into the shadows.

'Tonight?' he whispered.

'The reverend has asked me to meet him in the chapel, at eight,' I told him.

'What for?'

I told him that he had not informed me.

'Are you afraid?' he asked.

'Yes,' I said, for I would not lie to Thomas about anything. Whatever he asked me henceforth, I should tell him the truth.

'Then I shall come with you,' he said. 'I will call for you before eight, and take you there, and protect you.'

'He will not speak to me with you there,' I said.

'Then I shall wait outside, if you wish me to.'

I did wish it, and the thought of him waiting for me lifted my spirits, and I told him that he was a good, kind man, and I trusted him, and afterwards we should talk about everything. He said he needed to tell me something too. He said he did not want me to go to Arundel, but to stay here in Bromley.

I kissed him, then. However he should change his mind with the truth; for the moment he cares enough for me to ask me to stay. We shall see what this evening brings.

Monday, 6th November, evening

Frances and I have had a short but jolly sort of visit from Clara, and Thomas. Clara apologised that her brother was there, but he insisted on walking her across the Market Place; Frances told him he was welcome to stay, and so he did, although he remained sitting in the corner by the stove, and hardly said a word. Frances, having slept most of the day, was a little brighter, and perhaps the fever is passing, although her cough is persistent and her throat is very sore.

We talked of the school, and I said once more to Frances that her girls were a credit to her; she loves hearing this. She wanted to know everything they did, what questions each of them asked, how well they performed their drills, and whether I thought their singing had improved since the last time I heard them. I hope one day I shall be as conscientious, and as loved, as she is. Clara asked me about Arundel, and if I was very excited to go there. I told her I was, but I was anxious about Frances and would not leave her while she was unwell. I told them I would go to London first, and stay a day with Richard and Maria.

All the talk was very light and inconsequential, but my thoughts were pressing on me and making me feel almost dizzy with the weight of them. Only Thomas, sitting there quietly and watching me, made me feel any better. That I should have to tell him the truth! I had put it off for so long. If the reverend gives me money, or if Mrs Verrall does – or even if, at the last, I should tell Maria of my troubles and hope that she might help me – then I shall still tell the truth to Thomas, for he deserves my honesty if nothing else.

Clara left after forty-five minutes, saying that she could see Frances had grown weary, and Thomas left with her. At the door, he touched my hand, and I smiled.

I told Frances that she should get back into bed, and I would make her some gruel later, to help her throat and make her sleep more easily. She sat up in bed and watched me writing here, and asked me what I was doing. I told her I was writing a letter, and I meant it to go in the post tonight. This, at least, gives me an excuse to go out again later, but the act of writing it has given me another idea.

It is, perhaps, an odd one: but I shall take the coach to London on Wednesday, whatever happens tonight. I need to see Richard, and Maria, and if then I have enough money from whichever source to go somewhere and have my baby, then I shall do it; and if I have not, and if Richard and Maria will not take me, then I shall have to find a workhouse, and be brave and face whatever the Lord has in store for me.

Bromley
Monday 6th November

My dearest Maria,

Well, this is a peculiar letter to write! You must be wondering why I have sent you this parcel, and why I have written you another letter today, and sent it separately. The first letter is one that I expect Richard will open, and read; he will not be expecting a parcel, and perhaps then you will open it and see this letter before he has a chance to intercept it.

I find myself in very desperate circumstances, and, whilst I should have wished very much to confide in you from the beginning, Richard has led me to believe that you are weak, and fragile, and have been unwell since the birth of your son, and that to do so would be to put your life at some degree of risk. I kept this secret from you so as not to burden you with it, but I find I have reached the very limits of my desperation, and there is nobody left to whom I can turn. Perhaps I should have ignored Richard, and confided in you from the very beginning. I know you to be no feeble woman, after all.

Do you remember that night you sobbed in my arms, because you had reached the point at which your own pregnancy was impossible to ignore? I find myself now in the same position, but without the solace of a good friend. Without doubt the child is Richard's, conceived before I left London for your sake, and yet you will see from the letters which are held between the pages of my journal that he has shown no inclination to help me, and in fact has been most unkind.

However, I hope you will also see, from this journal, that your very natural fears are entirely unfounded. Whatever his faults and whatever his behaviour towards me, Richard clearly has your interests at heart – he loves you. And you will be reassured too, I hope, that I have no desire to separate you, or to cause strife between you.

All I ask is for some help and a little kindness in this, my hour of need. My desperation and fear are feelings that you will recognise, dear Maria; and for me there is no prospect of a marriage to legitimise the child I carry. Therefore I beg you to remember the way I stood aside for you, and left London so that you and Richard could pursue your love without any distractions, and to please, please intercede with Richard on my behalf, if you are at all able.

Please believe that I do not send you this journal to cause you pain or hurt, but from respect. My dearest wish is that all three of us might together find a solution, and my hope is merely to spare you the shock of hearing the news from my lips, and to give you and your husband time, if you wish it, to discuss the matter privately between yourselves before I am with you. I shall still come to London in the week, if I am spared, although in my condition I will be unable to continue on to Arundel.

If you cannot or are not minded to persuade Richard to help me, then I shall go to a workhouse in London and trust in the Lord to take care of me. Please do read the journal, and keep it safe for me, and I will retrieve it when I see you. Until then, I remain your most loyal and loving friend,

Harriet

Thursday, 7th May, 1846

Frances Williams

Without my noticing it, the lamps had burned all their oil, and the light by which I read Harriet's final words came from the grey light of the dawn.

Tears had flowed from my eyes, and dried, and flowed again, and at various points during the night I had risen, and stretched, and tended the fire; towards dawn I had opened the curtains, the better to see by. And, at six o'clock, I heard from upstairs the thin reedy cry of a newborn. Maria had been delivered of her second child.

Richard came back into the room shortly afterwards, and told me that she had a son, and both mother and child were exhausted but safe. The woman, whose name I never learned, hurried down the stairs, and was paid by Richard, and left: and not long after that the servant girl, who had been entirely unaware of the dramatic turn of events during her day of absence, came back into the house and set about making breakfast.

Richard brought tea, and said that I should have eggs, or kippers, or kidneys. I had not felt hungry at all until he mentioned food, and then my belly grumbled, and I agreed that a poached egg would do me very well. He seemed quiet and contrite, as I think he should be, considering the behaviour that Harriet had described in the journal.

'You see, Miss Williams, I do not come out of it very well.'

'No, Mr Field, I declare you do not. How did you come by the journal? Did you even show it to Maria?'

He told me that Maria had it first; that, as Harriet had intended, he had been fooled by the letter and not expected the parcel, so Maria had opened it and read it privately, and then, when Harriet did not appear as expected, and Verrall's letter arrived instead, she had shown him the journal and bade him read it from cover to cover.

'I see you are moved by the contents,' he said.

I am not an emotional woman by nature, and it is rare that I am moved to tears. At that moment, the recollection of Harriet's words, and the horror of her situation, sliced through me afresh, a knife-blade to my very heart. 'She was so very brave,' I said, 'and she came so very close to freedom. I believe that if she had just told Tom Churcher the truth, he would have accepted her, and your child, and done everything in his power to keep her safe.'

'You believe so?' Richard said. 'I rather thought he might have been the one to do it, myself.'

'Tom? Of course not. He adored her; any fool could see it. I think the evidence of Harriet's own words suggests that you are more of a suspect than Tom Churcher, Mr Field.'

He nodded, and did not deny it. 'I agree; I betrayed her in every possible way. At the time I thought of nothing except Maria, and my own reputation, and it cost Harriet her life. In that way I am profoundly guilty; but in the real sense I had nothing to do with her death. In fact, the day she died, I was travelling back from visiting friends in Northumberland. If the police had asked, I should have brought witnesses to prove it. But they always seemed to suspect Mr Verrall and Tom Churcher above me.'

'And Maria? I assume she could not have travelled to Bromley overnight?'

Richard let out a bark of a laugh. 'With a baby? I believe she did not leave the house until the child was half a year old. She was severely weakened by it, and has never fully recovered.'

I drank my tea, and found myself much revived. At length

he said, 'Harriet's intention in sending the journal might have been a desperate one, but I believe the result of it was that it saved our marriage.'

'How could it possibly have done that?' I asked.

'Apparently Maria had known about Harriet and me from the very beginning, just as Harriet had known about Maria. I supposed I had been very discreet, but I underestimated both women's intellect – which is indeed a very bad habit I seem to have developed. Maria loved and hated Harriet in equal measure, but hearing the whole story in the words of the woman who was first her friend... well, she saw that what Harriet had done was a very noble thing. And she also saw that what I had done was foolish and cruel, but that I had done it with the best of intentions towards her. That I was loyal to her, having chosen her.' He looked at my face and shrugged. 'Not much of a mitigating virtue, I agree, but one that is important to a wife.'

'I am glad for it,' I told him. 'I do not believe Harriet wanted to come between you and Maria.'

He rubbed his fingers across his eyes, and I thought he was feeling the loss of Harriet very acutely in that moment. And, perhaps, the loss of his own child, who had died with its mother on the floor of the privy at the Bromley Chapel.

'Who do you think did it, Miss Williams?'

I had been pondering that very thought all night, with every word Harriet wrote.

'I rather fear, Mr Field, that I am more confused than I was at the start. I had thought Verrall the strongest suspect, and perhaps still he is the man. I believe the coroner thought him responsible. And yet, there are others: Tom Churcher, of course, though I do not believe it is he; and Emma Milstead, who is now his wife. And even Harriet's own sister was against her. Any member of the congregation, fearing the scandal. If any of them had found out, or suspected, that Harriet was carrying a child, they might have been angry enough to do it.'

Richard sighed, and placed his coffee cup back upon the table. 'Perhaps we shall never know,' he said.

'I rather hope the detectives will find it out,' I said.

He looked at the journal, which was still in my lap. 'Would you like to keep it?' he asked. 'I had intended to destroy it, but I have been unable to bring myself to do that. And I rather think the person who comes out of it the best is you, Miss Williams.'

I smiled, and held the journal close. 'I should love to have it. I feel that I have met and loved Harriet all over again, for having read it.'

'And you will keep it safe, and not share it with anyone? I am sure you understand why.'

I thought of Richard, who believed himself in love with my Harriet and yet had seduced her just the same – should I protect him, now, despite the faith he had shown in me? And what of Verrall? Here was the evidence that he had lied to the coroner, that he had assaulted Harriet again and again, and had asked her to meet him on the very night she died. I had thought myself the last person to see her alive, and now here was Harriet's own testimony to report that it was Verrall, and not I. Did I not have a duty to share that information? But I had given Richard Field my oath, in that moment when he held the journal out to me and gave me permission to read it.

'Of course,' I assured him. 'I promised you that, and you must know I am a woman of my word.'

'Very well, then,' he said, getting to his feet. 'I must go and see Maria. Please do have breakfast, and the maid shall find a cab for you. Will you return to Bromley?'

'No,' I said. 'I am going home. To Shifnal.'

He said, 'Then I wish you Godspeed, Miss Williams. Mistress Warrior.'

I shook his hand. He looked at the journal, and at me, and then he smiled, and left the room.

V:
1843

Monday, 6th November, 1843

Harriet Monckton was dead. Any fool could see it, even by the light of the candle that Tom Churcher held in a shaking hand over the shape of her.

He was breathing hard, and fast, and dropped to his knees, clattering the candleholder to the flagstones and taking her up in his arms, shaking her. 'Harriet! No ... oh, no, God, no ...'

She was still warm. He pressed his ear close to her chest, but all he could hear was the rapid pounding of his own heart, and the rustle of her dress, and something else, unidentified – a movement that might have been a ghost or a mouse or someone on the road outside. And then a wail, ending in a sob. He placed her carefully down. Her mouth was dark with blood, her eyes still a little open, clouded; her bonnet, pushed back.

Tom sat back on his heels, his hands tucked tight into his armpits, rocking himself back and forth, fighting to know what to do. He wanted to stay, in case she opened her eyes and spoke; he wanted to hold her to him while she was still warm, tell her he loved her now, although it was too late; the harm had already been done. He stroked one trembling thumb over her cheek, wiping away a tear that had fallen from her eye. The tears were falling from his own, so that he could barely see.

But then the anger rose in him and he got to his feet. This was wrong, all wrong. He left the candle by her side, so that she should not feel alone, and ran from the chapel, the door swinging on its hinges behind him. The night outside was as it had been, just a few minutes ago, when he had waited outside the chapel, hidden beside the Cage, deep in the shadow cast by the full moon that watched everything from a cloudless sky. But now, everything had changed.

He had seen Verrall go in. He had seen Harriet go in. They had been inside for twenty minutes, perhaps more – he had no real grasp on the time – and then Verrall had come out, alone, and had turned right out of the gate, heading up Widmore Lane towards his house.

Tom had waited. He had counted the minutes off in his head, and lost count, and given up, and gone to find her. He had thought she must be praying, or perhaps upset and crying, or even simply waiting for him, hoping that he had come to protect her as he said he would, even though she had gone from Miss Williams's house without him and had not waited for him. He had searched the town for her, and then remembered that the meeting was supposed to be at eight, and had gone to the chapel and waited for her there.

For a moment he stood outside the chapel gate, whimpering, looking left and right as if Verrall might be there still, waiting for him. But he had gone.

The fury flooded through him again, and he began to run up the lane, faster and faster, the breath burning in his lungs; his side caught a cramp and he clutched it and did not stop. Ahead, he saw a couple walking and he kept running, even though the woman said something to him and the man made to stand in his path and he had to dodge to the side to avoid him, and he ran and ran all the way to the Verralls' house.

He grabbed at the railing and swung himself on to the path, and ran up it, and as he did so he was yelling, the words coming from the pit of his stomach and coming up into a roar: 'Where are you, you devil!' Then he was hammering on the door with the flat of his hand, once, twice, and it opened and there he was, Verrall himself, fully clothed and carrying a lamp which was so bright it made Tom shrink back and shield his eyes. He could not breathe. He stood back on the path, his hands on his knees, panting hard, thinking he might be sick.

'What on earth——?' Verrall said. 'Tom? What is it? Is it your father?'

That he should deny it!

Tom launched himself forward and caught at Verrall, and the lamp fell and smashed on to the path. He propelled the man back until his foot caught against the step and they both fell backwards against the door, crashing together in a horrific sort of embrace. He was too close to hit him. He struggled and tried to strike him with his forehead, but Verrall brought up his knee and pushed him over onto his back, and then he was too exhausted to do anything, and the pain had risen once more and taken the place of the fury, and all that was left was a sob that sounded a little like, 'Harriet.'

'What on earth do you mean by this?'

George Verrall got to his feet carefully, feeling the bruised flesh on his calf and his shoulder and brushing the dirt from the seat of his breeches. At his feet, Tom Churcher was sprawled, panting. The man had clearly had some sort of fit. He had not smelled the drink upon him when he wrestled him to the floor, but to all appearances he looked drunk. His eyes, in the dull light from the pantry, looked wild, staring, tear-filled; his lip curled back, showing his teeth.

'You killed her,' Churcher said, and then again, louder, 'You killed her, you bastard!'

'For God's sake, man,' Verrall said, 'what language is this? What are you talking about? Killed who?'

'Harriet,' Tom said, and again it sounded like a cry of pain.

'Harriet? But she is alive and well. I saw her in the chapel, not half an hour ago.'

Then the cold reality of the situation, of Churcher's behaviour, seemed to drench him, and he shook. There was no doubt in his mind that he had left Harriet alive. She had been living and breathing and upright, leaning back against the wall of the chapel against which he had just gripped her around the throat, lest she try to move away, and fucked her into a stunned sort of silence; but she had definitely been alive. He had had money with him, two half-sovereigns – a token amount – which he had offered her in exchange for, as he termed it, 'the honour of your Holy Fire, one final time'. She had thought about it and nodded her assent, lifting her skirts and spreading her legs like the good, pious, desperate little whore she was.

So he had done it, waited for the rush of joy and inspiration as the Holy Spirit doused him. But it did not come. Twenty shillings for nothing. And she had snivelled in his ear, at the end.

Perhaps it was the feel of her hard belly against his stomach, the swelling of it; the thought of the child inside her. Whatever it was, the route by which he obtained his spiritual ecstasy had vanished.

'I say to you, Churcher: she is alive. Unless *you* have done something to her?'

The thought had just occurred to him in that moment, seeing the man in such a very bad way. If Harriet was indeed harmed, Churcher had done it himself and now was here to try and place the blame at his door, to make him a scapegoat. Yes! That was the size of it.

He reached down and grasped Churcher's jacket, and hauled him to his feet. 'Let us go together, then, and see it, whatever it is.'

He strode up the path to the lane and turned back to the town, not even caring to look if Churcher was following him or not. Perhaps the man had gone mad. Perhaps he had seen something in the darkness, and mistaken it, and in his peculiar little brain he had conjured up the image of a dead girl. There were explanations aplenty, but none that could be dealt with from the front step of his own home; he had to go and look.

After a while he heard Churcher hurrying to catch up, and then the younger man fell into step beside him, and without a word the two continued along the moonlit roadway, the lantern hanging outside the Three Compasses the only other illumination, some distance away, at the end of the lane.

Churcher must have acted in a fit of anger, and hurt her; perhaps he had overheard the fucking, and taken his fury out on Harriet? But why, then, would Churcher run to the house and blame him for it?

The gate to the chapel was open wide. Both men went through it, and Churcher followed Verrall round to the back door, which was shut. For a moment they stood in silence. The door was in deep shadow. For the first time, Verrall felt afraid.

Then he turned the iron ring that served as a handle, and the door opened.

Inside, the single candle that Churcher had brought from the porch burned low and guttered at the sudden draught. It illuminated a shape on the floor, which looked to Verrall like nothing so much as a bundle of laundry. He approached and crouched, as Churcher had done, and lifted the candle to look at the face.

'Good God,' he said. 'What on earth can have happened?'

'You did not do it?' Churcher asked.

'No, I did not. Was it you?'

'No, sir, no! I found her just as you see her now.' His voice rose to a shout. 'Just as you left her, not a couple of minutes before. I saw you go!'

'I assure you, Tom, she was in fine good health when I left her. If it was not you, then perhaps she was overcome with a fit – or perhaps she took something – see, here, her mouth is bloody.'

'Took something?'

'I don't know. But look at her! Something happened, did it not? Sometimes people do terrible things when they are sad, or unhappy, when their troubles seem to leave them no way out.'

Churcher, crouched beside him, had begun a low, animal-like moaning. His mouth was open wide, ugly, a fine line of spittle trailing from his lip. Verrall could not bear to look at him.

'Pull yourself together, man!'

The younger man made no response, rocking gently on his heels, staring into the face of the dead girl.

'Churcher!'

At last his eyes turned, unfocused, on to the reverend.

'Listen to me. Go and find some more candles, or a lantern – there is one in the vestry, on the windowsill behind the door. Fetch it now. Go on!'

Given a task, Tom Churcher seemed to come to his senses; he got to his feet and scrambled off down the aisle towards the vestry. Verrall lifted the candle and searched the floor around the body for the glint of a coin; there was none. He found the pockets of her gown and pulled out what he found: a letter, a penknife. Thimbles. Ah! A purse! But inside, just a few coins – loose change. The half-sovereigns had gone.

The chapel was illuminated then by the wildly swinging lantern carried aloft by Tom Churcher. He did not come all the way but hung back, casting a sickly yellow glow over the ghastly scene.

'Did you steal from her?' Verrall asked. 'She had money. Did you take it?'

'No! No! Of course not!'

He believed the boy, in spite of everything. Perhaps the coins had been dropped; he would search again, in daylight. Think! He had to think – to get matters straight in his own head. Something terrible had happened. Whatever it was, he had been the last man to see Harriet Monckton alive, and Churcher had been the first man to see her dead. Whatever had happened in those intervening minutes, the two of them would be the ones to fall under the greatest suspicion.

'We have to move her,' Verrall said.

Churcher's voice, high, almost a wail: 'What?'

'She can't be found here. In the chapel, of all places! We have to move her.'

'No.'

'Put the lantern down. You lift her shoulders. I will take her feet.'

He did as he was told, but made a noise about it, crying and snivelling.

'Stop it, Tom. Pull yourself together, I say! That's it – now, lift.'

She was heavier than she seemed, the deadest of dead weights.

'We are going to carry her outside. To the Cage, yes? Ready? Watch the step!'

Between them they carried her through the back door of the chapel, awkwardly, her right hand swinging free and hanging beneath her, knocking against the door frame. Down the steps. Out into the moonlight. Churcher was gasping and sobbing like a girl.

'Stop that!' Verrall hissed. 'Someone will hear!'

They went down the path, Churcher stumbling on the uneven path for he was walking backwards, and then a leg slipped from Verrall's grasp and the lower half of her tumbled to the ground. From the lane, just a few yards from where they stood, there came the noise of a woman's laughter and a man saying something in response. Both men stood motionless, staring at each other in panic. Somewhere, a door slammed. Silence.

'We can't take her out into the lane,' Verrall whispered. 'Someone might see. We'll have to conceal the body here.'

'Why?' Churcher whispered back. 'Why hide her, if you've done nothing wrong?'

'Because she was in the chapel!' Verrall said, frustration building inside him. 'Don't you see? We have worked so hard to build the reputation of this place, and a girl decides to kill herself in it? Why, we should lose everything!'

The realisation of it seemed to dawn on Churcher. 'But if we can't take her out there,' he said, waving vaguely at the gate, 'what is to be gained by leaving her? Can I not just run for the constable now?'

Verrall stepped over the body and met Churcher, eye to eye. 'And say what, exactly? That I had a private meeting with her at eight o'clock? That you had a private meeting with her after that? And now she is dead? I – I am a respectable minister, but you would be arrested immediately, Tom, and hanged within a week! Don't you see it? I am trying to protect us both. Now, we need to move her, and quickly, before someone else passes by and sees us both standing here with a body lying between us!'

All the questions seemed to sag from Churcher's body, then, and without another word he bent and put his arms under Harriet's neck, and another under her knees, and lifted her. Her head lolled and he let out a whimper.

'The privy,' Verrall said. 'She will be out of sight, at least.'

He held open the wooden door and Churcher shuffled through the narrow gap with some difficulty, before placing her gently upon the floor. He was still making that sound, a low keening, and in between breaths he was muttering, 'Sorry, sorry.' The whole thing was a terrible, terrible mess. Verrall could scarce believe that he was doing this, that the night had unfolded so dramatically from his slightly disappointing fuck and his walk home in the dark, during which his only concern had been that he was two half-sovereigns poorer for it. He remembered thinking that he might as well find a proper whore and be done with it; it would be much less expensive to do so, and likely more effective.

Churcher made to shut the door, but Harriet's foot blocked it. He opened the door again, and pushed up her knee, and tucked it behind the door, whimpering. And the door was shut.

Churcher took a deep breath, and straightened, and said, 'I'm sorry. It's better now I don't have to look.'

476

'Come inside. We need to think.'

Verrall took the lamp back to the vestry and lit the candles, so that it was light enough for them to see each other properly. Churcher's face was a red mess of tears and mucus and dirt. Verrall thought perhaps he did not look much better. He sat behind his desk, and closed his eyes, and thought of all the possible things that might happen the next day, and how they should best be managed, and what the consequences of each choice might be. When he believed he had as clear a vision of the day as he could possibly see, he sat forward in his chair.

'Tom, you are going to do exactly as I tell you. If you do it, you will be safe, and I shall be safe, and the chapel will come to no harm. You will need to be very strong, and keep to the same story every time you are asked, and then all will be well. Can you do it?'

'I don't know.' He was sullen now, his head bent.

'If you don't, there is a good chance you will hang, whether you killed her or not. Do you understand?'

Perhaps Churcher had not been listening, for he did not move; but then, eventually, he nodded.

Harriet was dead.

Thomas could think of little else, even the instructions given to him by the reverend, and repeated, committed to his memory; those had faded, and her face was back. The eyes dulled, still open a slit; the dark blood bubbling from her lips.

She had still been warm! If he had come in a moment sooner, he might have saved her. If he had gone into the chapel when the reverend did, if he had waited in the shadows inside the chapel and not out on the lane as he had promised, he might have saved her. If he had told her the truth, that he loved her more than he had ever loved Emma Milstead, and that he would do anything for her, he might have saved her.

So many mistakes, heaped upon mistakes, and each one of them his fault. He had failed her at every turn.

Even distracted as he was, his feet carried him swiftly to the Market Place, keeping to the shadows cast by the moon, although nobody was about. Earlier in the evening he had seen Mrs Humphrey, and the Hopperton girl standing at her window, and others, too – but now there was nobody. Nothing but the Devil himself to notice as he slipped through the gate that led into the back yard, wincing at the noise made by the bolt, and through the back door. The family were all in bed. He crept up the stairs and into the bedroom he shared with James and his father. Both of them were already asleep. He got into his narrow, creaking bed, and lay there, his eyes open, thinking of her. So many things had happened in such a short space of time, he should never sort it all out in his head enough to understand. And at the heart of it all was the poor, dead girl, whom he had loved, and who was now gone.

In a nearby bedroom he heard his sister stir, and he quickly closed his eyes.

Verrall had watched Tom Churcher until he turned the corner into the Market Place, and then gone back and closed the gate behind him. He had made to lock it, and then thought better of it. It should be left unlocked; for Harriet would have made her way into the chapel of her own volition. She would have gone alone, for the purpose of ending her life, and perhaps whoever had used the gate last had neglected to lock it behind them. Such carelessness was not uncommon.

He made his way up the lane at a more sedate pace than his previous two walks this evening, still thinking of the instructions he had given Tom Churcher and hoping that the lad would be able to follow them. He was not certain of it, but it was their only hope. He would need another plan, of course, for if Churcher broke down and tried to blame him for it he would need to be ready to prove that Churcher was unstable, mentally deficient, and a liar. Between the two of them, Verrall liked to think he was more readily to be believed.

Sarah would be in bed, asleep. He'd thought she might have woken with the racket that Churcher had made against the door, but it was not unheard of for a member of the congregation to call upon him urgently, late into the evening, to offer comfort to the sick and the dying.

As he walked up the path, he saw that the front door was slightly ajar. Had he left it like that? He saw an odd shape at the edge of the path; as he went to it, his shoes crunched on something and he realised it was broken glass – his lamp, smashed by Churcher in their struggle. He picked up the remains of the lamp and a few bits of glass, before giving up. He would attend to it in the daylight.

The lamps were still lit in the kitchen, as he had left them, for the pounding at the door had interrupted his intention to heat some milk upon the stove – and, to his surprise, his study door stood slightly ajar, and he could see light coming from within. That was definitely something he had not done; the study had been left in darkness, with the door closed.

His brow furrowed, he pushed at the door. Nobody was in the room, and everything looked as he had left it. He turned to go, and then stopped.

Wait. Not everything…something was different. Something had been moved. There was an odd smell in the room, too; a sweetish smell, not unpleasant. Almost as if someone had baked a cake, and the scent of it had lingered.

He went into the centre of the room and looked about him, trying to determine what it was that seemed out of place. The fire was swept and laid, ready to be lit by the maid first thing in the morning. His desk was tidy, although piles of papers, sermons and notebooks, were stacked neatly upon it. On the centre of his desk was the previous day's copy of *The Times*, roughly re-folded, just as he had left it.

On top of the newspaper was a bottle, a glass bottle, and another, smaller, beside it. He went to it and almost picked the larger bottle up, but something stopped him. He bent to look at it more closely, and to examine the label upon it.

HST: ACID
HYDROCYAN:

It was half full of a colourless liquid. Beside it, a smaller bottle, with a label that he had to squint to read:

THE CORDIAL BALM OF SYRIACUM

For treatment of those who have fallen
into a state of chronic disability.

Nervous disorders of every kind, sinkings,
anxieties, and tremors which so dreadfully
affect the weak and the sedentary will, in a
short time, be succeeded by cheerfulness
and every presage of health.

Provided by R. and L. Perry, and Co.
PERRY'S PURIFYING SPECIFIC PILLS
19, Berners Street, London

This smaller bottle was entirely empty. Between the bottles, neatly stacked, were two half-sovereigns.

Verrall heard a sound from the hallway behind him. He looked back, startled, and saw that Sarah had entered the room. The first thing he noticed was that she was fully dressed. The next, that her face was fixed upon him with a smile, such as he had never seen before. She looked almost elated.

He placed his trembling hand upon the desk for support, and said,

'What have you done?'

Epilogue

18th June, 1880

Here I sit, an old man, waiting under a rat-coloured sky for Death to claim me.

I have long since given up the hope that I shall meet Jesus in Heaven; rather, I think it is oblivion that awaits, and I believe I shall be glad of it. I have spent my life praying for forgiveness, and the words have grown cold on my lips, and meaningless; my life has been spent on others, and it was all to try and make amends.

Oh, we all make mistakes, I know that. Small ones, great ones; little white lies, dangerous untruths: I am not the only one guilty of it. But I have borne the weight of my own sin, and that of another, for nearly forty years, and it has made me stoop, and cry with the pain, and wish for it all to be done with. A lifetime spent on good works is not enough to redeem a man. Confession, and repentance, and absolution, and whatever else it is that the High Church tells you will lead you to God, washed clean in the Blood of the Lamb, and none of it is worth anything – anything at all – without a simple apology.

I am nearing the end. My eldest son has taken my place, preaching God's Holy Word and Divine Love to the world. I am proud of him, for he is truly the godly man I always wished to be, and now see that I never was.

Every day I wonder if I should tell him – tell all three of my boys, fine men that they are now – what really happened on that night in November, 1843, so many years ago. How it was that young Tom Churcher and I suspected each other, and because of my foolishness how we entered into a grand scheme of deception, to throw the blame away from God's house and place it at Harriet's own hand; and how, later that evening, I discovered that the truth was far darker.

It has been nine years since Sarah died, taken by a fever as the old year gave way to the new. My wife: voiceless, unheard, unasked. In all that time, her opinion was never sought. She was never called to the inquest, never asked about my whereabouts on the night in question, much less hers. How would she have responded, if the coroner had thought to call her to give evidence? We should all have been undone, perhaps.

What would they say, my boys, if I were to tell them that their mother was a murderess? That she had become so very exhausted by her husband's filthy sin that she took it upon herself to end the latest threat to her reputation, her father's money, and her life as a minister's wife? For it was Harriet, asking for help, that had caused her to act. She had seen so many women taken by her husband, and she had known of them all – but not until Harriet came, brazen, desperate, to the door of her own home did her final thread of forbearance snap. She balked, finally, at the continued price of my dalliances, or at the cost, rather, of keeping at bay their consequences. For it was not my money that had bought us the fine house, that paid off the debt on the building of the Bromley chapel; it was hers. I was a man of very modest means until I met Sarah. Her father's money had bought us everything; and charity was one thing and freely given to those good souls who deserved our pity, but her husband's whore was not going to take a penny of it.

What would they say? Would they blame her, for losing her patience? No! They would blame me, for I was the sinner.

I have paid for those sins every day of the last thirty-seven years, in Sarah's silences and in the look of cold disgust upon her face every time she beheld me. I have paid for it in her hatred and her scorn, in her bitterness and in the beating of her miserable heart, and I deserved it all. I have paid for it in the nine years without her, when I had nobody left to hate but myself.

That night, as I moved Harriet's body out of the chapel, believing her to have taken her own life, or perhaps that Churcher had harmed her in some inexplicable fit of anger, I swear I had no knowledge of my wife's part in it. I had left the house, thinking her upstairs, to visit Harriet in the chapel, and all the while Sarah had been there already, hidden in the shadows, waiting to see what might pass between me and the girl who had come to her in desperation, four days earlier. And she had seen the very worst of me. The cruelty and the meanness; the cajoling, the wheedling, the asking for favours, the offering of money. The girl, crying, despairing, but quietly accepting. My fingers, gripping her throat. The act of lust itself, filthy to behold. And after it, I had left.

What had she done, then? Come out of the shadows, or pretended that she had just chanced to pass, and seen that Harriet was within? Offered her a solution, a tincture to rid herself of the problem? And had Harriet taken it willingly, or was the liquid forced upon her? I like to think, at least, that it must have been quick.

The act is done; it cannot be undone. All I can do now is something I should have done many years ago.

Harriet, dear, brave girl: I am sorry. I sit here in my final days of life, weeping for you, and for the life that was so cruelly taken from you. For the life of your child, entirely innocent of any sin, taken and discarded as if worth nothing at all. I treated you so very badly, and you deserved none of it. Forgive me, Harriet, for I have nothing left now but sorrow, and shame, and despair.

And all I have to hope for, now, is that I might see you translated into Glory, and, if not that, then at least that you sleep in peace.

Afterword

I stumbled across the first two (of the three) documents that tell Harriet's story when I was researching another novel at the National Archives in Kew, London. These documents (which can be read at the National Archives, reference TS 25/218 and TS 25/208) consist of correspondence between the coroner, Charles Carttar, and the Home Secretary, via the Attorney General and the Solicitor General, dating from December 1844 and January 1846. One of the jurymen, Richard Hodges (also known as Barbarossa, apparently because of his impressive red beard) had written to the Home Secretary to ask for him to prompt the coroner to resume the inquest, and reach a verdict, as it had been, by then, nearly three years since the murder. One of the jurymen had died, one had gone abroad, and the rest of them were certainly very frustrated at the lack of a conclusion to their efforts. The Home Secretary requested the circumstances of the case from the coroner, and a comprehensive account of the 1843 inquest was forwarded, along with the explanation for the delay, namely that, owing to his suspicions of a particular person (George Verrall), he had decided to adjourn in order to allow the police to investigate thoroughly. The Attorney General and Solicitor General were consulted as to whether the coroner had been criminally negligent, and eventually after much correspondence back and forth the decision was reached that the Home Secretary should just tell him to bring the matter to a rapid conclusion.

Fascinated, I googled 'Harriet Monckton'. To my surprise, having read so much about Victorian crime, nobody else appeared to have written about Harriet and the circumstances of her death; the only relevant hits (despite trying different spellings) were the two documents I had already seen plus, intriguingly, a third, also in the National Archives, entitled 'Murder of Harriet Monckton at Bromley Thomas Churcher suspected' (document reference MEPO 3/48).

My reaction to those documents was almost a physical one. I felt breathless with excitement. A cursory online search suggested that none of the people mentioned in the documents I'd read had been arrested or tried for Harriet's murder. Verrall and Churcher, in particular, went on to live relatively long lives and so had clearly not died at the end of a hangman's rope. I felt a desperate sense of injustice for Harriet, and for her unborn child. Such a terrible thing had happened, an act of violence whether by accident or design. But why was Harriet the victim of that violence? Why was her murder never solved? I was determined to find out, hoping that the documents were going to help me achieve some sort of justice for Harriet.

In his reply to the Home Secretary, the coroner, Charles Carttar, listed nine reasons why he suspected George Verrall of the crime (*see* p.497). Whilst these reasons certainly raise questions, there is little in the way of the sort of evidence that a modern investigation would require to establish a case against him.

Whilst the coroner was fixated on Verrall being the guilty party, the two Metropolitan police detectives who arrived in Bromley to investigate quickly decided that Thomas Churcher was a far more likely suspect. The police notes in the archives suggest that their suspicion was based on Churcher's own reluctance to speak to them; and that in an early interview he had claimed that he knew Harriet only vaguely from her attendance at the chapel, but then several residents of Bromley came forward to report that he had been seen on numerous occasions walking with Harriet, including late in the evening, and on the night she died.

The police concluded that whilst Verrall had undoubtedly acted suspiciously in the time following Harriet's death, this might have been due to his efforts in protecting some other member of his congregation, i.e. Churcher.

Intriguingly, there was a third named suspect: one Thomas Cranfield. The case against him seems to consist of the fact that he was in Bromley on that night, and that he committed suicide shortly after Harriet's death. From the newspaper reports at the time of the second inquest, I discovered that Cranfield 'dined' (probably meaning luncheon) with the Verralls on Monday, 6th November – along with several others. The police ruled him out of further investigation, for there was no other evidence to connect him to Harriet.

What struck me about the case was that, in addition to these three, there was an abundance of other suspects: the Fields, Thomas Churcher's betrothed, Frances Williams – even Harriet's own family seemed hostile. There seemed to be many people who could have had a reason to want her out of the way.

The hardest thing was trying to work out the best way of telling the story. I spent a long time trying to decide if I was going to write a 'true crime' book, or to embellish the details of the case with historical details I had acquired through my research; or whether to fictionalise it, either completely, by changing all the names and the location, or by retaining as many of the facts as I could. I tried to write all of these versions, and struggled. My goal was always to try and find some justice for Harriet and her son; to reveal the crime and then leave it unsolved, or to give her a made-up name and disguise the town, would fail in this aim. In the end I decided to stick to the facts, and to write in the spaces between; this does, at least, allow for Verrall to apologise for what he did, or failed to do.

I have tried my best to keep to as many of the facts of Harriet's case as I could, as far as they are provided by the coroner's documents and by the contemporary press reports. The details of the inquests are as close to the facts as I can get them; as far as possible, I have used the words the witnesses actually said before the coroner and the jury.

The details for the first inquest come from the documents in the National Archives, and the contemporaneous news-paper reports; the details for the second inquest come only from the many newspaper reports at the time, which are available to read online thanks to the British Newspaper Archive. Everything that takes place after the second inquest finishes is, therefore, entirely imagined. Harriet's diary is entirely fictional, as is, of course, Verrall's confession.

It was a challenge to differentiate the voices of the narrators. As these were real people, it felt wrong of me to imagine their voices. It's very different from making up characters and getting them to speak. But, after inhabiting the documents and the newspaper reports for some time, I did get a feel for them; from his interactions with the coroner, Verrall came across as very self-assured; Thomas Churcher did not want to speak to anyone without his father present. Miss Williams clearly had the measure of the townspeople in the way only an outsider would. Richard Field, who shared his house with young women and married one who was thirty years his junior, seemed to me to be at once charming, and predatory. I felt that his behaviour towards Harriet amounted to what would be described now as grooming.

George Verrall remained in Bromley for the rest of his life, dying at the age of 83 in July 1880. His wife, Sarah, predeceased him and died in 1871 at the age of 79. They had been married 46 years. The Bromley Congregational Chapel was rebuilt in the 1880s and remained as a landmark in the town until it was destroyed during the Blitz, on 16th April, 1941. After the Second World War, a new building designed by Raymond Wilkins became the town's United Reformed Church, consecrated in 1957. The current church has several meeting rooms, one of which is called Verrall Hall in honour of their first minister.

Verrall's sister, Ruth, married James Churcher (Thomas's brother) in June 1852, when she was 37 and he was 32. The first of their two sons was born nine months later.

Thomas Churcher married Mary Ann Milstead (see 'A note on the names', below) on 25th July, 1844. They had six children, and in 1851 moved the relatively short distance to Sydenham. Thomas died there in 1876, at the age of 58. Mary Ann died in Lewisham in 1902, at the age of 83.

Clara Churcher married Richard Humphrey in 1854, when she was 41. They do not appear to have had any children, and Clara died in 1902 at the age of 93.

Richard and Maria Field had six children, including Richard, who was born before Harriet's death, and Ebenezer, who was actually born in 1847, although for the sake of the story I have moved his birth date forward to 1846. Richard appears on the 1851 census as a collector to a charitable institution, and in 1861 as a clerk at a wholesale grocer's.

According to the newspaper reporting on the second inquest in 1844, Frances Williams moved to Shifnal, in Shropshire, at some point after the first inquest. A record in the 1851 census shows a governess called Fanny Williams as a visitor at the house of unmarried brother and sister Edward and Ann Williams, in Wellington, near Telford. No other trace of her has yet been found.

When you're dealing with real people, it's very easy to get distracted by the details of their lives. I loved finding out about all of them. One of the ways in which I tried to investigate from this distance was by researching all the suspects for Harriet's murder, not just to see if any of them had been prosecuted for this offence, but to see if any had gone on to be convicted or suspected of any offences in the years afterwards. As a result of this, I found that one of the suspects was also involved in something that, whilst perhaps not criminal, was certainly morally dubious. I am not going to say too much about that because I am slipping down that particular rabbit hole as we speak, and potentially it might turn into another book.

From the moment I read the documents I got a thrill of excitement at finding something unique and important, I knew I would have to tell Harriet's story. The impact on my life has been profound, to the extent that I feel as if I have inhabited Bromley in 1843 myself. This was helped in some degree by acquiring a suitcase full of family history material a couple of years ago. I discovered quite recently that my own great-great-great grandparents lived at 6 Fieldgate Street, in Whitechapel, in 1841 – at the same time as Harriet was living there with Richard Field, at No. 33. Researching my own family tree helped me a great deal, as it gave me a connection to that time in a way that meant something to me personally.

As it turned out, I knew Bromley fairly well, having worked there as a medical rep in the early 1990s. These were streets I recognised, even though, of course, much had changed. I took a research visit back to the town and identified many of the locations that would have been familiar to Harriet, and of course this is something that the reader can also do. The United Reformed Church now stands where the Congregational Chapel formerly was, and a very lovely and welcoming place it is too. Widmore Lane is now Widmore Road, and is a busy thoroughfare. The place where the Verralls' house once stood is now the junction with Homefield Road. The Three Compasses public house is currently a pizza restaurant at which I had the best pizza I think I have ever had, although the building is recognisable from the three compasses in the plasterwork above the door. The Market Place still exists, although is considerably changed. But at least four buildings are still the same as they were in Harriet's day: the Archbishop's Palace, now the

Bromley Register Office; historic Bromley College, opposite where the Workhouse stood before it was demolished; the Swan Inn, used for the second inquest, which is still on the corner of the High Street and Beckenham Lane; and of course the parish church, where Harriet is buried with her father and her mother, which is still largely as it was, albeit somewhat extended over the years. Alas, there is no way of telling exactly where Harriet is buried, but, as I walked through the churchyard with my friend Sarah, a whole load of receipts inexplicably fell from the purse I was carrying tightly in my left hand. They scattered behind me and, as I picked everything up, I wondered if Harriet had taken that opportunity to tell me where it was she lay.

A note on the names

The newspapers vary considerably in their reporting, not least in the spelling of the name of the surgeon who performed the post-mortem. I have seen his name reported variously as Stott, Scott, Hott and Ilott. The 1841 census is corroborated by books on the history of the town, and I have thus established that, although there was an eminent surgeon in Bromley by the name of Scott, the young man who performed the post-mortem and appeared accordingly at the inquest was James William Ilott.

For the purposes of avoiding confusion, I have taken some liberties with names.

Emily Graham, who is living with Frances in Shifnal in 1846, is a character entirely of my own invention.

Thomas Churcher's sweetheart, who later became his wife, was in fact Mary Ann Milstead. I changed her to Emma (her younger sister's name) to avoid confusion with Harriet's sister Mary Ann.

The two police detectives who came to Bromley to investigate the case at the instigation of the Home Secretary were Superintendent Nicholas Pearce and Inspector Charles Frederick Field. Both of these men are well known as being among the earliest members of Scotland Yard's detective branch, set up in August 1842, and they were contemporaries of the now famous Jonathan Whicher. Field in particular may have been the inspiration for Dickens's Inspector Bucket. To avoid any confusion with Richard and Maria Field, I have given him the alias of Meadows in Harriet's story.

In the interests of furthering the plot, I have also changed the dates of some marriages and pregnancies:

Harriet's brother William and his wife Ann had their first child in October 1844, which would have been too late for Harriet to hear of the pregnancy in the weeks before she died. They named their daughter Harriet.

Richard and Maria actually married on 24th July 1842, a year earlier than suggested in the novel. Their second child, which in my fictional version arrived immediately after the verdict in May 1846, was actually born in 1847, a boy named Ebenezer. Maria's maiden name, according to the marriage records, was Grieff; discovering this enabled me to find her in the 1841 census, where her occupation is given as 'FS' — female servant. That she was a schoolteacher, and previously a friend of Harriet's, is therefore also my own invention.

For interest, the letter following is a transcription of one of the contemporary documents mentioned in this Afterword (part of TS 25/218). There are undoubtedly further documents in relation to Harriet's case in existence, and I am sure that there are many more omissions and inaccuracies than I have mentioned here. Any mistakes in relation to the text are, therefore, due to the limitations of my own research as well as to the need to produce a dramatic fictionalisation based on a true story.

To: *The Right Hon'ble Sir James Graham Bart., M.P.*
Greenwich, 12th January 1846

Sir,

I have the honour to acknowledge the receipt of Mr S.M. Phillipps's communication of the 29th ulto respecting the Inquest on the body of Harriet Monckton wherein [...] I am decided to state for your Information the name of the person suspected and the circumstances which were communicated to me from time to time that the party suspected evinced great anxiety for the termination of the Inquiry and also the mode in which those circumstances were communicated to me and further to transmit a exact copy of all the Evidence taken at the Inquest.

I beg to state that the person suspected is The Reverend George Verrall the Minister of the Chapel at Bromley in the Privy at the rear of which the body of the deceased was found.

The circumstances of suspicion attaching to this Individual and the manner in which they have from time to time been brought under my knowledge and consideration are these: That prior to the cause of the deceased's absence from her home being ascertained this party suggested that she had committed suicide.

That the body having been discovered under circumstances detailed in the Evidence the same party at the first meeting of the Jury expressed a desire to avoid a post-mortem examination in a manner so earnest as to lead me to make a Note of it.

That the post-mortem examination having been made it was ascertained that the deceased was about six months advanced in pregnancy and had died from the effects of Prussic acid.

That the party was a constant and apparently anxious attendant at every meeting of the Jury suggesting from time to time questions to be put to the Witnesses for the purpose of leading to a belief that the deceased had committed suicide altho' the state in which the body was found and the whole tenor of the Evidence at that time given were quite opposed to any such conclusion.

That the party having become a Witness in the Inquiry it came out that the day preceding that of her absence from her home the deceased and himself had been closeted together in the Vestry

Room of the Chapel for some time under circumstances that could not fail to make a strong impression on my mind.

That having come to a determination that for the furtherance of the ends of Justice the best course to adopt would be to adjourn the Inquest for a sufficient Interval to admit of additional evidence being produced or new facts bearing upon the case discovered, during that Interval, an anonymous Letter signed 'Chemicus' was addressed to me under cover to the Revd. Dr. Scott of Bromley the Magistrate – this letter was suspected to be the production of the Revd. Geo. Verrall which suspicion was subsequently confirmed by comparing the Letter with the party's handwriting.

That a more extended adjournment having been decided upon the High Constable of Bromley Mr Joyce (who had charge of the Case) communicated to me that the party had expressed to him annoyance at the further postponement, and an anxious desire that the proceedings should be closed as no additional evidence was likely to be produced, alleging also that he wished to leave Bromley for a time but could not go until the enquiry was over for if he did 'people would say he was the man'.

That since the last adjournment the High Constable has on several occasions mentioned to me the continued anxiety of the party for the termination of the Enquiry stating also that some of the Jury had expressed a similar desire, but as several of them were Members of the Reverend George Verrall's Chapel and it was known to me that some one or more of them had divulged to him the private deliberations of the Jury with myself which it had been agreed should be kept secret, pending proposed inquiries, I hesitated to act upon any recommendation from that quarter, tending to close the enquiry upon the present unsatisfactory state of the Evidence whilst there appeared to me a hope that time might throw further light upon a Case wrapped in so much mystery and suspicion.

I forward a copy of the Letter signed 'Chemicus' bearing the post mark of Nov. 18th 1843 also a copy of a Letter received by me from the Revd. George Verrall dated 23rd January 1844 with copy of its enclosure [...] and I also forward as requested a correct copy of all the Evidence taken at the Inquest.

Chas. J. Carttar, Coroner for Kent

C Division, Divisional Office
Greenwich

1st March 1846

Gentlemen,

I beg leave to report that in Consequence of some information that Mr. Superintendent Mallalieu had received relative to the Death of a Female named Harriet Monckton which took place at Bromley on the 6th Nov. 1843 he was induced to send me down to the above place to watch the proceedings of an Inquest which was held on the 4th Feby. 1846. Accordingly I attended and from the Evidence which came out upon that investigation it was considered by Mr. Supt. Mallalieu that an Enquiry should be immediately made into the Circumstances Connected with the Matter. I was therefore Employed and from the Information I obtained I saw that some suspicion was attached to three persons viz. The Revd. George Verrall, Mr. Thomas Cranfield, and Thomas Churcher, Legal Enquiry which has since been instituted by myself and Mr. Insp. Pearce of the F. Division who was ordered to be Employed with me, we jointly consider that there is not the least doubt that Thomas Churcher is the party who was the cause of the deceased's death. With respect to Mr. Cranfield every enquiry has been made in the neighbourhood where he resided and also from the Various persons connected with his Establishment and there is not the least Evidence to affect him.

With regard to the Revd. Mr. Verrall there is Certainly heavy points which Remain to be cleared up by him relative to the Writing Anonymous letters which there is no doubt have been written by him, whether he has taken up the cause for the purpose of shielding other parties or his attempting to bring the right parties to Justice that yet remained to be explained, but it is the opinion of Mr. Supt. Pearce and myself who have gone through the Matter, most minutely, that the Various Circumstances that had come out with the Information that has been obtained throws the greatest suspicion upon Thomas Churcher.

Charles Fra. Field, Inspector

Acknowledgements

First and foremost my best thanks to Candida Lacey, editor, publisher and friend, who has championed Harriet from the very beginning. She helped me explore the possibilities of the story whilst insisting that I was, in fact, qualified to write it. Thank you for all of the encouragement, the Skypes, the unfailing commitment to bringing Harriet back into the light.

Thank you, too, to my genius editor and friend, Linda McQueen, who transformed my words from a hideous tangle into something coherent and glorious, whilst remaining serene and calming at all times.

Additional grateful thanks to Dawn Sackett for her conscientious and skilful proofreading.

Many people had my transcriptions of the original documents thrust upon them, and provided encouragement and ideas as a result. For this, my grateful thanks are due to Gina Haynes, Lindsay Brown, Katie Gatward, Paul Hiscock, Linda Weeks, Lisa Cutts, Vicky Allen, Denise West, Donna-Louise Clarke, Jo Hinton Malivoire, Helen Nash and Danny Gregory, and of course my fabulous agent, Annette Green.

Grateful thanks to Nicki Herring and Helen Treacy, who both provided midwifery expertise in relation to Harriet's and Maria's pregnancies. Nicki also helped me trawl through the Kent Archives.

Very special thanks to Sarah M'Grady, who accompanied me on a memorable research trip to Bromley, took much better photos than I ever could, and helped me pick up all the receipts in the parish churchyard when Harriet pulled them out of my purse.

In the course of that same research trip I visited Bromley United Reformed Church, and was welcomed by Stephen Fellingham, Local Church Leader, who gave me a tour and furnished me with a book about the church's history, which proved to be invaluable to my research. The book also included a picture of George Verrall in later life – the only photograph I have seen of any of my protagonists, as far as I am aware. I am so grateful to him, not only for the assistance, but more importantly for his kindness and genuine warmth. I had been expecting to find the church chilly and haunting, but it is in fact a vibrant, inclusive and welcoming place, which I highly encourage you to visit. In the interests of telling Harriet's story I have taken liberties with the characters of George and Sarah Verrall, who cannot now answer for themselves; and in particular with George's use of the Bible to justify his nefarious behaviour. My sincerest apologies for this, and I trust the reader will understand that my story casts no reflection whatsoever on the church and its work in present day Bromley.

I would also like to extend my gratitude to Lucy Bonner and Anita Luxton at the Bromley Historic Collection, who were extremely helpful; they pointed me in the direction of the Baxter cuttings and ELS Horsburgh's *Bromley, Kent: From the Earliest Times to The Present Century*, both of which proved most enlightening.

Thank you to Sally Ann Taylor, who provided some useful insight into the events surrounding Harriet's death, and her relationships with those around her. I felt much closer to Harriet as a result of our meeting.

Grateful thanks are due also to Susan Allen, who has helped me enormously with genealogical research, and thank you to Andrew Taylor for answering a crucial research question at a very late stage.

Thank you to the Writers' HQ and to the brilliant Alexa Radcliffe-Hart, whose encouragement at one of the

Cambridge Writers' Retreats enabled me to write the entire Confession in a single day.

As always, the process of writing is made easier by the support and encouragement of my fellow Norfolk novelists: Vicky Allen, Denise West, Donna-Louise Clarke, Jo Hinton Malivoire and Hayley Webster, thank you all. Thank you to everyone at the Alby Tearooms for allowing us the space to be creative, and keeping us sustained with tea and cake while we do it.

In particular, I am immensely grateful to the fabulous Jo Hinton Malivoire for creating the beautiful map at the start of this book. I cried happy tears when I saw it. Thank you.

Thank you so much to my coach, the brilliant Andrea Bell, who has quite revolutionised my way of working; that Harriet was ever finished at all is entirely down to her. Thank you, Andrea. I hope you like the book!

Special thanks are due to my dear friend Samantha Bowles, who shared Harriet with me from the very beginning. If Harriet had lived today, I like to think she would have enjoyed an afternoon with cocktails in our company, and been a good friend to us both.

Finally, posthumous thanks to Harriet, for allowing me to write your story. I hope I've done you proud.

Elizabeth Haynes is a former police intelligence analyst. Her first novel, *Into the Darkest Corner*, has been published in 37 countries. It was Amazon's Best Book of the Year and a *New York Times* bestseller. She has written a further three psychological thrillers – *Revenge of the Tide*, *Human Remains* and *Never Alone* – and two novels in the DCI Louisa Smith series, *Under a Silent Moon* and *Behind Closed Doors*.

to for, or sold any Prussic Acid and I cannot find that they have

wit/ **Richard Field** of Whitechapel Varnish Manufacturer Sworn Says I knew the deceased the last time I saw her alive was some time in the month of August last at my own House in Whitechapel On Tuesday (the 7th Novr/ the Letter which I now produce was delivered by the Postman, it is in the hand writing of the deceased and is directed to my Wife

To have reached me on Tuesday the 7th Novr it must have been posted on Monday the 6th Novr in Bromley It bears the Bromley Postmark The Letter put in and read the following is a copy

"My Dear Maria

"I received yours on Saturday and was a little surprised not "expecting to hear from you so soon I am however much obliged by your "kindness I shewed it to Mr Verrall and he said it was a very nice Note "I cannot come to Town this week as I am attending to Miss Williams' "School she being very ill herself but on Wednesday next I shall hope to "see you and the dear Baby once more I am rather unsettled and hope you will "excuse this short note, I shall hope to see you if I am spared my Dear "Maria I often remember your words "All things work together for good" I "trust this will be, but I must say adieu My Mother and Sister desire their "kind respects to Mr Field and thyself

                    "Ever yours most affectionately "Harriett"

"P.S. A kiss for baby I long to see him, I have a great deal to tell you "when I see you; Good bye"

I expected deceased at my house on Wednesday last, I knew that she had obtained a situation at Arundel at which she was much pleased Her visit to Town was preparatory to her going to Arundel I was not at all aware that until after her death that she was pregnant I am surprised to hear it At the time she was staying at my house I believe she was much attached to a person of the name of Samuel Phipps whom she met at my house but she was told that he was engaged to another Lady I heard of the death the deceased by Letter from The Revd Mr Verrall, the Minister of the chapel at Bromley The deceased had frequently met at my house several Gentlemen Students of Hackney College, but I never heard of her being intimate or attached to either of them I have not been in Bromley before today for some months I have not sent or written to the deceased at all I never saw anything in her conduct or manner or disposition to lead me to think she was likely or capable of

(13)

wit/ **Thomas Churcher** of Bromley Shoemaker Sworn Says I knew the deceased I went to Miss William's house on Monday evening the 6th November I there saw the deceased Miss Williams had sent for my sister to go and take tea with her my Sister was engaged and could not go and I went to say so The deceased was apparently in good health